Q

BETHANY RAE SALWAY

Cover art by Priscilla Kim

ISBN: 978-1-7345794-4-4

for Sonata Arctica

ACKNOWLEDGMENTS

Special thanks to my sister, Rachel Garcia, for helping me navigate a tumultuous first draft. Thanks also to my husband, Talin, for his unceasing support.

CHAPTER ONE

People said a lot of things about the Baron of Geid. They said he lived underground, spoke with spirits, and could put out a fire just by looking at it. Some said he was born in the Otherworld. Others claimed he was banished from it altogether. No one could quite agree.

Most of these conjectures were rather silly. Fenwith was a recluse and a lunatic, but Senna did not suspect him of being a supernatural creature. As she stood before him, though, it was easy to see how these rumors got started.

The Baron looked like a ghost, with his jaw shoved up too far, making his lips curl against his nose. His skin was so pale she could see the veins underneath—especially in his thin hands, which were clutching the arms of his chair like claws about to snatch away prey.

The Baron's eyes scanned Senna for one brief, indifferent instant, then drifted to the armored man at her side. "What is this, Lodin?"

Lodin was the Captain of Fenwith's Guard. Captains seemed to change fairly often as the Baron became displeased with the old one and had him banished or beheaded. Most of the Guard had stopped vying for the position. Lodin was about three times stupider than his predecessors, and a good deal less ruthless, but so far he had managed to keep the title longer than anyone else.

Lodin bowed awkwardly as he pointed to the maiden. "Her name is Senna, Lord."

"I don't care what her name is. What is she doing here? If I want a whore to entertain me, I'll let you know, understand?"

Senna bit her lip. She was counting on her poor looks to save her from that fate.

Captain Lodin fumbled with the sword at his side. "She's your new housekeeper." Senna had bribed him to consider her for the job. He looked as if he were regretting it.

Fenwith laughed in a way that made the hair on her skin stand up. In the weeks that followed, Senna would notice that he had a habit of laughing when an occasion least called for it. "She's only a child," he said.

That was an interesting objection, from his perspective. The Baron was maybe twenty. He had an unlined face, though his hair was a strange color for someone his age. In direct sunlight it looked like bleached grain; in the torchlit shadows of the castle it reminded Senna of dirty snow.

Senna forced herself to look demure as she bowed. "If it please you, Lord, I'm a hard worker and I have experience managing my uncle's inn." She kept her eyelids lowered as she spoke, playing to his sense of authority.

The Baron stopped looking angry for a moment, and Senna was relieved to see his jaw settle into a reasonable position. "The Ironfoot Inn?" he asked.

Senna bit her lip again. "No, Lord. You had my uncle's inn burned to the ground last month." She should have phrased her reply less accusingly, but he was too callous to notice.

"Fine. You can get started by dusting this room." He lowered a finger and ran it across one of the curls that adorned the base of his chair, then flicked the black residue off with his thumb. "I don't think that it has ever been dusted before."

❖

Jedomar rested his cheek against the rough bark of a branch. His eyes scanned the road a hundred spans in either direction. There was no movement, save that of a treeskunk that ran across the road and shot a curious look into the leaves, probably displeased at the six men displacing it from its home.

His accomplice Grath pointed to the animal. "Skunks on the ground and men in the trees. That's an amusing reversal."

Jed shrugged. He didn't consider a tree to be out of his element. He was perfectly comfortable with the twelve spans of empty space between himself and the ground.

The branch swayed as Jed's friend shifted position beside him. "If I were Lodin," said Rimick, "I would petition to have this road rebuilt away from the forest. That would make it a lot harder to ambush these carts."

"By the Queen, Rimick, don't curse us with such an idea." Grath kept his words low, even though there was no danger of being overheard.

"The cart should be here by now," someone else said. "Maybe our information is wrong."

Young Mister Hack stuck his tongue out. "Or maybe the cart's so stuffed with grain they can't get the horses to pull it."

The Baron of Geid regularly confiscated a portion of the grain harvest in lieu of hard currency, which the farmers were unable to provide for legal taxes. It was taken to Candige for sale and eventually made its way north to Mackabine, where they suspected that most of it left the country. Four times out of five, Jed let the cart go through, but the tax was so harsh that full payment left nothing to sustain the farmers through the winter. Quite often the theft was tolerated, but every now and then the Baron would urge Lodin to set up some scheme for their capture. These schemes were occasionally troublesome, but none of them had worked. In his head, Jed could hear the retort Rimick would use to counter that thought. *It only has to work once.*

"There they are." Rimick pointed down the road at the group of Guards coming into view.

Jed's mood lightened. Waiting was always the hardest part for him. But his spirits sank again as he counted nine Guards. That was more than expected. In fact, it was nearly half the standing Guard. The Captain wasn't opting for secrecy today.

"Still think we can take them?" Rimick asked. He didn't appear doubtful, only interested in Jed's opinion. He might as well have been asking about a game of Six Feet.

Jed smiled with more confidence than he felt. "Simple as School-Day pudding, my friend. Let's do a one-man rabbit."

Rimick nodded. "I'll do it."

Jed acceded with a nod. He would have liked to do it himself, but the truth was, he trusted Rimick's judgment more than his own.

Six against nine wasn't great odds. Besides the competent aid of Rimick and Grath, Jed had brought three others for secondary support: Hack, Sable, and Brade. However, Brade was rather elderly, and Sable was barely fourteen. Jed's posse had anywhere from five to as many as fifty members. There were a few core people that Jed trusted, and the rest he picked up when the need arose for large numbers. He just hadn't realized this would be one of those occasions.

Rimick dropped gracefully and concealed himself in a copse of undergrowth. Jed signaled for the rest to follow. Dohack pulled against Jed's shoulder. "Are you crazy? We can't take on that many Guards!"

Jed glared at Hack's hand until he removed it. Then he answered nonchalantly, "Don't worry. I won't make you risk

10

your life any more than you're willing."

Hack could take this as an invitation to leave, but Jed doubted he would. Jed and Hack had grown up on neighboring farms. They'd both been active, carefree boys, almost the same age, seen as best friends by everyone who knew them. Neither had disputed the label, but time and temperament had distanced them, if they had ever been close to begin with. Despite his complaints, Hack insisted on being near the center of the action. He would follow Jed as long as there was fun and glory to be had.

"Grath?" Jed said.

"I want Sable to stay here," Grath said.

"That's what I thought."

Sable was Grath's son, joining them today for the first time. No one was ready to risk the boy. Sable looked at his father and frowned, but he didn't protest his exclusion.

Grath was arguably the most respected member of their group. The Baron's men had never pegged him as a Queensman. That generally meant Jed kept him out of fights, although he wasn't sure they could afford to do that today. Grath eased Jed's concern by pulling a small sack out of his pocket and stuffing it over his head. A rough hole across the middle revealed his eyes and nose. It wasn't the most elegant disguise, but it was doubtful Grath would be recognized.

"O...kay," said Jed. "That's fine."

"That's hilarious," said Hack.

When the Guard escort was close enough, Rimick expertly nocked an arrow and aimed it at the wooden plank that ran along the front of the cart. This was the easiest trick they knew how to pull, so they tried not to pull it too often. Lucky for them, the Captain of the Guard wasn't the ripest peach on the tree. Rimick shot a couple more arrows for good measure, one into the ground and one into the trunk of a tree opposite a startled Guard. Then he scampered into the forest.

"There! Go quick!" Captain Lodin shouted to the other Guards.

One by one the Guards charged away until only the

11

Captain and one other remained to watch the grain cart. Lodin ordered the driver to pull the cart away from the trees, but it was slow work to move horses off the road.

Jed waited until the crashing of the Guards in the underbrush had receded. He kissed his ring once for luck, then jumped down in an attack posture. Jed hoped to knock Lodin out with his first blow, but the Captain's head proved resilient. Lodin fell to his knees, still conscious.

Grath and Hack tackled the second Guard from behind and drove him to the ground. Mister Brade pinned Lodin to the side of the cart. The cart driver put his hands up and scuttled down the road away from the fray.

"Hoke," Lodin squeaked through clenched teeth. "Rodebath!"

Jed had a small second to recognize the names of the absent Guards before one of them ran back from the forest into the open. He ducked just before Guardsman Rodebath's sword swung over his head and embedded itself in the wood of the cart. Jed kicked hard into the Guard's chin, propelling him backwards. Lodin screamed in frustration. Another Guard, close behind his comrade, threw himself against the closest target, who happened to be Brade.

Jed tried to clear his head. Lodin hadn't fallen for their ruse after all. He kept his Guards back. All of them? Lodin had only called two names. Jed spared a nervous glance back at the forest, but didn't see any more. With luck, the other five Guards were still following Rimick.

After buffeting Lodin on the head to keep him down, Jed scanned the scene. Grath was unconscious. Sable was out of the tree. He was holding his bow out in confusion, a look of panic on his face, but at least no one had tried to attack the boy yet. Hack had managed to take out two Guards on his own. One lay skewered in a bloody pile behind him. The other was hunched over in agony, but clearly still alive.

As Hack met Jed's eyes in an expression of triumph, Guardsman Rodebath dragged himself angrily out of the road, sword raised towards Dohack's exposed back. Jed called a warning and Hack started to move, but not fast enough to escape a blow to the shoulder. Hack crumpled. Almost at the same time, Rodebath tumbled back with an arrow in his neck.

Good shot, Sable, Jed had time to think. He turned on Brade's opponent and subdued him with a sword against his throat. "Help Hack," Jed called to Sable as he methodically bound the last Guard to the wheel of the cart. Sable was already on his way. Lodin and Guardsman Hoke offered no more resistance.

"Sorry about this," Jed murmured half sincerely to the angry, trussed-up Captain.

The Captain hacked a red-tinged gob of spittle into the dust. "Don't apologize. It's stupid. You're a bandit."

"I prefer Queensman."

"You steal things. That's what you do. You're a bandit."

There was a truth to this that Jed could not deny. But he was pleased with the title the townsfolk gave him: Jedomar the Queensman. In the old days, a Queensman was someone appointed by Queen Benta. Saying someone was a Queensman meant they worked directly for the government. Since the Revolution, this term no longer held any meaning. But gradually folk had come to apply it to those few who openly opposed the Regent.

Grath came to and compulsively hugged his son. The Guard that Sable had shot was still alive, convulsing with tremors down the length of his body. It was obvious he wasn't going to make it, so Jed put him out of his misery. He cast a brief curse at the Otherworld for making him do it.

Hack rose from the pool of blood that he and the dead Guard had contributed to. "I'm all right," he groaned at Jed's touch. This could have been bluster on Hack's part, but a quick examination convinced Jed otherwise. Hack's wound was superficial. His collarbone had stopped the blade, which had damaged little but skin. He would be able to walk.

"Let's get out," Jed called to his comrades. He didn't care to think of the position they would be in if the other five

Guards returned. They took what grain they could carry and vanished into the leafy refuge of the forest.

Senna's installation occurred without ceremony. Captain Lodin handed her the keys to the cupboards and the upstairs rooms. He made a gurgle in his throat, as if he couldn't believe she was foolish enough to take them, and then left. Senna stood uncertainly examining the keys in her fist.

Another Guard eyed her critically from the entryway. Lodin must have mentioned her because he didn't demand to know what she was doing there. She summoned her courage. "Excuse me, do you know where I can find Lord Fenwith's steward?"

The Guard wrinkled his face, then spat emphatically on the tiled floor. Senna admired the viscous puddle as it dribbled slowly into a crack. It occurred to her that she would have to clean that up. "Outside," the man grunted, "as usual."

Senna nodded and stepped past, trying to look like she knew what she was doing.

The courtyard was about as large as the market square, with a low wall at its border. A Guards' quarters, a stable, and a few smaller buildings whose function Senna had yet to guess opened onto it. A pair of Guards pointed at her from the easternmost wall. Her interview must have been big news.

A hairless, wrinkled head bobbed in and out of view behind a barren hedge—the castle steward. Corvan was an ancient, eremitic little man that Senna had previously seen only from a distance. He'd been attached to the castle longer than most people had been alive, which may have been why the Baron kept him around.

The steward was on his hands and knees when Senna approached, paying no attention to the world beyond the mulch in his fingers.

"Good meeting," Senna began.

Corvan winced as she spoke. A glance seemed to satisfy the old man that she wasn't worth speaking to, and he went back to his work.

Senna cleared her throat. "I understand you're the steward? I'm the new housekeeper here."

This declaration at least got the steward's attention. He stood up and examined her with small, beady eyes. "Housekeeper?" The steward's manner was hesitant and timorous. He drew back from her as if afraid she might hit him.

Senna held out a hand and gave the old man her brightest smile. "My name is Senna. I hope we can be friends. I think I could use one in this place."

Her strategy worked better than expected. "Oh," Corvan mumbled. He suddenly made eye contact with her. "The new housekeeper. Oh, oh." The old man was still too shy to take Senna's hand. He pulled his own hands inward and ineffectively wiped his muddy fingers over his trousers. "That's good! I'm not a very good housekeep myself. I prefer to keep my business out of doors." Corvan gestured to the sky, as if Senna might not have known where it was. He scratched his head, mumbling more words of mild approbation. "Good, yes, good. Do you need me to show you around?"

Senna pretended not to notice the steward's reluctance. She took his arm as if she were a young woman supporting her grandfather.

Corvan opened his mouth awkwardly, showing more gaps than teeth. "Well, well," he started, "if anyone can tell you about this place, it should be me. This castle is four hundred years old, and I'm almost that old myself."

Corvan led her to the garden shed, and explained how he had built it some years ago, and what tools he had used. Senna let him go on for quite a while as he described the maintenance of the stables and the Guards' outhouse.

Eventually he turned her attention to the garden, where he told her how long each plant had been there, and how long he expected it to live. Senna hoped her polite attention was building goodwill with the steward, but she had little interest in plants, and it took some convincing to coax him out of his botanic reverie.

"The castle?" Corvan turned at her prompting. "Oh! The castle, yes," He turned towards the colossal stone structure as if disappointed to find it there. "I suppose you want to see that."

Corvan showed her a side entrance that opened into the kitchen, which allowed them to avoid another encounter with the Guard. Senna cringed when she saw the room. Dishes were piled high over soiled surfaces. What scanty reserves of food remained showed signs of vermin infestation. Corvan waved her through into the hallway. Senna felt amused that the steward had so little to say about the room where she would be spending most of her time.

"You are from Geid, aren't you?" Corvan went on without waiting for an answer. "Did you know this castle is four hundred years old?"

The castle was called so out of ceremony. It was too small to be used as a dependable fortress. There were only two halls — a main one and a subsidiary—and a mere five or six bedrooms. Even so, it was easily the largest building in the county, and its two stories were intimidating to the citizens of Geid. Senna took detailed mental notes while Corvan chatted away, providing details that weren't necessarily helpful.

"There are four windows in this hall, two in the east hall, and one over the entryway. I'm sure you've seen that one. It's the one with the crown of Dunguth in eight colors." Corvan was clearly proud of working for an estate that boasted stained glass in eight colors. He pointed to the closest window. "This one got broken last year and we had to send all the way to Gault for replacement glass."

Senna bit her lip, remembering the angry mob that had been the cause of the break. She nodded politely as she followed the steward into the next hall.

The east hall, though large, held only an ornately carved desk with fat legs and a small stool, set against the far wall. It served as Fenwith's personal office, Corvan informed her. He did most of his work here. As much as the Baron aspired to power, he wasn't much for luxury.

The fireplace was empty. "It's a nice enough temperature for now, but the castle gets cold during the winter," Corvan said. "This hall was kept much warmer when Themson was here."

Senna was a little surprised to hear the steward refer freely to the castle's former Baron. But perhaps Corvan was one of those people who cared so little about what happened in the world that no one noticed what he said about it.

"There were wonderful parties then," he said. "If we didn't have forty-eight candles, we made do with forty-six. An even number is always best, of course." Corvan grew somber, remembering old times. "There used to be a Revordian armchair here, and a mantle hung over that fireplace."

Senna knew immediately what mantle he referred to. It was a fur pelt with the crest of the Queen stitched onto it. It had been discarded in the square, symbolizing the new Regent's dominion, when Fenwith first came to Geid. Senna had been a young girl then, not old enough to be considered for work outside the family inn. She remembered walking past the Queen's mantle as it lay rotting in a pile near the market stalls, further defaced with dirt or other undesirable substances until Fenwith finally had it burned. The Gault Revolution had been an uncertain time. Heads were rolling, and people were eager to prove their affection for whatever authority happened to hold power over them at the moment. Senna dug her nails deep into her palms.

In the three years since the Revolution, the country had gone from bad to worse. Few people pretended to welcome the Regent's reign any longer. The Regent handed most of their wealth over to Gault, and squandered the rest. Most of those in Mackabine were either homeless or starving.

Corvan's voice, urging her upstairs, pulled Senna back to the present. They took the back flight near the kitchen and emerged at a point overlooking the castle's front entrance. The main hall stretched up into an atrium, and the second-floor balcony wrapped around the inner walls of the hall with a stairwell at each end.

"Nobody ever uses this room." Corvan pointed lazily down the south wing. "That room either. You can pick whichever you like for sleeping." He gestured toward another door, then another. "That one used to be for tailoring and that one down there was for the Baroness's tea parties. Themson always gave her plenty of spending money to entertain her friends, just so she would stay in her parlor and not bother him."

"What about Lord Fenwith?" Senna asked.

"Uh...he sleeps in the north wing, but I won't take you there. You'd better stay out of it altogether. The Baron likes his privacy."

Senna frowned. If Fenwith had gotten along by himself this far, he wouldn't appreciate her sudden interference. "Where do you sleep?" she asked.

Corvan blinked. "Oh not here, by the Queen! I've got my own place outside, near my animals, and far enough away from the Guards' quarters. It'll just be you and the Baron inside the castle."

Wonderful, Senna thought with only half-hearted sarcasm. It would be easier to spy on him this way. Lord Fenwith was a clumsy tyrant, but it wasn't for lack of trying that Geid hadn't fallen to pieces in his hands. Senna was going to do everything in her power to make him pay.

CHAPTER TWO

The next morning Senna found Mister Corvan in the kitchen, washing potatoes, and greeted him warmly. Corvan backed away from her. He blinked, his expression cold and unregistering. Senna's confusion might have gone on unabated if Captain Lodin hadn't poked his head into the room after her.

"Corvan! You dummy," he barked. "You don't have to make the Baron's food anymore. Senna is doing that. You get back to the stables."

The steward shot Lodin a disappointed look, then turned to go, after a frown of suspicion at Senna. The Captain gave a laugh at Senna's expense. "He doesn't remember you," Lodin said. "Corvan suffers from a riddled head. Gets worse every year."

Senna stared forlornly at the empty space Mister Corvan had just vacated. She had been looking forward to a warm rapport with the odd little steward.

"There's a reason Corvan's not the most friendly fellow. Don't worry. He'll get used to you after a few weeks. You may have to remind him who you are a few times, but eventually it'll stick."

"Wait!" she called as Lodin turned to leave. Her questions were too numerous to voice at once, but she managed to form one. "Where do I serve Lord Fenwith's meals?"

Lodin shrugged, displaying either a lack of knowledge or interest. "Just leave it on the table. That's what Melga used to do." He started away again, then stopped and pivoted back. "Be careful," he advised. "The Baron is not an easy man to work for. He expects perfection, and he'll ignore you if you give it to him, but he's quick to anger at mistakes."

Senna nodded somberly.

"I'd warn you of more, but I don't want to scare you away," he said and left quickly.

Senna was scared; she couldn't deny it. On the other hand, she didn't think the Baron's expectations could be high, after living in squalor for so long. The halls were dank and smelly. Nothing had been cleaned for months. The Baron appeared to wash his own clothes, if they were washed at all. Meals prepared by Corvan consisted of raw vegetables and bread. Senna was surprised Fenwith hadn't crawled into town on his hands and knees, begging for a housekeeper. She picked up the closest rag and got to work.

Senna didn't actually see the Baron again until her third night in the castle. He tended to seal himself in the east hall in the evenings. She found the door to the hall ajar while walking the interior perimeter of the castle. Some visitor was still inside. She could hear unguarded voices drifting into the hallway. Senna slid along the wall and peeked around the corner. The Baron was inside with one of his Guard.

"We're not even sure if it *was* Jedomar," the Guard ventured.

"Why do you use that name? I told you I hate that name!"

"Yeeess, Lord. The…uh, bandit—"

Fenwith held up a hand to silence his Guard. His eyes

fixed upon the side of Senna's face visible in the doorframe. Striding angrily to the entrance, he slammed the door. The wooden slab quivered an inch from her face.

Senna swallowed as she assessed how close he had come to taking off her nose. Mentally she congratulated Jed on whatever distress he'd caused since the last time she'd seen him.

Curiosity made Senna linger outside the door for another quarter hour. Eventually the Guard emerged. He turned without seeing her and walked back towards the entryway. Senna had to hurry to keep up with his brisk pace.

"Cafin," she called.

The Guard halted and whipped his head around to look at her.

"That's right, isn't it?"

He narrowed his eyes suspiciously before nodding.

"I'm Senna," she volunteered.

"I know," said Cafin. He examined her with curious eyes. He was one of the youngest Guards, although misfortune in his line of work had already left him with a limp.

Senna smiled and tried her best to look harmless. "Real slave-driver, isn't he?" She tossed her head towards the Baron's closed door.

Cafin tentatively returned her smile. He was probably trying to decide how familiar he was supposed to be with the castle's housekeeper.

"Listen," Senna said lightly, "I do laundry on Horse-Day and I was wondering if any of the men wanted their shirts washed. There's plenty of room on the line."

The Guard's mask of caution dissipated. "You'd wash our shirts?" he asked, incredulous.

"Well, sure. It's hardly more work for me," Senna lied. An extra twenty shirts would take the entire morning, but she hoped their goodwill would be worth it. "Anyway, you fellows look like you could use some help. How long has it been since you washed that thing?" She waved at the fabric underneath his harness.

Cafin shifted his eyes and gave her an *I'll never tell* smile.

"Well, any Guard who wants a clean shirt can drop it off in the kitchen and pick it up the next day. It's just an offer. Tell your friends."

Cafin nodded. "No one will turn you down," he promised.

"But, uh…" Senna lowered her voice. "Don't tell *you know who*. Not that he'd care, of course, but he sure can be cranky sometimes."

The Guard broke into a grin. Now they were accomplices.

"What was he yelling about, anyway?"

Cafin's grin faltered ever so slightly.

Don't push, Senna admonished herself. *Walk away if he doesn't answer.*

"Just some problems with that Queensman. You know the one, right?"

It would be foolish to play dumb, so Senna nodded. Everyone knew about Jedomar. "What'd he do?" The question was out of her mouth before she could check it.

Cafin snorted. "He just makes our lives difficult."

Senna shrugged to say it wasn't her business. "Well, good luck." She didn't have to pretend to look busy. She still had an armful of chores to complete before bedtime.

On Spools-Day, Senna received a few hours of her own for personal business or family visits. She was so anxious to get out of the castle that she got up early to do her morning chores and finished them a little more haphazardly than usual. She put on her good tunic, and spared ten minutes to pin up her hair. It was still first light when she left the garden by the servants' entrance. She hardly expected to see a soul, so she was very surprised when she ran headfirst into Lord Fenwith. He came in through the gate the same moment she walked out of it, and in such a hurry that he nearly pushed her to the ground. He recoiled instantly and for a moment looked as if he didn't remember who she was.

Senna felt obliged to give an explanation. "It's my day off. I'm going to visit my broth—" She broke off as she realized he didn't care. The Baron was about as disgusted at being spoken to as he was at being run into.

Those blank eyes prompted a memory. It was the same expression the Baron wore when he dismissed her uncle's plea for her parents' bodies. A flash of sorrow seized her heart, almost overpowering her composure.

During the Gault Revolution, Senna's parents were among the few to voice opposition to the new reign. They told anyone who listened that the Regent was a robber and that they were proud subjects of Queen Benta. A few days later they were among the handful of defiants hanging from the castle walls, right alongside the bodies of Lord Themson and his wife, the former Baron and Baroness of Geid.

"I'm sorry," Senna apologized in a neutral tone. She backed carefully out of his reach, breathing shallowly.

Did Fenwith know he had killed her parents? Did he care? Senna was sure he didn't. It never occurred to him that a serving girl might be plotting her revenge.

Senna kept her eyes on the garden tiles as she backpedaled. She hoped she looked obedient, inconsequential, dominated. She swore to herself she was none of those things. The Baron's sour gaze followed Senna until she passed the end of the rose hedge, where she was grateful to be out of sight.

Jed tilted his chair onto its back legs, balancing himself

at a forty-degree angle while he used one foot to steady himself against the table. He rested his neck on the rim of the chair's back and let his gaze wander over the ceiling, reading patterns in the grain to pass the time. He had stared at this cottage ceiling enough times that the markings were familiar. He slept here sometimes. Carly cottage was supposed to be abandoned. It had once belonged to a witch doctor, and people stayed clear for fear his spirit still lingered over the place. That made it perfect for a hideout and occasional meetings of Queensmen.

Jed couldn't pinpoint the exact moment he began to self-identify as a Queensman. When the Gaultian shock troops were sent into Geid, Jed was just as confused as anyone. There had always been injustice, even before the Gault Revolution. Guards who abused their power. Tax collectors who thrived on bribes. With Fenwith in power, these things had become expected, even legal. Jed was branded a criminal early on. Little by little, he started confronting the injustices he saw. Now he was the most famous man in Geid.

Dwen's behavior was a distraction. He kept getting out of his chair and looking out the window towards the riverbank. He fidgeted, whistled bits of half-remembered tunes, and tried to engage Rimick in conversation. Rimick had his attention stuck in a book, and responded only grudgingly to Dwen's prattle.

They knew Senna had been successful in her mission to become Fenwith's housekeeper. They did not know when exactly she would be able to meet them. Jed thought there was little chance of Senna appearing sooner than midday, but that didn't stop Dwen from camping hopefully at the door. His anxiety was understandable; Senna was his half-sister.

Jed was probably as anxious as Dwen, though he hid his feelings better. Senna was a grown woman. She could take care of herself. Besides, she would either come or she would not. Any extra worrying was pointless.

"Do you know the difference between a rabbit and a footstool?"

Jed sighed. "I don't know, Dwen. Enlighten us. What is the difference between a rabbit and a footstool?"

Dwen shrugged. "I don't know either. Mister Dodran asked me that riddle and I've been trying to figure it out since yesterday."

Jed chuckled. It was worth keeping Dwen around just for a few cheap laughs. At nineteen, Dwen was a year older than Senna, though he acted half his age.

"Come on, Rimick, you must know, since you're so clever. What's the difference between a rabbit and a footstool?"

Rimick answered without moving his eyes from his book. "A rabbit is alive and a footstool is not."

Dwen squinted and turned to Jed. "Do you think that could be it?" Before Jed could think of an answer, Dwen's expression brightened. He sprang towards the window. "She's coming!"

Jed followed and spied Senna's figure walking along the edge of the riverbank. She moved at her usual brisk pace, cloak trailing in the mud behind her. Jed held Dwen back from running out to meet her. There was no point in being careless. The young man stuck his tongue out at Jed's caution, but he restrained his loud greeting until his sister was at the door.

"Senna! I'm so glad you haven't been executed." Dwen held his arms open for her.

Senna smiled back. "Well before I am, I fully expect you all to come and rescue me." She hugged Dwen, shook hands with Rimick, and hovered uncertainly in front of Jed.

Jed hugged her. "It's good to see you, Senna," he said.

"Likewise," she murmured as she pulled away. "All of you. You're a sight for sore eyes." She sank into her chair in a way that made it look like she hadn't sat down for some time.

The flood of questions came quickly. Dwen started them, and Rimick kept them up. How had she been treated? Did the Baron talk to her? What was the Baron's schedule? Did she know when the Guard changed? Had she found where the tax records were kept?

In Jed's opinion, most of Senna's answers were unsatisfying. Except for some minute descriptions of the layout and provisioning of the castle, she was unable to provide very much in the way of useful information.

"Did you see his office?"

"Not really."

"Did you see his room?"

"It's off limits."

"You don't know anything!" Dwen clicked his tongue matter-of-factly. "I knew it! I knew this was a bad idea from the start," he reminded everyone.

"I need more time, that's all," Senna said. "I can't look like I'm sniffing around. The Baron doesn't trust me yet."

Jed hummed. "Surely he'll never get to that point?"

"No, but he might get used to me."

Jed didn't want to push her any more. He started rummaging through his knapsack for their spoons. Rimick had brought a meal his mother cooked and Senna was happy to eat something she hadn't labored over personally.

"By the Queen, I'm so tired," she complained. She looked it. She had dark circles under her eyes and her eyelids drooped heavily. Her hair looked as if it needed a wash.

"You're working too hard," said Jed.

"I know," she said. "I'll slow down next week. I think I can get away with it, now that the floors no longer stink."

The meal momentarily interrupted the conversation, then Senna made an obvious effort to change the subject. "Did you get the last grain cart?"

"Yes!" Dwen thumped his cup down with enthusiasm. "You should have been there, Senna. It was marvelous!"

Jed snorted dubiously. Dwen hadn't been there either. But the young man had a secondhand account and Jed let him share it. Dwen surely loved to tell a story. He got most of it right, and when facts failed him, he embellished with details from his imagination. Jed closed his eyes, his gut tightening as he remembered the fight. It had been a close one.

"Jed pushed the Captain into the mud," Dwen was saying. "He sits up, angry as hell. He's got mud plastered to his face, so he can't see a thing, and he points up at his own Guard and says, '*Get them!*'"

Senna laughed appreciatively.

Jed felt the need to correct him. "That didn't happen."

Dwen waved Jed off, unconcerned. "If Senna digs up enough dirt on the Baron, are you going to overthrow him?"

"Probably not," said Jed. There wouldn't be much point. The real threat was Regent Gote, an usurper with no blood claim to the monarchy, and who wasn't even a woman! The Regent wouldn't care what dirt they found on Fenwith. He was the one distributing it to his Barons in the first place.

"Mister Noreth says he saw Fenwith out in the hills, doing a strange dance. He was making a deal with spirits from the Otherworld!"

Here Rimick interrupted. "I told you not to repeat that nonsense, Dwen. No one speaks to the Otherworld."

"Albinos do," Dwen insisted. "Mister Noreth says—"

"Don't go spreading wild stories, Dwen," Jed spoke up in support of his friend. "It's hard enough trying to calm people's fears without involving the Otherworld."

"But Jed! You know the Baron is a villain."

"He's a villain because he's villainous," muttered Rimick, "not because he's albino."

Dwen turned to his sister for support, but Senna claimed to have no opinion.

Jed wondered if Senna had more to fear than Rimick believed. There were always rumors, of course, and Jed wasn't gullible enough to believe half of them. But he didn't dismiss the possibility that Fenwith practiced some form of dark arts.

Jed had to hold his peace in front of Rimick, or he would never hear the end of it. Rimick wouldn't listen to conjecture on anything he couldn't see, hear, or touch. Privately, Jed decided to give Senna a rosemary token as soon as he could. A good thick one, to scare away bad spirits.

If only it were that easy to scare the Baron and his

men.

Senna's spirits were fortified as much as her stomach by the simple meal. The people she cared about most in the world were in this cottage with her.

In between gesturing to his audience, Dwen idly picked up her hand and gave it a squeeze. Senna counted her good fortune to have a brother who wasn't ashamed to show affection.

Her eyes absently swept the room as she listened to Dwen's familiar, carefree chatter. It was hard not to keep them from settling on Jed, especially since he was looking at her. It was embarrassing, how much she relished his attention. A bit of stubble accented Jed's strong jaw, indicating that he hadn't bothered to shave for a day or so. Every so often, his features converged into an irresistible twitch of a smile.

Senna had loved Jed in one way or another since she was a little girl. At first, he was simply the most exciting of her playmates, and older enough that he seemed wise. As they grew, she allowed herself to love him as a friend. There was always some part of her that wanted to be more, but she kept that part well hidden. Jed was too good for her. He was the ideal for most women: strong, good-natured, ruggedly handsome. His red-brown hair and laughing eyes drew attention wherever he went.

Jed noticed her scrutiny and gave her a wink. Senna bit her lip to keep her heart in check. Jed was only being friendly. He was always friendly.

Senna searched for another topic to distract her thoughts. "What about Dohack? Will he be all right?"

"In bed for the time being," said Jed. "But mostly as a precaution against infection. Brade said he'll recover in a few days." Jed's composure told her there was no fear.

Senna couldn't muster too much sympathy for Hack. When Dwen was a child, Hack used to tease him and make him cry. She had never forgiven him for that. Dohack had a selfish streak. He was inherently lazy, and didn't bother himself about anything unless it added to his own enjoyment.

Jed continued to snack on peanuts after the main course was finished. No one else had so hearty an appetite so he took the bowl into his lap. "We're doing the Baron a favor, whether he knows it or not," he mumbled as he unshelled one of the fat little nuts.

"His policy is completely insensible," agreed Rimick. Illogic was one of the few things that could drive Rimick to express his opinion. "Where does he expect to get the next year's grain if we all starve to death during the winter?"

Rimick was in stark contrast to his friend. Nothing about Rimick drew attention. He was slight, balding heavily, and timid-looking. If you spent some time with him, you discovered that he was clever with numbers and good in a fistfight. Beyond that, Senna felt she understood him very little.

Jed threw one of his peanuts at Rimick. "No one accuses the Baron of being sensible."

Rimick caught the peanut as it bounced off him. He returned it across the table with a serious little nod. Rimick was an extremely serious person. But there was no denying his unqualified loyalty to Jed. For that, Rimick had Senna's respect.

"There was something else the Baron was upset about," Senna said, remembering suddenly. "I thought it was the grain cart at first, but the Guard said they weren't sure whether it was you or not."

Jed shrugged.

"She probably means the cloak incident," Rimick suggested.

Jed smiled crookedly. "Oh, that. That wasn't me."

"What was it?" she insisted.

Dwen's explanation was the fastest. "Someone stole

29

the Baron's cloak off his horse. And stuck it on the proclamations post in the square. And piled a load of goat dung on it."

"Before you ask, I don't know who did it," said Jed. "But it was rather funny. Everyone decided I did it anyway, so I suppose I may as well have. I'm surprised you didn't hear about it," Jed told her, "the way everyone was talking."

Senna blinked. Perhaps Dwen was right—she was learning even less inside the castle than she would outside it.

Jed hummed mischievously. "The Baron raised the price on my head again. Thirty silver pieces," he said proudly. "A pretty little sum. I bet I can double it again before the year is out." He scratched at his ear, a sign Senna recognized that he was trying to be polite. "Rimick and I have business to take care of. We should probably be going."

Rimick perked up, and Senna felt a prick of annoyance that Rimick was bored by her company.

"It doesn't matter," she sighed. "I have to get back to the castle in time to fix dinner."

Dwen pouted. "You used to make *me* dinner."

Senna leaned over to kiss Dwen on the cheek. "Jed? Make sure my brother gets something to eat, won't you?"

Jed shrugged. "I think Madam Haw feeds him from time to time," he quipped.

Dwen got a salary of sorts running errands for Jed, but he would be happiest spending most of his time in the town. The loss of the inn hadn't left them without friends. Senna was glad of it. Homelessness didn't suit Dwen very well.

Jed didn't let her leave the cottage until Rimick had given the all clear. It seemed overly cautious to Senna. No one had followed her. As far as she could tell, no one at the castle cared two figs what she did.

She'd gotten as far as the first fork when she heard Dwen calling her name. She turned around and watched him run to catch up.

"Senna, Jed told me—" he panted a bit, out of breath "—not to ask you, but I gotta."

"What is it?" Senna prepared herself for drastic tidings.

"Stay here, Senna. Don't go back to that place."

"Oh for pity's sake, Dwen!"

"I don't want you in that castle. It's so dangerous. What would Mother say about it?"

Dwen's concern was sweet. Though he was slightly older, Senna had always been the one to keep them on track. Dwen's mother had died when he was an infant and their father remarried soon after. Senna's mother cared for Dwen as well as his real mother could have done. When she died, Senna considered it her responsibility to watch out for her wayward brother. *Keep his face shiny,* as Mother would have put it. Had Dwen suddenly decided it was time to take charge?

"I'm being as careful as I can, Dwen."

"The Baron is crazy. Mister Noreth says—" He stopped, seeing her expression, and changed tactics. "Even the Guards say he's dangerous. When he's in a bad mood, he takes it out on whoever is closest. Anyone who stays around him long enough gets executed."

This was not entirely so; there were many people who'd served Fenwith for years. Corvan was a prime example. But there was enough truth in it to keep her on her toes. She started to shake her head.

"Just promise you'll stay as far away from him as possible."

"I'll try," said Senna. She patted Dwen's cheek fondly. She hoped the spirits wouldn't hold her accountable for her small lie.

CHAPTER THREE

For the amount of labor involved, Senna's job offered little in the way of compensation. Her week's pay was less than she used to make as an inn maid. Small wonder there were so few applicants. For the first week in her position, Senna got up at the crack of dawn and didn't retire until after midnight. Housekeeping was ambitious, grueling labor. Her duties included cooking, cleaning, and organizing household activities.

Most castles engaged a throng of servants to support the leisure of their occupants. Only the Baron's indifference allowed him to keep such a humble number of staff.

The Baron didn't like people. He lived alone, ate alone, slept alone, and had low tolerance for company of any kind. He never entertained. The only visitors permitted on castle grounds were officials from the Regent's estate. They were seen occasionally passing through town. They came by ones and twos, were always strictly business, and never stayed for very long.

Senna was permitted to hire extra hands when necessary, but aside from Corvan and a widow who came to help with the laundry, she rarely saw another person. Even the Guards were allowed to enter the castle only by invitation, which Fenwith seldom proffered. They spent most of their time in the Guards quarters, either on or off duty.

Senna received neither suggestions nor complaints from her employer. She saw him very seldom. He was out most of the day, even in poor weather, and when he was at home, he always seemed to be in another part of the castle. Senna would have thought he was willing to vacate a room to avoid meeting her—if that thought did not attach more importance to her presence than she dared credit herself with.

Her first opportunity to spy came when the Baron informed her that she no longer had to leave the dining room after setting out his meals. She was to stand on hand while he ate and attend him if he needed anything. This was a tedious and demeaning task: standing immobile against the wall, and stepping forward on occasion to pour wine. However, it did guarantee her a glimpse of Fenwith at least once a day. Twice if he didn't travel.

It was during one of these mealtime vigils that she learned about the new taxman. Lodin barged into the dining room to announce the arrival of a note from Mackabine. It ordered Lord Fenwith to receive a Gaultian replacement for the usual clod that came to collect quarterly profits.

Fenwith took it as a personal intrusion. "Nosy little Gaults," he muttered over his potatoes. "When he comes, tell him he has to speak to me in my own language. It's bad enough listening to that gibberish in the capital; I won't have it here."

Lodin left the note with his master, where it lay crumpled and forgotten on his plate. Senna had already gleaned tremendous information from the Baron's unguarded conversation, but the note would hold specifics—names, codes, instructions.

"Do you need more soup, Lord?" She nodded at his empty bowl.

Fenwith reacted to her unusual breach of silence by turning away. "No," he grunted.

Senna had a brief opportunity while his eyes looked elsewhere. Without thinking overmuch, she tipped the pot and poured a portion of soup directly into his lap.

She squealed as the Baron leapt up, and her look of terrified apology was hardly feigned. If he had screamed or threatened, it would have been bearable. Instead he gave her a glance like a man might give a cockroach right before he stomped on it.

"Forgive me, Lord," said Senna.

He went wordlessly into the kitchen and Senna followed, offering to boil clean water. It was not until he ordered her out that she dared pass alone through the dining room and spare a moment with the note. She flattened it against the table and committed the contents to memory.

The Baron reentered just as she finished replacing the letter. She froze, and began to back away when the Lord spoke to her. "Sit." Senna looked up, not understanding. "Sit," he repeated in a low voice.

Senna did not dare disobey him. Trembling, she lowered herself into the Baron's dining chair. Fenwith crouched to eye level, put a hand over her mouth, and clenched her face tightly. She voiced a brief, muffled objection. Fenwith picked up the soup pot with one hand, held it over her head, and deliberately poured the contents over her. Senna held very still. The soup was not quite hot enough to burn her, but it was close. She dug her fingers into the sides of the chair.

Fenwith dropped the pot with a thud and braced himself against the table to look at her. "Don't cross me."

Senna was trying not to cry. Did he know she had done it on purpose? A drop of soup fell from her nose onto his knuckle. Unable to speak, unable to shake her head with the hand against her jaw, she merely stared at him.

The Baron finally released his grip. He didn't waste further words with her. He slid the note into his front pocket, seized a scrap of bread for the road, and left her dripping creamed vegetable broth.

Senna spent the next hour washing her hair and clothing. When she located a mirror, she found her face marred by the red imprint of Lord Fenwith's fingers. Dwen was right, she thought. That man would kill her one day on a whim. She would have to finish with him first.

Reluctant to leave the comfort of her kitchen fire, Senna waited until next afternoon to set out to market for midweek supplies. Her hesitation vanished when she opened the door into the fresh still air, and felt the welcome of a new spring sun. Senna hoisted a basket onto her shoulder and started through the courtyard. The last bits of snow melted to soft wet oblivion beneath her feet.

Corvan was at work on his garden, tending what he hoped to salvage from last year's growth. Senna gave him a good meeting as she passed. Corvan showed no interest in conversation.

The Guards were expending some of their leisure time out of doors in the unexpected warmth of the spring thaw. A handful were engaged in a game of Dinigo in the middle of the courtyard. Senna paused and hovered over the shoulders of the men.

"What do you want, Senna?" one of them asked her. She ignored their comments about her soiled apron.

"Hoke won again, didn't he? Pay up," she said.

They ignored her, busily gathering their coin into pouches. Senna insistently stuck her hand into the game ring. Toby sighed and passed her a fifth piece.

Senna pocketed it happily. "Thanks, Hoke. I won't doubt you next time you say you're the best player here."

"I never said that," Hoke protested modestly. This earned him a number of dirty looks, because he had.

She was about to leave the Guards to their vices when they heard the sound of a horse approaching at high speed. Senna leaped aside quickly enough to escape danger but not the loss of dignity as mud splattered over her clothes. Baron

Fenwith reared the animal to a halt a few feet in front of her, displaying his considerable skills as a horseman. Senna was sure he had sprayed her on purpose.

"What's going on here?" Fenwith said to Lodin. The Captain backed a step away from the horse. Senna couldn't tell if he was uncomfortable with the horse or if he was trying to hide his pile of coins. There were Guards' boots strewn across the pavement around the game ring, alongside several empty cups of beer.

"Just off duty, Lord."

"Does this look like an inn?" The Baron dismounted as he spoke, and unstrapped his saddlebags. "I want this yard cleaned up before the tax collector gets here. And get your men into uniform," he snapped, shooting a look at Guardsman Toby, who was standing in little more than his underwear.

His fellows snickered as Toby sheepishly shifted back and forth.

"Is that funny?" the Baron asked in a low voice. "Are you laughing at me?"

The snickers choked off abruptly. They eyed one another until Captain Lodin pointed out the obvious. "They were laughing at Toby, Lord."

"That Guard is insubordinate and undressed." Baron Fenwith pointed an accusing finger at Guardsman Toby. "Lodin, kill him for me."

The order left the Guards stunned in place.

"*Now, Captain*," said the Baron, his voice tight.

Lodin may have been lazy and unprincipled, but he was fully obedient. The Captain knelt, lifted his sword from among the others, and moved to carry out the order. Toby was late in perceiving his fate. He turned his back to run just as the Captain's sword went through him.

Senna gave a squeal, shrill and instinctual. She clamped both hands over mouth, stifling the sound. Her outburst drew no attention. Most of the Guards yelped as well.

After a pause, the Baron continued. "As I was saying, I

want my Guard in top form for the tax collector's arrival."

The Captain broke through with immediate assurances. "We'll get sorted out right away—"

"Good. Get rid of the body." The Baron turned away, shouting his last order from the door of the castle. "And someone take care of my horse!"

Senna took a few minutes to recover. The old steward appeared, slinking silently out of the rows of barren bushes. Corvan gave eyes to no one. He calmly patted the horse and loosened its saddle.

Senna picked up the basket where she had dropped it and hurried out of the courtyard.

Jed was cold and his feet hurt. He didn't dwell much on the first condition. When you lived in a country like Mackabine, cold was a part of your being. Sore feet were a more obnoxious problem. Jed glowered resentfully at the dainty embroidered things on his feet. He had left his own shoes and clothing with Rimick some miles behind.

On his back were garments crafted of fine material. Jed wondered why any Gault would be so stupid as to wear this type of flimsy apparel outside their own country. Yet they often did so. Jed had taken this outfit off the back of a Gaultian merchant two years ago. He didn't feel bad about it, since the merchant had been trying to blackmail some farmers out of their life savings.

Jed stopped short as the seam in the toe of his shoe ripped clean out. The thin soles were made for dancing on carpets, not tramping about out of doors. Jed took the shoe off and examined the stitching. It was yellow with age and should have been repaired years ago. No one would believe these were his shoes. Disgusted, he removed the other and hid both shoes beneath a bush.

Ah, the things I put up with for a little glory. Jed smiled to himself, satisfied with his own cleverness. He was happiest when his heart was pounding with adrenaline.

If they hadn't intercepted the letter, the idea probably would have come to naught. The Baron was expecting the real Counselour Tellemie, after all. Rimick could have delayed him —maybe. But the collector would have his own Guard, and probably a carriage. People tended to give eyes to those kinds of things.

But by a stroke of fate, the postman who came on Mercy-Day was Finch, and Finch generally let Jedomar read any correspondence that came for the Baron. The letter from the tax collector was nice and succinct.

Fenwith. Being delayed in Banth. Three days. Expect me on New-Day. Tellemie.

Finch refused at first to surrender the letter, but under an enormous bribe he finally agreed to let them "borrow" it for a few days. Jed took it as a sign from the Otherworld to proceed with his plan.

If you had asked Jed at fifteen what he wanted to do with his life, he would have told you that he planned to travel to the end of the world and marry a foreign princess. His family tried to dissuade him of these notions, but it did no good. Eventually they decided he should enlist in the army. A soldier would get to see and do things that a farmer in a backwoods county could only dream about.

Jed's younger brother was happy to take charge of the farm. Jed had only to wait until the boy was old enough to shoulder the responsibility of caring for himself and his parents. For years, Jed dreamed of the day when he could leave the county of Geid in the dust.

Then the Gault Revolution came. The conflict was settled and over in the Mackabine capital before their county even got word of the Queen's death. The people of Geid prepared for a mourning procession and instead they got an invasion of Gaultian shock troops. Some folk tried to fight. Baron Themson tried to run. Jed defended some of his fellows

38

and ended up killing one of the soldiers.

The death of a Gaultian soldier could not be forgiven. While Jed took refuge with friends at the Bonidon Inn, the new Baron sent troops to Jed's farm with orders to punish him. The Gaults didn't bother to knock on the door when they arrived at the farm. They barred the house shut and set it afire. It burned to the ground with Jed's brother and parents still inside. There was nothing for Jed then. Not even an army to join.

Jedomar was a man with nothing to lose. Which was probably why he got himself into situations like this one.

The wall surrounding Geid Castle was not the kind that required skills or equipment to climb. It was four spans tall and barely obscured Jed's view of the castle. Jed walked through the gate without being noticed. A bit miffed at the lack of reception, he glanced about and stormed boldly up to the first Guard he saw.

Jed could tell the Guard didn't know what to make of him. He wasn't anyone Jed recognized—perhaps he was one of the new Guard brought in from Anseth. It was general practice to move Guards around as often as possible. Men were usually less concerned about abusing folk they hadn't grown up next to. This Guard was about forty and his physique was starting to go. He huffed a little as he jogged to intercept. He put a hand up to discourage Jed from coming farther.

"Lord...Mister? Where do you think you're going?"

Jed puffed himself up importantly. Numb and tired, it wasn't hard for him to look cranky as he snapped at the Guard, "I am going to see Lord Fenwith. Is there a problem?" He spoke with the airy, nasal accent associated with Gaults, though he tried not to lay it on too thick. He didn't actually speak a word of Gaultian, much less understand the phonetics.

Jed was sure he made a fantastic spectacle, dressed in his dilapidated robes with a filthy, wet turban on his head. He'd darkened and lined his face with ash to age it, and added a bit of trimmed mustache and a slightly paunched belly to complete the disguise.

The Guard opened and closed his mouth, unsure whether there was a problem or not. "Is he expecting you?" he ventured slowly.

"If it means that much to you," Jed said, "you could inform him that Tellemie is here for collection."

The Guard stared some more. "Please wait here, sir."

Jed nodded brusquely. The Guard ran off and reappeared soon after, on the heels of Captain Lodin.

Lodin was, if possible, even more confused than his subordinate. He didn't try to hide his incredulity as he stared. "Counselour Tellemie?"

Jed rolled his eyes skyward and took a moment to massage his face, as if trying to soothe some terrible anger. "That is I."

"What's the pass code?"

"Pass code? Fenwith gave *you* the passcode? What an imbecile! Take me inside and I'll give it to him myself."

The Captain looked too confused to respond.

"Oh, for pity's sake! The pass code is 'Peabird's Northern Treasure.'"

Lodin relaxed and waved for assistance. By the time they reached the doors, Jed had been honored with a full escort. He tried not to look too many of them in the face. Some of them had seen him up close before. He was especially worried about Lodin, but the Captain seemed too preoccupied by his arrival to submit him to very much scrutiny.

Jed had never been inside the castle. From Senna's descriptions, he wasn't expecting to be impressed, but his first view of the main hall drew his breath in. The arched ceiling was as high as a great tree and the sight was magnified by the light from glass-set windows. Jed quickly shook away any signs of awe. Counselour Tellemie would have seen better castles than this.

He summoned his confidence as the Baron came

striding into the hall. Fenwith had seen him up close too, but never for long and never, he hoped, with much attention on his facial features. He bowed like a good official and raised his eyes without betraying recognition. "Baron Fenwith?"

Jed watched Fenwith take in his appearance. After a brief silence, Jed rambled off his false name and the pass code before asking to be shown a fire and a hot meal.

Fenwith squinted and said slowly, "Are you all right, Counselour Tellemie?"

"Do I look all right?" Jed snapped. "I am sorry to say, Lord Fenwith, that the hospitality in your county leaves something to be desired."

"Is that so?" Fenwith said cautiously.

"It is so. I'd scarcely taken one step into this wretched county when I found myself surrounded by bandits. Of course I had to give them everything. Do you know what it's like to fear for your life? That Jedomar fellow had an arrow pointed at my throat. He took my horses, my carriage, my servants—" Jed pointed angrily at his wet stockings. "The mad villain even took my shoes."

Luckily Fenwith wasn't much brighter than his Guard. His expression shifted from suspicion to embarrassment. "My apologies, Counselour," he said, seemingly genuinely concerned.

Senna chose this moment to come into the hall with her arms full of laundry. Jed hadn't seen anyone call for her, so she was probably looking for an excuse to see what was going on. With her head up high and her focus on the front door, Senna looked convincingly disinterested. Jed wondered how well his disguise would hold up.

He was disappointed. Senna gave a little squeal when she saw him and dropped her load of clothing on the floor.

All eyes turned to watch her scramble to gather the dropped laundry. "I'm sorry, Lord. I...I saw a mouse."

Good girl, Senna.

The Baron lost interest in her immediately, but the overturned basket gave her an excuse to linger and overhear more of their conversation.

"This bandit, Jedomar," the Baron said. "I know of him. He's been a problem for a few weeks, but he'll be caught soon."

Weeks, indeed! Fenwith had been trying to get rid of Jed for years, though that seemed to be something he was unwilling to admit.

"I don't know what kind of order you keep around here," said Jed. "I don't consider it my business. But when an honest official can't travel the roads, it paints a sad picture of your governance."

The Baron seemed to take this chastisement to heart. "I understand. It's only a matter of time—"

"Keep your platitudes, Lord Fenwith. Just get me some dry clothes."

"Of course," the Baron said smoothly. "You, woman —prepare a room for my guest."

"Yes, Lord," said Senna.

Jed felt a good deal better with his feet soaking in a tub of hot water. His chances of coming out of this venture alive were looking good and he was beginning to enjoy his lavish surroundings.

The room he'd been given was at least twenty spans wide, with two large windows overlooking the town. They were both set with real glass, a festive green pieced in only three or four places. They cast an emerald tint over the firelit chamber. The furniture was sparse, but plush. Jed had already tested the giant four-poster bed. He would have to stay in the castle for one night, at the least. Jed would have taken the money and run if he thought he could get away with it. But tax collectors often lingered for several days, and a tax collector with no belongings would naturally require time to recuperate.

He was beginning to wonder if Senna would manage to visit, when he heard a rap at the door. Senna opened it without being invited and entered with a basket of towels and some fresh robes. Jed couldn't resist the urge to shoot her a quick wink.

Senna dropped her load unceremoniously on the floor. "What in the name of the Otherworld do you think you're doing?"

Jed raised his eyebrows haughtily. "I'm washing my feet, Madam."

"You need your brain washed," she exclaimed. "What if someone recognizes you?"

"Madam, please! I don't know what you mean."

"There's no one to hear, Jed. The nearest Guard is four walls away."

"Still!" he squeaked, willing her to lower her voice. "You could refrain from using my name."

"I assumed you would waylay the collector, not take his place!"

"But you sent me all that wonderful information. So precise. Even the pass code, by the Queen!" Jed stroked his new mustache. "I've never had so much fun!"

"But what about the real collector?"

"Don't worry. I've taken care of it."

"What did you do, kidnap him?"

"Not quite. I'll tell you later. This isn't the place for that conversation." Jed dried his feet and slid them into the set of slippers Senna had brought. They were brand new and blessedly roomy.

Senna stammered as she tried to come up with a new objection.

Jed hushed her. "You worry too much, friend. Now you'd better go. The Baron wants me to have dinner with him. Unless you want to stay and watch me get dressed?"

Senna's mouth twitched unhappily. "I'll see you at dinner." She swept out the door and banged it behind her.

❖

Fenwith's manners were a surprise to Jed. He had never seen Fenwith anything but cruel and blunt when dealing with his tenants or subordinates. But it seemed he was completely capable of being civil toward important company. Not charming, perhaps—but civil.

"I hope your room is satisfactory?"

"It's fine," Jed replied politely, but he kept his tone curt. He wanted to appear disinterested in conversation.

"That room was used by the former Baron. It's a little large for my tastes, but it does make suitable guest quarters."

Jed was tickled by this news. He had never managed to meet Baron Themson. It was something he had always regretted. Perhaps Themson had not been the most lovable of Barons. During his forty year tenureship, his greatest accomplishments had been drinking and playing Dinigo. But people named him a friend and a saint when compared with Baron Fenwith.

Fenwith outlawed solstice and birthing ceremonies because he claimed they were a drain on the economy. He confiscated music and literature, dismantled the helping circle, and squashed anyone who had the audacity to look joyful. By Jed's estimate, Fenwith was a thoroughly miserable man who wanted everyone to be as miserable as himself.

Fenwith gave Jed a shallow, wooden smile. It probably irked him that he wasn't allowed to squash visiting tax collectors. Instead he asked Jed what he wanted to drink, and leaned over to make sure his guest's cup was full.

Senna stood against the wall and pretended not to listen. Jed wondered how she could bear the indignity of serving this man, day after day. Jed was impressed by her discretion. Her eyes were blank and did not stray towards them during the meal.

Jed thought it safest to say as little as possible. Fenwith expected an aloof and disdaining foreigner, and that was precisely what Jed gave him. The Baron mirrored his behavior for the most part. They paid more attention to their food than each other.

Halfway through the braised goat, Fenwith worked himself into mentioning the robbery. "That bandit. It's not worth worrying too much about him. A very minor nuisance."

Jed raised his eyes, hiding his amusement.

"Jedomar has never tried anything of this magnitude before, and he certainly would not have harmed a government official. You were never in serious peril," Fenwith said.

Secretly, it was a relief to Jed that the Baron wanted to downplay his Queensmen problem. It was a challenge to remain stiff as he replied, "I hope you're not dismissing the seriousness of the event. It was not a joke."

"Not at all," the Baron said hastily.

"Being robbed was a thoroughly unpleasant experience. But I suppose," Jed added thoughtfully, "there's no need for me to mention this incident to the Regent."

Fenwith's smile looked even less joyous. "How much?"

"Fifty pieces will be sufficient. Naturally, you will provide me with a new carriage and escort."

"Naturally."

"Then there's no need to worry. I'm sure this sort of thing won't happen again."

"Of course," said Fenwith. "I've sent some men to retrieve your escort, in case they have trouble finding their way to the castle."

Jed coughed. He had hoped Fenwith would overlook his fictitious servants. "That's not necessary," he said. "I don't think any of them survived."

A cloud fell over the Baron's face. "What do you mean? Jedomar killed them?"

"What else would I mean?"

The cloud darkened. He seemed to ponder the matter

with serious concern. Jed didn't understand why he should. Despite Fenwith's blathering about the harmless bandit, the Baron had always played up Jed's escapades to the town. From the way Jedomar was presented on wanted posters, you would think he was a raving, bloodthirsty maniac.

"Have you been in Mackabine long?" Fenwith asked.

"No. That is, no and yes. I was recently on furlough in Gault, but before that I was in Mackabine for several years."

"I'm impressed by your command of our language," Fenwith said.

"I prefer to speak the local language when I travel." Jed quietly begged the spirits of the Otherworld that Fenwith wouldn't test him. He barely knew two words of Gaultian.

"You must be tired after your adventure today," the Baron suggested as Senna began to clear their dishes. "The collection can wait until morning, don't you agree?"

"Make it early," said Jed. "I wish to leave as quickly as possible."

Fenwith said of course he understood. They finished the rest of the meal in relative silence. Jed wasn't sorry when Fenwith stood and wished Tellemie a good night.

CHAPTER FOUR

It was cold in the hills near Geid. Gaults complained of it often—that even in summer Mackabine was a land unfit for warm-blooded creatures. Tellemie often scorned his countrymen for their lack of grit. The pampered nobles at home sniveled over a bit of rain. Tellemie took pride in facing adversity, and liked to consider himself above such concerns as the weather. But weather in Mackabine was a serious business, and even he wore two cloaks on an early morning.

The scene outside the carriage was a dismal one: vistas of barren fields and hills broken only by small patches of forest. The skies had been too dry to dispense any snow this season. The farmers needed snow to protect their soil from freezing. This morning there was only a thin sheet of frost over the empty grasslands.

Tellemie should have liked this country. It was made of good hard land and good hard people. But there was too much ruin in the present landscape to engender his affection. Too many starving children, too many wandering men without jobs or land. It was a poor season for tax collecting. People needed to reserve what they had to keep themselves alive until spring, and instead they were forced to relinquish the bulk of their wealth to their greedy Regent. These conditions would never have been tolerated in Gault.

"It's a shame we have to stop in Geid," the

47

Mackabine beside him was saying. "It's very dull there, you know. And its Baron is very dull too. But at least it won't be necessary to stay for long."

Tellemie shrugged noncommittally. He was sorry he had offered to let Lord Bale share his carriage. Bale was a short, plump man who had the honor of being the Baron of Banth. It was a babbling set of consonants if you asked Tellemie, but the Baron took pride in his title.

"It has a musical ring, don't you think?" Bale had remarked upon their introduction. "It makes up for not getting Aog county, even if that is closer to the capital. I'm glad not to be called Baron Bale of Aog. No, no. *Baron Bale of Banth,*" he sang. "It sounds so much better."

For a fat man, he had a good voice.

Tellemie had made his stop in Banth two nights ago. The plump Baron hosted him lavishly and then claimed to be going the same way. He dropped so many hints about being a conversable companion that Tellemie finally invited him along.

Lord Bale probably wanted to curry favor with a ranking Gaultian. Too bad no one in Gault cared for Tellemie's opinion. His service in Mackabine was more a form of punishment. He wondered whether he should tell Bale that becoming his friend wasn't likely to boost his career. Not that they were in danger of being friends. Baron Bale was fairly uninteresting—a shallow person with shallow ideas. Tellemie watched him bite at his fingernails.

"He is something to look at, though. Lord Fenwith, I mean. He's an albino. Did you know?"

Of course Tellemie knew that. Did Bale think he was totally uninformed? Mackabine tradition probably would not have allowed the appointment of an albino Baron, but Gaultian sensibilities were more enlightened.

"The first spirits of the Otherworld were supposed to have been albinos. Not that, uh, Gaults believe in that sort of thing..." Bale finished on a high note, as if posing a question.

Tellemie opened his mouth to answer. *Yes, you*

insignificant little busybody, he thought. *I've been in your country for three weeks and I've decided to relinquish the true faith of Achenes in favor of your aimless superstitions.* Pointless.

Tellemie shut his mouth. He leaned out of the carriage and addressed his driver. "How much longer until we reach Geid?"

"We're in Geid now," the driver answered.

"I meant the town, not the county."

"Another hour at most."

"Well, move a little faster, why don't you? The horses can't be tired."

"Yes, Counselour."

Tellemie rolled his eyes as he leaned back into the carriage. It wasn't the first time he'd had trouble with these redundant naming conventions. The natives relied too much on context. The word Mackabine, for instance—depending on how it was used, could mean the name of the country, the name of its monarch, the name of its capital city, or the name of the county where the capital city was located. Tellemie thought that his country's capital, Gaultillemo, was very appropriately named. It wouldn't hurt these Mackabines to add a suffix here and there.

Bale was saying something about game fixing in a dog race. The man had hardly closed his mouth the entire journey. Tellemie put a hand to his temple and muttered that he was getting a headache. The effect on Lord Bale was minimal. He only lowered his voice slightly. "There was no reason for Handor's dog to fall over that way," Bale whispered.

 Out of nowhere, a whistle heralded the arrival of an arrow. It briefly disturbed the curtain of the carriage window. Baron Bale screamed as the arrow embedded itself in the seat between his open legs.

Tellemie took only a second to verify that his companion was actually unharmed and to yell at him to take hold of his senses. Then he crawled out of the carriage.

Tellemie's four Guards were up in their stirrups, trying to make sense of the attack. Tellemie ignored their entreaties that he return to the safety of the carriage. They didn't seem to notice how unsafe it had already proven.

"Which way did it come from?" he asked.

They pointed into the trees.

"Are you Guards or aren't you?" he demanded. "Get after them!"

Fenwith ordered a pair of slovenly Guards to take the false Counselour Tellemie to the border. It took two days for the escort to return. Senna was sure they dawdled on purpose, probably spending time at an inn after Jed released them early. Senna was able to breathe normally before that because Jed took pity on her and sent a note with the word *safe* scrawled on it.

In her relief, Senna forgot about the existence of a real taxman. She was as surprised as everyone else when he showed up suddenly at the gate. The real version of Counselour Tellemie was nothing like the one Jed had portrayed. His clothes were Mackabine, but his fine features, dark hair, and swaggering confidence gave him away as Gaultian. Used to moving in the wake of authority, the Guards made way for the Counselour to enter. Senna battled briefly with her sense of self-preservation, then followed the party at a distance.

Fenwith had gone to sit in the main hall, letting the trouble come to him. No one took notice of Senna as she slipped silently into the stairwell by the corner. She pressed her hands against the cold wall and watched the scene unfold.

Tellemie strode forward unannounced, trailed by his entourage. Lodin followed behind. Senna could see the Captain's face crumpled with worry.

"Where is Lord Fenwith?" Tellemie shouted. As he spoke, the Counselour's eyes fastened on the Baron without any doubt of whom he addressed.

Fenwith slowly got out of his chair while the man announced his name and gave him the same pass code that Jed had used three days ago. Fenwith answered the Gault cautiously. "I've already had one Counselour Tellemie this week. That was quite enough for me."

Tellemie shook his fist at the Baron. "You are the greatest fool I have ever seen. Is it true you gave your tax money to a bandit?"

Senna held her breath for his reaction. The Baron walked forward until his back was to her, but she still had a good view of the Gaultian Counselour. He looked furious.

"If you really are Tellemie, then you are late," the Baron said carefully.

"I am not late," the man insisted. "I sent you a letter of intent."

"What letter?"

Lodin had the unhappy duty of coming forward and producing a letter that arrived at the same time as the Counselour.

The Baron snatched the paper and read aloud until his voice trailed off. "Being delayed in Banth. Three days..." There was a crack in the Baron's confidence. "How do I know this isn't forged?"

"It has the Regent's seal on it." The Gault spoke slowly, as if explaining to a child. "Did the other Counselour have the Regent's seal, Lord Fenwith? Tell me, did the other Counselour have *anything at all*?"

Before the stunned Baron could answer, Tellemie marched forward and handed him a second letter. Senna could only imagine what it contained, but the Counselour very considerately enlightened them all. "That note was shot into my carriage this morning," he announced. "Apparently, someone named Jedomar wanted to thank you for your hospitality."

When Fenwith had finished reading the note, he opened his hand and let it drift to the floor. Senna held her breath, waiting for the explosion. It didn't happen. Not right away. Fenwith turned purple and then blue. He must have been aware of everyone staring at him. "Excuse me," the Baron said quietly to Tellemie. He turned, walked towards the cellar door at the end of the hall, and went inside.

Senna was momentarily bewildered. The cellar was a dead end; there was nothing inside except cold storage.

For a moment there was complete silence in the hall, then Fenwith began to laugh. The heavy wooden door muffled the sound at first, but it rose in volume until Senna was certain the whole castle could hear. High-pitched, absolutely hysterical laughter. It went on for several minutes.

The Guards exchanged looks. Every face carried the same diagnosis. *Crazy*.

Tellemie stared at the cellar for a while in disgust, then he called his servants and marched unceremoniously away. Lodin just as quickly ushered the rest of the Guards out of the hall, leaving Senna alone with the laughing door. She stood there until she realized she didn't want to face the Baron when he emerged, and fled away into the kitchen.

Senna wished one of the Guards was around. She would have liked to ask someone at that moment: "How did we get stuck with a crazy Baron?"

Bale wanted to leave right then, but Tellemie needed an excuse to take to the Regent, so he parked himself in a drab and undersized dining room. A nervous-looking serving girl brought them some wine. Bale went over his disbelief at their appalling reception and the ineptitude of Lord Fenwith. Tellemie listened without paying much attention.

"He lets those Queensmen run about on purpose, I venture."

"Fenwith seems awfully young for his position,"

Tellemie said, more to himself than to Bale.

Bale looked as if this hadn't occurred to him before. He paused, then grasped readily at the notion. "You're right! He's a dirt-sniffing teenager, by the Queen!"

Tellemie smiled in amusement at his companion's oath. Even these Barons, who owed their fealty to Regent Gote, still swore under their old monarch. Mackabines didn't even have a proper word for a king, only a title for the Queen's husband. It would take decades to erase such thinking, even after they found themselves subject to the King of Gault.

"What was Gote thinking," said Bale, "giving a Baronship to a runt like that? It's no wonder he has all the leadership skills of a baby chicken." From Bale's tone, you would think some great offense had been committed against him.

But a bit later, when Fenwith got over his hilarity and joined them in the dining room, Bale changed his tone to one of sympathy. Poor Fenwith, he commiserated generously. How did he put up with these horrid Queensmen wreaking havoc in his county? Fenwith nodded, and looked half-heartedly attentive to his fellow's unsolicited advice on county policies.

Tellemie snorted under his breath. It was obvious these two men loathed one other, although they both seemed to think they were hiding it. Between the self-absorbed silence of Baron Fenwith and the self-absorbed chatter of Baron Bale, Tellemie sharply wished he was somewhere else.

Not for the first time, Tellemie wondered why Gote chose to fill his positions of power with the dregs of humanity. Perhaps you couldn't expect much of a man who sold out his own country. On the other hand, perhaps it was necessary. If your goal was to bleed a land dry, you would have to make use of scoundrels.

Tellemie's mind wandered further.

It was almost tempting to cheer for these unlawful elements. He wondered what the mysterious Mister Jedomar planned to do with the tax money he had absconded with. Tellemie had been impressed with the way the missive was signed: *Queensman of Geid, Jedomar.* As if the title were the important part, and the name only an afterthought.

Before the Revolution, "Queensmen" was a term for the closest servants and guardians of the monarch. After the Mackabine Queen was replaced, the term had gradually been usurped by those who opposed the Regent's claim to rule. These "Queensmen" hoped to reinstate a course of legal succession. They weren't doing that, but they did undermine some of the Regent's destructive policies. The Gaultian court would have preferred the Mackabine government to collapse quickly. The sooner Lord Gote fell, the sooner Gault could assume control of its new colony.

Lord Bale declared he was hungry and Lord Fenwith had no choice but to call for dinner. The chatter died once the food arrived. Lord Bale directed his jaws towards a more appetizing labor. It was a wonder the man wasn't fatter than he was. It was a half hour before Bale's gluttony was sated enough for him to speak again.

"Very good, Lord Fenwith, very good." He waved the leg of a fowl he held in one hand to accentuate his compliment. "A bit simple, but satisfying. How many cooks do you use?"

Fenwith shrugged. He didn't seem to be listening. Tellemie hadn't seen any help besides the one serving girl.

"I have nine altogether," Bale continued, "but they rotate out, you know, so I don't think there are ever more than five of them in the kitchen at one time." He dropped the mangled bird leg and reached for his drink. "The hard part is making sure they don't steal food."

After a long swallow, Bale nodded at Fenwith. "Do your tenants try to tell you that they don't get enough to eat?"

Fenwith frowned in confusion. Tellemie suspected his tenants never told him anything if they could help it.

"Mine do. All the time. 'Lord Bale, we're so hungry! Lord Bale, please give us half a piece for the baby!'" Bale pitched his voice an octave higher than normal to mimic the whine of his tenants. "Do you know that a worker will eat a pound of grain in a day, if you let him? They can live on half that, and be just as efficient!"

Tellemie was glad that Fenwith was too ill-tempered to respond.

Lord Bale changed the topic, leaning forward in a posture of unusual interest. "I don't suppose you have any executions scheduled for today?"

Fenwith shook his head.

The Lord sagged back into his chair. "That's too bad. I really wanted to see one. Do you think you could arrange one for me before we leave?"

Fenwith shrugged indifferently. "I suppose." His eyes scanned the area for likely targets. The serving girl was out of the room.

"Keep them on their toes, that's my advice," said Bale. "I had five hangings last week. Three short and two long."

Tellemie wondered why Bale was so interested. "How does Lord Fenwith dispose of his criminals?"

"Oh!" Bale's eyes widened. "Don't you know? He throws them into the ocean at high tide. The doomed souls are swallowed straight up into the Otherworld!" Bale shuddered a little in gleeful fascination.

Tellemie formed a sly smile. He did not believe that the Otherworld was located at the bottom of the ocean, or even that the Otherworld existed in the same sense that Mackabines did. "Are you sure that's what happens?" he asked. "Maybe they just swim away."

Tellemie was being facetious, of course; anyone properly bound would be easily drowned. But Fenwith and Bale both stared at him as if he had lost his mind.

"Of course," said Tellemie. "I'd forgotten. Mackabines don't swim."

Tellemie didn't know how a people who lived so close to the ocean could be so afraid of it. Mackabine was an island. Their commerce was dependent on ships and sailing. But

Mackabines only seemed willing to traverse the water so long as they never touched it. It might have had something to do with the temperature of their ocean. No one swam for pleasure in waters below freezing.

Bale turned back to Fenwith. "I'd try it myself, but my castle is too far from the water."

Tellemie did his part to try to spare some random person's life. "I don't really feel like watching anyone be devoured by the Otherworld today. I thought you were in a hurry to get to Candige, Lord Bale?"

"Ah yes," Bale sighed. He seemed to resign himself to missing the experience.

Tellemie stood and announced himself ready to depart when Fenwith gave him leave to do so. He was eager to put space between himself and this castle.

Fenwith softened his demeanor. Perhaps he realized he had made a blunder for which he could be punished. Perhaps he would be. Tellemie didn't know and didn't care.

"I'm sorry you came all this way for nothing," Fenwith said. "You realize I can't provide collection under these circumstances."

"Give me a letter of explanation. I will take that to Gote in place of your collection."

Fenwith had the letter already prepared. Tellemie looked it over and smiled sadly at the notation of the sum owed. Geid was small and poor. But he had not realized until now quite *how* poor.

"A shame, by the Queen," Bale added. "It would have been a good show."

CHAPTER FIVE

Jed had a kink in his neck. His head was pressed against the low ceiling, forcing him to stare at the floor. Courtesy told him to keep smiling, and he was trying, but the urge to leave was getting stronger.

"I think...I think he was an Ansethman. A person from Anseth."

Madam Cadweth had been plying her slow banter at him for a good half hour. There was enough space in her speech for Jed to cut in, but the Madam was so intent on her conversation that she hadn't noticed his efforts.

"I try to," the woman was saying. "Uh...I try to pay attention. To new people. New kinds, uh, new kinds of people are...well, I think new kinds of people are always interesting."

Jed nodded as best he could. Madam Cadweth had once owned a prosperous business, but the family had fallen on hard times since her husband's death. All that remained was a one room hovel that smelled of damp and must. There were no chairs, only two stick beds and a fireplace. Nothing else could be shoved into a space nine spans square.

Madam Cadweth was easily the oldest living woman in Geid. She lived in the hut with her daughter, Madam Cadweth the Younger, who was not particularly young herself. The younger Cadweth was pinched in the head. She didn't speak more than one- or two-syllable sentences. The elder Cadweth could speak intelligibly, but she did it at an excruciating pace, as if her words were being squeezed from a rusty hand pump.

"There's not always...not always a lot of new people anymore," she said. "Not so much. But I do remember. The other day...ah. There were two, two travelers. Two travelers from Candige. I don't know, uh, I don't know where...in Candige. Mhmm. But they, uh...they were from Candige. Both of them, I think. I do think they both were."

The old woman looked up while she strained to remember the next thing she had planned to say. Jed seized the chance to interject his thanks. How could so much delay be caused by one old woman? "I need to be going, Madam Cadweth. It was good to visit with you."

"Oh no! We...ah, we must be the ones...the ones doing the thanking. It means...you know, it means so much for us." Madam Cadweth patted the pouch of new coin in her lap. She had already thanked him half a dozen times, using much the same language.

"And the roof, by the Queen! I'll never forget that. You did the roof too," she added. "Caddy, you saw how Mister Jedomar...how he fixed our roof for us."

The younger Madam regarded her mother with bulging eyes. "Mama yes," she gurgled, presumably without understanding what her mother had said.

Jed smiled. It was two summers ago that he'd worked on their roof. "You're very welcome, Madams." He bowed his farewell. "Until next time."

"It must have been Goat-Day that I saw them," Madam Cadweth went on without noticing that Jed was leaning out her front door. "Nice fellows. I didn't, uh, didn't talk to them, really. But they seemed nice. They were...in a hurry. They were from Candige—they were from Candige, so they must have been in a hurry. I went to Candige once, before I was married..."

Jed decisively closed the door. He put his ear to the door and heard the woman's voice droning on in his absence.

He laughed quietly as he rubbed wood dust from his hair, glad that his rounds were done for the day. Jed did rounds once a week or more. Sometimes he shared only news and company. Sometimes there was something more substantial to share.

Jed inspected the house from the outside and noted that the roof was again falling into disrepair. Madam Cadweth's praise may have been a subtle hint. The central beam was rotted and needed to be replaced. He made a mental note to bring one on his next pass through the town. With any luck, he could do the job without Madam Cadweth noticing and spare himself her loquacious gratitude.

Jed refastened his cloak as he stepped into the lane. Today Jed had two cloaks, one to cover his body and another to cover the three pouches of coin stuffed in his shirt. It was good fortune that the customary apparel of his county made it easy for a fugitive to hide. Especially in winter, when it was expected that a person cover their face out of doors. Jed turned towards the market square to pick up something to eat before the shops closed.

The township of Geid covered a comparatively small area north of the cliffs and west of the hills. Geid was barely a step up from a village, but it comprised a fourth of the county's population. Jed was comfortable within the confines of the town. He knew the occupants of every house, specifically which ones to visit and which ones to avoid.

"Boss!" A whisper shot out of an alley as he passed. Jed backed up. Dohack was alone in the alley, half concealed by a man-sized barrel. He peeked out of his cloak and gestured furiously.

Jed sauntered over to him. "Why're you calling me boss?"

"You'd rather I shout your name all over the marketplace?" Hack smiled. He had a crooked smile that made him look devious.

"It sounds funny. Don't call me boss."

"Can I call you Supreme and Holy Master?"

"Sure."

Hack grinned. It was common knowledge that Hack was idly jealous of Jed's leadership. He whined about it on occasion, but Jed felt certain that Hack would never actively seek to supplant him. Too much work for a job he couldn't have handled anyway.

"I see you're feeling better."

Hack pulled his shirt over and exposed the sprawling black scab on his shoulder. "It's my battle scar. Pretty, don't you think?"

Jed genially agreed.

"You're distributing spoils, aren't you?" he said. "Can I help?"

Jed raised his eyebrows. Usually Rimick was the only one he trusted with treasury. Hack wasn't what you would call a model citizen. He rough-housed his neighbors and cheated at cards when he could. But Jed had never heard of Hack committing an act of actual theft...which in fact couldn't be said for Rimick.

Jed decided to take a chance on his comrade's integrity. He shook a pouch loose and released it with an indulgent smile. Hack's eyes gleamed, either from a desire to be helpful or a chance to handle ready money.

"This all goes to Grath. He'll take what he needs and tell you what to do with the rest."

"Aw," Hack complained, "I want to give it to the little people."

"There's plenty of little people on the oceanfront. Grath will show you. Or would you rather give it back?"

Hack hastily pulled the purse out of Jed's reach. He stuffed it down his pants, and gave a triumphant yelp as he scampered back down the alleyway.

While Jed was in the alley, he took advantage of the seclusion to count the balance of his booty. There were twelve coins remaining in the first pouch and roughly thirty in another. One of the pieces fell from his hand into the dirt. Jed picked it up lazily and ran his fingers over the clunky metal. There was a chip on the front side, right through the engraved stamp of authenticity. Jed recognized it, and realized he had stolen this same coin some months before. He felt an urge to laugh. It was all the same money moving in pointless circles.

Rimick said their country would go bankrupt if something didn't change soon. Mackabine pieces were losing foreign exchange value. Villagers rarely used coin to trade anymore. Instead they bartered basic goods and hoarded their currency to surrender to the Baron on Tax-Day. From time to time, Jed's stolen influxes would flood the economy and make everyone rich again. But debt accrued easily, and relief was short.

Jed stowed the coin away and made his way back onto the street. The market was throbbing with morning activity. Jed chose a stall tended by a pretty young woman named Yamat. Her family put her in front of the stall because she drew customers. Yamat was the sort of delicate girl poets wrote songs about. It was a pity she had all the intellect of a pumpkin.

"Good meeting, Yamat."

The woman's smile put little dimples in her cheeks. "Good meeting, Mister! Are you hungry?"

"Indeed. But what am I hungry for? That is the question." His eyes perused her scanty collection. There was a small assortment of ready-made breads. Besides that, it was mostly sacks of coarse stock—milled grain, unmilled grain, and grain for distilling beer. "The choice appears to be with dillweed or without," Jed observed to the waiting young woman.

"Yes, Mister! I recommend the dillweed," she offered.

Jed smiled. "Do you know me, Yamat?"

"Oh!" Yamat looked mildly confused. "Well, yes, I know you. Are you one of my cousins?"

Jed's smile grew as he shook his head. He wrangled his purse and paid for five loaves with two silver pieces. "Keep the change," he said.

"Thank you, Mister! You must be very rich, I think— oh!" Her expression changed suddenly. "Oh, I do know you!

Are you Jedomar?"

Jed hushed her by putting his finger to her mouth. Yamat raised her eyes in pleasure. The girl's full pink lips were soft against his skin. Jed forced his hand to withdraw.

"Mister Jedomar!" Yamat's excitement carried her away to bouncing on the balls of her feet.

"Be still, Yamat. And call me Jed," he added with a wink.

The woman covered her mouth with the fingertips of both hands, a charming enough gesture, but it did nothing to stifle her giggles. Jed decided to take his leave before Yamat drew attention. He gave her a last smile as he swept the loaves off the table.

He was halfway out of the square, still stuffing the bread into his sack, when a heavy hand fell on his back. Jed startled slightly as Rimick stepped into pace with him. It was the second time he'd been startled that morning, and it wore on his nerves. Someday, he thought, he was going to get stabbed in the back before he knew what was happening.

Rimick frowned at him. "Were you flirting with that floozy, Yamat?"

"That's not a very nice thing to call her." Jed was always working on improving Rimick's temperament. In six years, Jed couldn't say there'd been a lot of progress.

"She's engaged to Mister Orlack, did you know?"

"What? Oh." Jed dismissed the few feeble thoughts he had been entertaining of Yamat.

Rimick and Jed were an odd pair, brought together by fate rather than inclination. Their friendship began when Rimick stole a goat from Pitch and his brothers. Someone had seen him, and tipped off Pitch for three half-pieces. They grabbed Rimick after supper and pinned him outside the slaughterhouse. The brothers wouldn't have killed him, but they were looking to take ten years off his life.

Jed happened to be passing nearby. If he'd had any sense, he would have pretended not to see anything. Rimick was a known thief at the time. Anyone could have told you he was getting what he deserved. But Jed was sixteen and cocky and for some reason, he decided to intervene. He stood, arms akimbo, over the brothers and ordered them to stop their assault.

The brothers turned around—out of disbelief, mostly—giving Rimick a second to slip out of their grasp. Rimick hardly spared a glance behind him before disappearing into the night. Then Jed was engulfed in a flurry of angry fists.

After that, Jed had intended to avoid Rimick.

He was nursing a drink outside the inn a few days later when Rimick walked up to the door. Jed had a black eye, a dislocated shoulder, and a puffy lip that looked like a plump caterpillar. Jed eyed Rimick suspiciously with his good eye. But he didn't complain when Rimick sat down, and Rimick had been hanging around ever since.

"How much do you have left?"

"I'm done," said Jed.

"I know," Rimick quipped. "But how much do you have left?"

Jed smiled. "Forty and change. We've never had a surplus before. What shall we do with it?"

"Store it away until we need it."

"You mean hoard it." *Like tax collectors,* Jed thought.

It would be more fun to run off to a port city and spend all their fortune on a good time. Jed said so aloud, and Rimick passed him a look of befuddlement.

"I've known you for how long, Rimick?" Jed laughed. "And you still can't tell when I'm joking."

Despite the early life of thievery, Rimick was more principled than a clam. These days, he wouldn't even spit in the street. Overcompensation, in Jed's opinion. The honesty didn't do much for his personality.

"We should give a few pieces to Senna," Rimick suggested. "She may need them as bribes."

That was a good idea. Jed should have thought of it sooner.

"She should have weapons, too," said Rimick.

"Weapons?" Jed protested. "I don't want her fighting anyone."

Rimick countered with, "If she does have to fight, would you rather she have them or not?"

Jed frowned. Rimick was right, as usual. Senna's position in the castle frequently unsettled his mind. It was her choice of assignment, and a good idea, too. But he couldn't help feeling that if anything happened to Senna, it would be his fault.

Jed had known Senna since she was a wee thing. Her family would often visit his parents' farm during the dormant season. He couldn't remember a time when she hadn't been there—a bright-eyed child tripping over things and demanding to be involved in every scheme where she wasn't wanted. In his youth, he never gave her much thought. Jed was attracted to the spectacular, and Senna was far too ordinary to be very interesting.

But as time went on, and fortune narrowed his alternatives, Jed began to think of what he could settle for. Senna was not beautiful, but...well, it didn't pain him to look at her. She was at hand; she was pleasant; she had a strong will and a lively mind. *What more can I ask for?* Jed wondered.

Senna woke at first light, stirred by the bracing drone of brass as a Guard in the courtyard rang the morning gong. She forced her eyes open against the weight of less than four hours' rest. She blinked once, remembered she still had to clean out last night's dishes before she could start breakfast, and then slipped back into sleep.

She dreamed of long hallways and dirty railings and a half-spectral Baron who followed her endlessly, screeching that she was stealing his silverware. Senna awoke rather indignantly, recalling that she had never stolen anything from

Fenwith, and furthermore, that he didn't even have nice silverware.

Her sleepy eyes flicked to the barren wall and admired the slivers of sunlight splashing a pattern against the gray mortar. A gentle, lazy moment passed before she realized how high the sun was.

Senna was on her feet the next moment. Without washing and almost without dressing, she ran downstairs with her shoes in her hand. She reached the dining room in time to see the Baron glide in. Senna very quickly put on her shoes and stood tall, prepared to face his wrath. It was past time for the morning meal and she had not even cold bread to give him.

The Baron did not seem angry. He barely looked at her. He threw his gloves on the table without noticing that it was empty. "Tell Corvan I went to Indor," he said. "I'll be gone most of the day. No breakfast today."

Senna held her breath as Fenwith traipsed briskly away. "Yes, Lord," she murmured, long after he'd moved beyond range of her voice.

Soon after, she followed him outside and watched the Baron march towards the Guards' quarters. The Guards were engaged in drills, led by a subordinate while Lodin lounged on a bench. Lodin stood up when he saw Fenwith and immediately joined the other Guards. Some Barons joined or led their Guard in weapons practice, but Fenwith had no affinity for that sort of thing.

Senna saw him stop briefly at the quarters to have words with his Captain, then move on. Corvan appeared at the stable door and wordlessly handed Fenwith his riding gloves. Senna had never seen the Baron mistreat Corvan the way he did Lodin or the others. She was sure Fenwith didn't actually *like* anyone, except perhaps his horse, but he seemed to tolerate Corvan.

The drill broke up after Fenwith rode away. The Guards milled about in the aftermath, conversing as they collected their gear. They were relaxed enough that it seemed a good time to approach the Guard quarters.

Guardsman Hoke gave Senna a greedy look as she came into range. "Housekeeper! Come to clean out our room for us?"

Senna ignored him and addressed Lodin. She needed a hand moving an obstinate piece of furniture. The Guards booed. "Let the steward do that! It's his job, ain't it?"

"Corvan is too old to lift the cupboard," Senna explained sensibly. The steward could barely lift his own tool chest anymore.

"Patch!" Lodin shouted at one of the men. "Go help the housekeeper."

Guardsman Patch grumbled a bit, but he followed her. She led him into the dining area and showed him where she wanted the cupboard to go. The cupboard was almost too much for one person, but Patch refused to let Senna carry the other side. He threw his arms around both sides and heaved.

"How does Fenwith give you orders?" she asked him. "Do they always go through Captain Lodin?"

Guardsman Patch hesitated and lowered the cupboard for a moment. Panting, he gave her a funny look. Senna began to panic. What was she thinking, asking such an overtly suspicious question?

"Say, I just realized something," said Patch. "Aren't you the girl who used to work at the old inn? What was it called?"

Senna let out her breath. "The Bonidon Inn."

"That's right. I liked that place. It was better than the Ironfoot."

The Bonidon Inn had been owned by Senna's father before her Uncle Inwick took it over. It was the pride of Geid for two generations. Dwen would have inherited it eventually, if the Baron had not condemned it to ash.

Senna smiled in a weak attempt to conceal her anger. Somehow Inwick managed to shield the children from blame. He took responsibility for hoarding the tax grain, and made a pretty speech about his loyalty to the Queensmen.

Her smile made Patch wince. "Sorry," he said. "I...uh, sort of liked your uncle."

Senna wondered if Patch was there when they paraded her uncle in front the burning inn. The Baron had wanted Inwick to watch the destruction of his life's work. "It doesn't matter. No use talking about it," Senna said quickly. She didn't need Patch reminding anyone of her connection to a condemned relative.

"He died well, you know. No crying or nothing," Guardsman Patch told her, as if that was going to make Senna feel better about the whole thing.

Her smile reformed—more genuine, because she knew something the Guard did not. Her uncle was very much alive.

CHAPTER SIX

In the speckled light of the forest, Jed danced the rapid steps that kept him out of range of Rimick's wooden sword. He gave a playful cry, swinging widely against Rimick's flank. Rimick parried and pushed Jed's arm aside.

"Be careful with me. That's a real sword you've got."

Jed's sword was stolen from a Guard years earlier. It was an older model, traditional Mackabine with a short hilt. Newer swords were often made with long hilts for the option to use two hands. Jed liked the old sword, not for any technical reason, merely because he was prejudiced in favor of anything Mackabine-styled.

"I knew you would block it." Jed shrugged. "You're better than me."

Jed was being modest. They were fairly evenly matched at swordplay. Although to be honest, either of them would have a hard time against a trained Guard. They depended on stealth and surprise, not to mention ranged attack. Jed's fondness for swordfighting was mere romanticism. He still entertained a slim hope of one day becoming a soldier in the Queen's army.

Jed nicked a wedge of bark off a tree and used it to scrape his teeth. "Had enough for the day?"

Rimick didn't look tired, but he didn't have Jed's passion for practicing. "I'd go some more. But you might

68

prefer to see the entertainers."

Jed dropped his wedge of bark and picked it up again. "What entertainers?"

"I saw their wagons on my way here. They're probably in the square by now."

Jed sputtered an incoherent response. He discarded his bark into a bush. "Do you want to come?" he asked, although he knew the answer was no.

Rimick shook his head, and Jed wasted no more than a quick farewell as he scampered away towards town. Jed felt a wisp of irritation at Rimick for keeping this information from him, but that was no doubt because he knew Jed would disappear when he heard it. Fair enough.

There were multiple routes to the town through the forest. Jed took the most direct path, emerging into a press of excited people as soon as he met the road. A horde of children ran across his path, threatening to trample him. Jed dodged nimbly. He jostled elbows with Geidfolk, visitors from Indor, and the followers who trailed the entertainers from town to town. The flow of people led him to the square, where voices filled the space, each clamoring to be heard over the others.

The entertainers had set up a circle with their wagons, and partially dismantled parts of them to create stalls and a staging area. A bushy-haired woman directed action from the center. It was clear the entertainers had only just arrived. Some were laying out their gear, others preparing a meal. One of the women went around to every stall and posted signs advertising a performance of *Pickpan's Run*.

The entertainer closest to Jed spread a mat of whistles over a stone, and another picked one up to market its appeal to a passerby. He played a melody from olden times. When sung, the lyrics had insulting overtones, but the instrumental version was universally popular.

When Jed was younger, the purple-colored wagons of entertainers signified the best part of his year. But it had been a long time since entertainers came regularly, and some of the excitement seemed to have perished with time. The purple wasn't as bright anymore. Was that an illusion? Had youth given him golden eyes? Or was the entertainment truly sparser, less exuberant than it used to be?

Jed approached the wagons and presented himself to the bushy-haired woman. "Good meeting, Madam. Your troupe is welcome in our small county."

The Madam held her chin and awarded his courtesy with her full attention. She answered him in a rich, welcoming timbre, one which was used to making itself heard. "Indeed. A kinder greeting than I received at the border, where a pair of overfed men in uniform proceeded to rob me and called it taxing." The Madam Director's laugh was deep and appealing.

Jed laughed with her. "Perhaps we shall do something to repay the burden."

"You speak as one who represents his countyfellows," said the Director. She cast a cynical eye over Jed's well-worn appearance.

"In no official capacity, of course. But I do what I can." He gave her a half-piece as a peace offering. The woman accepted his statement and his money with a smile. "It's been a while since your kind passed through here," Jed added.

"My apologies. We usually aim to entertain the Barons. They're the ones with the money."

Jed immediately saw how this arrangement might deprive their county. He couldn't imagine Fenwith taking joy in a showing of *Pickpan's Run*. "And now? You are working out of season, I believe?"

"We're on our way to Banth at the invitation of Baron Bale. He has a host of exotic visitors, who must be shown proper Mackabine hospitality."

"When must you arrive?"

"Not for two weeks. We'll stay in Geid several days to relax ourselves."

"And us, I hope."

"Of course."

His curiosity satisfied, Jed bid farewell to the Director. Two or three youngsters who had come to investigate their conversation scampered away when he turned, and the slight distraction left him prey to an encounter with a grotesque metal grin.

"Garaagh!" said the fanciful face.

Jed flinched in surprise before the face pulled away and revealed the more human smile of young Mister Dwen. Dwen greeted him happily, and applauded his own joke. "Didn't see me coming, did you?"

Jed looked dubiously into the studded mask his friend had obviously just purchased. "Dwen, you know better than to buy from entertainers."

"But look! They have whistles."

One of the entertaining players overheard the remark and came to offer Dwen a sample performance. The player had tied little bells onto his feet that jingled as he walked. He was quite skilled, and his practiced dance made the bells chime in time with the music.

Dwen did not know how to play a whistle, but he pretended. He held the instrument to his mouth and hummed, nodding his head in a mirror image of the player. The player reciprocated with a toothy grin. The whistle spun expertly in his mouth. He took Dwen by the hand and pulled him onto the dais, where they both did a silly, unrehearsed dance.

Jed watched a short time before leaving Dwen to his own enjoyment. He followed the road away from the square. The line of entertainers slowly petered off, replaced by those from the town who were coming to see them.

The appearance of the entertainers had not cheered Jed the way he'd expected. Even Dwen's minor trick with the mask felt more bothersome than clever. It used to be Jed who pulled the best tricks. When had everything become so serious? Was Rimick rubbing off on him? Jed tried to keep up the appearance of cheer, to ease his mood and the mood of those around him. But he seldom felt the carefree vigor he once did. The weight of the town burdened him. So many souls depended on him for things he could not provide.

In the midst of these somber thoughts, Jed's eye was

drawn to an old man lounging near the outskirts of the market. Jed didn't know him on sight, which meant he could not have been a Geidman. And yet he didn't much look like he belonged with the entertainers.

Jed stopped walking next to the bare feet that hung in the road. "Good meeting, Mister," he said. Deciding that such an elderly person must be in need of assistance, he slipped a coin into the man's frayed garment. The old man squinted, and raised his head to look at Jed. His cheekbones were crooked and his skin hung from them like dead weight. His body showed no adornment but a single necklace of bone, carved in the shape of a rising sun. Jed recognized the symbol. It was the token of an ancient sect—a group of wise old ones who made lives better with a little magic and a little healing skill.

"You used to be part of the helping circle, didn't you?" Jed asked.

"Oh, helping is always nice," the old man mumbled. "Help you, I may."

Jed lowered himself gingerly, as if sudden movements might frighten the old man. "How?"

Instead of answering, the witch doctor extended a frail hand and took hold of Jed's fingers. He kept his eyes on Jed's face and felt his way over the bones. "I know you," the man whispered. "You look for trouble. Be careful or it will find you."

Jed swallowed away the dry spot in the back of his throat. "Sometimes it does," he admitted.

"Run towards the waves. Otherwise they will catch you."

Jed pondered this cryptic counsel. His knees began to ache, but he dared not shift position for fear of breaking the witch doctor's concentration. "What else can you tell me?"

"There are things you want to know. Ask me."

"Do I have a destiny?"

"Ah…" the old man crooned. "That you know. You do not need to ask."

"What of love, then? Is there a woman for me?" Jed leaned forward to listen intently.

The old man frowned, hesitating. Finally he tilted his head and shook it slowly. "There is much to say. Much you want to hear. Sadly, I can say only this: you must make your own luck in love."

Feeling dissatisfied with these answers, Jed tried once again. "Can I restore Mackabine to what it once was?"

The witch doctor moved his grip from Jed's hand to his wrist. "You cannot finish what you start. You may break the kindling, but not light the fire. Beware, young man. The white one haunts you."

"The Baron?"

"Yes, that one. Beware that one. He will bring you down."

The slight warmth of the afternoon was sucked away in the witch doctor's prophecy. Jed held his breath as he asked, "Down where?"

The witch doctor squirmed. "To the Otherworld."

Jed was gone by the time Dwen raised his head to look for him. After a small argument, the whistle player refused to let Dwen purchase a whistle at cost, and he wandered away to admire what else he could among the crowd.

The entertainers had disrupted all the work of the day. There were children playing unattended all over the square. He spotted a girl who had a whistle of her own. He knew her well. The girl's name was Clane and she was one of the miller's daughters. Dwen followed her for the pleasure of hearing her play. She wandered out of the square towards her home at the edge of town, her whistle singing out brightly with each step. Her tune was repetitive and caught the ear for dancing. Dwen skipped in time to her song as he walked. Clane looked back and smiled to see him there, although she did not stop playing. Dwen smiled back. Clane was getting to the age where she was starting to be very pretty.

Dwen had just convinced himself to go and speak with her when a group of younger girls came across the bridge from the other direction. They called for Clane to join them and within a moment she was swallowed up in their group. Disappointed, Dwen watched the girls giggle their way towards the mill on the other side of the river.

For a minute, Dwen didn't know what to do with himself. Then he noticed two strangers standing in the middle of the bridge, whispering to each other, their words lost in the roar of the river. Their brightly colored vests told Dwen they were from the troupe of entertainers.

"Hello, hello!" Dwen called. He approached them without fear, and introduced himself as a frequent walker of this bridge.

The pair was surprised but not unwelcoming. The larger one offered his hand. "I'm Dander. Good meeting."

The second tossed his chin up at Dwen. "Junillo."

"That sounds like a Gaultian name." Dwen frowned suspiciously.

The man puffed his chest out. "My mother was Gaultian. Good woman, too. You got a problem with that?"

"Maybe I do," said Dwen.

"Stuff it," his companion counseled, as much to Dwen as to the offended man. Dander stood a little straighter, reminding Dwen that he was outnumbered. "Jun's as much Mackabine as anyone," he assured him. "Anyway, his mother died before he knew her, poor sod."

Dwen took this as an omen of friendship. His mother too had died in his infancy. "What are you fellows doing?"

The entertainers exchanged looks, and Junillo smiled. "Are you a wagering fellow, Geidman?"

"Maybe." Dwen tried not to gamble because he tended to lose. But there was always the temptation to check whether his luck had changed.

"We're playing sticks. You can take a turn, but it'll cost you a fifth-piece."

Dwen felt in his pocket for his last scrap of coin. "How do you play?" he thought to ask before committing his money.

Dander pointed at the stream below them. "You pick a stick, and throw it into the water when we say 'mark.' Whichever comes out first on the other side is the winner."

It was the sort of game Dwen preferred: one that did not require very much skill. He agreed to a match. The entertainers bid him fetch a stick, and he marked it with a length of red string that Junillo offered him.

Junillo had a thicker, heavier stick, and Dander had a very pointy branched one. Dwen believed his lightweight stick would be less work for the river to carry.

When "mark" was called, Dwen's stick hit the water later than either of his competitors'. They raced to the other side of the bridge and waited as the slow-moving water pushed the sticks out—Dander's first, then Junillo's, then finally Dwen's.

"Bonker!" Dander shouted, and tapped fists victoriously with Junillo.

"I want to play again," said Dwen.

The entertainers looked at each other, grinned, and shrugged. "Another fifth-piece?" Dander asked.

Dwen held up his hand. "This is all I've got."

Junillo made a grab for the coin.

He pulled away. "But I want two plays for it."

"Two plays for one coin?" Dander clicked his tongue.

"The first one was practice."

It wasn't exactly a fair offer, but it was Dwen's last coin and he didn't want to play it without an edge. Rather to his surprise, the two men agreed. "I suppose we can give you one for free."

On the next play, Dwen launched his stick with all his might, and it landed almost the same time as the others. "Bonker!" Dwen cried in fun, imitating the entertainer. He crowded beside his opponents on the other side of the bridge. To his disappointment, his little red string came last by several feet.

"Tough luck, friend," said Dander. "One more try, then?"

Junillo was already heading below the bridge to retrieve the sticks. Dwen spotted a long, worn stick on the bank that he thought might do better than his own. "I'll go. I want to switch sticks." He pushed ahead of Junillo.

"Hey!" Dander called after him, sounding startled.

Dwen was quick. He reached the stream before the other two, who were trailing after him rather anxiously. Dwen saw why as soon as he looked underneath the bridge. There was a third entertainer huddled on a stone in the middle of the stream. It took Dwen a second to understand why. Then he realized the man was in a perfect position to intercept the sticks and rearrange them in whatever order he wished. Dwen felt his face grow hot.

"All right, Geidman," Dander placated him, "we'll give you your money back."

"You cheated me!"

The fellow under the bridge showed no remorse. His mouth puckered as he looked to his comrades to share in their amusement.

Dwen's fist clenched of its own accord. He took a step forward and knocked the entertainer in the jaw. The man howled. Dwen wanted another shot, but his friends grabbed Dwen from behind and held him as the injured man angrily returned the blow.

Dwen tried to protest. Three against one wasn't very fair.

"All right, that's enough," he heard Dander say. They pushed him to the muddy ground.

Dwen was so angry he didn't even stop to catch his breath. He crawled back to his feet and rammed his head into Dander's stomach. His foes scattered and regrouped. Dwen swung at empty air until a punch sent him sprawling.

Screaming insults, they swarmed and kicked at Dwen until Dander called them off again.

"Leave him be. Let's go."

"Dumb lad. He wasn't winning anyway," the entertainers grumbled.

Dwen chose to stay down. It was clear he wasn't going to win today. Even with his eyes closed, he could feel the world spinning in one direction. He waited for the voices of the entertainers to fade away.

"Are you all right?"

This was a new voice, entirely unexpected. It was light and feminine. Dwen opened his eyes to the round face of young Clane. The girl stood over him, bent slightly forward in concern, her hands tucked modestly behind her back. Her friends were not to be seen.

"Oh…oh," Dwen sat up immediately. "I'm fine." He lazily stretched his arms, hoping to convince her that he'd just happened to take a nap at the bottom of the bridge.

"Those men attacked you, didn't they? We should tell the lawyering circle."

"No, we were just playing," he insisted. The story of Dwen beaten senseless by a pair of entertainers wasn't something he preferred to have spread around. "A game. It's a…" Clane was looking at him curiously, a sly little smile on her face. By the Queen, she was pretty "…a game with sticks. You throw them off the bridge and watch them come out the other side. Want to try?"

Clane looked shyly about her, found no peeking eyes, and her smile deepened.

CHAPTER SEVEN

Senna's next day off was Spring-Day, and for once, the day lived up to its name. She enjoyed the crisp air all the way to Carly cottage. The neglected little dwelling was engulfed by new growth that would soon reclaim it as part of the forest. The sun lit up the untended garden, and the gnarled vines around its decaying walls gave it a charming air of disrepair. Senna ran the last few spans up to the cottage.

Jed must have seen her coming, for he opened the door before she could knock. "Senna, come in and have a look at this!" While neglecting the politeness of a greeting, Jed's words were animated enough to express some felicity in seeing her.

Senna checked the room behind him. "Where is Dwen? And Rimick, or Hack, or whoever else you've got following you around these days?"

"Oh, busy," said Jed. "Except for Dwen. I'm not sure where he is. But I have something to show you." He brandished a piece of inked paper under her nose. "I'm now the official leader for the Queensmen of Geid."

Jed was that already, and she said so, only half interested. Senna loosened her cloak, even though it was no warmer inside than out. No fire today. Where was Dwen? Didn't he know she was coming?

"Yes, but now it's official. Look here!" Jed tried again

to offer her the paper.

Senna looked. The document was precise, and well-written. If she were less informed, Senna could have believed it came from an official source. "Q.M.?" she said, smirking. The initials figured prominently on the document.

"It's a shorthand they're using instead of Queensmen. Very popular in the capital. Rather cute, don't you think?"

Senna rolled her eyes. "Yes, terribly. I'm sure no one will be able to guess what it means."

Jed laughed.

"Where did you get this? Don't tell me Rimick wrote it for you."

An *official* title of Queensman could only be bestowed by the Queen herself, or an adjutant she commissioned for that purpose. It was doubtful there were any such agents left.

"I got it from Gayna," said Jed.

"Gayna," Senna repeated. She bit her lip to restrain a mocking smile. Madam Gayna was Jed's counterpart in the neighboring county of Candige. Senna heard stories of her boldness. But she was no more official than Jed.

"Gayna got it from some other Q.M. in Pannerack, who got it from a retired Counselour in Aog. I see what you're thinking, and you're right. We're all ragtag outlaws. But don't you see what it means? There are groups like this connecting all over Mackabine. Together we might stand a chance to put down the Regent."

Senna was beginning to feel at least marginally impressed. "What are these Q.M. groups planning to do?"

"Obviously, the first thing is to install a new monarch, a real one."

"Like who?" Senna couldn't hide her skeptical lilt. The Gaults' appointment of a male ruler was an insult to Mackabine. Only women could be trusted to rule a country. Men couldn't see past their aggressive impulses. Gote was proof enough of that. But except for some foolish rumors that Benta's daughter was in hiding across the sea, no heirs had survived the carnage of the Gault Revolution.

"That's the crux of it. We've got candidates ranging from a fifty-year-old great aunt to a six-year-old second cousin. The most popular idea is to find a wife for Benta's widowed uncle, Roman."

"Well, that leaves it open. They could make anyone Queen."

"If they got Roman to marry her. It could even be you, Senna. Want me put to in a word for you?"

"Don't tempt the Otherworld, please," she warned. As fascinating as the idea might be, she was not anxious to marry a man more than thirty years her senior. "Has anyone discussed this with Roman?"

"Not easily done. He's sort of in league with the Regent."

"Which makes it very likely he'll listen to *us*," she said sarcastically. "This is a run around the water wheel. We can't set up a valid government without having control, but we can't get control without the support of a government."

"Don't pull me off the roof, Senna. Even Rimick is excited about this."

Senna laughed at the notion of Rimick being excited. Still, it was hard not to catch a measure of her friend's optimism. "I've heard your news," said Senna. "Do you want to hear mine?"

Jed sat down with an eager smile. "Absolutely," he said.

Senna straightened. Her news wasn't earth-shattering, but she was proud of it anyway. "There's another grain cart moving on Craft-Day. Usual route. Only three Guards, I think."

"Hmmmm." Jed ran his fingers over his cheek. "I don't know if I want to attempt an ambush just now."

"You didn't get very much from the last cart."

"No, but the tax money is doing its job. I want to keep a low profile for the next few weeks. Do you think you'll be able to find out when the next one leaves too?"

"Lodin posts his schedule in the barracks," said Senna.

"It shouldn't be difficult."

"Excellent," said Jed. "The news keeps getting better. I might send a coin or two to the Otherworld in thanks. Don't tell Rimick."

Senna thought they could certainly use the Otherworld on their side.

A few days later, a winter storm crashed through Geid and demolished everything not rooted to the ground. Senna sat up half the night, listening to the wind howl. For once she felt glad to be safe behind stone walls. When she ventured out in the morning, the courtyard looked like it had been dragged through the Otherworld and back. Senna's laundry line was missing, along with the posts that held it, and so were some of the trees.

The town had weathered worse in its history. Most of the buildings in town were sturdy enough to withstand the tempest, though small repairs were necessary. Yards had been ruined and animal pens knocked over.

Corvan was in a frenzy over losing the spring saplings that had just started to sprout. Part of the Guards' quarters had been damaged. The wood was old and needed to be replaced anyway, so Corvan asked for permission to rebuild it. The Guards flat-out refused to take part in any manual labor. They fetched some hired hands out of the town.

Senna felt sorry for the workers who had to mend the Guards' lodging before they could see to their own homes. She fixed a meal in the afternoon to bring to the hired men while they worked.

"Madam Senna." The senior workman nodded politely as she approached.

"Good meeting," said Senna. "I thought decent folks should be working on filled stomachs."

She began distributing vessels for the soup she would pour. Most of them thanked her as they took the bowls. One hesitated, and only accepted his meal when a coworker passed it out of Senna's hands. Senna looked at him in surprise. It was Mister Wade, a long-standing friend of her father, and of her uncle Inwick.

"Mister Wade," she said, "I didn't know you were here."

Wade neither answered nor looked at her. She was baffled until she realized he was snubbing her because of her position in the castle. He thought her a traitor for serving the Baron. She tried to think of something better to say to him, but in the end she only waited silently to take the dishes away.

As she carried the remainder of the hot soup across the courtyard, some of the Guards made faces at her. "Where's our lunch, Senna? You got any more of that?" they wheedled.

Senna shook her head at them. The Guards had a long-standing arrangement to take their meals at the Ironfoot. Senna did not feed them. That was one thing she would never do for any Guard.

There had once been a similar arrangement at the Bonidon Inn. Guards got their food first, and they were always the worst customers. Senna hated waiting on them. Uncle Inwick would clean out the second floor and serve them the best cuts, but they were rude and rowdy, and demanded extras without paying for them. As cordial as Senna pretended to be here in the castle, she never truly forgave them for condemning her uncle.

Senna went back to her kitchen and stared at the window, feeling lonely as night fell. She watched enviously as the workers filed out of the front gate towards their families and their warm fires. The fire in Senna's kitchen was pitifully weak. Her firewood was stored outside, and after being drenched in the storm, most of it wasn't dry enough to be used.

Senna reserved a plate of soup and some peaches for

the Baron's meal. When the kitchen was cleaned, she made her last trip out to the pit. The Guards cleared out of the castle by sundown, but the courtyard was fair territory. She passed a pair of them tossing coins near the kitchen entrance. Senna paid no attention. She was developing a decent working relationship with most of the Guards. She ignored them and they ignored her.

Senna held her breath as she waded towards the pit. It reeked with the stench of trash and human waste. She threw her load of peelings in, and came back as quickly as possible. The Guards had ceased their idle gambling and were watching her. Senna returned their gaze for a moment, but the moon was new and gave little light to help her distinguish their faces. She quickened her pace. The two forms moved as well, and Senna saw that they meant to intercept her. She tensed. It was a good place for an ambush. Between the wall and the castle there was nowhere to run except into the Guards or back towards the pit. Before she could weigh the appeal of that second option, they had her cornered.

"Hold there, woman. How about a little company?"

Senna was close enough to both to see and smell them now, and her heart sank as she identified the speaker. It was Guardsman Skole. Up to now, Senna had carefully tried to avoid the beast who'd attacked her uncle. Skole was the most widely disliked of the Guard. He abused his authority by demanding services from the townsfolk, and threatened to arrest anyone who disagreed with him.

The other Guard she recognized by face only. His cheeks were fat and red from too much beer. Emboldened by Skole's remark, he reached out a hand to touch Senna's hair.

She smacked the fingers before they got close. "Keep your ugly hands away. Does Lodin know you've been drinking on duty?"

Skole laughed. "We're not on duty—are we, friend?"

The nameless Guard shook his head. Senna doubted whether Skole knew his friend's name either. Skole loomed nearer, putting his nose in her face and sniffing. He licked his lips as though contemplating a dessert.

Senna was equal parts fear and ferocity. Her heart beat rapidly as she reached into her apron pocket and found her vegetable knife. She kept it there under the excellent pretense of using it for vegetables. Senna didn't know what the penalty was for attacking a Guard, but at this point she didn't care. She was not going to be raped without a damned glorious fight.

Her fingers gripped the handle without revealing the weapon. Surprise was her only ally against a man trained in arms. She clenched her teeth in the hope that bravado could still save her from the situation. "If you value your manhood, Skole, you will keep it in your pants where it belongs."

The nameless Guard was impressed by her savagery. He backed away with a frown. Skole did not intimidate as easily. He put a hand on her shoulder and clenched it tightly enough to hurt. Senna was ready to thrust the knife into his gut when a loud voice stopped them both.

"Skole! What are you doing?"

Skole jumped nearly half a foot. He let go of Senna's shoulder and whirled around to face Lord Fenwith, who was standing behind them with his arms crossed. Senna could not think how the Baron had gotten there. He was like an apparition, appearing here or there at will.

"Nothing, Lord," Skole stammered.

"Nothing? Who is that?" Fenwith pointed vigorously at Senna.

Skole looked as confused as Senna felt. Surely the Baron hadn't forgotten what she looked like?

"It's your housekeeper, Lord."

"Exactly," he snarled. "*My* housekeeper. Mine. And you don't touch anything that's mine, do you?"

Skole shook his head. "No, Lord."

"Good. Scram."

The Guards ran off together, leaving Senna plastered to the wall. Fenwith appraised her coldly. Senna shuddered. Fenwith's claim of possession frightened her more than

Skole's lecherous leer. But she needn't have worried. Fenwith wasn't interested. He looked as if she were no more valuable than a goat in his livestock pen. He walked away without a word to her.

Ugh, disgusting man, thought Senna. It took a few moments before she could collect herself enough to move. Then she carefully dragged herself back to the kitchen. Grateful though she was for his interference, she wished it was possible to never see Fenwith or his wretched castle ever again. *I could manage it,* she told herself. *I'll go live in one of the northern counties. I'll hitchhike out of town tonight!*

She wouldn't. But it was fun to think about. Senna finished rolling the flour before she finally snuffed out the candles and sealed the kitchen for the night.

Senna didn't tell her friends about the incident with Skole. She didn't need Jed or Dwen jumping out of their socks with worry. When she passed Skole in the courtyard, he scowled and made it his business to pretend she did not exist. The red-faced Guard, whose name she learned was Anvin, was so anxious to escape her that he reassigned himself to scouting duty. Not many days after, he left Geid for a post in Chatskin.

Senna returned to keeping herself busy. The Baron took only as much notice of her as was strictly necessary, but he slowly gained a tolerance for her company. He stopped ordering her to leave when meeting with his Guard or reading reports. Fenwith didn't seem to care if she polished the same bit of floor fifteen times over. It was a common conceit among nobles - they assumed their servants were as uninterested as they were uninteresting. Senna was not the first to take advantage of their arrogance, and she certainly would not be the last.

One morning when Fenwith sat down to breakfast, he studied his plate of fruit and porridge and sniffed in annoyance. "This isn't enough food."

Senna let out a cough of surprise. Not enough? He rarely ate a fourth of what she gave him. In fact, she tended to make his portions too large because she was then free to distribute the remains amongst the hungry children who invariably waited behind the wall near the kitchen entrance.

"I want more variety," the Baron explained coldly. "Meat, potatoes, fish. You're a cook, you know what I mean. Hire more servants if you like. There's no reason for me to eat like a pauper."

Senna nodded submissively, even as she dug her nails into her palms. Most of Fenwith's tenants could barely feed their families through the winter. "Of course, Lord."

He waved a dismissive hand at the porridge. "From now on, I want this entire table filled in the morning. And that goes for the rest of my meals as well."

"Yes, Lord."

"I won't eat breakfast today," he announced as he rose and strode out of the room, leaving Senna fuming and wondering how she was going to conjure up a feast by dinnertime.

Senna knew the Baron cared little about food. She was convinced he made this request only to watch her fail. She wasn't going to give him the satisfaction. She would exceed whatever unreasonable expectations he was harboring. It took her the rest of the day and used up most of the food in stock, but by sunfall she had created a feast she would not have been ashamed to serve the Queen. There were stuffed cabbages, roast pork, roast duck, rolled bread, steamed turnips, two kinds of beer, and a pudding that rose nicely in the center. The Baron studied the table and sat down without a word. Senna was mollified. His silence was the highest praise she had hoped for.

It was impossible to maintain the new standard without help. Senna took the Baron's permission to hire servants quite liberally. She posted wages generous enough to draw applicants, despite the stigma of working at the castle. Overnight, she engaged four part-time cooks hired on rotation, and turned two of them into permanent staff. The first was Cafia, a quiet teen. The other was Emwid, a widow past forty, who was talkative enough for all of them and frequently entertained the kitchen with her tall tales. Both women were unattached, without children or other dependents.

From then on, Senna prepared meals for twenty instead of one. It required three extra wagons of food per week to maintain this ridiculous standard. The Baron signed off on the expense without comment, and Senna, for the first time, began to realize how much power she had to manipulate the budget. An extra set of wages to the dishwashing girl. An extra sack of potatoes smuggled here and there. Who would notice the difference?

The Baron did not derive much pleasure from his new epicurean style. If anything, he ate even less. Usually he sampled only one or two of Senna's dishes before throwing his napkin at his plate. Senna didn't mind. She enjoyed their new arrangement. In the first place, the help was sorely wanted. It lifted Senna's spirits immeasurably to have other hands in the kitchen. Cafia was an earnest student and Emwid did the work of almost two women. They teased each other that they should quit and open an inn together in some larger county.

In the second place, the leftovers of each dinner got shipped directly to Jedomar, who provided for its subsequent distribution. It was impossible to overstate the delight this arrangement caused in the town. Dwen laughed to everyone that the Baron unwittingly fed half the town out of his own pocket. This was not so. Even a wagon of food could only feed a few families, but the irony was not lost on anyone. Jed finally ordered Dwen to stop laughing, lest news of his inept generosity reach Fenwith's ears.

By springtime, Geid Castle was a far friendlier place

than it had been in the winter. The halls were swept, the laundry was fresh, and the food was good. Senna felt as if she had been promoted from a drudging woman-of-all-work to the head of household management.

The Baron made no acknowledgment of the fact that his standard of living had risen fourfold in the past month. Senna would have scorned his praise if he offered it. And yet, it was somehow aggravating to slave night and day for a man who refused to recognize her existence. Senna wanted to wrap her hands around that skinny white throat and squeeze for all she was worth.

CHAPTER EIGHT

Guardsman Cafin tugged on the hem of his uniform, trying to make his harness lie straight. There was a permanent crease in the bottom layer of leather that always made him feel improperly dressed.

Cafin was more than usually wary for his morning patrol duty. The roster paired him with Guardsman Rofus and Guardsman Skole. Cafin gravely disliked Skole, who was an upstart and a bully. Rofus was a different problem altogether. An unknown, someone Cafin had never seen. The new Guard had only just arrived from Aog, where he brought down a gang of bandits using only three men, or so claimed the rumors that Cafin heard third- or fourth-hand.

Cafin scattered a flock of ducks as he passed by the pond. The castle was the last place in Geid you could still find ducks. The wild ducks had all been caught and eaten some time in the last few hungry years. Cafin wondered how the animals here knew to stay within the walls that kept them safe.

One duck flew too close to the gate, where Skole and the new Guard were sharing conversation while they waited for him to arrive. Skole made a menacing snarl at the bird, and would have smacked it had the animal not changed its mind and altered course. Cafin briskly evaluated Rofus and was relieved to find him a fairly normal-looking fellow.

"You're late," Skole accused him.

Cafin was not late, but he didn't want to start an argument with Skole, who was temperamental and a strong fighter besides. He offered a brusque apology. Perhaps Cafin's insincerity was a little obvious. Skole looked ready for a confrontation until Rofus stepped in between them.

"Good meeting," Rofus said. He had a moderate voice and a visage that appealed to the senses. They exchanged names and backgrounds. Rofus looked interested when Cafin told him he was from the county of Thegar. Rofus claimed to have a brother stationed there, and wanted to know what the towns were like. They might have discussed Thegar in detail if Skole had not grown impatient.

"Enough gab," Skole insisted. "We're supposed to be on patrol."

"Quite right," said Rofus. "You should lead the way, Skole. You have the most experience with this town."

The suggestion pleased Skole, even as it irritated Cafin. Cafin had been stationed in Geid longer than most anyone. But he didn't have any status as a leader. He spent too much time trying to avoid the anger of people like Skole.

"We'll head south first and make a loop around the town. That way we'll hit the market before anyone sees us coming."

It was clear that Skole was trying to impress Rofus with this scheme. Half of the time the Guard just sat around drinking while they were supposed to be on patrol. This morning, however, Skole looked ready for business. Cafin fell in line behind the other Guards as they left the castle and followed the road into town.

"Ask Cafin where he got that limp," Skole told Rofus.

Rofus glanced back at Cafin like he hadn't noticed before. "Limp, huh? It doesn't seem to slow him down."

It didn't. Cafin could run as fast as any of the Guard.

"Ask him," said Skole. "He won't tell anyone."

Rofus laughed. "Then why would he tell me?"

Rofus didn't ask, which was just as well, because Cafin would not have told. Not because he was embarrassed, only because the truth was rather uninteresting.

It was early, and the townspeople were still setting up the market for the day. They shied away from the Guards when they saw them coming, some disappearing into their houses. Skole took delight in harassing the ones that were slow to evade him. An older man cut across their path on his way to a stall and Skole deliberately tripped him. He laughed, accused the man of clumsiness, and demanded an apology for being in their way.

Cafin hung back with detached distaste. Some Guards claimed that this sort of treatment would make the town more law-abiding. Cafin didn't think so, but he never tried to intervene. His only goal was to collect his pay at the end of the week.

Away from the town center, things were quieter still. The houses were situated between fields, long empty patches of land that lay ugly and brown until planting. They went all the way to the stream at the border of the town.

The stream emptied into the river on the other side of the road. Outside of Geid proper, most of the county's population lived along the river, which snaked along the coast, although it didn't empty into the ocean until it reached the neighboring county of Candige. Upstream, the current twisted through the countryside until it reached Indor, the closest village, only half a day to the south. The river created fertile farmland. The county borders were drawn along its path, making Geid rather prosperous for its size.

"This is farther than we usually go," said Cafin. There wasn't much to see past this point. The farther from town, the greater the distance between farms.

"Don't worry," said Rofus. "We'll be back for lunch. I want to get a look at the outskirts. I haven't adjusted to this land yet."

They crossed the stream. The water mill was the first building in sight, stuck halfway over the river. The wheel extended into the fastest part of the waterway, where the paddles struck water again and again. Cafin watched it for a bit, mesmerized by the steady motion.

"Let's check the barn," Skole suggested, presumably out of boredom. He stepped into the untended meadow before them. Rofus gave Cafin a shrug before falling in line.

The barn was unlocked, and Skole easily hefted the bar and swung the door inward. At first glance there were no animals, although the barn was large enough to hold several head of livestock. A few scattered tools and empty crates were the only occupants. Cafin was about to suggest they leave when Skole pointed to a pheasant cage resting on one of the crates. There were three birds in it. They were alive and squawking, flapping their wings.

"What fat little pretties," Skole said. He reached out in admiration and pulled his hand back before getting scratched by one of the aggravated birds. "Oh, naughty!" Skole drew his sword and held it point first against the cage, ready to skewer the bird through the twine slats.

"Hey!" someone called out from the open barn door.

The Guards turned their heads in unison towards the outraged voice.

A very young man, probably not old enough to take on adult chores, faced them with livid courage. "Those are ours!" the boy declared. "You get out of here."

Skole lowered his sword and the three of them stared at him. The boy was defiant a few seconds more, until he realized how far his authority was outstripped by three armed Guards. Skole got an evil glint in his eye.

"I mean," the boy stepped back, "we haven't done anything. You might as well go."

Rofus spoke up. "You aren't supposed to keep wild animals inside the town limits."

That might have been true for wolves, but not for any other animals Cafin knew of.

The boy looked momentarily confused. "They're not..." he murmured. "They're just birds. For my sister's wedding feast."

"That so?" Skole gave the boy a deliberate look. He

raised his sword, and in one violent downstroke, splintered the cage down to its base. One of the birds had its head severed by the blow. Another was smashed flat in the aftermath. Skole lifted the sword again and hacked his way into the mess of blood and feathers and twine. The last pitiful pheasant, injured and screeching, turned in circles about the floor.

"Stop!" The boy was hysterical. "I made that cage!" he cried.

Skole stomped on the limping bird, pinning it still, and used his other heel to grind its head into the ground.

With a howl, the boy launched himself into Skole's stomach. Skole was unprepared for this. The impact knocked him over and he dropped his sword into the dirt. He used an arm to push the boy off, but the boy caught his hand between his teeth. Skole screamed for help.

Cafin, who until now had been feeling sorry for the boy, came to his senses and pulled the wiggling lad off of his comrade. "Stupid child," Cafin muttered. He shook the boy a bit to calm him.

Skole recovered himself enough to stand up. He looked so furious that Cafin felt half frightened for the boy. He released his hold, allowing the boy to make a dash for the door. But Guardsman Rofus stepped forward to block his path. The boy fell back on his rump and nervously looked for another escape.

Skole showed them his bloody hand. The boy had bit hard. There was an obvious wedge of broken flesh across the front of his palm. Rofus was unhesitating. He dragged the boy aside and pinned his arm against the wall of the barn. Rofus nodded to Skole, who smiled evilly as he picked up his sword. "Help!" the boy muttered, struggling ineffectually against the Guard's strong grip. Skole oriented his weapon hilt-first and drove it into the boy's hand, crushing bones. The boy wailed the bloody cry of the Otherworld.

Cafin swallowed the bad feeling in his mouth. "That's enough," he got up the courage to suggest.

His words were drowned by the boy's caterwaul and

the sound of new voices outside. "Jondy? Jondy?" a man cried, his voice rising as he approached. The Guards looked up to see the barn door swing open. It was Mister Brade, the miller, who could only have been the boy's father. He was a large man with a full beard and a wide forehead. His big eyes grew bigger as they took in the scene. Rofus released the boy, and stood straight. He looked ready to explain, or possibly to reprimand. But before he could get that far, a second man came through the barn door. Bodies tensed in mutual recognition.

Skole growled under his breath. He identified the man for Rofus's benefit. "That's Jedomar."

Cafin belatedly remembered himself. His hand went for his own weapon. The miller rushed Skole and was confronted by both of Cafin's comrades. Cafin blocked out the distraction. This was the best chance he would ever have to take Jedomar on his own. The Queensman was unarmed, and after briefly considering the sword in Cafin's hand, the bandit took the coward's option. He ran.

"Run, Jed!" the miller encouraged him as he rumbled with the other two Guards.

Cafin took off. The bandit was fast, but Rofus was right about Cafin's limp. It did not slow him down. The Queensman had just reached the road when Cafin caught up. He took a flying leap, seized the bandit's ankle, and dragged him to the earth in a scuffling pile of limbs. His sword was lost in the process and Jedomar rolled over him to reach for the blade. They struggled, each trying to push the other away from the weapon. It was a contest of strength, which Cafin was rapidly losing. He berated himself for stupidity as he realized this scenario was going to end with his corpse gutted in the road.

Jedomar scored a punch that left Cafin gasping for air, and the next thing he was aware of was his own sword held against his chest. Cafin held still while Jedomar got to his feet. The Queensman assumed an offensive stance, sword out, but he didn't attack. He just stood, breathing heavily, and glanced nervously towards the barn. He'd even taken a tentative step in that direction when Skole and Rofus came out. They were slightly bruised but ready for trouble. Jedomar decided that three against one was poor odds. He took off in the opposite direction.

"Get up!" Rofus ordered Cafin. "Go for aid." They left him crumpled in the road as they ran after Jedomar.

Cafin eventually regained the will to stand. He stared at the disturbed ground, and then, rather slowly, limped towards the castle.

Senna generally received a lot of attention when she went to market. Few patrons were able to purchase as much as they wanted, and Senna tended to purposefully buy the most expensive things, from whoever looked like they needed the most business.

"Come this way, Madam," they would cry. "My potatoes are the largest!"

"Won't you look at my figs, Madam?"

"Take pity. My daughter is sick, Madam."

Senna did shopping for the castle twice a week, to supplement whatever Corvan unearthed in his garden. Today she was by herself. Cafia was sick, and Emwid had refused to come. Senna hired a boy instead and gave him a basket to carry her purchases.

The market felt uncharacteristically quiet as she crossed the first street into the square. Senna was one of only a few wandering the streets. At first she thought it was because she had arrived so late in the day, but eventually she noticed a crowd congregating at the other end of market.

The shopping boy called her attention to it first. "Something that way, Madam. Is it a Candige cart?"

Senna couldn't think what else could draw so much attention. She stepped closer. The folk did not sound excited about a shipment of new goods; they sounded angry. Some were shouting. The shopping boy lost patience. He dropped Senna's basket and scampered off. Senna called after him but he ignored her. The shouting increased in volume. Senna distinctly picked out the word "Jedomar."

Her heart skipped a beat. How long had it been since her last conversation with Jed? Several days, it seemed. Senna abandoned the basket where it lay and pushed forward through the crowd, fighting snapped rebukes and shoving shoulders until she won her way to a clear view of the square.

Five Guards blocked the intersection, flanking a single prisoner. A quick glance assured her that it was not Jed. One of the Guards had a horse, but the rest were on foot and looked tired, as if they had been giving chase. She recognized all of them except the Guard on horseback. He must be the new man from Aog.

"What happened?" Senna asked the woman next to her. The woman shook her head, apparently unenlightened.

Further inquiry was suspended by the arrival of Lord Fenwith. The Guards parted for him as he galloped his great horse into the square. The Baron was yelling before he even came to a stop. "Well?"

The new Guard was elected spokesperson. "We almost had him, Lord. We tracked him down the river—"

The Baron stopped the Guard by seizing his shirt and yanking him forward so that he nearly fell off his horse. "Almost?" he hissed through clenched teeth. "Is that the only word you fools can say? You said he was in the millhouse. Did you go to the millhouse?"

The Guard tried to respond, but Fenwith was still yelling.

"I want Jedomar! Not some unnamed dogfish!" The Baron reached down from his horse and took the prisoner by the hair. "Who is this?" he asked. He shook the man's head violently up and down. "Where is Lodin?"

The poor Guard hesitated, not knowing which question to answer first. Finally he settled on the most recent. "Lodin is at the millhouse examining the scene."

Senna spared a glance at the man sagging in the road. He gave up trying to stand after the Baron released him and knelt dejectedly in the mud. It was Mister Brade, the man who ran the watermill. Senna didn't know him very well, but she knew he ran with Jed on some of his escapades. He was the father of four or five children. The man stared at the ground with empty eyes. Senna tuned back into the conversation to hear the Guard accuse Brade of harboring Jedomar and helping him to escape.

Fenwith addressed the prisoner loudly for everyone to hear. "Let no one say I am unmerciful. Tell me where I can find the bandit Jedomar, and I will give you your life." A long pause ensued while Fenwith dismounted and approached the helpless miller. When Brade remained silent, Fenwith kicked at him savagely. "Why do you die for this man? Is your puny life worth so little to you? Answer me!" The Baron spun around and faced the spellbound crowd. He looked furious to the point of being unwell. "All of you! One of you could tell me where Jedomar is. Instead you choose to honor a man who defies your rightful Baron. It makes me sick!"

This was more than Fenwith usually said at one time. Senna couldn't help thinking his appeal was likely to have the opposite effect from the one intended. Fenwith quivered like a rabid animal, daring them to come down to his level. No one made a peep.

Finally the Baron motioned for Guardsman Cafin to hand him a sword. He fiddled with it as he considered the miller. Fenwith didn't like to do his own dirty work, but for a moment, Senna was sure he would run Brade through right then and there.

Say the sea. Please, please. Say the sea.

Fenwith pointed the sword at Brade as if perhaps that might make him speak. But it didn't and the Baron gave up. "Give him to the sea," he ordered.

"What about the boy?" the new Guard asked.

"What?" Fenwith barked distractedly.

"Should he be punished too?"

Guardsman Cafin broke in with an uncharacteristic boldness. "The boy was already punished, Lord. We broke his hand."

Fenwith swung around to remount his horse. "Have the miller's house burnt to the ground. The boy can take care of himself elsewhere. And the rest of his family, too."

A pair of folk broke away from the crowd and ran to warn the family.

The Baron's eyes fell on Senna, in the front of the crowd. He seemed momentarily embarrassed by her presence. Senna didn't try to conceal her hatred. It was a shame he didn't burst into flames from the force of it. The Baron frowned, muttered something else to the mounted Guard, then rode away.

Cafin spied Senna hovering on the edge of the crowd. He opened his palm invitingly, expecting her to join them. Senna felt sick to her stomach. She took a step back. A hole opened behind her and she melted into the enfolding crowd.

CHAPTER NINE

Rimick liked to look at the sea. Up close the sea was a deadly, frothing, stinging business. But at a distance, its beauty could be haunting. On a clear day, it looked like reflective glass draped over the earth. Today, the sea took on a different life. It splayed peaks of white against tones of deep blues and grays. Its temperament matched the sky, which Rimick feared was gathering momentum for a storm.

Rimick peered down the cliff into the churning water below. He was perched on a small section of rock leaning laterally into the ocean, creating a miniature harbor on its inward side. He shifted position and winced as a sharp stone tried to pierce the back of his pants. He reached back and extracted the loose piece from the rest of the outcropping. His eyes drifted from the bay to the slope below him, where a woman's figure approached from the angle of the town. Rimick lazily tossed the stone in the other direction. He wished she had not come, but he had no way to prevent her.

He waited until she was close before he tried to pitch his voice over the roaring wind. "Are they coming?" Rimick yelled.

Senna nodded as she clung to the rocky outcrop, huffing slightly from the climb. Her hair unraveled and streamed in the wind. "Only five Guards. The Baron's not coming. Too windy, he said."

"You shouldn't be here either."

Senna tossed her chin defiantly. He could tell she wasn't disposed to argue, so he saved his breath.

"It's too cold," she fussed. Senna was shivering, but Rimick knew she wasn't complaining for herself. He watched her play nervously with her fingers. Senna was always nervous when Jed went under the cliff. Rimick wondered if she noticed when it was his turn.

Sometimes it frustrated him that Jed was so popular. Rimick did half of the work and risked as much danger as his friend. But Jed managed to get most of the credit. It was a personality issue. Jed was more passionate and magnetic. Rimick should have envied him, but Rimick loved Jed as much as anyone.

He rubbed his hand along the length of his bow, generating friction for his fingers. He worried for Jed too. But his body was glad to be up here, wrapped tightly against the wind, and not down in the cave, waiting to brave the freezing ocean.

"I'm going," said Senna.

Rimick shrugged. He couldn't stop her. She passed his feet and headed towards the lamplit house behind them.

Minutes later, he caught sight of the company conveying Mister Brade to his fate. Rimick quickly confirmed Senna's head count. The Guards were fighting against the gale. They covered their faces with their cloaks. Their sad prisoner had no covering except for an undershirt and pants. He tripped on a patch of stone and stumbled. The Guards jerked him upright.

The procession was followed by a small group of spectators that Lodin had allowed to come. The condemned man's family, Rimick guessed. He couldn't see their faces from this distance. There were several dazed children of various ages, and an old woman who had given up keeping track of them. The woman held her shawl to her face, screaming laments that carried ominously in the wind.

Something cold and hard stabbed Rimick on the

cheek. He wiped it, leaving a wet trail along his face. It had begun to hail.

"Senna, darling!" Madam Haw was always quick to meet a new guest. Jed slyly peeked over his shoulder to see Madam Haw hurry over with a blanket from the shelf. Haw ran a motherly hand over Senna's hair as she wrapped the woolen blanket over the younger woman's shoulders. "We weren't sure if we should expect you. I'm so glad. I haven't seen you for months."

Jed was glad she had come too. He was used to her being here.

"Poor girl, you're freezing. Come warm yourself. This weather is terrible! It'll be a tempest soon enough."

Senna said she thought it had reached that point already. Her hair had come undone in the gale, the barrette once holding it tangled crookedly in the ends. "Two storms in one spring—that's a bad omen, isn't it?"

Madam Haw frowned with concern. "Especially when they come after the frost is gone."

Jed didn't suppose the weather mattered one way or another. The ocean was always the same—wet and windless.

Senna sat next to Jed and tugged on the barrette trapped in her tangled hair. "The water looks bad today. Are you sure you'll be able to manage?" she asked him.

Jed hid his anxiety with a smile. "Don't worry. I'm the best swimmer in the county."

Senna laughed. It wasn't much of a boast. The swimming skills of Mackabines were remarkably poor. Few would dare invade the entrance to the Otherworld, which was known to be guarded by contentious spirits.

Rimick had convinced Jed that the spirits wouldn't want him, so long as he was alive. The explanation held a sort of twisted logic. So far, it had worked. The spirits stayed deep enough in their world not to bother him while he dallied at the surface. Jed told himself if he did drown, his soul wouldn't have far to go.

"Did you see Mister Brade?" Madam Haw asked Senna. She offered the young woman a warm cup of tea.

"Yes. He isn't looking well, to be honest. Do you know him?"

Haw nodded sadly. "His wife and I were friends, until she died from sickness after the youngest babe."

"His family is up there too," Senna added. "His mother is having a breakdown. Can't I bring them here now?"

"No," Jed answered. "They need to be seen to mourn."

"But you'll smuggle them out together, won't you?"

Jed pressed his lips together. "Yes, it shouldn't be too hard. The Baron gave them a reason to leave town."

Concealing the survival of the people they rescued was the hardest part of the job. Jed dreaded what would happen if someday someone reported a dead man walking around the next county. The last man to go over the cliff had been Mister Inwick, Senna and Dwen's uncle. The exchange of refugees was part of Gayna and Jed's arrangement. They sent her any sod they managed to pull out of the ocean. So far Gayna hadn't had occasion to send anyone to Geid. The Baron of Candige went in for beheadings.

Mister Grath and Madam Haw's peculiar cellar had been fashioned generations ago, for reasons lost to time. It was deeper than an average cellar, and at one end joined a natural underground cave that connected to the bay. The upper half of the cave had been converted into a work and storage area while the seawater formed a pool below. A small tunnel underneath led to the open water.

When he was dry and warm Jed liked to boast of his battles against the sea. But when he was ice-cold and exhausted, he would remember that he hated this. Jed dipped his toes into the salty water and pulled them away as a chill bit through his skin. Most of his clothing had already been removed. He sat with a single blanket that could be easily discarded when the signal came.

Jed idly twisted his ring around his index finger as he waited. The ring was cheap and poorly made, but it had belonged to his father. It was the only thing he had managed to salvage from the charred remains of his parents' house.

Senna came and sat beside Jed. Her presence was comfortable, like the blanket on his shoulders. "You know Nebbath would be proud of you," she said.

Jed self-consciously removed his hand from the ring. He scraped up a smile for her benefit. He'd been told this before, but Senna had more right to say it than many others. She had actually known Jed's father. "Thanks for coming, Senna," he said. "You'll have some free time, with the Baron gone this week."

"Oh, he left me enough things to do."

Jed nodded uncertainly. Senna kept her burdens to herself as much as Jed did. She was really a remarkable woman, far braver and cleverer than most you would come by. He gave her hand a possessive squeeze. Senna had melded into her role so well that Jed doubted the Baron would easily do without her.

"Don't worry," said Senna, "Brade will be thanking you in a few minutes."

Jed was glad that it was his turn to swim. What happened to Mister Brade was his fault. It was poor luck that Jed had been visiting at the wrong time. When they heard the cries from the barn, coming to help had seemed like the proper thing to do. Instead Jed's presence turned disastrous. Without it, the Guards might have backed off. They might have let Jondy leave with his father. Now the entire family would have to move to another county. Jed wouldn't blame Brade if the man never forgave him.

"What's taking so long?" Madam Haw muttered behind them, worried.

As Jed opened his mouth to speculate, they heard a

throb of sound ringing low over the roar of the storm.

Senna's head snapped up to meet Jed's gaze. "Did you hear that?"

"That wasn't the gong?" asked Madam Haw.

Jed and Senna shared a moment of panic as they realized what a strong wind might do to Rimick's arrows. The gong was a ceremonious gesture, sounded by the Guards when their prisoner went over the cliff. But Jed should have been in the water well before that. They had never failed to save someone, and Jed did not want this to be the first time.

"Go!" Senna cried.

He watched her a split second before coming to his senses. Then he dove into the pool. That was a mistake. It was like getting kicked in the head. The cold squeezed like a vise. Jed almost resurfaced, but he forced himself forward instead. He used his fingers to trace his progress along the wall of the cave. Five spans, then ten, and he was out in the open bay. Jed didn't know how deep the ocean was. He had an idea that it went on forever, its depths cascading into the realm of the Otherworld. If Brade sank, he was already gone into that world.

Jed opened his eyes, bearing the stinging of the salt, and his heart lightened. Brade was struggling. His feet kicked up a flurry of bubbling water at the surface. Jed prayed that Brade had taken a good breath. He seized one leg and yanked Brade downward. Brade's response was fierce and immediate. Jed kept a tight grip as he pulled the resisting man down, hand over fist. When he found Brade's shoulders, Jed shook him hard. Brade became still, whether from acknowledgment or shock. But he took hold as Jed pulled Brade's arms over his chest.

Jed found his way back by feel and a sense of the light in the cavern above them. The whole ordeal took less than a minute. He barely noticed that he'd resurfaced until he heard the exclamations of the women above him.

"Good job, Jed," Senna murmured in his ear. He let her pull him out of the freezing pool.

The fire seemed scaldingly hot, but he welcomed the dry blanket that fell over his shoulders. Jed's thinking was fuzzy and it took him some effort to identify the people around him.

Rimick arrived, huffing and haggard-looking. "I'm sorry, friend." Rimick crouched at his side. "I shot every arrow I had, but none of them reached the window. I could barely keep my bow straight. I guess that gong was good for something, although I was afraid you wouldn't hear it either, over this wind."

Jed nodded, half listening. He glanced at Mister Brade. Brade was in worse shape than Jed. He'd been in the water longer. But he was alive.

Brade saw his gaze and returned it with a quivering smile. "I thought you were a spirit, trying to drag me into the Otherworld."

Jed forced his shivering jaw to relax for a grin. "The Otherworld isn't ready for us yet."

Madam Haw insisted on caring for the victims, so Senna put herself in charge of getting the traumatized family settled. She sent Rimick to fetch their things from a neighbor while she ordered the children into sleeping arrangements.

There were seven refugees altogether; Mister Brade had five children in addition to an aging mother. There were four girls and one boy. The youngest was only three. They huddled together like goats for warmth, with the older ones trying to hold onto the younger. Madam Haw had carefully wrapped the boy Jondy's hand in a cast, but it was doubtful he would ever be able to use it again. Senna couldn't coax much out of any of them—except for the mother, who wailed a stream of unintelligible grievances.

After Madam Haw came upstairs to eat, Senna went

down to the basement to say goodbye. Jed was looking better after a few rounds of hot soup and beer.

"Is Dwen here yet?" Jed asked before she could speak.

"Dwen?" Senna repeated in surprise. She seated herself in the chair next to Jed's bed. "Is he coming?"

Jed sighed, looking worried. "Look, you'd better not leave until he gets here."

Senna would have liked to see her brother, but she had already stayed as long as she dared. She promised to look for Dwen on her way out. Jed closed his eyes and lowered his head back onto Madam Haw's feather pillow. Senna put her fingers over his palm and squeezed. His skin was warm again to the touch, though he would still need the night to fully recover. He let her hold his hand without complaint. When she started to pull away, Jed held on with the merest resistance. Senna was unable to refuse him anything. She stayed, watching Jed breathe, enjoying the silent warmth between them. She didn't move again until she was sure he was asleep.

Upstairs, she gave Haw a parcel with a few stuffed rolls and some coin. "For the children," she said.

"Well, that couldn't hurt," said Haw. "They're leaving enough things behind."

Senna remembered how horrible it had been to lose her family's inn. When Inwick left, he had wanted Dwen to come with him. Senna probably would not have gone either, but it always hurt a little that Wick had not asked. Wick was Dwen's blood uncle, but not Senna's. Senna was only a step-niece. Inwick tried to be kind to both children, but it was easy to see that he favored Dwen.

Deciding she couldn't wait any longer, Senna stole out of the house without raising notice. The storm had dissipated almost as soon as it had come. The air was calm and there was a fresh carpet of late snow over the ground. The sun had already left the horizon, but the moon was so bright that it danced across the thin layer of white.

Senna saw a figure striding towards the house, kicking

106

up little puffs of sparkling powder. She recognized her brother by his shockingly bright orange pants. The pants irritated Senna almost without her realizing why. Dwen wouldn't tell her where he got them. Probably from an eccentric trader. He'd had them for years and wore them everywhere.

"Dwen!" Senna met him a few paces down and gave him a delighted hug. "I haven't seen you since Moon-Day."

"Thank the Queen you're here," said Dwen. "I wouldn't have been able to leave without saying goodbye."

Senna looked down at her brother's bag and realized he was packed for an extended journey. "What do you mean? You're not planning on going to Candige? I suppose you think you need a fling of adventure." Senna was working up more words of disapproval in her head.

"No Senna, you don't understand. It's not a fling. I'm going. For good, I mean. I'm going to live in Candige."

She started. It took a moment before she found the strength to mutter an exclamation. "What?"

"I'm in love, Senna. With the oldest girl, Clane. She and I are going to be married."

Senna was too stunned to answer right away. She summoned a mental picture of the tiny, doe-eyed girl. "Clane? She's only fourteen!"

Dwen looked affronted. "She's sixteen," he corrected.

"Why did you never tell me this? How do I find out now that you're in love?"

Dwen gave her his most Dwen-like look. It was like a puppy that was being punished and didn't understand why. "I wanted to," he said, "but you were busy."

She knew it was true before he said it. Her brother used to be her closest confidant. Now she saw him every other week in a good month, for a handful of minutes at a time. It was no wonder he'd found someone else to talk to. Her eyes stung with the realization that Jed had known about this before she did.

"Are you sure about this, Dwen? Really sure?"

"This isn't a quick decision. I've been serious about

Clane for a while now. I had already asked her before," he waved his arms to indicate the unpleasantness of the day, "all this happened."

"But how will you get by without me?"

Dwen laughed. "I'll be fine, Senna. I'll write to you all the time."

Senna smiled. She would be lucky if Dwen remembered her at all. She'd lost her hold on him, a little bit at a time.

"Listen, Senna, could you spare me some money? I haven't bought a wedding crown yet. I want it to be a good one, not just those cheap twigs with flowers stuck in them."

Senna would have given him something, but she'd just handed the last of her money over to Madam Haw. "Here," she said, thinking quickly. "You can have Mother's necklace." Senna pulled the silver chain out from under her tunic. Dwen tried to protest, but Senna forced it into his hands. "You deserve it as much as I do," she said. "You can sell it, and use the money to buy a crown for Clane."

Senna enfolded her brother in a tight hug that lasted until Dwen's anxiety to see his bride overcame his affection for his sister. They said goodbye, and Senna watched his back disappear into the house.

CHAPTER TEN

The Baron hated the name Fenwith. Every time someone called him by this name, he felt guilty for associating himself with it. But it was his now, and he was stuck with it. Perhaps he had sullied it more than necessary. Perhaps the original owner of the name would have treated it better, made himself less despicable to his tenants, or even to his peers. He hated his name the way he hated himself.

Sometimes it was good to pretend to be Cole. Cole was such a mild, amiable name. It tasted pleasant on the tongue. The Baron stood in front of his mirror and smiled, desperate to recall the sensation of being a mild, amiable person. "Hello, Cole. How are you?"

"I'm fine," the mirror answered back. "How are you?"

"I would be better, but Hemmon is coming and we're out of money again, so its going to be a rough week."

"I'm sorry to hear that."

"Me too."

"Lord?"

The Baron jumped at the last word, and looked with chagrin towards the entryway, where his housekeeper was examining him with a puzzled expression. The Baron had long ago discovered that the best way to recover from a delicate situation was to become vicious and irrational, but even as he got ready to work up a temper, Senna beat him to the punch.

"Lord, I finished the guest rooms, but we're out of firewood, so I sent Corvan to Mister Wiffin to get some. The ticket will be on your desk this evening."

She spoke with such composure that he decided there was no point harassing her. "That's fine. Thank you, Senna."

Clearly he'd said too much. The housekeeper's eyes widened before she bowed and left. The Baron realized it was the first time he had called her by her name out loud. Not to mention the fact that he'd thanked her. She must really think him unsettled. Ah well. Everyone in Geid already thought he was crazy. What did they care if he talked to himself?

Jed crouched next to Dohack behind the courtyard wall, fighting for control of a thumb-sized peek hole in the stone facade.

"Who invited you again?" Jed asked, brushing Hack's ticklish breath away from his ear.

"You did, because Rimick wouldn't come."

Jed grunted grudgingly. Rimick was useless for any endeavor that might be deemed reckless—or fun.

There was something about a rich man that compelled Jed to follow and ogle, so he could laugh at the ludicrous spending—if only to hide the fact that Jed secretly wished to be him. As Jed watched Lord Hemmon pull into the courtyard, he decided that no matter how wealthy he became, he would not spend money on solid silver carriage wheels.

According to Senna, Hemmon was an enemy of Lord Fenwith, and the Regent's most important Counselour. It was said that the enemy of your enemy was your friend, but that would likely not hold true in this case.

Jed could barely see Lord Hemmon over the heads of all the Guards who had come to gawk at his arrival. The Counselour's entourage was impressively large, and very well dressed. The carriage was escorted by four servants on horseback, all with matching cloaks and velvet gloves. An extra honor guard followed the support wagon.

The Geid Guards were a disorganized mess in comparison. They scattered back as Lord Hemmon descended from his carriage. The Lord turned to inspect the courtyard, and Jed was finally able to get a good look at him. Regal and not unhandsome, the man looked every bit the part of a capital dignitary. His hairstyle and clothing were selected for fashion. He wore a long inner cloak protruding from the short cut of an outer one, which he shrugged into the arms of a serving boy at his heels.

Lord Fenwith descended the castle stairs. He greeted Hemmon with a touch of obeisance, which Jed thought very becoming in him. The dingy little Baron was dwarfed by the tall splendor of Mackabine nobility.

Whatever answer the Counselour gave to Fenwith's welcome appeared ill received. Jed could hear nothing from this distance, but the gestures and facial expressions of the noblemen suggested displeasure all around. Jed covered his mouth, pushing a laugh back into his throat.

"What is it? Let me see," Dohack demanded. He nudged Jed ungently in the shoulder. Jed swatted back blindly, making contact with some unidentified part of Hack's face.

Jed ignored Hack's complaints until the fool threatened to get his share of the view by jumping the wall. Jed seized Hack's shirt and forced him back to a squatting position. "Keep your toes in your shoes," he said.

Jed stretched and leaned his back against the wall while Hack took his turn. He breathed deep, enjoying the sticky, floral scents of spring. The thin dusting of snow that came with last week's storm had melted with the dawn, leaving the dirt wet and fertile. New growth was everywhere. Eager vines hugged the wall and tickled Jed's neck with their soft leaves.

Jed imagined the ship he wanted to buy someday, when he was rich. Two masts, a fine deck, made from the best wood. Carbanthid wood was dark and strong. Of course, he'd also need to pay someone to teach him how to sail.

Hack gave an ineloquent description of what else transpired. The Counselour went inside; the Guards dispersed. Jed dug his heel into a knot of grass as he listened.

"There's a duck walking across the yard now. That's about it."

Hack surrendered use of the peek hole and Jed confirmed the assessment. The silver carriage had been drawn away and left naught but muddy trails in the courtyard. Jed shook his head again at the thought of silver wheels. You might as well use a silver hoe to dig the field.

Senna learned very little from Lord Hemmon's servants. They rebuffed her attempts at cordiality, and kept a disturbing silence even amongst themselves. Senna put them in the empty rooms in the south wing, and made sure they had a hot meal to themselves. Hemmon's Guards settled into their own tents in the front courtyard, as the Guards' quarters weren't large enough to accommodate so many.

Senna wasn't sure what the difference was between an inspection and a tax collection. Whatever Hemmon was inspecting, he wasn't using his eyes to do it. After meeting with Fenwith for a short period, the Counselour went to his room and stayed behind closed doors for the rest of his visit.

The Baron came to dinner by himself. He made no comment on the second place setting Senna had laid. Afterwards, she took Hemmon's share of the evening meal to his room. A polite knock granted her admittance by one of several attending servants. The Counselour welcomed her with a beckoning finger. He watched her set the meal tray on the table.

Up close, Lord Hemmon was more intimidating than

he had seemed from a distance. His face, while handsome, had a feral aspect. At Hemmon's feet, a serving boy arranged a tray of bottles of various petite sizes. Senna recognized him from the yard. He was tiny for a manservant, no more than ten years old. The boy returned her gaze with curious eyes. Hemmon noticed, and slapped him for the lapse of attention. Senna felt profoundly sorry for him.

The Counselour gave her a coin in appreciation for the tray. "Tell me, woman of Geid," the Lord crooned at Senna before she could leave, "are the people here happy with their taxes?"

Senna wrinkled her nose. "Not really, Lord," she said. Any other answer would be ridiculous.

The boy sat up to tend to the food. He opened Lord Hemmon's napkin and tried to place it for him. Hemmon shooed the boy's hand away. "Of course they are not. All folk begrudge a tax, no matter how high or how low it may be. That is human nature. But do they have a real cause for complaint? Is Geid more than usually put out by the hardship of their tax?"

Senna wondered what the Counselour wanted to hear, and whether he would believe the truth if she offered it. "Yes, Lord. I would say that."

Hemmon looked at her. He gave no outward sign, but she got the feeling he didn't like her answer.

She bowed, a little lower than she would have for Fenwith, and backed out of the room. Safe in the hallway, she shook the eeriness from her bones, feeling as if she'd just escaped a den of wolves.

Hemmon's entourage left mysteriously at the break of dawn. Senna was expecting to help with preparations for the departure, but she almost missed them by the time she was up and dressed. She exited the castle in time to hear Hemmon address Captain Lodin from the seat of his carriage.

Torpid and purple-eyed, Lodin had not completely woken for this exchange. He nodded listlessly at the Counselour's instructions. "Don't deliver it until after I'm gone," Hemmon said, passing a letter to him.

Senna guessed that it was the inspection report, and developed a burning desire to read what it said. She watched Lodin as the carriage and all its attendants drove away. He turned the letter over and over in hands. The Captain didn't see her, or else didn't care that she was there. He poked at the seal and tried to peer down the crack between the folds. Senna couldn't tell whether he was having any success. Yawning, he finally turned to the castle, passing her on his way inside.

"Good morning, Captain." Senna bowed politely in greeting.

He gave her half a glance and mumbled something that attempted to have the word "morning" in it.

Lodin didn't feel any obligation to deliver the letter right away. He wandered lazily to the main hall. Oblivious to Senna's hovering presence, the Captain glanced at last night's reports, and then settled on a bench for a brief morning nap. Senna was really annoyed with him for keeping the letter in his pocket while he slept.

Fenwith came down rather late, and didn't look as if he'd slept well. He seemed angry that Hemmon had left without notice. He paced a few feet in front of Lodin while the Captain related the Counselour's words and offered him the letter. Fenwith snatched it and then disappeared towards the east hall.

The Captain took a moment to gather his courage, then followed after the Baron. Senna took only slightly longer to decide. When she reached the east hall, the Captain was standing in front of the Baron while he studied the freshly opened letter. Both of them lifted their heads in her direction as she entered.

Senna bowed apologetically. "Forgive me, Lord. Do

you want breakfast this morning?"

The Baron grunted in answer. He went back to his letter, studying it intently for a few moments.

"You're still here. Did you want something else?" Fenwith asked, not to her, but to Lodin. When Lodin didn't answer, Fenwith looked up from the depths of his reading.

"I—"

"You want to know what's in this report," Fenwith answered for him.

"No—" Lodin started to protest, but to Senna's great surprise, the Baron flipped the report around and offered it to the Captain.

Lodin looked surprised too. He took the paper and read its contents, unfortunately without sharing any of it out loud.

"Are you satisfied?" the Baron asked gruffly.

"Nn—ye—nn—" Lodin waffled between consonants. Finally he gave up and tried to return the report. Fenwith grabbed it out of his hand, crumpled it, and threw it lazily in the direction of the fireplace. It missed, and rolled into a pile of discarded ashes.

"Fine." Senna looked up as she belatedly realized the Baron was addressing her. "I do want breakfast. Go see to it."

Defeated, Senna turned to go, but Fenwith stopped her again at the door. "Clean that mess up before you go," he said, gesturing towards the ash bucket at the base of the fireplace.

Senna tried not to let her eyes widen with glee.

"And Senna?" Fenwith added.

"Yes, Lord?"

"Tea with breakfast."

The Baron had finally learned her name. Senna couldn't decide whether or not this was a good sign.

❖

Cole liked his horses. He had several, of course, but his favorite was a gray and white dappled stallion named Whip. The Baron spent as much time in the stables as he could get away with. Horses were dignified creatures, tractable, and less judgmental than human beings. Their companionship was a singular comfort to him.

Cole left his riding cloak on the hook at the door as a sign to Corvan. The steward knew to give the stables a wide berth whilst his Baron was inside.

Whip took note of his master's entry by tossing his head. Cole reached up and stroked the animal's long dark nose. Whip snorted and nudged against Cole's chest, hoping for a peach or some sugar.

"You want to get out of here, don't you, boy?" said Cole, "Me too. Let's go for a ride."

He yearned for an hour of freedom and real solitude. Something to blow away the stench left by Hemmon's visit. Cole had to remind himself not to waste more unspoken outrage on a man he had no dominance over.

He slipped on a bridle and adjusted it for Whip's comfort. A small noise distracted him, and he turned to find the housekeeper at the stable entrance. Cole wondered what she was doing here. It sometimes seemed that she followed him. "Are you lost?" he barked.

The housekeeper pressed her front teeth to her lip. She had a habit of doing that when she was annoyed. He found it rather endearing. Senna was not attractive in the conventional sense. Her face was a little too round, her body a little too heavy, and her nose was spread over too much of her face. Cole once overheard a Guard describe her in precisely those terms. It had irritated him. He liked Senna; there was a softness to her he found pleasing.

Cole positioned himself on the left of his horse so that he wouldn't have to walk by her on his way out. "As long as you're here," he said to Senna without looking at her, "you

116

can polish these saddles. I want them shining when I get back."

"Yes, Lord." Her voice was compliant, but he peeked back to see her mouth twist in anger. Cole frowned hard to keep himself from smiling.

CHAPTER ELEVEN

In the middle of Geid forest, nestled against the trunks of two younger trees, an enormous stump towered five spans high over the undergrowth. The tree it once supported might have once heated the entire town through a week of winter. If so, the event must have occurred sometime in the distant past, because the forest had since grown outward, obscuring the stump from the casual observation of townsfolk. This made it convenient for Jed and Rimick's purposes.

Jed climbed the giant stump with both hands and stuck his hand into a deep crevice on the top. "Aahhhh!" he screamed.

"What is it?" Rimick leapt to attention, hastily scrambling up the dead tree behind his friend. "Did something bite you?"

Jed chuckled at his own joke. He withdrew his hand from the empty hole and showed it to his friend.

Rimick's sense of humor was grievously underdeveloped. "You should be careful," he cautioned Jed. "There could be a treeskunk hiding down there for all we know."

"No," Jed lamented. "No treeskunk and no letter, either."

Rimick checked the crevice and confirmed the matter for himself. "I guess that's that," he said.

Jed had no choice but to agree. It had been months since the last missive. For the past couple of years, Jed and Rimick had used the stump to receive occasional notes from an informant. They didn't know anything about him, except that he signed his notes *Falcon* and that he worked inside the castle, probably as a Guard. When the notes stopped, they continued to check the stump every few weeks. But it was time to admit the loss of their anonymous source.

"Perhaps he got caught," Rimick suggested.

Jed shrugged. Arrests were usually publicized, but not always. He preferred to believe that Falcon's disappearance was incidental. Their spy might have merely moved on. Guards were transferred often enough. "Well, there's nothing for us to do. Falcon didn't want us involved, so we're not. May the Otherworld send him luck."

"It's a good thing we have Senna to take his place," said Rimick.

That was inarguable, thought Jed. Senna's intelligence was proving more valuable all the time. She had already made friends with some of the Guards and mapped a schedule of their patrols every few days. Sadly, most of their communication now took place in notes between runners. Jed was surprised by how much he missed her. He looked forward to their infrequent bouts of personal contact.

"I hope she gets here soon." Jed swung his feet over the edge, banging his boots into the bark facing the river, in the direction he expected Senna to appear.

"Try not to flirt with her today," Rimick suggested.

"What?" Jed frowned self-consciously. "I do not flirt with Senna."

"You flirt with everyone."

"I do not!"

"Well, be careful. She takes your friendship more seriously than you do."

Jed contradicted it, although he knew his friend was right. Rimick would occasionally display unexpected insight into the human condition.

"I think she only went into that castle to impress you."

"Are we going to have a fight about this?"

"It's none of my business," Rimick said. "The King of Gault couldn't care less than I do. I just thought you should figure it out one way or the other."

Jed felt hot inside. He kept his romantic sentiments tightly guarded where Rimick was concerned. Jed's sentiments regarding Senna were held even tighter. Jed realized he would probably end up marrying Senna someday. But not today, and not tomorrow, either. Right now, the only thing he wanted was to avoid this conversation.

Rimick held up his hands. "I'll just pretend I never said anything."

Wind brushed Senna's face as she followed the riverbed into the forest. The cool air tasted good after a morning with a hot oven. Her feet were warm from walking, and she liked this stretch of river, where the bank was wide, and the water eased from a sprint into a comfortable crawl.

When she reached the appropriate bend, Senna turned inward and followed a nearly nonexistent trail into the forest. Few people came this way, and those that did tried to keep their footsteps discreet. After a short while, Senna heard her name called through the bushes and unconsciously slowed her steps. Her friends were near but she couldn't see them yet. She tried to catch their number by the voices. Jed's rich timbre mumbled something she couldn't catch, but her ears were open when Rimick's clear answer came through. "Senna's a good woman," he said.

Senna felt a flash of warmth at this praise, coming from Rimick of all people. It vanished when she heard Jed's haughty response.

"So? Why don't *you* marry her then?"

Senna's heart ceased beating. She came to a stop, one heel poised in midair, afraid to let it make contact with the ground. These words weren't meant for her. She wasn't supposed to hear them. But she had, and there was nothing she could do about it now. Senna held her breath, terrified that they would discover her, and terrified she would cry if they did.

Senna tried not to hear Rimick's next words, but she could hardly help her ears. "Because she isn't swing to the moon in love with me," he said.

Blessed Queen, was it so obvious? Senna wished she could vanish into the wind, and never be seen or heard of by anybody ever again.

Senna could see Jed's shape through the leaves, perched above the ground over the great old stump. He formed a sound somewhere between a sigh and a hiss, then jumped down, crashing onto the decayed leaves of the forest. Senna took it as her cue to run. She pulled her cloak up and fled as though the trees themselves might chase her.

It took Jed until midmorning the next day to locate Senna. He knew she came past Madam Magg's house on her way to market, so he waited by their door until he spied her with one of her kitchen maids.

"Senna!"

Senna was facing away from him, and she turned around so abruptly she almost dropped her small basket. The slender, shy girl behind her took Senna's bundle and added it to her own considerably larger basket. Jed graced the pretty kitchen maid with a smile. It was in his nature to charm first and ask questions later. He wondered if Senna had told her about him, or if she knew who he was.

Senna took a moment to come round to her senses.

"Cafia, thank you. Could you wait for me at the corner, please?"

Cafia pursed her lips, then dutifully did as she was told.

Jed waited until she was out of earshot. "Where were you yesterday? We waited at the stump but you never came."

"Oh," said Senna, "I had some errands. I couldn't get away."

Her nonchalance irked him. "Well, you could have sent word. I was worried."

"I know. I'm sorry. I thought you would find me here."

Jed was unable to argue with the outcome. He had found her, so he let it pass. "What about the Counselour's visit, then?"

Senna appeared half distracted. She gave him a concise answer. "It was short. He made an inspection report." Senna pulled a note from her cloak and offered it to him. She had the actual report? Jed was continually impressed with her craftiness. He unfolded the paper and read the few lines written there.

Town appears disorderly. Large beggar population; likely feeding criminal movement. Suggest removal of homeless individuals. Roads require maintenance.

"That's not the real report," Senna was saying as he looked up. "Hemmon left that shorthand for Fenwith. In exchange for a bribe, I think."

"Fenwith bribed someone for this? What a waste of money."

Senna shook her head, seemingly annoyed. Jed didn't blame her; the report wasn't very flattering. He grew quiet as he thought some more.

"Homeless individuals...removed to where?"

"Murdered, no doubt," Senna scoffed. "What else could be done with them?"

Jed looked at her seriously. "Do you think he'd do that?"

She frowned. "I don't think Fenwith puts a lot of stock in this Counselour's opinion, but...that doesn't mean he wouldn't."

Jed surrendered to his own thoughts until he noticed Senna staring at the ground. "Can I keep this?" he asked, rolling up the letter.

She shrugged indifferently, as if the conversation bored her.

"What about you, Senna? Are you all right?" Something had put her in a foul mood, and she didn't seem eager to tell him what it was.

Her scowl flickered briefly. "I'm fine."

"Are you sure? If there's anything I can do, let me know." Jed's concern was genuine. Senna meant something to him, no matter how much he denied it to Rimick.

"No, nothing," Senna shot an anxious look at Cafia, who was waiting passively at the end of the lane. "I'd better get going." She turned without farewell.

Jed sighed. His conscience prodded him as he watched her disappear down the road. If Senna were in some kind of trouble, she would tell him. Wouldn't she?

The Baron awoke late in the night and couldn't go back to sleep. It happened often; he was not a good sleeper. Sometimes his dreams woke him, but this night it was the cold more than anything else. He lay awhile, letting his toes freeze between the thinly quilted sheets until he decided the most sensible thing to do was to fetch another blanket.

Cole winced as his feet touched the cold stone. Some moisture had seeped into the tiles during yesterday's fog and frozen into a crust. He glanced regretfully at the empty hearth across the room. He didn't let Senna come up here and he often forgot to bring fuel for his own fire.

He moved one door down the hall to his study. The door tended to squeak, but there was little chance of being overheard at this time of the night. He ignored the mess of scrolls and books strewn across the table and knelt to retrieve a chest from beneath the bench. It was closed with a heavy lock, but that was only a decoy; the chest had no key. Cole twisted the brass fittings into specific positions and released the lid.

The blanket was on top, concealing a mess of personal items and documents, some bound with twine and others loose. Cole wrapped the blanket around himself. He was ready to leave when he heard a muffled cry, like that of an animal. Cole tensed before he realized the noise had come from outside. Curious, he moved to the narrow slit that served as a window and cast his gaze downward.

A man crouched at the castle foundation directly beneath him. He was wearing almost nothing, trembling from the cold, and hugging himself. Cole watched for a long moment. He recognized the man as the beggar who had come in yesterday, trailing after the traders from Hasset. Cole had ordered his Guards to chase him off the grounds, but apparently he'd come back. Perhaps Senna had been kind to him.

In one motion, Cole swept the blanket from his shoulders, rolled it into a wad, and tossed it out the window. It unraveled on the way down. The man against the castle wall didn't notice anything until the blanket landed on his feet. Not unsurprisingly, he looked up.

Cole ducked away from the window and pressed himself against the wall of the study. He held his breath for several counts before he allowed himself to peek down again. The beggar was hugging the gift in happiness. He got to his feet and raised his arms to the sky. Perhaps he thought the stars had taken pity on him.

The Baron watched a little more, satisfied that he had not been seen, then returned to his bed chamber. The exercise had warmed him, and he fell right to sleep.

❖

Mister Inwick knew his way to Gayna's house in the dark. He trod the three uneven steps to the back door, avoiding the weak ledge, and turned the hidden bolt that released the door. He found the refugees in the kitchen, already fed and washed, with nothing to do except wait for him. Well, they could wait a moment longer.

Wick removed his shoes, caked with the mud of several hours' walking, and tapped them against the fireplace. One at a time, Wick peeled off his wet socks and hung them over a dowel. He fetched the best chair in the room, the one with the feather-stuffed cushion tied to its backrest, and placed it next to the roasting coals of Madam Gayna's oven. Then, slowly, Wick stretched his feet over the firewood stacked by the wall, and smiled at his young fool of a nephew. "So, Dwen. You've come to start a new life in a strange place. With this lovely person." Wick nodded graciously to Madam Clane. "How do you intend to support each other?"

Dwen took the hand of his very young wife. The rest of the family was retiring for the night, but the girl was apparently unwilling to part with her husband. She held Dwen's hand as if it were the anchor that kept her from floating away.

It had been more than a year since Inwick's exile from Geid. The time had transformed Dwen from a bumbling youth into a budding scrap of a man. He had the same scrawny set of bones, but his height seemed to have stabilized, and his face had sharpened handsomely. His hair was still wild, and kept him looking as unkempt as ever. He had an indentation on one side of his face left by the straw he'd slept on during the long wagon ride.

"Oh, we'll find something or other," Dwen spouted carelessly. With no money and no skills, Dwen's optimism was overblown. Wick would have to take care his nephew didn't starve.

Candige was different from Geid. It was a port city, the largest one on the northern border. Its large transient populace made it easy to hide people. Putting them somewhere wasn't usually the problem. Feeding them was.

"I can probably get you a job working on reconstruction, at least temporarily," said Inwick. Part of the town had been damaged in a recent fire. No one knew how it started. The Q.M. and the Guard both blamed it on each other. The only consolation was that it gave willing workers access to the Baron's money.

Inwick was far from unhappy with the responsibility of caring for his nephew and new wife. Wick had no children of his own and few souls to absorb his affection. His sister's children had been the focus of his life before he was forced to flee Geid in the same manner as Mister Brade. Poor Brade. The fewer souls forced to take a dunk in the ocean, the better.

Gayna stepped out from the back rooms where Brade's family was settled down to sleep. She wiped her hands on her apron as she reported on the well-being of the family. They would be temporarily housed until a new home was secured. The little ones were exhausted from their trip, she said.

Despite the late hour, Gayna had no thought of lying down herself. She busied herself shelling beans at the table while she directed conversation around her. The task made her appear deceptively ordinary, even though she was arguably the most powerful person in Candige. Gayna was wiry and well past middle age, with a small frame and fast hands. No one knew how old she was, exactly.

"If I count one year for each gray hair, I must be 150," she liked to say. Admiring her silver head, Wick couldn't tell if she was joking or if she was that poor at math.

"Well, little Geidman," said Gayna to Dwen, "I hope you take after your uncle. Wick is one of the few refugees who fixes more trouble than he causes."

Dwen got over the speechless awe with which he had been eyeing the old woman, and spoke nervously. "Uh...Jed wanted me to tell you he's sorry for making all this trouble."

Gayna huffed to herself. "Jed works too boldly. He irritates his Baron. My Baron doesn't even know I exist."

Inwick chuckled. "He certainly knows there are Queensmen in his county."

"But he doesn't know who they are," she said, "and that's a great difference."

Gayna's adult son appeared from the hallway and leaned against the doorframe on her left side. She invited him to join her, but he was above such domestic chores as shelling beans. He amused himself by tossing a sackball back and forth between hands.

"So you're a Geid fellow, then?" the man said, nodding at Dwen.

"That's right."

"Ever been to Candige before?"

"No, never. I've never been anywhere."

"I haven't been to your county either, but I hear good things. They say there's food in Geid. They say the tenants have somewhere to sleep at night."

"It's true. Jedomar takes care of us," said Dwen.

"Right you are. I've met your man Jedomar. A slick one, isn't he?"

"Nobody slicker," said Dwen. He looked proud at the just praise of his friend.

"I'm Sid," the young man said, "Gayna's youngest." He seemed to think that would explain him. In a sense, it did. Gayna's reputation was powerful among Queensmen, even outside her county. Her several children were leaders in their own rights, and they all obeyed her absolutely.

"Sid," Wick called to him, "why don't you let me talk to my nephew? I haven't seen him since I left Geid."

Sid looked willing to excuse himself from the room, but Gayna called him back. When her son hovered between her and the hallway, Gayna directed a look at Dwen. "I expected Jedomar to come with you. I'm disappointed he didn't."

Dwen spouted something about the dangers of the journey.

Gayna waved her hand impatiently. "I need to send Jed a message. My usual runner isn't available right now, so I need a volunteer to make the journey." Gayna shifted her eyes towards Sid. Sid showed no great enthusiasm for the assignment. He made a pained face.

"I can do it," Dwen proposed. Clane renounced this idea with a jerk of her hand.

Inwick sympathized with her immediately. He caught Gayna's eye. "Send me."

"Uncle!"

"Dwen, you have a brand new wife. It's not fair for you to leave her this soon." Wick frowned resolutely.

Gayna looked thoughtful. "There are others who can go, Inwick."

This was true, but the notion stuck in Wick's head rather stubbornly. He had been inert long enough, and the sight of Dwen gave him a pining for his old life. "It's been years since I left Geid. No one is thinking of me anymore. Besides, I want to see my niece."

"Is she the one working in the Baron's castle?" asked Sid.

"Well, I won't see her there, obviously." Wick had made up his mind to go, and Gayna wasn't going to stop him. Perhaps she sensed this, because she changed the subject.

"Since that's settled, Sid, I want you to take the wagon and fetch the goods I ordered from Madam Sebbet."

"I'll go tomorrow."

"Now," said Gayna.

Sid expelled a long-suffering sigh as he left the room.

Wick winked at his nephew. "I'll wait until tomorrow to leave, if that's all right with you, Gayna."

Gayna's mouth turned upwards on one side. It was as much of a smile as he usually got from her. She gave him a judicious, half-tender look. "Don't stay too long."

CHAPTER TWELVE

A tap on the carriage roof roused Cole in his sheltered enclosure. "We're arriving now, Lord Fenwith."

Cole opened the window to signal to the Guards that he was awake. Four days of bumpy roads and travel inns left him almost eager for his destination. Tomorrow was the Regent's birthday celebration. The Regent called his Barons into the city at least once a year, so he could play king with a full court. Cole looked out at the spires rising over the bustling streets of Mackabine city. The castle towers were draped with colored banners, bright enough to be seen from outside the walls. It looked very expensive. No doubt some important Gaults would arrive to appreciate it.

The Regent had many years of experience pandering to the Gaults. At one time Gote had been the Mackabine Ambassador to Gault. In the twentieth year of Queen Benta's reign, Lord Gote quietly suggested to King Jamel the IV that he could conquer Mackabine through a bit of underhanded diplomacy. The King provided Gote with men at arms to remove the Queen. In return for throwing his country to the wolves, Gote gained all the money and power a man could want. The Regent maintained the illusion of Mackabine independence, while siphoning off a large tribute to the King. It couldn't last. Everyone knew it. Even Gote must know it, Cole sometimes thought. He wondered if the Regent had any sort of long-term plan.

While the carriage rolled into the main gate, a choir of heralds belted out an old patriotic ballad.

In our lovely home of Mackabine
Roads of red and forests of green
There is one wiser than all have seen
He is our Regent, Lord Gote.

The song had lost much of its cadence in the last revision.

One of the heralds asked the Baron to wait in his carriage until he could be properly announced. Cole sighed his annoyance. Nicer carriages than his had been arriving all morning, and he doubted his arrival would draw very much attention. The carriage of Geid was equipped with only minimum accoutrements, and led by an unimpressive escort of two Guards. Cole would have preferred to ride, but Lords were expected to put on a display of rank for these occasions.

At length, Cole was allowed to descend from his carriage. He followed the gestures of the house servants directing him into Mackabine Castle. Any castle could be said to be larger, better staffed, and better maintained than the castle of Geid. But no castle in the country outclassed Mackabine. The grounds themselves took up a substantial portion of the capital city and housed servants capable of servicing a nearly unlimited number of guests.

Cole went directly to the main hall to pay his respects to the Regent and draw attention to the fact that he had done his duty in attending. The room was decked in the finest tulle silk, pursuant to Gaultian fashion. Several guests had arrived at the same hour that morning. Cole had to stand in a line to make his address. He watched the Regent receive Lord Renton of Pannerack, a Baron who governed one of the mining counties to the north. Gote's face proclaimed his good mood. He laughed at whatever Lord Renton had to say. Gote was well groomed, but otherwise unremarkable in appearance.

He was wide-shouldered, and less plump than might be expected from a life of eating sweetmeats.

Beside him, the Regent's wife, Lady Orila, was propped upright against a stack of pillows. She spied Cole from across the room and beckoned him forward. Of all the smiles being flashed about, hers alone spoke of genuine welcome. Cole forced a smile in return. Lady Orila was one of the few people in the court whom Cole actively sought to placate. She had long been an object of intense study to him.

Orila was the sister of a worldly woman named Ivina. Their family was nobled, but decades of poor management had left their fortunes middle class at best. Both girls were such pretty things, however, that their parents held out hope of their marrying well. Ivina married the first man who ever asked her, a sailing merchant named Magath. The merchant was handsome enough not to laugh at and decent enough to buy her an expensive wedding crown. Their marriage produced one child before the merchant got himself drowned by pirates.

Orila fared a little better in her marriage to Gote. He had just been appointed Ambassador at the time of their engagement. Gote had been wealthy to begin with, and he used his position to become richer still.

Ivina never recovered from the embarrassment of having an albino for a son. As soon as the boy could read, she sent him off to study in an obscure part of Gault, while she went to join her sister in the opulence of the Gaultian court. There she was lucky enough to catch the eye of an ancient Lord who, although not quite willing to marry her, was able to support her in the style she desired.

The most thought Ivina had spared for her son in the last five or ten years was to casually mention to her sister, "Oh, Orila! If you're going back to Mackabine, won't you take Fenn with you? He keeps writing me these dreadful letters saying how bored he is, and how much his professors all hate him."

Orila was actually more tender-hearted than her sister,

and had promised to set her nephew up with something nice, if her husband could be applied to for assistance.

Even though most of the Regent's agents had arranged their position through some connection or favor, Fenwith was the only one to benefit from pure nepotism. It earned him his fair share of scorn at court.

"Fenn," Gote spoke with false warmth, welcoming Cole as the previous Baron backed down. "I'm very glad to see you."

Cole was confident that the Regent was no such thing, but he accepted the greeting and bowed before his patron. "A pleasure, as always, Regent."

"Fenn, it's been too long," cooed the Regentess.

"Yes, Aunt," Cole replied emotionlessly. "I hope you are well."

When someone once asked Cole to describe the Regentess, he replied that she sparkled. Which she did, in the sense that her clothes were lined with small gems. Orila was a handsome woman, but when youth failed her, she overcompensated with so many oils and perfumes that her skin glowed fluorescent from the use of them. This, plus the many hats and scarves that she managed to wear at the same time, made her look like a giant ornament that ought to be hung in the dance hall.

The Regentess patted the stool beside her and bade him sit. "Come, dear. Tell me, how are things in—oh dear, where is it?"

The servant leaned over on cue and whispered the answer into her ear. "Oh yes, Geid!" she exclaimed. "A large county, is it?"

"No," Cole replied, at the same time the servant was correcting her.

"It's quite small, Madam," the servant whispered just loudly enough for Cole to overhear.

"Oh," said the Regentess. "Well, no matter, I'm sure small counties are much nicer than large ones." She batted her eyes and appeared to not have anything else to say. Orila must have felt how little she had in common with her nephew, but she did not let that hamper her efforts to dazzle him. Orila had few occupations in life beyond a desire to dazzle everybody. Cole pitied her. She was a foolish, selfish woman, but she was not mean-spirited.

He sat down in the place the Regentess indicated. "Have you heard from my mother recently?"

"Not recently," Orila muttered. "How is dear Ivina?"

"She was well the last I heard from her," Cole lied. He had never heard from the woman in his life.

Cole often wondered whether Lady Orila and her sister had quarreled, given how little they seemed to communicate. The first time he ever saw the Regentess, she embraced him and told him how much he had grown. He supposed Orila must not have seen Fenn since he was very young, not to harbor any suspicions of his identity. Lucky for him. Cole lived in dread of the day when Ivina came to visit her sister and informed Lady Orila that the sullen albino in the corner was not her son.

The Regent's tenuous attention to their conversation ceased as his favorite Counselour approached. Lord Hemmon bowed a greeting to his patron and a briefer one to his wife before sliding into the seat next to Gote, a place of honor reserved especially for him.

"Hemmon, you know my nephew," said Gote. "Did you straighten him out when you went to see him?" They both turned slightly in Cole's direction.

"Yes, indeed. Lord..." Hemmon hesitated, as if he might have forgotten the name. An affectation, unfortunately. It would have been comforting to imagine holes in Hemmon's memory. "Fenwith. He's still having trouble with Queensman."

"Is that right, Fenn? Are you having trouble?"

"Some, Lord."

Lord Hemmon took over the line of interrogation, and Cole was forced to follow it through to its humiliating conclusion. "You know how important it is to keep an aura of control."

"Of course."

"You can't do that with some miscreant running around undermining your authority."

"I know that."

"Well, take care of it."

Cole promised to do everything in his power.

Hemmon smiled. While Lord Hemmon's rank was ostensibly no greater than a Baron's, his power was enhanced by being Gote's close friend. Hemmon was too valuable to be given a post that would take him away from the Regent's daily confidence.

"Lord Hemmon, did you copy your hat from the Hasset Ambassador? He wears one in the same style," Cole remarked.

This insult, which seemed frivolous to Cole, hit its mark with Lord Hemmon. The Counselour reached up and stroked his headwear. "I didn't think you had enough fashion sense to recognize a hat, Fenwith."

The Regent observed this exchange with interest, and Cole regretted acting on an impulse which had likely curried him further disfavor. It was not useful to make an enemy out of a man who had the Regent's ear.

"Pardon me please, Uncle," Cole addressed the Regent. "I promised Lord Renton a chance to take my loose money at cards."

Although Gaultian in origin, Dinigo had been popular in Mackabine long before the Gault Revolution. Cole wouldn't get out of playing it six or seven times before he left Mackabine.

"Let's play the next round Mackabine style," Renton suggested. "Double winnings per match."

Lord Renton smiled as he collected his share of the coin on the table. Renton was a Gaultian by birth who'd lived in Mackabine since early childhood. Somehow he managed to pass himself as Gaultian to the right people and Mackabine to everyone else.

Cole made a match and took a card from Baron Renton's stack. Renton gave him a slightly dirty look. "Everyone is talking about your Queensman, Fenwith. What was his name?"

Cole pursed his lips in annoyance. No one had heard of Jedomar before he was forced to explain the disappearance of an entire quarter's taxes. Now gossip seemed to be everywhere.

"They are not Queensmen," Lord Terrus interrupted, objecting to Lord Renton's choice of words. "Queensmen are official appointees of the Great Lady. These are just bandits."

Across the table, Counselour Lallimus gave Terr a baneful smile. "There is no 'Great Lady' either, Terr."

Lord Terrus looked unhappy at being corrected. Terrus was one of the few Barons to survive the change in regime when Queen Benta was killed. "I know that. It's a misnomer anyway," he murmured.

To his right, Lord Renton made a match and exchanged a card with Lallimus. "How much did he get away with? Was it really the entire collection?"

"My, my," Lord Terrus cooed. He scratched at the hair on the point of his chin. It was becoming fashionable to imitate Gaultian styles. Terrus had shaved the facial hair over his cheeks and left a long dark strip along his jawline. The result was something called a Quinellit. It made Terrus look like someone had tried to cut his throat.

"Everyone has their rabble to put up with," the player to Cole's left moderated diplomatically. Lallimus was a court adviser, not a Baron. He offered advice whether anyone asked for it or not.

"So how many pieces did you bring in this quarter? Enough to make up for it?"

Cole made another match with his cards and took two pieces from the pot. "Eighty score," he answered truthfully.

Renton gazed enviously at Cole's growing pile of coins.

"Eighty score pieces, that's about what? Two hundred falla? My dogfighter brings in more than that per month."

"Perhaps if I had some rich tenants, I could do as well as you, Renton," said Cole.

The monetary difference did not embarrass him. Geid's grain shipments were far more important than its currency. Farmers in southern counties had been made to stop growing food in order to work in the mines. The Regent considered silver a top priority. But without the contribution of grain from the north, counties such as Pannerack would shrivel like overcooked figs.

"You could try sharing some of your silver with them, Fenwith. That might make them richer."

The table broke into laughter until it was silenced by the approach of some corridor women. Corridor women were one of the customs the Regent had borrowed from Gault on his inheritance of the Queen's castle. The name came from the old practice of lining a designated hallway with prostitutes. Guests who were so inclined could select from them on their way to retire.

The Regent, who found the pickings of royal ladies rather slim, improved the idea by dressing the women in court attire, giving them pseudo-titles, and letting them mingle freely with the castle's inhabitants.

"Ooh, how exciting!" squealed one of the women, "I love Dinigo!" She bobbed up and down to prove her affection for the game.

Renton craned his neck back in order to smile at her. "Do you want to play, Lady...?"

"Balla," she cooed, extending her hand for him to kiss. Her two companions were introduced as Ladies Rona and Taquim. The women did not want to play. They wanted to admire the skill of the existing players.

Lady Balla was a dark-haired thing with a dimpled face. She reached a hand down Renton's jacket and left it there for the entire next round. Cole hoped she found something to steal inside.

A soft voice spoke to him in Gaultian, and he turned to find the taller woman at his side. Cole shifted awkwardly in his seat. He had not understood. The first words were "Je me malla." *Are you always?* But Taquim was obviously a native, and the rest of the sentence disappeared under her fast tongue.

"I'm sorry, what?"

Taquim laughed and repeated in Mackabine, with a thick accent, "What I say is, 'Are you always this quiet like a sweet mouse?'"

Cole wasn't sure how he felt about being compared to a mouse. "Yes, always," he answered, which was a silly thing to say, but it was the first thing that came to him, and he wanted to speak quickly.

"I don't know how your Gaultian can be so poor, Fenwith," Lord Terr taunted him from across the table. "Didn't you go to school there?"

Cole frowned. His inability to speak Gaultian was the greatest hole in his camouflage. His childhood tutor had taught him only the barest basics—enough to spout "please" and "thank you" and "where is the outhouse?" Now he studied the language every chance he got, but he still found it difficult to follow the substance of a fluent conversation. Cole's only defense was appearing to have a very dull mind. Which probably meant he shouldn't be winning at cards.

He threw down his portion of the deck. "I concede," he said. "I'm going to get some air." He pulled away from Taquim, who was leaning far too close to him, and escaped into the nearest hallway.

The hall led primarily to private residences, and was empty this late in the morning. There were windows every three spans, offering a good view of the grounds. All of them were open to the air on a fine day like this. Cole situated himself by one of them.

The bustle of the city was subdued from this height in the tower. The buildings appeared small, and stretched almost endlessly around the castle. Cole turned his head and saw the city disappear on one end into the sea, and on the other into the distant sloped hills that spread out along the horizon.

Cole closed his eyes and relished the moment of peace, brief medicine for a headache that never really went away. His solace was interrupted by the high chime of a female voice.

"Good evening, Lord Fenwith."

Cole looked up with grace for someone taken by surprise. "Lady Rona," he murmured without facing her. It was a broad interpretation of the word "Lady."

She flashed him a shy smile. "I saw you were brooding here by yourself, so I came to see if I could cheer you up."

Cole answered in an even, uninterested tone. "I'm not brooding. I'm enjoying the view."

"But of course," the woman agreed, willing to take his answer for granted. "The garden is very lovely," she continued. She turned her gaze over the spacious field of rose and caranthyn bushes, closed her eyes, and drew in an unnecessarily noisy breath. "Especially in the springtime."

Cole had not, in fact, given notice to the flowers before now. Although he didn't doubt the floral arrangements would be of the highest quality, Rona's exaggerated appreciation struck him as comical. Still not deigning to acknowledge her openly, he examined her out of the corner of his eye.

She was very beautiful, in a lascivious sort of way. With deliberate grace, she brushed a strand of hair under her ear, and let the lowering fingers trace the contours of her neck. Then, under the dubious pretense of studying the blossoms on a vine below, she craned herself so far forward that the majority of her bosom was exposed to his line of vision.

Cole wondered if there was a time when he would have been aroused by her behavior. Now he felt nothing but

139

disgust. Rona's reputation preceded her. She wanted to grind him up and spit out the pieces. For some reason, his mind conjured up an image of his housekeeper, scrubbing the hall under the stained glass, where the sun shone through her brown hair and cast little pieces of light over the dirty water on the floor.

He realized Rona was still talking to him. "What do you think, Lord?"

Cole brought his attention back to her face. "About what?"

Rona's mouth melted into a smile, no doubt mistaking the reason for his lapse in concentration. "About the Revordian tapestries in my bedroom." She leaned her face against his ear and lowered her voice. "I would love for you to come and take a look at them for me. I'm greatly interested in your opinion."

Cole turned his head away from her. "I'm afraid that style of art doesn't interest me."

Rona looked so confused that Cole decided he had better make his rejection more clear. "There's nothing you could show me that would excite my interest."

The crease in the Lady's forehead disappeared instantly. Her lips drew into a thin line and he noticed something in her which she'd been careful to conceal until now: a degree of intelligence.

"No one believes you're a hermit, Mister Fenwith. People talk. Of course, it's none of my business if you prefer —" she paused for effect "—something else to the company of ladies, but I don't think the court will be so forgiving. You'd better keep up appearances. I could assist you," she offered. "You'll find my demands are reasonable enough. It would be such a shame if reports were to circulate."

Cole raised his eyes at this change in tactics. He wondered whether there was any basis to her allusions, or if she intended to initiate the gossip herself. "Perhaps, Lady Rona, I have higher standards than the daughter of a goat slaughterer whose appearance is not as improved by a piece of

140

fine jewelry as she thinks it is."

Her face blanched, telling him the insult had hit home. He mirrored her earlier posture and put his mouth next to her ear. "If you think me an indifferent friend, you will find I can be a devoted enemy. If I catch word of any reports against my character, I will assume you are the origin and I will act accordingly. So if I were you, I would do everything in my power to make sure that doesn't happen." He turned brusquely back to the window. "Now get away from me. You still smell of goat."

Rona swallowed, bowed stiffly, and quit the room, leaving Cole to wonder when he had gotten to the point where threatening people no longer upset him.

CHAPTER THIRTEEN

Madam Emwid burst into the kitchen with a whoop. She was brandishing something above her head with such pomp that Senna instinctively ducked out of her way.

"By the Queen, Emwid! Is this an attack?"

Laughing, Emwid moved some vegetables aside and placed her item centrally on the kitchen counter. It appeared to be a jar she got from a traveler's stall in the market. "The vendor said it was special honey. Said I wasn't to use it on bread, only fruit. Can you imagine? What cheek! If I buy it I can damned well do what I want with it, can't I?"

Cafia leaned over the little jar and admired the color of the golden liquid.

"Is that what took you so long?" asked Senna. Senna had been expecting Emwid for nearly an hour. She considered chiding the older woman, but that would have been a waste of words.

Impulsively, Senna took a spoonful of the sticky treasure and added it to her simmering sauce. The smell of honey and raw wheat powder blended beautifully. She dipped a thumb into the spoon and licked the delicious sauce from her fingers. One of the benefits of cooking for a rich man.

"Not that," said Emwid. "It was the bustle the Guards are making outside. I stopped to listen. Something about Queensmen! Only not ours. They were talking about

Candige."

Senna came to sudden attention. Dwen wouldn't have joined the Candige Queensmen, would he? Not so soon after being married. He barely maintained association with the Q.M. in Geid. Yet somehow, she was able to imagine her brother being part of whatever trouble sent rumors across county borders. She gave the spoon she was holding to Emwid and made an excuse to leave the kitchen.

The commotion was still going strong. Senna found Guardsmen Hoke and Patch with a crowd of men around them. They were boasting about waylaying a stranger they found on the road. Senna arrived to hear the last fragment of a question someone had asked Patch.

"You really steal that from a Queensman?"

"Q.M. code's not very secret." Hoke chuckled.

Senna tried to exercise caution when entangling herself in any matter with the Guard, but this affair felt too important to ignore. She walked up to Guardsman Hoke and extended her hand. "Let me see," she ordered.

By some miracle, he did. Hoke might as well have been handing her a recipe for cake, for all the concern he showed. She uncurled the wrinkled paper before someone could overrule him. It wasn't a code of any kind; the language was plain.

I hope you'll forgive me for sending this with Wick. He's a stubborn dogfish and I don't know what to do with him once he gets an idea.

The first lines turned her gut to ice. The rest of the letter was news from Q.M. contacts in Pannerack and elsewhere, but Senna barely scanned it. Could her uncle really be so foolish?

Hoke was watching her. Senna faced him with what she hoped was a look of profound unconcern. "Huh," she grunted. She surrendered the letter without reading any more.

"I guess I have to pay the informant those three pieces now," said Guardsman Patch. "I shouldn't have offered him so much! I thought I was going to be out in the mud all day, stopping travelers, and wasting my time."

Senna wasn't surprised there were folk in Candige ready to betray their own, but Uncle Wick shouldn't have given them that opportunity. Her uncle was always more brave than he was careful. Senna closed her eyes, her breath stuck in her throat. Inwick had been a prominent figure in Geid. He was sure to be recognized, if he hadn't been already.

"Fenwith is going to have your neck for letting him get away," said Guardsman Cafin.

Senna found the strength to breathe again, but only until she realized the Guards were organizing themselves for a search party. Lodin sent a promise of reward to the first Guard that spotted the Queensman. Hoke said they had him trapped in the copse outside town.

"If we catch him before Fenwith gets back, no one loses their neck," Hoke encouraged them.

Senna didn't stay to watch the Guards wrangle for their cloaks and weapons. She was out the gate before any of them.

Even as she dashed down the road, Senna understood there was little she could do. Inwick was supposed to be dead, sentenced to the Otherworld more than a year ago. If he was caught, someone was bound to notice that he wasn't. Senna's terror was not just for her uncle. It was also for Mister Grath, Madam Haw, and their underground cave. No one would be able to save them if their secret was discovered.

Senna couldn't bring herself to sit down and wait for news beyond her control. Emwid and Cafia could manage the Baron's homecoming dinner without her. Or not. She didn't care anymore.

Senna was very familiar with the copse of trees before Rengor's farm. It was the same bit of forest that held the stump where she sometimes met Jed. If Inwick was truly there, the best place for him to sneak out was a gulch on the far side. There was underbrush he could hide in almost to the river. She went there by a roundabout path that avoided the road altogether. It brought her to a hill overlooking the gulch.

Indecision tormented Senna every step through the tall grass. Wick was probably caught already. She should have stayed at the castle, where she could have at least seen him being brought in.

She crawled the last few spans to the crest of the hill. Senna stayed low, and gave eyes to the patch of weeds that grew close to the river alongside the trees. She was not alone here. A single man stood watch at the edge of the trees. Senna felt cold inside as she recognized Baron Fenwith. He was hidden from the gulch by an outcropping, but not from her. He seemed to have gotten the same idea she had.

The Baron stared into the gulch as if watching or waiting for someone. Senna followed his line of vision and found what Fenwith was looking at. It was hard to make his face out at this distance, but Senna knew it was her uncle. Inwick crawled on his hands and knees, inch by inch through the grass. He was being so careful that Senna hadn't seen him at first.

Senna tried desperately to order her thoughts. The Baron was alone. If Senna could somehow overpower him, Inwick might be saved. But she was too far away. Senna wished she had an arrow she could shoot at his heart. She waited for the Baron to call for help. But he didn't. He stared curiously at Wick. Senna wondered if it was possible that Wick was still unrecognized. Her uncle had made himself rather memorable at his arrest, giving impassioned lectures to the Guards, and to Fenwith in particular.

Senna saw the Baron, and the Baron saw Inwick. But Wick hadn't seen either of them. He was moving like drool down a baby's chin, trying not to disturb the leaves beneath him. *Go, Uncle! Run!* Perhaps Wick could get a running start while the Baron was stunned stupid. Her hope vanished as some branches parted behind them and two Guards emerged from the trees.

Fenwith picked up a stone the size of his fist and hurled it at Inwick's head. The stone missed, falling short by several spans, but it startled Wick and sent him sprawling into the brush. He lay on his face in the tall grass, invisible both to Senna and the Guards behind him.

The Guards looked towards the noise, but they were distracted by the appearance of Lord Fenwith, who emerged from his perch and met them halfway into the gulch. They were too far away for Senna to make out words, but she could see Fenwith gesturing dramatically, giving orders. The Guards turned in the other direction. Senna blinked, not understanding, as they ran into the hills beyond the river. A call went up that the fugitive had been spotted, and more men spilled out of the forest to follow. Fenwith didn't glance back as he sauntered off after his Guard.

An hour later, Senna arrived at Grath's house, having taken the longest way to avoid meeting any frantic Guards. The last of the light fell away minutes before she arrived, and she felt her way to the door under the glow of starlight.

Inwick was there, in the front room. It seemed he had only just arrived, as Madam Haw was helping him hang his wet cloak and shoes by the fire. Wick looked at Senna, then pulled her in to his broad chest. His familiar shoulders smelled of rain and beer. "Dear sweet girl," he said.

Senna hadn't realized how sorely she missed him until just then. She abandoned composure and let herself cry for a few unheeded minutes. Madam Haw graciously left the two of them to conclude their reunion.

Wick pulled Senna back to look at her. His face was scratched from hiding in the brush and his beard had grown thicker since the last time she'd seen him. "No...not a girl anymore, I see. You're quite a woman now. You would have to be, for taking on that whole castle by yourself."

"Yes, Uncle," she smiled through her fading tears. "You can no longer toss me over your shoulder like a sack of grain."

"Oh, I don't know about that," said Wick. His bushy beard shook as he laughed. Laughed! After escaping by a toe-hair. Why were men in her life always pretending they were immune to consequence?

"How is Dwen?" she asked. Senna still had no news of him. She wanted to know that her brother was healthy and well received in Candige.

"He seems happy," said Wick. "His wife is the shyest slip of a girl I've seen, but she seems to like him."

He produced a letter that Dwen had written for her. "I had this letter in one pocket and Gayna's letter in the other. The Guards just happened to check that side first. It's funny. After they found the first one, they forgot to bother searching the rest of me."

Senna opened it.

Good sister,

You're probably worried I've gone and fallen into a hole somewhere. Don't worry. All the holes in Candige are too small to fall into. Really! They're so organized here, they've got workers to patch up pits in the road. There is so much to see and do here, I hardly know what I'm up for. Clane's father is teaching me about milling, so maybe I'll do some of that. I promise to write you every week, or at least every month, if I'm busy. Stay safe, little sister.

From your favorite fellow, Dwen

As little as the letter managed to say, she could at least perceive the happy spirit of her brother. She pushed the letter deep into her pocket, where she could take it out and read it again when her most urgent chores were over.

Madam Haw brought them tea. She said they were welcome to stay as long as they liked. She promised a good mattress and plenty of clean blankets in the basement. They thanked her, though neither had the intention of sleeping soon.

Senna told her uncle about life in the castle. She

147

described her duties as a housekeeper, her connection to Jedomar, and the small things she did to help the townsfolk. A great part of her still yearned for her uncle's approval.

Wick listened politely and nodded at all she had to say. But he was uninvolved and offered no particular advice. Wick had his own world of problems. It was clear he was ready to avoid hers.

"Uncle, do you think the Queensmen will really overthrow the Regent?"

"Of course I do. Why else would I risk my life running letters for Madam Gayna?"

Senna swallowed back her bit of doubt. From what she saw, most of their scrambling about had little to do with overthrowing anyone. It was a matter of mere survival.

"Are you feeling disheartened, dear girl?" Inwick hesitated briefly. "Would you...do you want to come back to Candige with me? We could all be together again."

There it was, finally, the offer Senna had been waiting for. For an instant, her work at the castle didn't seem that important. But she didn't think her presence in Candige would be valued any more than it was here. Dwen was married now; he had other things to worry about besides Senna. Life was always changing, no matter how much you didn't want it to.

"I'm fine," she promised. "I have things to do here."

Wick didn't push her.

Jed turned up sometime near midnight, long after the chase for Inwick had resolved into nothing. He was relieved to find Wick in one piece. Wick apologized for the loss of Gayna's letter, although no one could say it was very much his fault.

Wick begged Jed to find out who the fellow on the hill was—some poor fool who had been mistaken for him. Jed told them no one had ever been found.

Senna was too confused to offer comment. When questioned, she confessed nothing except to being privy to the ruckus at the castle.

"There was an informant," Senna said. "Someone

148

named Danry or Dorby, I think."

Wick's face darkened. "Dorby! That blighted little dogfish. I should have thought so. He disappeared fast enough."

"Does he know your name?" Jed asked, looking worried.

Wick shook his head. "I doubt he knows much of anything. He's a beggar skunk who likes to listen at doors, that's all. Even so, Gayna should be told as soon as possible. I dare not stay very long."

Wick decided to start his return journey then, in the cover of darkness. Senna encouraged the inclination. Geid was the last place Inwick belonged.

"Be safe, Uncle." She hugged him a last time before they parted to unsimilar destinations.

"Same to you, Senna. Be seeing you."

Senna smiled at him, even though she couldn't begin to think of when that might be.

CHAPTER FOURTEEN

Senna snuck into the courtyard just as the sun began to rise. The Baron was up early, ordering the Guard Captain to resume daily drills. He was as irritable as usual and inflicting his mood on everyone he saw. "Cowards, lazy sods, children of treeskunks"—Fenwith threw insults at every Guard.

"I practically handed that Queensman to you," he said. "I might as well run this castle myself, for all the help I get from you."

The Guards seemed to suspect that the Baron's sighting of the Queensman was a figment of his imagination. They exchanged long-suffering looks.

Senna had always suspected the Baron's mind was unwhole, but how befuddled could he be?

Fenwith spotted Senna trying to slip into the side entrance and gave her an underhanded stare. She steeled herself, prepared to be his next target. "Senna," he grunted. "At least I have *one* competent person about me. Fix me something to eat while I ride."

Senna blushed. In the kitchen, she hastily threw some bread and dried meat into a bag and left it for the Baron on the stable door. She was glad the Baron had been too busy to notice that she was absent without leave the entire evening prior. She discovered that Emwid and Cafia had fled yesterday when Senna disappeared, under the impression there'd been some calamity. She found the kitchen in a mess. The undressed bird she'd abandoned yesterday was spoiled, and shrouded in tiny black flies. It took her the morning to dispose of the mess and scour the stench from her kitchen.

The lack of sleep caught up to her in the afternoon. She stole an hour of rest and woke with her head full of strange thoughts. The Baron hadn't been aiming for her uncle. He had thrown that stone to warn him. It was the only thing that made sense. But it made no sense at all.

Senna went outside to gather fresh herbs for supper and ran into the steward fertilizing his plants. "Corvan?" she spoke softly so as not to startle him.

Corvan looked at her reluctantly, and wiped his earth-stained hand against the side of his pants. The steward wore the same thing every day: a brown tunic over pants that Senna suspected had once been white. She once tried to wash his clothes for him, but the steward wouldn't let her. He seemed to think she was planning to burn them.

"Corvan, whatever happened to the last housekeeper here?"

Corvan's eyes got big and watery. He gave her the barest glance of suspicion before answering. "She got out of line with the Lord." He made a slicing motion across his neck. Senna didn't press him for details.

It was late when the Baron returned from his riding. He skipped the supper she had prepared and went straight to the east hall to ruminate. Senna started to put away the unused dishes. Her fingers shook a little as she slid the plate into her hand. Her body was still suffering the effects of exhaustion and panic. All that effort, preparing an elaborate meal, and the Baron couldn't be bothered to look at her food. She could have slept the day away, had she known. A precarious fire lit inside her, nameless and inexplicable. She dropped the plate and set her feet towards the east hall.

The wooden door of the office made a thunk as it fell closed behind her. Fenwith looked annoyed by her entrance, but he didn't ask her to leave. Neither did he ask what she wanted. She stood ignored at the threshold for more than a minute. Senna suddenly realized how tired she was of being ignored. She walked across the room until she reached the edge of his desk. She stood there watching him scribble lies on his paper.

The tenants are greedy, but easy to subdue. Rebellion is still confined to minor outbursts.

The Baron dropped his pen when he reached the end of his sentence. He grudgingly looked up and gave her a pointed stare. It was a cross between *What do you want?* and *How dare you read my letter?* But still he said nothing.

Senna understood this was as much invitation as she going to get. Her courage deflated as quickly as it had arisen. She stumbled. "I...I wanted to...ask—"

"Get out," he interrupted her.

Senna's breath stopped short. When she tried to speak again, nothing escaped but a small coo.

"Now."

Senna swallowed hard and then spoke again, almost before she knew what she was doing, in a fast rush of words. "Why did you rescue my uncle?"

The Baron truly looked as if he did not know how to respond. He seemed astonished and somewhat worried. "I didn't," he answered tersely, and picked up his pen again.

"Yes, you did," Senna said. She could scarcely believe her own gall.

The Baron froze, hunched over his letter, stubbornly refusing to look at her. His manner would have betrayed him, if the truth had not already done so. "I don't know what you're talking about," he mumbled.

"Why did you do it? Last night you chased those Guards away. I saw you."

The Baron stood up very brusquely, knocking his chair over in the process, and clamped his hands against the edge of his table. "What I do is none of your business, and if you persist in asking me stupid questions, I will put your head on a pike to prevent you from doing so. Do you

UNDERSTAND?" He was shouting by the end of this declaration, and Senna, entirely overcome, bolted from the room.

As he watched her go, Cole decided he had never dealt with a situation more poorly in his life. He couldn't leave it at this. Who would she tell? Who had she already told? Cole looked down and saw he was gripping the edge of the table like he wanted to grind it into powder. He let go, ran a shaking hand through his hair, tried to sit down, then realized his chair had tipped over.

Think, Cole told himself. Senna was a clever woman, but how much did she know, really? That he was aware his executions didn't always work? That he purposely led his Guard on wild goose chases? He should have tried to reinterpret events for her.

I didn't know who that man was—of course not. I rallied my Guard for some other purpose. Why, I didn't even see him. He didn't think she'd buy it now.

This information would go straight to Jedomar. Strange rumors would spread. The Regent's men would not ignore them. Any careful investigation would eventually reveal the truth. Cole pictured himself being hung in the near future.

He left the hall and proceeded straightaway to the front gate, where a surprised Guard assured him that Senna had not tried to leave the castle in the last few minutes. He walked back inside and calmly climbed the stairs to the south wing. There was lamplight under her door and Cole felt secure to know that his housekeeper was contained, at least for now. He went back to the stairwell and sat on the top step to consider his next move. What were his options?

Kill Senna.

Cole dismissed this notion. Let him hang first.

Lock her up?

Not much better. He couldn't do that forever, certainly.

As far as he could tell, there was only one real alternative. He would have to tell her the truth. Cole felt a little giddy. Part of him had long ached to tell her. To tell anyone, really, but especially so wise and useful a confidant as Madam Senna. He also felt sick to his stomach. She would probably hate him anyway.

Courtesy would have dictated that he wait until morning, but having decided upon such an extreme action, Cole wasn't willing to put it off. He walked the distance to Senna's room in sporadic bursts, half-convinced he should turn around. But he wasn't going to get any sleep in this state of mind, and he couldn't afford to be tired for whatever came next. Cole took a breath and knocked on her door.

For her part, Senna had come to no miraculous conclusions. She learned nothing tonight she hadn't already known. The Baron was completely, irretrievably insane. She resolved never to speak to him again if she could help it. Rattled and miserable, she changed quickly into her nightgown and jumped into bed, where she lay quaking with fear.

The tap at the door startled her dreadfully. In all the months she'd been here, no one had ever thought to bother her in her room. She got up cautiously and eased the door open a small crack, afraid of who she would find. The Baron of Geid was in her hallway. At first, she wondered if he had come to make good on his threat about her head on a pike. Then she thought of another reason why a male Lord might visit a female servant in the middle of the night. She hoped it was the first reason.

When the Baron opened his mouth, the first thing he

said was, "I'm sorry."

Senna stared at him. Oddly enough, he did look repentant.

"I'm sorry I yelled at you. You asked me a question I didn't want to answer. I say ugly things sometimes, but I rarely mean them."

Whatever Senna might have been expecting from the Baron, she had never imagined anything so strange as an apology. His lack of sanity was more evident than ever. But she didn't trust his attempt to get on her good side, and she narrowed the crack in the door between them.

"I'm ready to answer your question now. Can you meet me back in the hall in a few minutes?"

Speech eluded her. Senna nodded, not seeing another choice. She closed the door without a word, and put her ear against it as the Baron's footsteps echoed down the stairs. She threw on her clothes, rumpled and filthy from the day, without a thought. But she took care to slip her knife into her skirt pocket, with the handle in ready reach.

When she reached the east hall she found Fenwith standing by a chair, staring into the fireplace. When he saw her, he motioned for her to sit. Senna hardly breathed as she did so. The Baron took the chair across from her and tried to smile. It was not a very good smile—it only reached half of his mouth and it died away quickly—but it was the first effort she had ever seen on his part, so she was impressed.

"What I'm going to tell you is in the strictest confidence. You must give me your word that this conversation goes no further than this room."

Senna hesitated a slight second. She disliked taking an oath that she had no intention of keeping. "I swear," she said finally.

The Baron appeared satisfied. He leaned back in his chair. "My name is not Fenwith," he told her.

Senna was past being surprised at this point; she merely waited.

"I'm not supposed to be the Baron of Geid. My real

name is Cole. I'm the son of a steward to a Lord in Lammark. The Lord took an interest in me as I was growing up. I had a few lessons in books and etiquette, enough that allows me to impersonate a member of the nobility."

He paused, looking for a reaction. Senna gave him none. She wondered if there was a grain of truth to this. She supposed it was possible. But that didn't explain why he would bother to tell her about it. Did he think Senna cared who his parents were?

"At the start of the Gault Revolution...before everything fell apart, I was approached by a Queen's adjutant. She said they'd intercepted one of the Regent's new henchmen, nephew to his wife, who'd been living abroad for years and wasn't likely to be recognized by anyone at court. And who just happened to be albino. Fenwith had been bequeathed the county of Geid, but he broke his head open in an altercation with the Queensmen, so he wasn't going to make his appointment. The adjutant thought I would make a perfect spy. Not many albinos roaming the country, and certainly none in the Queen's service. No one could suspect I was other than Mister Fenwith.

"It was supposed to be a temporary position. No one thought the Regent would retain power as long as he has. The plan worked at first. I got a total of two messages back to the adjutant. Then she was captured and killed along with every other Queensman. I found myself in an impossible situation. I'd spent weeks trying to convince everyone I was the Baron of Geid. Everyone who knew me from my previous life was either dead or very far away. I couldn't hide and I couldn't leave, and the Regent was ordering me to collect taxes. I began to compromise."

He paused again, and Senna wondered if she could appear as astonished as she felt. She shook her head. It was incredible, but she believed him. In all the time she had known Fenwith, Senna had never heard him say anything as sincerely as what he had just said to her. Certainly there was no reason for a man to lie about being an impostor. In a flash, she realized she held as much power over the Baron as he did over her. Her fear vanished at once.

"You compromised," Senna repeated icily. "I see. You turned into the very thing you were trying to save us from. Well done."

A cloud passed over the Baron's face. "That's not so," he said. "I try to make things better here."

Senna wanted to laugh, but anger squelched the impulse. "Really?" she said. "What a wonderful job you've done! Is that why you let people go hungry? Or perhaps that's why you like to execute people who help Jedomar?"

He sighed. "None of those people die, Senna, and you know it."

She stopped short. Of course—her uncle. She felt her jaw open and close several times as she tried to phrase her next question.

"Having a reputation for ruthlessness helps draw attention away from the relative good welfare of my tenants. Not to mention the lack of contribution I make to the Regent's cofferhouse. Your friend Jedomar takes care of that, thank the Queen." He flinched a little. "It's true I don't do very much. All I really do is rant and look mean, then look the other way while you people help each other. But if I wasn't keeping this castle in check, you wouldn't be able to do that much. I have no illusions about this. I'm not a good man. But if I thought for a moment that Geid wouldn't be worse off without me, I would leave in a heartbeat. I can't think of anyplace I would less rather be."

Senna felt like a fish out of water, and her gaping probably contributed to that image. She stared and then stared again. She was looking at a person she already knew, and discovering they had never met.

"You know, don't you, about the way I help Jedomar?"

"Of course I do," he said softly. Then he smiled. It was an actual, honest, and surprisingly good-looking smile. "Why do you think I give you access to everything?"

Senna glanced at the floor. *Why indeed?* It couldn't be that she was actually as clever as she thought she was. A moment passed before Senna gained the strength to peek back at the Baron. "What...who are you?" She furrowed her brow as she recalled with effort the name he had given her.

"It's Cole." He spoke with a patience that was so unlike him, it gave her chills. A man named Cole might be a remarkable actor who was able to create the persona of Fenwith, but Fenwith would never play the part of this humble, unaggressive person in front of her. He simply was not capable of it.

"Mister Cole. I think I'll call you that instead of Lord Baron," she taunted.

"I'd like that. But not in public, if you please." Before she could laugh at this, he became very grave. "I mean it, Senna," Cole said. "What I told you was somewhat out of necessity, but you gave me your word of silence. You can't reveal this to anyone. Not even Jedomar."

Senna hesitated. She felt a little more obliged to honor her word than she did before, but there were serious repercussions to this. She needed a moment to think them through.

Cole seemed to sense as much, because he pressed further. "I was commissioned by a member of the Queen's active Guard. That commission was never revoked, so it is still valid. I realize the irony of this, but I am an *actual* Queensman. I'm invoking that authority when I tell you to keep silent. On top of that, I'm asking, as a man with a secret—let me be the one to decide how my secret gets out?"

Under the Queen's law, Senna was obliged to follow the directions of anyone who had a commission from the Queen. Unless, of course, she decided that the Queen's government was dead and in no effect, but that was not something she was willing to admit.

Senna nodded. "I'll keep my promise," she swore, and meant it this time. "Not even Jedomar?" she pleaded.

"*Especially* Jedomar."

CHAPTER FIFTEEN

Cole woke the next morning with an emotion so foreign, it took him some time to place it. Finally he decided it was optimism. The morning was cool and pleasant, and he sat by his window for a half hour without feeling oppressed by the view. Rows of herbs and small potatoes poked their noses hopefully from the soil. There was a row of freshly turned dirt where Corvan had dug a new trench to catch rainwater so it wouldn't puddle at the castle's foundation. The steward's dedication went largely unappreciated. No one besides Corvan seemed to mind if the ancient castle rotted to its last stone. It was almost a shame. It must have been beautiful here once.

He went down to breakfast not knowing what to expect. Senna stood by the table as usual, presenting the dishes of the morning. Cole sat down and tried to look as if nothing had changed since last night. He had never felt more embarrassed about the circumstances of their relationship—the stateliness with which Senna attended him, the absurd quantities of food, even his clothes, which were modest by the standards of nobility.

He managed not to look at her for a few minutes, pretending to be deeply interested in his food. The first time he raised his head, she caught his glance and winked at him. Cole started to choke on his piece of bread. One of the kitchen workers chose this moment to bring out a fresh pitcher of milk. She hesitated in the threshold when she found her Baron coughing his guts onto the floor.

Cole could feel himself turning red, and unconsciously delved into character. He recovered, sat up, and made an impatient gesture at the servant. "If you want to die, by all means, keep staring."

The poor girl jumped with fright, placed her burden on the table, and hastily disappeared.

Senna give him a glare. Cole sighed inwardly. Fenwith often overdid things. With the maids in the kitchen waiting to overhear, he didn't dare do more than turn his hands over in apology.

Senna disappeared when breakfast was over. He saw her walking down the lane away from the castle into town. He didn't know if he could trust her to keep her promise, but he'd done what he could. There was no point worrying himself to death over it. He looked for Corvan instead.

The morning was half over. Cole shielded his eyes from the force of full sunlight as he crossed the courtyard. Mister Corvan was by the stables, turning hay for the horses. The old man crossed his hands when he saw Cole coming, the dutiful sign of steward to his master. Cole remembered his father making the same sign to Lord Gretin.

Cole stepped briskly into the shade of the stable, eager to rest his eyes from the light. If an aversion to sunlight did not earn albinos their reputation as creatures of the dark, it certainly did not help, either. Cole tried not to let anyone know how very apt the superstition was. He was glad to live in a country where fog was prominent.

Corvan followed submissively, replacing his tool as he retrieved a parcel from his cloak.

"I have the riding gloves you asked for, Lord," Corvan held the item with two hands, like some reverent offering. They were fine gloves, soft leather. The tanner's best work.

"Thank you," said Cole. "Did you meet the Hasset traders?"

"Yes, Lord. I gave them your payment for the field

161

cutters. They will sell to the Geid merchants for half cost."

"Good. Are you going into town again today?"

"If required, Lord Baron."

Cole hesitated. With Senna in his confidence, it might be a relief to rely less upon Mister Corvan. The old steward's dependability suffered more every year from his age. Corvan could retain a task in his mind for several hours, but ask him again the next day, and he would have forgotten performing it. From one point of view, this was beneficial. Corvan could not betray what he did not recall. However, the length of time the steward could be trusted to focus was growing shorter.

"No, it's all right," said Cole. He regarded Corvan thoughtfully. "Do you remember when I first came here?"

The steward blinked. Of course he didn't. He remembered twenty years ago like Cole remembered yesterday, but beyond that, memories were lost to him. Cole was no longer sure if Corvan still understood who he was, that he worked for the Queen, or what that meant. They didn't discuss it much anymore.

"You showed me what to do, how to function. You were my guiding star, Mister Corvan." Cole wondered if the compliment would sink in, if he repeated it often enough. "Thank you."

Corvan took it in stride. "Glad to be of service, Lord. Shall I ready a horse for you?"

"No." Cole wouldn't travel today. It was nearly Tax-Day.

Senna had an armful of sewing that evening, and she decided there was no reason for her not to do it in the east hall. She found the Baron in his customary position, huddled over an endless stack of papers. Senna walked directly past him. A dozen benches were stored in stacks against the wall, kept for festivals and ceremonies held in days past. She turned one upright, sat boldly, and glanced at the Baron to see if he would object. He gave her an expression of mild interest, then went back to his writing.

Senna took up her basket and began mending the tear in Guardsman Hawforge's vest. Lately the Guards had been asking her to do random favors for them. Mend a shirt here, pick up a delivery there. Senna generally felt compelled to accept such jobs. It meant she could demand some sort of recompense: either a coin or a scrap of information.

After a little time passed, the Baron complained of being thirsty. As far as she knew, there was no understanding between them that they might behave as something other than master and servant. Senna got up and went to the kitchen.

Not much later, she returned bearing a cup of warmed water with calomar leaves. She cradled the cup in both hands and set it reverently on his desk.

The Baron smiled warmly. "Thank you, Senna."

It seemed to please him enormously to thank her. Senna wondered whether or not it would ever occur to him to fetch his own water. Her returning smile was the beginning of a laugh, and she covered her mouth to hide it.

"What?" he asked, after taking a long swallow from the cup, "Is something funny?"

"I didn't spit in it," Senna said.

"What?" It took him a second to register her words, but he drew the cup away and regarded it suspiciously.

Senna beamed down shamelessly. "I used to spit in your food," she said matter-of-factly. "But don't worry. That one is clean."

The Baron looked confounded. It made Senna's confession very satisfying. His stare moved from her to the cup and back again. Finally he gave a shrug with his eyes and drained the rest of the liquid. The cup landed on the table with a bang. *"Thank you, Senna."* His voice was heavy with sarcasm and not a little disgust, but he looked grateful that she had done away with the habit.

"You're welcome, Mister Cole." She tried to sound sincere, but her words came half stifled between giggles, so he probably thought she was mocking him.

Senna went back to her bench. For a while there was silence again. Senna concentrated on making progress, but her mind was occupied and she had trouble making her stitches even.

The Baron dropped his pen with a clang. Senna looked up to see him rubbing at his eyes. "What's wrong?" she asked.

"I'm just tired."

"Why, trouble sleeping?"

Cole glared at her. "Yes. You can stop gloating; I get what I deserve."

She raised an eyebrow imperiously. "You must really sleep poorly, then."

"You don't give me very much credit, do you?"

"Only as much as you give your tenants."

The Baron laughed outright. Senna was surprised to see him take her wit with good humor. "Would you like to see my credit book?"

Senna halted mid-stitch. She had been wanting to get a look at his credit book since the day she stepped into the castle. "If you insist," she said.

Cole retrieved the well-worn volume from the single giant drawer in his desk. Traditionally, a Baron often did give out loans, which were tracked in a credit book. The phrase had evolved to include all of an estate's records, including the income and taxes, not to mention any other information the Baron found useful. Cole rifled through the pages for a moment. Then he turned the book around and pushed it in her direction.

Senna leaned over and squinted at the tiny letters on the page. Families were listed with an estimate of current wealth, percentage-based collection, and amount paid. Everything was recorded with a neat, even hand. The records were difficult for her untrained eye to follow, but Cole let Senna peruse the book at her leisure.

"I get most of this from the lawyering circle," he said.

She scanned the township for names she recognized. Yes, there was Mister Camindar, Mister Morick, Madam Haw. The Baron seemed to have a respectable idea of what each family owned. The list included family relations, family sizes, professions, and disabilities, if any. The book even showed that Madam Winid had a new baby.

"This is..." Senna searched for the right word, "thorough."

"I like to write things down. It's comforting to me. Besides," the Baron admitted, "I feel in charge of them somehow. The least I can do is try to remember who they are."

Senna regarded him impassively. "You're our Baron. You're supposed to be in charge of us."

Mister Cole tapped the desk as he considered this.

Senna turned a few pages and found records for the county beyond Geid proper. All of them were dated and sorted according to village population and land area. Local collectors must have supplied the data, but Cole had obviously organized the work himself. Somehow, it was never suspicious to her that the Baron did not keep a personal scribe. It seemed to match his obsessive nature. But she supposed it was necessary if he intended to falsify his reports. There were hundreds, perhaps thousands of entries.

The Baron hovered a finger helpfully over the book. "You see the most recent quarter here. There are still two collections to account for," he explained, pointing to a pair of empty columns. "It's a pretty standard report, but you might find this part interesting," He turned the pages to a chart near the front of the book. "I've been keeping a ledger of everything the Regent collects and spends. That I can track, anyway. All sixteen counties at the top, showing population, income, tax rates, and vassal percentages."

"Vassal percentage...what's that?"

"How much the Lord gets to keep for himself. Gote's standard is ten percent. Most Lords weasel off more than that,

165

and hide the balance in their reports. Gote knows it, of course, but he pretends not to so he can threaten all of us with treason if he wants."

"How much do you keep?"

"For myself? About two percent."

"Thief," Senna said. "That's our money."

"What?" The Baron looked taken aback. "Do I look rich to you?" He yanked on his tunic, gesturing as if to expose its inferior quality. "I have to pay the Guards and keep this damned castle from falling down. You're the one who keeps asking for more allowance!"

Senna rolled her eyes, wondering how she might calm him down without proffering an apology. She had spoken without thinking. Honestly, he ought to spend a little more. It was absolutely ridiculous for a Baron to only own two sets of clothes.

Cole sighed. "On paper, I keep the ten, of course. And then I conceal as much as I can, just like the others, so I can funnel it back into the economy."

Senna was feeling more and more confused. "Then why is Geid's tax rate higher than that of Candige and Anseth?"

"That's just for show. The account of what was earned is reported too low, so it comes out the same. But it's easier to look like I'm trying if I inflate all the numbers."

"It also makes people hate you," she pointed out.

"Yes, but that's to my advantage too."

"Why?" Senna looked intently at him. The urge to issue this challenge had been gnawing at her since yesterday. "Why do you appear so cruel? Why do you want us to hate you?"

Cole breathed deeply before he answered. "I can think of three reasons," he said. "First, the Regent would not tolerate any of his Lords being liked by their tenants. Can you imagine what would happen if people started immigrating to Geid because they thought it was nice here? I would lose my job, to say the least.

"Second, you can get away with a lot more charity if people think you don't mean it. They assume you're being foolish or inattentive. They give you no credit, and therefore, no attention.

"The third reason is the most obvious, and also the most maddening. You see, now that I've started, I can't stop. When I first took the role of Fenwith, I thought it would be easiest for people to accept my story if I overacted the part. A soft-hearted spy is always the first person suspected. The Fenwith boy was reported to be irascible, so I built into that. I made him the worst sort of character I could imagine. Now that I've lived with the disguise for years, I can't suddenly alter his personality."

Senna digested this explanation. You could tell he'd put a lot of thought into the matter. "You could have a miraculous change of heart," she suggested with toneless sarcasm.

Cole dismissed her proposal offhandedly. He slouched forlornly in his chair. "This isn't fun for me, you know. I'm friendless here. You might have more sympathy."

"Am I supposed to offer to be your friend now? That's such an obvious ploy."

The Baron sat up and looked suddenly less pathetic. "You are far too clever for a housekeeper, Senna."

"Don't you forget it."

Truthfully, she did feel a little sorry for him. But she wasn't about to let him know it. The man had planted his own tree and he had to sleep under it.

Senna wasn't expected at Carly cottage the next morning. The muffled voices within dropped into surprised silence as she knocked.

"It's me," she called, hoping that the building's

occupants turned out to be the ones she expected.

The door opened at once. Dohack blocked her way with a fiendish grin. Disheveled and groggy-eyed, he perked up enough to flex his muscles at her, an attempt at flirtation that impressed her not at all. She was sure Hack knew she didn't like him. "What's this?" Hack exclaimed. "The woman leading a double life. Are you supposed to be here?"

Senna stepped back, half chagrined. Her double life was getting more complicated than she'd bargained for.

Jed pushed Hack out of the way and greeted her more cordially. "Senna, come in. I didn't think you'd be able to get away today."

Senna gave an indefinite response as she scanned the cottage interior, subconsciously checking for her Uncle Wick. She was relieved to find him not present. "Any word from Inwick?" she asked.

Jed gave her a sympathetic smile. "He ought to be back in Candige by now. But we don't really know yet."

Of course not. Gayna hadn't had time to reestablish contact. Senna paused, feeling strangely out of place.

"Senna, sit down," Jed prompted kindly. He put a hand on her waist to carry through his point.

"Thank you. It wasn't hard to get away," said Senna with some satisfaction as she settled into a cushioned chair. The Baron was no longer a check on her mobility. "I have something to share. I got ahold of Fenwith's credit book."

Senna immediately had their attention. Even Rimick seemed interested. "How did you do that?" he asked.

"The Baron got careless," she said. "I checked the desk last night and it was open, so I wrote down what I could."

No one in the cottage gave eyes to her nerves. It was strange. If you'd asked her, Senna would have said she was a bad liar. Of course, she'd done well enough lying to her enemies in the castle. She thought it would be harder lying to people she loved. Apparently it wasn't.

Rimick took out a pen and began copying her crudely

scribbled figures. Senna had naturally poor handwriting. At least she had a fictitious excuse for haste in this instance.

"There wasn't much time, so I just got what I could."

"You did well," said Rimick.

Mister Cole had basically told her which figures to copy.

Hack tried to lean over Rimick's shoulder to get a look at the paper, but Rimick pushed him away.

"What else was in there, Senna?" Jed asked.

"There was a long list of expenditures. I can tell you Captain Lodin makes three pieces a week," she huffed. He was overpaid, in her opinion. Expenditures weren't big news. Senna was in charge of most of them anyway.

Jed nodded, half listening to her as he scanned the paper. "Blessed Queen, the Gaults took five tons in silver this year?"

The Baron wouldn't let her take the tax figures, which weren't really interesting to Jed anyway, but she did get a lot of data on exports, monetary contributions, and other favors in and out of Mackabine.

"Those Gaults are getting fat as skunks on our silver." Jed's voice rose as his temper boiled. "We should spread these numbers everywhere. People should know what the Regent's been doing with their taxes."

Rimick waved a dismissive hand. "I think everyone already knows, Jed. It's pretty obvious."

Senna agreed with Rimick. There were plenty of reasons to hate Regent Gote. Nobody needed any more.

"And," Rimick felt the need to bring up, "if we disseminate this information, suspicion may fall on Senna."

Jed's anger deflated. "Right," he said, sitting down, "we don't want that."

Now that they were looking it over, Senna couldn't remember why the credit book had seemed so important. They didn't learn that much from it. Nothing that helped them defeat the Regent or alleviate the strain on Geid.

They talked some more about useless things, the

weather, and how various folk were planning to pay their upcoming tax. Senna sat through it quietly, feeling strangely removed from the group. It was like watching a scene on a stage. Last night's information begged to burst out of her. *The Baron is a Queensman! He gave me those figures himself!*

Hack broke her reverie with a jab to her shoulder. "Are you going to eat that, Senna?"

She looked at the small loaf of bread Jed had handed her. "No, I'm not really hungry."

Hack eagerly relieved her of the unwanted food. He mumbled something with his mouth full of bread. Senna didn't try to understand him.

"Are you sure you're all right? You look tired."

It took Senna a few seconds to realize Jed was talking to her.

"I guess I am," she said. It was as good an explanation as any for her absence of mind. They persuaded her to go home for a few hours of sleep.

"We could all use some rest," Rimick said tranquilly. "You know what tomorrow is."

Jed and Hack answered in unison, with equal groans of displeasure, "Tax-Day."

CHAPTER SIXTEEN

Tax-Day was chilly for late spring. Every man and woman outside the castle was huddled into as much fabric as they could afford to bring with them. Jed settled his back into the wall against a shallow groove, an imperfection wrought by time and bad weather. The groove made him seem that much more inconsequential. No one identified Jedomar among the mass of hooded, shivering folk.

Tax-Day was a trial that had been endured by generations of Geidfolk. Each family was required to send a representative to account for its wealth. The lines were terrible. There were close to five thousand people in Geid. The outlying villages had their own collectors, who brought their accounts separately to the Baron. Only the citizens of Geid proper reported directly to the castle. One fellow usually spoke for four or five people, so the gathering of souls at the castle rarely exceeded three hundred. Even so, it was enough to clog the road for the day and ruin the mood of the town.

Jed paid taxes every cycle. Not his own, of course. No amount of silver would negate the debt against Jedomar's name. But there were always people unable to pay for themselves. Usually he just gave them what they needed, or, if they were too sick to come themselves, enlisted someone else to pay. This was the first time he could remember coming in person.

Jed lifted his head marginally over the crowd in search of Rimick. His friend was half a dozen spans farther up, nearly at the head of the line. He looked behind and briefly caught Jed's eye. Jed nodded just as a bored Guard waved Rimick forward. Jed focused his ears to overhear their exchange.

"Name?"

Rimick put a slight tremble in his voice. "Morick," he said.

"I have two Moricks here."

"Yes, sir, I'm the first one. The second is a fellow from Indor."

Jed inched forward over the irritated objections of the crowd. "Sorry," he whispered, "excuse me." He slipped between two farmers and dodged a woman trying to whack his shoulder.

"Is the other Morick here?" asked the Guard.

"I don't know," Rimick said simply.

Jed smiled. If it had been him, he would have added something more dramatic. Maybe that it wasn't his job to keep track of that no-good young upstart who stole his name. Rimick was a minimalist, but he was doing a good job. His taut, hunched posture made him seem much older than he was.

"You have a lot of tax due, Mister Morick. You were short last quarter, and you agreed to pay the difference with interest." The Guard raised his eyes, looking doubtful.

"Yes, sir," Rimick conceded with a nod. "I have the tax with me." He presented the Guard with a pouch.

The Guard made a pleased noise in the back of his throat. He reached down to examine the bag. Jed took this as his cue. He closed the few feet between himself and the table and banged his fist onto the wooden surface. The coin pouch jumped out of the startled Guard's hands and spilled some of the shiny medallions on the table.

"Morick! You dogfish! You stole that coin from me. I knew you couldn't pay your own tax, but I didn't think you'd stoop to taking mine. Give it back!"

Rimick remained calm at the insulting accusation. "I did not take your tax," he said.

The Guard obviously didn't care whose coin it was as long as it ended up on his receipt list. He warned Jed away from the table and waved for help to back up his order.

Jed took his chance before the Guards could outnumber him. He sank his fists into Rimick's garment and lifted him bodily off the ground. "I said give it back!"

The Guard stood up, eyes darting between the contenders. Jed summoned his strength and tossed Rimick into the collecting table. He rolled twice and plunged off the end, right into the collected stash of coin. Jed didn't give him time to sit there. He picked Rimick up again and held him off the ground while Rimick slipped a bag into Jed's left pocket. Rimick had the nimble fingers of a seasoned thief. Jed barely felt the change of weight.

The new Guards were arriving with drawn swords. Jed let Rimick collapse onto the ground. He backed away with his hands up, but his pretended rage remained. "I won't let you get away with this, Morick! You'll see me again!" Jed shouted. He turned and ran before anyone got the idea to detain him.

Jed got past the gate and out of sight before he stopped to wait for Rimick. He climbed a tree and watched to make sure no one followed him. Rimick came down the road a few minutes later, still stooping and scuffling as if his weight were too great for his bones. He didn't see Jed until Jed threw a twig at him.

"You can probably stop that now," Jed suggested, "unless you enjoy it. You'll end up looking that way in a few years anyway."

Rimick came to a halt and lowered the hood of his cloak. "How much did we get?"

"Almost forty pieces," said Jed, weighing the stolen bag in his hand.

"Ah," Rimick sighed. "That's not much. You didn't give me enough time."

Jed shrugged. "It'll do."

It was hardly more than they had paid for old Mister Morick's taxes. It had been fun, anyway, Jed told himself. He loved a chance to play-act in front of the Guards.

"Did they search you?" Jed asked.

Rimick nodded. "They seem to have noticed that I landed in their collection. But they weren't thorough; I don't think they were suspicious."

"They will be soon enough," Jed said.

That afternoon, Jed and Rimick ate dinner with Morick's family. They brought a pheasant they'd shot and let his daughter-in-law cook it for them. The house held three sons, three daughters, and a large dog who had just given birth to puppies. Madam Nanta was working desperately to pawn the dogs off on someone. Her family couldn't afford to care for them, and Nanta didn't have the heart to drown them.

"Come now, Mister Jedomar. Everyone knows you're the richest man in Geid. Surely you could manage one little puppy," she said as she set down a plate of vegetables.

He tried to ignore the cries of the pup yapping at his heels. "I appreciate the thought, Nanta, I really do," Jed assured her. "I just don't have a place to keep a dog."

"You could keep it here, Jed!" one of the younger children volunteered.

Nanta waved the child into silence. She was wise enough to realize that was the same thing as keeping the dog for themselves.

"Thank you again for paying our debts, Mister Jedomar." She served Rimick's plate next and quickly corrected herself. "And Mister Rimick, too, of course."

Mister Morick had actually died the week prior, a combination of illness and old age. Unfortunately, taxes were inheritable. The family sold off what it could to meet the debt, but a lifetime of farming passed on little to the next generation.

"I just hope you don't get into trouble over it," Jed answered. He expected a dead man would be hard to blame when their mischief was revealed.

While the older children helped their mother with the meal, the younger ones crowded around Jed. Their grubby hands pawed at his leg in a contest for attention.

"Want to see a trick?" he asked them.

"Yes!" the children answered one after the other.

"This is my magic stick." He showed them a short twig, as long as his thumb, and about as wide as a bird's beak. There was nothing special about it except that it had been trimmed straight and dyed purple with featherberries. The children were sufficiently awed. They took turns passing the magic stick amongst themselves.

"Don't break it," he cautioned, retrieving his twig from the grip of an enthusiastic toddler. "Now watch as I make the stick disappear!"

Using both hands, he slipped the twig behind his palm and tucked it behind his ring. The children couldn't see it from the front when he splayed his hands wide for them. They cried out in delight. The youngest girl reached for his hands. He let her hold the empty one, and before she could get further, Jed let out a breath of mock surprise. "Oh-ho, there it is! Inside Jojo's ear!"

Jojo squealed as Jed reached alongside her head and revealed the stick.

The children begged him to do the trick again. "Put it in my ear next," one said.

He didn't have time to answer them because their father returned home at that moment. The children moved to the door with single-minded purpose and clasped their hands around Mister Timbad's legs. "Daddy!" they cried.

Morick's son picked up every child in turn and laid a kiss on each of their little noses. "Hello, Kens. Hello, Jojo." Timbad said. Jed felt strangely jealous of their affection. He would have liked to come home to such a welcome.

"How did the...business go?" Mister Timbad asked. He looked down and to the side, as if the question were embarrassing. The toddler in his arms wriggled wildly.

Rimick answered first. "School-Day pudding, as Jed would say."

"That's good," said Timbad. He made brief eye contact and then went back to gazing at the floor. Timbad was a deeply shy man.

Madam Nanta knew how to fill in where her husband lacked. "Will you sleep here tonight, Mister Jed, Mister Rimick?"

Jed declined politely. He didn't see a spare place for them anywhere. "I have to go see some of the villages next. I hope to reach Indor by tonight."

The Baron took taxes from everywhere in Geid, not just the township. The villages in the countryside needed help as much as anywhere. Jed sometimes felt overwhelmed at the responsibility the county intermutually bestowed upon his shoulders. Other times he looked at the good he was doing—the easy smiles as Nanta shepherded her children to the table, assured of food and a place to live until next tax cycle—and knew he didn't want to do anything else.

CHAPTER SEVENTEEN

Cole spent the day sequestered with the collection results. He savored the comfortable smoothness of paper under his fingers. His hand moved over the paper, tracing straight rows with his fingernail. Each row was filled with numbers and labels—so orderly, so satisfying. It was the one thing Fenwith and Cole shared: a love of record keeping. It was nice to have *something* in common with his alter ego.

Cole snorted at his own thoughts. Fenwith wasn't real; he only had whatever qualities Cole had invented for him. But Cole had nurtured the idea of Fenwith for so long, he sometimes felt Fenwith was a ghost that haunted him.

The noise of the opening door made him start, even though he realized quickly that it was not a ghost. Only Senna. Lately Senna had given herself free rein to come and go as she pleased. Cole didn't think it was wise to argue with her.

The housekeeper smiled at him. "I like that you're so easy to find. You spend all your time in the same place."

"Yes, it's nice to be predictable. One of the things I strive for."

Senna had no retort to this sarcasm. "Jed wants to know when the next grain cart is leaving," she stated.

Cole set down his pen and smiled. He used to have to pass information to Jedomar using that stupid tree stump.

Senna was wonderfully more efficient. "When does he want it?"

Senna laughed. "I don't think he expects to be consulted."

"Actually, you should tell Jedomar to hold off. The people in Pannerack are close to starving. There's only enough grain for two shipments over the summer."

"Is that where it goes? Pannerack?"

"For now. Production of food has been halted in most counties where mining is possible."

Senna turned a grim gaze to the floor. He tried to gauge the critical aspect of her expression.

"I know Geid isn't getting everything they need," said Cole, "but other counties have it worse. At least the food is grown here."

Senna nodded slowly. She promised to carry the message.

"Is there anything I can help with?"

Cole hoped she would stay, but Senna shook her head. "I'm tired," she answered. "Good night, Cole."

Cole tried not to admit to himself how pleased he was by her use of his name. "I thought you were going to call me 'Mister Cole,' at least?"

"You don't call me Madam Senna. I'm just leveling the field."

Cole looked at her calmly. "Be careful, Senna. This castle is quiet but it's not dead. We can't start acting like we've become friends."

"Have we?" Senna asked impertinently.

Cole didn't miss a beat. "Yes," he said. "I'll send you a letter on your birthday and everything."

Senna smiled crookedly, shook her head, and left—but not without a mocking bow to show that she hadn't been put in her place. *Intractable woman,* thought Cole. It was hard to overstate how much he liked her.

❖

An hour after sending Emwid home, Senna heard the singsong voice of her maid announcing a return from the kitchen window. "Hoodaloo. What did I hear? Let me in and I'll tell you!"

Emwid often gleaned gossip from her nephews as she picked them up from the market on her way home. Sometimes, when news was sensational, she retraced her steps back to the castle, nephews in tow, to share with the rest of the kitchen.

Emwid rapped at the window in impatience. "Jedomar is at it again!" she exclaimed. "That's what I heard."

The other maids, who were preparing to leave, opened the door to let her finish her story inside. "The town's going to be well-off again," declared Emwid. The loose flesh on her chin jiggled as she spoke. She described, in imprecise terms, how the county Queensman hoodwinked the collectors on Tax-Day.

Senna's initial worry evaporated. Emwid was behind on her news. Senna had never explicitly explained her relationship with Jedomar to her maids. They did know that she was on his side when rumor came through. Of course, there was hardly a soul in Geid for whom that was not the case.

"Oh no, no one saw him," Emwid assured her. "No one is that crafty. But it would have been Jedomar, for sure. They say the Baron is going to extract the lost amount from Guardsman Perr's salary. It's going to take him thirty years to pay that off!" She broke into uncharitable laughter.

Her nephews were complaining about the delay and so Emwid was off again in a hurry. Cafia and the other maids followed quickly, exchanging exultations amongst themselves. The women had family and obligations at home. The last remnants of dinner were packed into their baskets to smuggle away.

179

"Would you like to come to my parents' for dinner, Madam? We're having baked eggs." Cafia shuffled her hands over her travel basket, clearly venturing outside her comfort zone to ask this question.

Senna shooed her off affably. There was plenty for her to eat here. Cafia's brothers didn't need another mouth to compete with for their dinner. Besides, there was still work to do. The maids were only paid to work part-time.

With the kitchen free of other eyes, Senna untied her soiled apron and draped it across an empty stool. For a moment, it felt good to be alone. Then the silence reminded Senna of the intrigue waiting down the hall. She got a clean cup and took a bottle of wine from the shelf. It was the best wine in the castle, imported from Yfreife, and the Baron's favorite. She poured half a cup before the bottle ran empty. Senna went to the cellar to get more. She came back trailing dust and had to shake it from her cloak onto the porch. She made a note to herself to give the cellar a good summer cleaning. Senna finished filling the cup, arranged it on a tray to make it more presentable, and took it to the east hall.

The Baron was engrossed in a thick volume. He seemed neither pleased nor displeased to see her, but he smiled a weak greeting. His smile was so subtle, it was more in his eyes than his mouth. *He might be handsome,* she thought, *if he were anyone else.* After a few minutes of conflicted introspection, Senna convinced herself she had often thought the Baron handsome, but had been too prejudiced to admit it.

Senna leaned over to catch a glimpse of the title of Cole's book. It was something in Gaultian. "Ugh, how can you read in that language?"

"Reading is nothing. You should try speaking it."

Senna replaced this morning's cup with the fresh one. "Well, don't drink this too fast. I can see you'll need your senses about you."

"Yes, Madam," he said absently. Cole took the wine without lifting his eyes from the book.

Senna bit her lip, uncertain whether to stay. His

180

demeanor seemed a plea for solitude, so she returned to the kitchen. The evening was cooling fast. She added coal to the fire and then drew hot water for the dishes. The ladle was still in her hand as she turned for her apron, and found a man standing a few spans behind her. Senna squealed and dropped the ladle.

"Whoa there." Dohack grinned and crossed his arms arrogantly.

Senna's eyes swept the kitchen to see where he had come from.

"I was hiding in that pantry over there." Hack pointed behind him. How or when he had gotten there remained a mystery.

Senna picked up the apron and started beating him with it. "You—scared—me—to death!" She gave him one swipe of the apron for each word. Hack laughed at her feeble attack.

"What are you doing here, anyway?" said Senna.

"You'll never guess," Hack boasted as he cracked his knuckles. "Go ahead and try!"

"What? Have you given up gambling?" Senna jeered. She wouldn't be surprised if he'd snuck in here on a bet.

"I'll tell you, but don't be mad, okay? I would've told you first, but I was afraid you would act nervous or something."

"What, what, what?" Senna insisted.

"I just got rid of Baron Fenwith."

Senna colored a little, and might have been frightened, had she not left the Baron some minutes before.

"What do you mean?" she said. She put the dishes into the water, trying to look as if nothing he said bothered her.

Hack drew a tiny bottle from his vest pocket. Out of her peripheral vision, Senna could see that it was empty. She pulled her wet hands out of the barrel and yanked Hack's hand towards her face.

"Don't try to take any of the credit. It was my idea. I can't wait to see Jed's face when he finds out."

Senna dropped all pretense of indifference. "What is that?"

"Dragonweed," Hack said. "I put it in the wine just before you took it out."

Senna was out of the room before Hack had finished speaking. Ignoring the cries that pleaded with her to wait, she flew down the corridor, through the main hall, and almost impaled herself on the door latch trying to get it open.

Cole was standing facing the door. It was clear he had only just turned to see who entered. His book rested easily in one hand, and the fatal cup in the other. Without a word, Senna launched herself at him, and smacked hard at the back of his hand. The cup fell with a clang, draining its contents onto the floor.

"Did you drink it?"

Cole was flabbergasted. His eyes got wide as her urgency awakened his suspicions. Senna didn't dare to hope he would answer in the negative. But he did. A simple "no" fell from his mouth.

Senna was feeling woozy so she sat down on the Baron's stool. He didn't seem to mind.

"Senna?" he began.

"It was poisoned."

Cole might have turned paler if he was capable of it. He took the other stool and stared at the wall. For several seconds, the room was silent.

"What made you change your mind?" he said finally.

Senna's head snapped up. "It wasn't me!" she cried. "It was Dohack. I found him skulking in the kitchen. He must have done it when I was in the cellar."

Cole mulled this over a moment longer. "Did Jedomar tell him to—"

"No," said Senna. "Jed would never do that. He knows he could never control someone else the way he does you."

Cole snorted just a tiny bit. "Good."

"Jed will be furious. It would mess up his system if

182

you died, and the chances of the Regent appointing someone better are marginal."

Cole nodded. "You'd better go find Mister Dohack before he gets into more trouble. And chase him out of the castle. It'll be a bother for me if the Guard catches him here."

Senna nodded. She picked up the fallen cup on her way to the door. "I'll get something to clean this up," she said, shaking the splashed wine from her fingertips.

"Senna." The Baron gave her a meaningful look. "Thank you."

Senna searched for words on her way back to the kitchen. Dohack's egotism appalled her beyond words. Did the fool not realize how he was implicating her in his deed—almost framing her?

She could have reproached Hack with all the reasons why it was not appropriate to assassinate their Baron. But as Jed was bound to do that anyway, and to more effect than she could, she decided that what Hack really needed was a healthy dose of grief. She wanted to be certain he never tried this again.

Hack appeared ready to throttle her at first look. He fumed like a small child. He actually jumped up and down as he demanded to know what had happened.

"That wine *wasn't* for the Baron, you dogfish." Her performance was convincing; Senna was already close to tears. "One of the Guards brought his daughter to the castle. She wasn't feeling well and I was bringing her some wine to calm her nerves."

"What?"

"The poor girl is having a nervous breakdown and her father decided to bring her to me. He's not married, and I was probably the only motherly figure he could think of." This had actually happened last week, so Senna felt that it must have the appearance of truth.

Hack seemed to be buying it. The color left his face. "Sweet Queen," he swore softly. "Is she dead?"

"No, I got there in time." Senna rubbed her red eyes.

Hack swore again. "I...I'm sorry, Senna," he stammered.

"Get out," she ordered.

He licked his lips, "Look, just because—"

"I said get out!" She nearly screamed these words, making Hack glance nervously about. He chose the course of discretion and left. Senna followed him out to the end of the garden and slammed the gate behind him.

In fading light, Captain Lodin trudged towards the castle with the gait of the slightly inebriated. His eyes were heavy after a long evening of gossip at the inn. His considerable weight dug uneven holes into the mud. Lodin was a big man in every dimension. His stature was the primary reason he became a Guard, and possibly the only reason he was ever promoted. He patted the new loaves of bread in his sack, the latest bribe from Gambad. Lodin sometimes took unfair advantage of the innkeeper, but the Ironfoot made enough money off the Guards that it could afford to give something back. Captain Lodin considered Innkeeper Gambad a personal friend. He was a jovial man, a useful font of information, and he kowtowed to Lodin in a manner that Lodin enjoyed.

A pair of Guards passed Lodin on the road, going in the opposite direction. Guardsman Patch gave him a salute and an airy comment about being off duty. Guardsman Rofus, less flippant, paused to deliver a report.

"Captain," Rofus said smartly, "there's a man at the castle, a Gaultian. I think you should speak with him."

Guardsman Rofus had improved the order of the Guard since his arrival. The other Guards seemed to take notice when he reminded them of their duties. Lodin wasn't sure what to do about it, so he made it official by promoting

Rofus to second in command. He hoped that decision wouldn't come back to bite him. He got the feeling Rofus didn't think much of his current Captain.

"Uh, all right. Thank you, Rofus," Lodin muttered. His mood dampened at the prospect of duty and dealing with diplomats.

Lodin lived for three things: food, friends, and a desire to not work very much. The trouble was, it was a lot of work to get into a place where you didn't have to work very much. In theory, Lodin knew what he needed to do to get the men to listen to him. But it was so much hollering and throwing his weight around, Lodin didn't always feel up to it. With a little cajoling, and a great willingness to let things slide, they managed to get along.

The visitor was waiting for Lodin outside the front gate. He was skinny and gangly, and possibly the ugliest Gaultian Lodin had ever seen. No wonder Rofus had passed this problem on to him.

"Hello there, Captain Captain!" The visitor spoke in a heavy Gaultian accent. He saluted Lodin in a way that made him suspect he was being mocked. "I'm looking for Fenn."

It took Lodin a minute to realize he meant the Baron. "Lord Fenwith isn't at home. Perhaps I can help you," he spoke respectfully because the man was Gaultian. But his clothes were scruffy, and if he didn't come up with a good story fast, Lodin was going to help him out of the castle yard on his ass.

"No, no, no. I need to see Fenn. He knows me." His speech was slurred, and his breath stank of orange beer. He was young, still in his teens probably, with a head full of orange hair to match his breath. His smile showed a mouthful of the crookedest teeth Lodin had ever seen. "Name's Elimilo," the fellow continued, extending a hand. "Me and Fenn went to school together."

Lodin hesitated, considering. Lodin really doubted that the Baron would be interested in conversing with this smelly young man. But he also couldn't think of a reason why anyone would say they knew the Baron unless they did. It was possible Lodin would get into trouble if he dismissed a valued acquaintance. Leaving Elimilo's hand in midair, Lodin nodded for the Gaultian to follow. "You can wait inside," he suggested.

"Thanks, Captain." The boy was unperturbed by any lack of civility. He followed Lodin up the lane.

As Lodin turned the key to the castle door, the boy slipped past and whistled at the dark emptiness that waited. "Where's the fire?" he asked.

Lodin put his lantern down on a bench. "You understand, if he doesn't want to see you, you'll have to leave immediately."

"He'll want to see me," the young man insisted. "I told you, he's a buddy of mine. Old gassy-passy Fenn."

Lodin immediately had two thoughts. One, he would bet a year's wages the Baron never had a buddy in his life. And two, if this idiot called him gassy-passy to his face, he was never going to see the light of morning.

Lodin left the Gaultian to the hospitality of the empty hall while he went to tell the first watch to watch for Lord Fenwith. Lodin wanted time to explain the existence of Elimilo before the Baron got a look at him.

He didn't get the chance, unfortunately. Fenwith arrived as Lodin was shutting the door. "Lord Baron!" Lodin exclaimed.

Unfazed by the sight of Lodin in the doorway, Fenwith pushed past into the foyer. The Captain clucked nervously, hoping to get Fenwith's attention as he turned around to follow. No sooner had he managed to say, "There's someone here to see you," when the Gaultian appeared in front of them.

"Fenn!" the boy called. His crooked teeth spilled out all over his grin. Fenwith looked at him, and Elimilo's grin slid off his face. "You're not Fenn."

Lodin nervously tried to gauge the Baron's expression. It was confused at first, and then cold.

186

The Baron cursed softly. "How dare you come here?"

The Captain sensed his employer's overtly dangerous mood, but Elimilo was unmoved.

"Who the bogsnatch are you?" cried the boy.

"The last person you're going to see for some time," said Fenwith.

"Look, I'm here to see Fenwith," the young man went on.

"Lodin, throw this visitor in the dungeon. No one is to talk to him, including you."

Elimilo's jaw dropped open as the Captain moved to obey. "What? You can't do that. I'm a friend of the Baron, buddy!"

Lodin shook his head in sympathy for the young man. *Not anymore,* he thought.

Cole waited until Lodin retired before he went to see the prisoner. The Gaultian was securely detained in the largest cell. He had not been chained, and someone had left him a hot meal. The young man hadn't touched it, but the gesture pleased Cole nonetheless. Lodin always acted in the most magnanimous way possible unless specifically ordered otherwise.

Elimilo leapt up as Cole came into sight and became instantly impertinent. "You again! Who do you think you are?" he demanded, clinging to the bars with a sort of angry desperation.

Cole did not answer right away. He settled into a practiced look of bored disgust. He took his time drawing a stool from against the wall and placing it in front of the Gault's cell. Then he made a show of wiping it down with a handkerchief before he condescended to sit on it.

"I am the Baron of Geid," said he. "That is all you

need know of me."

Elimilo sneered at him. The boy's hair hung in his face like a greasy mop—too long to keep out of his eyes and too short to be tied back. With a casual gesture, he brushed back a strand and tucked it behind his ear. The strand was restrained for a few seconds before it fell back like a withered leaf. "You're *not* Fenwith."

"And you're not the same friend I knew four years ago, Elimilo. You've changed. You were always a little unstable, but I think you've lost your head this time. Why, you don't even remember your old schoolmate!"

The young man's bravado fizzled somewhat. He eyed Cole with a wary expression.

"Don't think it would go any different, boy. No one will be disposed to hear your story." Cole leaned forward and lowered his voice a pitch. "I've worked hard for what I have here. I won't let it be jeopardized by some foul-looking Gaultian brat. Now I have three choices regarding you. I can kill you, I can let you sit in this dungeon until you rot, or I can trust you to keep your mouth shut."

Most of the color had left Elimilo's face by this point. Cole watched as common sense finally penetrated the boy's alcohol-saturated senses. "I like the third choice," Elimilo said.

Cole waved his hand carelessly. "I thought you might. I suppose you came here hoping for money?"

Elimilo's eyes shifted back and forth as he pondered the wisdom of being honest. "Yes," he said.

Cole took a pouch off his belt, slid it through the bars, and tipped it upside down. A rain of coins fell onto the floor, where they clanked and rolled in all directions.

"Come back next month, and I'll give you more of the same. Speak of this to anyone, and I'll make you wish your mother drowned you at birth."

Elimilo showed his acceptance of this deal by chasing the coins around the floor of the cell. Cole examined his fingernails while he waited. "Do we understand each other?" he asked, when it looked like Elimilo had clutched upon every

188

piece.

The young man stood up and pressed his face into the bars. "Yes, sir," he said. "I won't cause you any problems. I swear it on my mother's dead rotting eyeballs."

Cole grimaced at this macabre image. He was very ready to get rid of this troublesome young Gaultian. He unlocked the cell and steered the acquiescent youth through the exit, up the stairs, and towards the kitchen entrance. He doubted the night Guard patrol would be paying very much attention.

"Next month," he reminded Elimilo. "Come to this door and ask for Madam Senna. She'll match what I just gave you."

Elimilo looked weak with gratitude at the thought of a steady income. It was all Cole could do to pray that greed would keep his tongue in check.

Stung with curiosity, Cole ventured a final question. "Were you really friends with Fenwith?"

Elimilo answered sheepishly. "Well...kinda sorta."

"What was he like?"

"He was a whiny son of a whore. I didn't like him. He's dead, right?"

The Baron stared. He inclined his head yes, and gestured for the young man to be off. He watched the bright orange hair careen down the lane. Cole spent the next hour wondering how good a judge of character a man like Elimilo could possibly be.

CHAPTER EIGHTEEN

Dwen sat on an old stool and stared at the rain through the window. It had been falling in sheets for hours, sounding against the roof like a herd of galloping horses. The ground had swallowed its fill, and now allowed the remaining water to pool into small ponds over the yard. Dwen watched one expanding puddle overflow and merge with a larger one.

Behind him his wife read her book while the senile grandmother in the corner sang macabre Mackabine poems. *"Turn and bite, the spirits said, Muckus will take your bloody head!"*

"Grandmom," Clane prompted quietly, "could you sing the one about the Madam in the garden?"

The old woman didn't acknowledge her request. Madam Nabetha's mind hadn't been sharp for years, but the recent upheaval seemed to have pushed it over a precipice. Clane had started caring for the little ones in her place.

Dwen spent most of his time indoors since his arrival. He wished he were at the harbor with Brade and Mister Leron. There wasn't a demand for millers in Candige, so Mister Brade was learning the boating trade from their new neighbors. In general, he left early and returned late. By this time Brade was so late they no longer expected him. He would probably sleep in the boat shop to wait out the rain.

The knock on the door startled Dwen off of his stool. Brade wouldn't bother to knock, but who would visit on a night like this? Cautiously he went to the door and opened it a crack. He found a fist poised over the door to knock again.

"Oh-ho. It's you." The owner of the fist quickly lowered it. It was Sid, the young man he'd met in Madam Gayna's house on his first night in Candige. Sid looked like he was trying hard to remember Dwen's name.

"I'm Dwen," Dwen offered helpfully.

Sid smiled as if he knew this all along. Sid was tall and friendly-looking, with a wide mouth that invited trouble. He seemed a less careful version of Jed. "Course you are! This is my sister Werd." Sid tapped his fist against the woman standing next to him. "Werd, this is Brade's son, Dwen."

Dwen opened his mouth to correct them, but the brother and sister ignored him as they pushed past into the room. Their dripping clothing left instant puddles on the wood flooring.

"By the Queen, what weather!" cried Sid. He shook his cloak in the direction of the doorway, spraying drops of water back into the soaked porch.

Dwen held the door in confusion until Sid took the initiative and closed it. "Have a letter for Brade," Sid claimed.

Clane rose from her place next to Madam Nabetha. "My father's not here," she said quietly.

Sid's smile pinched into a round mass. "Don't tell me we came over here for nothing."

Werd snatched the pouch out of Sid's hand and turned it over to Dwen. "Just give it to him when he comes back."

The pouch held coin as well as correspondence. Gayna was supporting them until Mister Brade's trade took hold.

"You came in the rain just to deliver this?" Dwen felt momentarily honored until Sid clarified.

"Don't be silly. It was on our way. We're on an important mission. Very secret. Queensmen business." Sid gave Dwen a hearty clap on the back. "Want to come?"

Werd's eyes rolled in annoyance as Dwen nodded.

Clane looked nervous. "But it's raining," she objected.

Sid laughed. "That's what makes this a good time.

Rain is the least of our worries," he said.

Dwen was delighted to be included. "I'd like to come," he said, without thinking to ask where they were going or why.

Sid rewarded his enthusiasm with a wide smile. Werd's expression was less welcoming, but she didn't object. She didn't seem to care whether Dwen was in one place or another.

Sid threw Dwen an oiled cloak from off the wall, and cocked his head in invitation. Then he followed his sister out the front door, leaving little time for goodbyes.

Dwen kissed Clane on her cheek. "I'll be back!" he promised. Clane voiced a weak objection, which Dwen pretended not to hear. He hurried out the door before the others could disappear.

The downpour was getting heavier. Dwen quickly slipped the cloak over his shoulders as he ran after Sid. "Where are we going?" he asked.

"To the docks," said Sid. "There's a ship bound for Gault on the morrow and it hasn't passed inspection yet."

"Inspection?"

Sid winked grandly. "Our inspection," he said.

Werd turned around to explain. "We're going to look at the cargo, see if there's anything we can liberate."

"Oh," said Dwen, nodding his approval.

Sid and Werd leaned their heads together to make conversation. Dwen strained his ears, hoping to contribute something that would make him look smart or jocular. But he couldn't hear over the pouring rain, and in the end he fell back.

The rain died down as they neared the harbor. A sliver of moonlight managed to sneak past the clouds from the north and revealed the open planks of the dock. Dwen had visited the harbor many times during the day. He liked to sit on the shop benches above the dock and watch foot traffic. Candige was the second largest port in Mackabine and sometimes it was hard to move for the press of human flesh. It was a place of wonder, brimming with energy, strangeness,

192

and excitement. At night the harbor was a different world, dismal and barren in the darkness.

Water was leaking through the top seams of Dwen's cloak. He cheered himself by remembering that terrible weather was a blessing for this kind of adventure. It would discourage anyone from following them.

Werd tapped Dwen's shoulder and motioned him off the dock.

"There's no one to see us," Dwen complained.

Werd pointed wordlessly at the city wall. Dwen saw a faint glimmer of lights from the tower. He obediently followed as Werd took the lead, and the pair dropped into the narrow ditch between the dock and the shops.

"Keep up, new boy. No lagging," she said.

"I have a name," Dwen reminded them. He expected Sid to be on his side, but Sid was too busy motioning for them both to be quiet. Dwen worked his way through the mud while trying not to ruin his shoes.

Eventually Sid came to a halt and Dwen stumbled into his back. He raised his eyes and found the hull of a ship looming imposingly on one side. Sid darted across the dock to the ship's gangplank and crouched in the shadows, waiting for Werd and Dwen to join him.

In his haste to follow, Dwen accidentally stepped on Werd's heel. Werd cursed quietly as they huddled into the shadow of the ship. Dwen mouthed a silent apology, which Werd probably did not see in the darkness. Sid issued another hiss for silence. Below them spread the deep black well of the ocean. The water was eerily still, rebuffing even the light plink of raindrops.

Sid seized the edge of a porthole and used it to gracefully hoist himself onto the deck. Werd offered to give Dwen a boost, but Dwen waved her off. He made a jump to the porthole and pulled himself up with only mild difficulty. Sid grabbed Dwen's arm as he reached for the top of the railing. "Good jump," Sid whispered as he bent back over the railing for his sister.

Dwen sank against the railing and paused to marvel at his location. Dwen had never liked the idea of ships; he wasn't sure he trusted a colossal wooden bowl to float. But the deck felt surprisingly steady.

From one pointed end to the other, the ship spanned the length of several houses. The deck was littered with coils of rope and piles of debris. Down the center, giant poles were draped with net and cloth. Some of the cloth was painted with the image of a large dog, symbol of the King of Gault. Dwen shivered. It was a Gaultian ship.

Werd arrived panting and ushered them through a hatch and down several flights of stairs. The mandate for silence seemed to have been lifted. Sid made a joke about the absent crew spending the evening ashore at the Bird's Nest Inn.

"All of them?" asked Dwen.

"Better opportunities for happy company than there are on a rotting ship." Sid grinned, poking Dwen in the ribs. "Speaking of which, how do you like married life?"

"I like it," Dwen replied. "Are you married?" he asked Sid.

"Not me. I like keeping my options open. I find happy company wherever I can."

Sid's sister made a disgusted sound in her throat. Dwen silently agreed with her. No one was going to marry Sid if he did that! He was glad for the conversation, though, which distracted him from the eerie atmosphere of the abandoned ship.

They descended into deeper blackness, where the portholes let in minimal light. It took several seconds for Dwen's eyes to adjust before he had an idea of what he was seeing. They were surrounded by looming stacks of rectangular crates. Dwen touched the hard wooden surface of the closest shadow. Each crate was about one span high and twice as long.

Werd smashed one open with her hatchet and examined the interior with satisfaction. Dwen squeezed past

Sid for a peek. It was hard to be certain in the dim light, but the contents appeared to be nothing more than a pile of rocks. "What is that?" he asked.

"That's the reason Gault is after Mackabine," said Sid.

"Silver ore," said Werd.

"Mined in Pannerack."

"Slave labor."

"Gaultian dogfish."

Dwen picked up a chunk of silver for examination. He didn't see how they were going to steal more than a few bricks of the stuff. It was extremely heavy.

Without discussion, Werd and Sid crouched on either side of the crate and lifted it arduously off the floor. "Blessed Queen!" Sid swore. "This weighs more than my whole family." Together, the pair managed to get the box to the side of the ship. Then they tilted it sideways against a porthole and poured the entire cache of ore into the sea.

Dwen clamped his hand over his mouth to keep from bursting into laughter. He got his hands around the next crate and tested it. It weighed far too much for one man, but he wrenched at the load until Werd appeared to help him. Together they slid it across the hold and likewise dumped it into the ocean. The rain had picked up again and swallowed the sound of plunking silver. They took turns, every third person resting, and worked this way for nearly an hour. It was tooth-grinding, sweat-pouring, backbreaking work, and Dwen was having a grand time.

"This is great!" he told Sid. "What if we get caught?"

Sid gave him a dirty look over his shoulder. "Why the bogsnatch would you ask that?" he asked. He knelt down for the crate in the farthest corner.

Dwen was not really worrying about getting caught. He was not even paying attention, but the timing of his question was inauspicious. They heard a sound that none of them had made—a slight, scuffling noise from the stairwell. The whole party paused. A second later a glimmer of warm light flashed briefly over the walls of the hold.

"What was that?" whispered Sid.

The light reappeared as its bearer came around a stack of crates and faced them head on. An unwashed, middle-aged man in uniform stared at them, the look on his face as dumbfounded as their own. There was a mutual stunned silence as the torch cast its light over the cargo hold. Less than a third of the cargo had been dumped, but there were large empty patches where many of the crates had been stacked. The Guard searched for something to say. Then he dropped the torch and ran.

"Stop him!" Werd's injunction was barely a squeak in her hurry to rise. She lurched forward half unbalanced, then sped off as she gained momentum. Sid was close behind.

Dwen watched Sid and Werd disappear in pursuit of the Guard. He was left alone. The dark cargo hold seemed far less friendly without his companions, but he was afraid to go on deck if there were Guards on board. Dwen rebuked himself for his selfish thinking. If there was trouble, then Sid and Werd were already into it. He should be helping, not hiding in the dark. Dwen searched his belt and drew a little penknife, a gift from Clane's father. He held it in front of him as he stumbled up the closest stairway.

Dwen arrived on deck not knowing one end of the ship from the other. Disoriented, he squinted through the rain. He wanted to call out, but he was afraid of attracting the wrong attention. A shadow moved in the curtain of rain, coming fast, straight towards him. Dwen was too stunned to get out of the way. The fleeing man didn't see him. He raced towards Dwen before he flailed, tried to stop, and skidded into Dwen's feet. Dwen fell on top of him, his nose coming to rest a mere inch from the face of the unwanted Guard.

It was only when the Guard started to tremble that Dwen realized he was holding the little knife near the Guard's throat. "Please," the Guard whispered in strongly accented Mackabine. "Please! I have a family!"

Dwen froze in indecision. Was he supposed to kill this Guard just for coming around at the wrong time? He didn't want to. Dwen wished Sid and Werd were here to tell him what to do.

"I'll just leave," the Guard said in a hushed voice. "I won't tell anyone you were here, I promise."

Dwen considered this proposal and decided it was fair. He sat up to release the Guard, and at the same time felt something sharp inside his gut. Dwen looked down in disbelief where the Guard had stabbed him. The hilt of a knife, six times the size of Dwen's miniature one, stuck out of his tunic. Dwen choked, tipped over backwards, and hit his head against the deck of the ship. He reached for the knife to try to pry it from his wound. His hands slipped over a shocking amount of blood.

Help me. Clane?...Senna?

The Guard left. Dwen barely noticed. His thoughts slipped into illusion. He saw the faces of people that weren't there, dancing synchronously over the clouds.

A little later he felt Sid put his hand over his chest. "You poor sod, Dwen," he heard him whisper.

"Is he dead?" asked Werd.

"Not yet, but we can't save him," said Sid.

Werd spit out a curse. "Let's go before the Guard brings others."

Dwen tried to make his mouth work, to ask them not to leave, but his throat wasn't working. He closed his eyes, and the sound of their footsteps faded into the pulse of the drowning rain.

The late summer sun shone a welcome ray of warmth onto Jed's back. He bent and ran his hands over the full tips of grain beneath him. Jed chose a stalk at random, removed the head, and popped a few seeds of grain into his mouth. The kernels tasted crisp, perfect for harvesting. The crop would be good, despite the late planting season.

During harvest time, the fields were as full of people as they were of grain. All around him rows of townsfolk huddled on their knees, engrossed in the work to get the grain gathered. Jed rearranged his sack over his shoulder and turned the sickle in his hand. Sometimes the most useful help was a little bit of manual labor.

"These cursed plants won't hold still," a disgruntled voice complained behind him.

Jed turned to laugh at his friend. Rimick was not a farmer. He spent his youth scavenging, not working the land. Jed almost envied him for it. The truth was, he hated farm work—the repetitive motions, the smell of goat manure, the dirt forever trapped under his fingernails.

Jed's father had nurtured a companionship with the land. Every stalk of grain was treasured as if it were a child. "Be good to the land, my boy, and it will be good to you." The words were as clear in Jed's mind as if his father said them yesterday.

Jed had never been able to cultivate his family's love for raw earth. Jed saw the land as an oppressor, weighing him down to drudgery and obscurity. Jed knew how to turn the soil, but that was as far as the relationship went. He tolerated the land, and it tolerated him back.

"Tell me a story, Rimick. It'll help pass the time."

Rimick was an adept storyteller. He read enough books that he could speak competently on most subjects.

There was a pause while Rimick thought. "Did I ever tell you about the time I tried to steal from old Carly?"

Jed was surprised. Rimick didn't usually select an event from his own life. "Carly the witch doctor?" Jed didn't care to think about the dead man whose empty cottage they regularly slept in. They used the legend of Carly to scare away passersby. It wasn't comfortable to remember him as a real person.

"That one."

"I can't believe you would steal from a witch doctor,

Rimick. Have you no fear of the Otherworld?"

Rimick shrugged. He obviously did not. "It was a commission," he said. "A patient of Carly's wanted his charming bauble. He thought he could cure himself with it better than Carly could."

A woman cutting grain in the next row became interested. "You stole Carly's bauble?" she asked incredulously. She showed no shame for eavesdropping on their conversation.

Rimick answered her with a cold stare.

"Well it's no wonder he died," she said.

Whatever response they might have given was delayed by a scream that rose from the far end of the field. Jed turned his head. A black, formless emission spread across the sky in the distance. People in the next field were converging on the barn.

"What's that?" asked the woman.

Rimick gave the obvious answer. "Smoke."

Jed broke into a run.

The fire was out of control. Folks gathered frantically around the door of the barn in a losing battle against the orange heat. By the time Jed arrived, flames had engulfed most of the building.

"What's in there?" he asked the closest person, who happened to be Madam Nanta. She was sprawled over the road, too overcome to assist in the efforts.

"Our grain," she wept. "All our crop. What's to become of us? We'll starve!"

Jed selected another, less affected bystander. "Go find the county Guards and tell them what's happened."

"What?" the girl seemed bewildered by his order.

"They have to help. It's their job."

The girl took a breath and ran off along the road.

Jed looked around for a bucket, but anything with carrying capacity had already been seized. Rimick was right behind him. He tapped Jed's shoulder as he motioned towards the other side of the barn. Jed followed Rimick to the trough used for watering goats. It was still full of water. The trough was too big for any one person to carry, but with a concerted effort, the two of them managed to get it off the ground. A few others came to help when they saw their struggle. With a great heave, they launched the water into the burning wall. Smoke and heat singed the skin of Jed's hands and face, and his clothing. He drew back coughing.

Jed felt sick to his stomach. Visions of his parents and brother flashed through his head. Crisped away like overcooked loaves of bread.

"Get back!" someone yelled as a piece of the roof collapsed beside the line of farmers.

Folk scattered. The fire was too great a beast to tame. Some gave up and stood back to watch it burn. Others stubbornly ran back and forth with their cups and spoons, anything to get the barn a little wetter. Rimick shook his head. No good. The grain inside was already burnt. Jed tilted his head back and watched the slowly darkening sky.

Cole once heard Senna say she had a fondness for Dwussar tea leaves. Some facts stuck in a fellow's head without his meaning them to, like the capital of Hanchapocad, the color of Lord Hemmon's dressing knife, or a well timed joke Senna told to Guardsman Daggin to avert an arrest. Cole couldn't have chosen a better accomplice if he'd planned it. Senna was tenacious, cool-headed, and just judgmental enough to keep him on his toes.

Cole reached into his cloak pocket for the second time since coming down the stairs. The tea leaves were still there, wrapped in a packet tied with colored twine. He hoped the present would please her. Dwussar leaves were hard to get since the Revolution.

After a brief pause to straighten his clothing, Cole

strode into the dining room and looked expectantly at his housekeeper. Senna's eyes looked bright in the tinted sunlight. "Good morning, Lord," she said, and winked at him.

Her wink had a salubrious effect. Cole smiled, then sat with his back to the kitchen so that stray eyes would not see him do it.

"Would you prefer duck eggs or chicken eggs this morning, Lord?"

"Don't bother me with questions," he said. Cole kept his voice gruff for the benefit of the kitchen staff, who he expected to be eavesdropping at all times.

Senna brought him duck eggs and winked again when she set them down.

Cole would have winked back, except he wasn't any good at it. When he tried, all he did was blink.

Senna disappeared again into the kitchen. She was gone long enough for Cole to wonder what was keeping her. He'd started to bite into his breakfast when he heard a heart-rending scream from beyond the door.

He left his chair without thinking and barged into the kitchen. Senna was crumpled on the floor, her two maids poised anxiously over her shoulder. She was cradling a crumpled letter in her hands. Whatever news she received must have been terrible. Senna looked like she was being dipped in hot oil. She took no notice of him. But the maids stopped in mid-crouch to gape stiffly at the Baron in their kitchen.

He didn't dare ask what was wrong. Fenwith blistered under the surface, waiting to say something derisive. Cole couldn't bring himself to be that heartless, so instead he left.

CHAPTER NINETEEN

Senna spent half of the day looking for Jedomar. Grath didn't know where he was, and no one had stoked a fire at the Carly cottage for several days. Senna got little response from her whispered inquiries at the marketplace. Few folk knew about Senna's particular relationship with Jedomar. All they knew was that she worked at the castle, which was reason enough not to talk to her. Eventually, Jed got news of her poking around and came to find her. He called her name from behind a house that she passed.

By this time, Senna had worked herself into a fit. "Jed!" she barked at him, hardly letting him pull her aside for privacy. "What happened? How could you let this happen?" As if he were entirely to blame. Part of her was waiting for him to tell her it was a mistake.

Jed didn't bother to answer. He just looked at her with a remotely sad expression.

The last shred of denial faded away. Her brother was dead.

"It's my fault," sobbed Senna. "I was supposed to protect him. I should have gone with him."

"There's nothing you could have done. You think he wanted his younger sister tagging along with his new bride?"

Senna wasn't interested in reasoning, she only felt an urge to keep talking. "Tell me what happened, Jed. I want details."

"I don't know much more. He was killed working with some Q.M."

"What was he even doing with the Q.M. in Candige?" Senna cried.

Jed frowned at her. "Obviously, he was with them because he wanted to be. Gayna doesn't send people on jobs against their will. Dwen wasn't a child, Senna."

His use of the past tense hit Senna like a blow to the stomach. She stood trying to breathe while Jed waited for her to calm down. Her last objection seemed suddenly trivial, but she voiced it anyway. "Why didn't you wait to tell me in person?"

Jed sighed. His lack of emotion irritated her. "What did you want me to do? Send a note that read, *See me when you can; I've got a little something to tell you?*"

Perhaps Jed's letter was the reasonable course of action. But she couldn't help feeling it showed a lack of respect for Dwen—or for her. He looked so solemn and composed. Senna had seen Jed fall down and weep for the death of a child he'd never met. Why couldn't he show more compassion for his own friend?

"All right then." Senna nodded. There was nothing left to say. She didn't know why she expected Jed to fix everything, why it ever seemed to her that he was able to fix anything.

Jed grabbed her arm as she tried to leave, but she jerked it away. She didn't look back. She didn't want to see Jed anymore. She didn't think it mattered if she never saw anyone ever again.

Senna's maids served dinner that evening. Cole felt it necessary to mention her absence so he asked the older maid where she was.

"She's not feeling well, Lord."

"She's sick?" he snapped.

"Yes, Lord." The maid looked really unhappy about having to speak with him. It was probably a clause in her job description: no direct conversation with Fenwith.

"Tell her to stay away from me then. I don't want to get sick."

"Yes, Lord."

It was a game of nerves to deduce the cause of Senna's distress. Cole hoped nothing had happened to Jedomar. If so, he certainly hadn't heard about it. He thought Senna would confide in him when the time arose, so he was relieved to find her waiting in the east hall when he retired to study. Senna barely looked up as he entered. She sat staring into a fireplace she hadn't bothered to light. Cole began to fear she really had been taken by some physical ailment.

"Senna," he began, unsure how to question her.

"My brother's dead," she said.

Cole respired. It was the best news he could have expected under the circumstances. Mister Dwen's death would discomfort no one but Senna. He offered the usual sympathies, only because it was polite to do so, not because they provided any actual comfort.

Senna shrugged his words away.

"Your brother was in Candige, wasn't he?"

"He went with Mister Brade," Senna explained. "He was going to marry little Madam Clane."

Cole had only the vaguest idea who she referred to. "The miller's daughter?"

She nodded.

"Well," said Cole, feeling more awkward at every moment.

"After my parents died," said Senna, "Dwen was all I had left."

"I know how you feel," he said.

"Do you?" Senna kicked resentfully at the firepit,

204

throwing cold ash into the air. "You know what it's like to lose your entire family?"

"Yes," Cole affirmed before he could restrain the urge.

Senna looked up at him, her face vapid and strained. She went on looking until Cole decided she was waiting for him to elaborate.

"Almost everyone I knew was killed in the Gault Revolution. I have a fair idea of how things went in Geid, and I knew it wasn't pleasant, but other counties had it worse. Lammark openly opposed the Gault incursion. The Regent sent an army at Lord Gretin. My family lived in the castle. No one was spared."

Cole realized it was the first time he'd spoken about it since it happened. There hadn't been another opportunity. No one to speak to. It sent a wave of heat through him. *You're not that special, Senna. Lots of people die.*

Senna answered, after a moment's reflection. "Is that why you agreed to become a spy? For vengeance?"

Cole shrugged. "Vengeance was a factor, I suppose. But that part didn't sustain me for long."

Senna curled herself into a ball on the bench, looking thoughtful and lonely.

"You still have your Uncle Inwick. Not to mention your friends," Cole added. From his perspective, Senna had quite a lot. He would have traded places with her.

Senna didn't look disposed to speak anymore. Her eyes locked on the floor, unmoving.

Cole hesitated. He was almost afraid to leave her in this state. Finally he reached into his cloak and threw the packet of tea leaves at the floor beside her.

"I got you something," he said. "A present."

"I don't want it."

Cole didn't argue with her. Senna sat with her face downturned, but eventually, curiosity got the better of her. Her hands collapsed around the packet and she ripped it at one corner. Senna took a minute to stare and then sniff the package, as if she couldn't make out what was inside.

"Dwussar leaves. You mentioned once that you liked them."

"I did?"

"To your maid."

"Oh. I do like them. Thank you."

Cole was afraid Senna was going to cry again. "I'll leave you alone," he offered.

Senna's face crinkled painfully. "No, I'll go. This is your office. No reason for me to be here…" Her voice trailed off into incoherent mutterings. She was gone before Cole had time to argue with her.

There were two general approaches to Grath's house. The obvious way went through town and over a few fields. The other route was a roundabout walk along the seafront, where one could look down into the barrier of water that separated Geid from the rest of the world. It was scenic, and traveled only by the adventurous types.

Jed and Rimick naturally chose the latter route on their way to Grath's conference. The conference was held every Lock-Day. Hack usually came. Brade used to, before he was spirited off to Candige. Often they got a visit from a member of the lawyering circle, such as Madam Jortha. It was a chance to check that everyone was still alive, to organize distributions, and to address issues in the town.

Jed rubbed his hands for warmth as he walked. His skin bristled at the cold metal of his ring. Unbidden, the sight and scent of smoke came back to him. He still remembered how he pulled the ring from the gruesomely charred hand of his father's corpse. Luckily no one had died in last week's fire. Only Dwen, and he far away.

Jed had observed death many times. He used to think he would get used to it, and sometimes he convinced himself that he had. Then it would happen, and he would reassess all over again. To have a fellow disappear from the world without a trace: it was startling, unnerving, disheartening. Dwen was too young to have gone.

Jed's heart felt heavy for Senna. He would give her some space over the next few weeks. If her grief bore out anything like his, she would appreciate the solitude. Jed and Logas had been close enough in age to be friends as well as brothers. His parents at least had lived the better part of their lives when they died, but Jed had never gotten over the death of his brother. Jed shook his head to clear the melancholy from his mind, and glanced back at his friend.

Rimick had taken Logas's place as Jed's closest companion. In many ways, Rimick was a poor substitute for his brother. Logas was so much like Jed they practically read each other's mind; Rimick was more an enigma. They often didn't understand each other even after hours of conversation. But Jed and Rimick had a bond based on mutual survival. In some ways, that was stronger than friendship.

"Rimick...whatever happened to Carly's bauble? The one you stole?" Jed asked.

"I still have it. Old Carly came in as I was searching his cupboards. Dropped dead right in front of me."

Jed stopped in his tracks, forcing Rimick to halt behind him. "Wait a minute...you killed Old Man Carly?"

Rimick frowned. "I wouldn't say that. He was very old."

"And so what, you kept the bauble out of penance?" Jed asked.

"No, but my client wouldn't take it. Cursed now, he said." Rimick gave Jed a wry smile. "Do you want it?"

"No, I don't want your cursed bauble. Are you crazy?"

Rimick was joking, Jed was sure. He must be. No one would keep a bauble from a dead witch doctor. It was hard to tell with Rimick, though.

Rimick got tired of waiting for Jed to continue, and moved to go around him. Perhaps if they buried Carly's bauble under the cottage, his dead spirit wouldn't hold a grudge, Jed thought. He made this suggestion, but Rimick showed no interest in continuing the subject.

"Look there." Rimick pointed down the rocky gorge ending in a narrow strand of seashore.

Jed obediently turned his eyes to the bay. There was very little beach in Geid; most of the land ended in hazardous cliffs, except for a few inlets where the shore sloped into the bay. A small group of youths was gathered in one of the reachable pieces of shoreline, combing the waves for clams. It was a rite of passage for young men to test their ankles to the forbidden water. The bravest boys scaled part of the cliff in search of the best clams. Their mothers would scold them if they knew what they were doing. It wasn't a very profitable endeavor. With hard work, the lot of them might find four or five clams in a week.

"I remember doing that," Rimick remarked casually.

"So do I." Jed remembered that he climbed farther than any of the other boys. "Let's go down and say hello."

Rimick didn't have any particular objection, so they left their path and took the steep trail down the gorge towards the water. The boys were starting a fire to stay warm and perhaps roast clams, if they'd caught any.

When they saw Jed and Rimick coming, they stood up and huddled into a group. One of the boys turned out to be Sable—Mister Grath's oldest son. He greeted them with a warm, embarrassed smile.

"Hello Jed. What are you doing here?"

Jed crossed his arms with pretended authority. "We're going to see your father. Does he know you're down here?"

Sable shrugged happily, which may or may not have been confirmation.

The other boys were curious, but not shy. Most of them recognized Jed and Rimick on sight. Sable quickly educated the rest.

Jed nodded to the over-awed youngsters. A small part of Jed was grateful for the Gault Revolution. Nobody ever bothered one way or the other about Jed the farmer. Jed the Queensman was somebody. People looked up to him, admired or despised him in turn—but by the Queen, they noticed him!

"Hey, we could turn them in for the reward," one of the younger boys suggested, probably in jest, but Sable snapped back at his comrade.

"Don't be stupid," he said. "You'd never see a fifth-piece of that money. Don't you know that Mister Andelwar turned in his neighbor for hiding tax money? There was a ten-piece reward, but the Baron told Andelwar to forget it."

Sable's story was true. No one had ever collected a reward out of the Baron. Jed liked to believe that Geid wouldn't betray him out of principle, but it helped that Fenwith's bribe was so implausible. He probably didn't even have two hundred silver pieces.

"It looks like you boys made a good catch." Jed inclined his chin towards their bucket, which held nearly half a dozen clams.

"We're saving them for the festival," the boys said.

"Festival?"

"On Grand-Day, didn't you know?"

"Geid is having a festival?" Jed didn't know what to make of that. In fact, he didn't quite believe it. The last festival in town was held before the Revolution, hosted by Baron Themson.

"That's what the signs say. And the Guards said so too."

"I heard it this morning," said another boy. "The castle housekeeper already bought up all the grain for beer."

"Is that so?" Jed's curiosity rose. "Sounds like good news!"

Jed tried to clap Rimick on the back, but his friend pulled away. Rimick had a thing about being touched. "We'll discuss it at the meeting," Rimick said.

His friend's slight didn't stop Jed's mood from improving. A festival would be just the thing to raise spirits after the barn fire.

CHAPTER TWENTY

The castle was the last place Senna posted her sign. The market and the inn were fully advertised when she walked up to the Guard's quarters and nailed her final and plainest poster to the door. She hurried away to the kitchen before anyone saw her. She told herself she wasn't hiding, even though her nerves suggested otherwise. There was plenty on her list, so Senna gave herself something to do, and started rolling flour for bread. The Baron didn't take any longer than expected. The dining room door swung violently open and he came to a halt in front of her flour-dusted kitchen bench.

"I hear I'm hosting a festival on Grand-Day."

Senna severed eye contact and busied herself with her dough. "Well, it's about time, don't you think?"

"Senna—"

She heard the warning in his voice. She had crossed boundaries—gone behind his back, made plans in his name. It was time to see how far she could really push.

"Is this about Dwen?"

Senna bit her lip hard. "No," she said. "I was already planning this before—" Senna didn't finish her sentence. She concentrated on beating her dough senseless. "Anyway, I can't think of anything he would have liked better, if he were here."

"It's a reckless idea, and a waste of money."

"It's a beloved tradition," she argued.

"What's more important to the townsfolk: indulging them in frivolity or keeping food in their stomachs?"

"Just because you can make do with physical sustenance doesn't mean everyone else can. Sometimes you've got to feed the spirit. People need to laugh! To wind down, to celebrate!"

It incensed her that because the Baron was a cold man, he supposed everyone else should be cold and mirthless too. But that was the way of most men. They assumed their own preferences were the only ones worth having. Cole regarded her with unconvinced stoicism.

"You are so callous," Senna complained. "Do you even have a heart? Maybe if you did, you would know what it means to be happy, and that it's a worthwhile thing now and then."

Cole stared at her. His face maintained a dark dispassion. "You really do think I'm unfeeling, don't you?"

Senna didn't answer. She had just said so, and she didn't know how to deny it now.

He sighed. "Maybe I am. I didn't used to be. At least I don't think so..."

The faint hint of remorse couldn't hold back her sarcasm. "You used to be all sugar and roses?"

The Baron continued to stand there while Senna worked her dough. The lack of reply gnawed on her. She cast about for something else to say.

"There was a field fire on the east side of Geid last week," she said. "Two families lost their harvest." More than anything, it was that tragedy that convinced her to go through with her plans.

"I heard. I also heard the other farmers pledged to sacrifice a portion of their grain to the deprived families."

"Yes," Senna concurred. She sometimes wondered where the Baron got his information. Jed was the one who talked the farmers into this show of benevolence. "The festival will be seen as an omen of luck. The townsfolk need this. They need to believe things will get better."

Cole blew a puff of air through his nose. She could tell he had already surrendered. Of course, Senna was confident he would. He wouldn't want to retract the declaration after it had been made. It was a rather low trick. Senna could sense his frustration.

"Hold your festival," the Baron muttered, and walked out of the room.

Senna's mood improved instantly. She finished forming the shapes of several raw loaves of bread, then decided there was time to get away for a brief moment.

She made her way past the gates, down the lane away from town, towards the memorial grounds. She found the carved block with Dwen's name on it. The acorns she put down yesterday were still fresh, and several unnamed mourners had added their own plant offerings—some flowers, some herbs and roots. She wondered if Dwen's memorial block in Candige looked more or less beloved than this one.

Senna felt a pang of pity for Clane, a sister she had scarcely known, and would likely never see again. There were no nieces and nephews to be born, no family reunions to look forward to. Her eyes burned, and she blinked to keep them dry. It was time to get on with her life. "That's what your brother would have wanted," Emwid had told her. Senna wasn't so sure. Dwen didn't mind upsetting other people's business for his own sake. But it had already been four days. Dwen's spirit must have arrived in the Otherworld by now, where her mourning could no longer please him.

"Goodbye, Dwen," Senna said aloud. She gave his memorial block a final parting kiss.

The festival was in as grand a scheme as any Jed had seen. There were upside-down lamps strung along the perimeter of the market square. Several people had been enlisted as musicians, with six flutes, four big-bottomed drums, and one three-stringed fiddle. Folk had traveled from all of the other villages to be here, and the square was so crowded that people were lined along the roads, trying to get in. The food was the largest attraction. There were small cakes, fresh beer, and two roasted pigs that were being sliced into strips on demand. Some of the food was offered freely, the rest at a discount. Jed had a feeling it wouldn't last long. He hid himself on a bench next to Rimick and dug into a pie Madam Tamonda had brought for them.

The musicians played as loudly as they could, and when that wasn't enough, people joined in by clapping, dancing, and singing songs they barely knew or made up on the spot. It was a great, raucous, joyful tumble of humanfolk. Senna was in the center of the business, keeping the beer flowing, and making sure no one got more than their fair share. Somehow she had managed to bridge a peace between the townsfolk and the Guard. The Guards weren't allowed to drink, but at least some of them were on their way towards having a good time. The town was in awe of Senna's apparent influence. It was rumored she was the one who had persuaded the Baron to host the festival.

Fenwith did not look particularly pleased. He presided silently from the dais, a shadowy blight that dampened the festivities near him. It was a mystery why he had come. Most people were managing to ignore him.

As the casks grew empty, the crowd drew apart to make room for more ordered dance movements. Senna was the first invited to join the dance floor. She was as gay as a flower and she looked like one in her blue dancing skirt. Jed watched the crowd gravitate slightly in her direction. Everyone wanted a chance to glimpse the ornament that shone unexpectedly out of Fenwith's castle. They sought to smile at her, to thank her, or to offer their own brand of advice. Senna didn't shy from the attention like Jed thought she would. She smiled back and laughed her way through the sea of happy people.

214

Jed was jealous of everyone who touched her. Young men, old men, and children alike took her hand and led her in a circle, while Jed could do no more than watch. If there had been less attention on her, Jed would have risked a dance, but there was one eye besides his own that kept vigil on Senna.

Lord Fenwith was as quiet as ever, but more than usually watchful. And in watching, his gaze never once deviated from the spot where Senna stood. It chilled Jed through to his heart.

Rimick would have preferred to stay far away from the festival. He found it tedious to sit amid the merriment of other folk. Not only that, but it was dangerous to put themselves within easy reach of so many Guards. He grimaced as another man thudded into their table on his way past. Space was tight and people were less keen on manners tonight. He lifted his feet as a cupful of spilled beer soaked the ground beneath them.

Jed could not be deterred from coming. He reveled in the midst of this raw humanity. "This is good music," said Jed. "Works you up into a dance, doesn't it?"

Rimick shrugged noncommittally. He didn't doubt that Jed longed to dance, to expose himself shamelessly, and draw the attention of every soul present. He was poised to rescue his friend, should he attempt anything so foolish. But for all his impatient looks and foot tapping, Jed did not stir.

Instead, he swallowed cup after cup of free beer. Several times Rimick suggested that there was nothing more to see, but Jed refused to leave. He wanted to enjoy every minute, or so he said. But as the hours wore on, and the festival took no notice of them, Jed's mood slowly deteriorated.

"Rimick, do you suppose if you died, the world would

still go on without you?"

Jed looked complaisant with his question, and Rimick wondered how much of the drink had gotten to his friend's head. "Are you asking if I think the world is a figment of my imagination?"

Jed squinted. "Huh?"

"There was an Ossetian philosopher who claimed that all existence came about from perception."

Jed looked more drunk than usual. "That's not what I meant at all."

"What did you mean, then?"

"Well, I'm the only means I have for seeing things. So if I die, that's it. The world may as well end."

"That's an egocentric view," said Rimick. He was surprised. Jed was not usually egocentric.

"Yeah," Jed looked down at his cup in shame, "it is." Rimick was also surprised that Jed knew what egocentric meant. "I was thinking," Jed continued, "about the Warrior Muckus. He was a great hero, but he died before he even knew whether they would win the Old War. So much has happened since then, and he'll never know any of it. What do you think he would say if he knew people still sang his name two hundred years later?"

Rimick knew his friend's ego, but even he was surprised to hear him compare himself to the Warrior Muckus. "No one will be remember your name a century from now," Rimick advised him. *Probably.*

Jed went on without appearing to have heard. "There's so much I'm missing! So much will happen that I'll never get to see. Across the ocean, on the other side of the world, there are whole places to discover. And here I am, stuck in the same no-name village I was born in. Did you know I've never traveled farther than Candige?"

"No one could see everything. It's not possible."

"I bet I could."

"No, you couldn't. The oldest man who ever lived, if he traveled every minute of his life, wouldn't see enough to satisfy you."

"Well at least I could see *something*."

"You can see something here."

Jed snorted. Rimick didn't understand why it wasn't enough for Jed to be the most famous person in his own county.

Someone tugged suddenly on Rimick's arm. He turned slightly, making room for an elbow to push between them. They both looked to see who had recognized them. It was an elderly woman, her hair dragging to her waist and covering half of her face. "You!" The woman confronted them with eyes of steel. She bent sharply at the waist, coming to eye level. She pointed a skinny finger in Jed's face. "I know you! You murdered my son!"

"I?" Jed examined her in consternation.

"My poor son," she wailed. "He was a Guard in the castle. He was doing his duty to the county, and you murdered him in cold blood!"

Rimick stood and took Jed's arm from the other side. "We should go," he whispered.

Jed hesitated. He looked concerned and possibly repentant. He might have tried to apologize if the woman hadn't started shrieking, "Guard! Guard!" The woman wasn't interested in platitudes. She wanted blood.

Rimick gripped Jed's arm more tightly, nearly yanking him off the bench. Jed broke from his trance and got up. They ducked around the table and zipped through the jammed marketplace. The cries of the woman rang out behind them.

"He went that way! Filthy murderer!"

By the time the Guards figured out the woman was referring to Jedomar, it was too late. The market was too big. There were too many places to hide, and too many people willing to hide them.

❖

In the wee hours of the morning, Senna rolled the last of the empty barrels into the kitchen. Most of the help she'd hired had already left, but Corvan the steward was still behind her, making sure there wasn't a mess left in his yard.

"What about the debris in the square?" Corvan grumbled.

Senna cut him off. "It's after midnight. We can do it in the morning."

Corvan grumbled something inaudible, but he backed out into the yard and let Senna close the door.

She took a last glance at the calamitous state of her kitchen. There was hardly a thing left, not even a scrap of bacon. Townsfolk were very free with their money during a festival. With a little more planning, they might have turned a profit. Maybe she could suggest that to the Baron as incentive for the next festival. Senna sighed. She wouldn't be ready for another one soon. Her bones ached from the work of the day. As she turned towards the kitchen door to leave, it swung open from the other side. Cole took a step in and folded his arms in front of her.

"You're still awake?" Senna observed in surprise.

The Baron shrugged. He must have been waiting up for her all evening. "Have you any word from Jedomar?" he began.

Senna shook her head. No news was good news for the time being. "That Jed. I should've known he would come." Almost no one had seen him, but very few doubted that Jedomar had been there. His phantom appearance broke up the festival entirely.

"It's just as well he turned out when he did," said Cole. "It was an excuse to send everyone home before they got so drunk they couldn't move."

Senna bit her lip to hide a smile. "Was the festival as bad as you feared?"

"It was fine," said Cole. "I wasn't expecting anything

disastrous. I don't loathe all form of amusement, you know."

"You could've fooled us," Senna quipped.

The Baron inclined his head. "I do try."

Senna laughed. "Why don't you pretend to be something else for a while?" she teased.

"Such as?"

Senna had no idea. She thought briefly. "Captain Lodin?"

Cole's posture changed. He could hardly convey the same physical presence as the Captain, but he thrust his chest out and tilted his head back the way Lodin did when he was trying to intimidate. "I'm gonna make you stand in line." Then he pretended to notice Senna and backpedaled. "Oh Madam, I didn't see you there." His intonations were perfect. He even mimicked the facial tick that Lodin got between his eyes when he was embarrassed.

Senna's jaw dropped low. "That's amazing! You should be an entertainer."

"It's too personal. Give me something general, not a real person."

A half dozen foolish scenarios ran through Senna's head. A traveling mute. An overworked goat farmer. "A charming noble?" she suggested.

Cole fell obediently into the role for her. He clicked his heels and gave a very courtly bow. "Gracious Madam, I've kept you awake too long. Allow me to bid you good evening," he said. He waved his hand like one of those heralders that she used to see announce things for Lord Themson. The performance was convincing and rather silly. Senna laughed. Cole picked up her hand and gave it a kiss. She thought he held it longer than courtly protocol required.

"Well..." Senna whispered into the remaining silence, "good night, then."

"Good night, Senna. If it's of any interest, I fully intend to sleep through breakfast."

"Good...so do I."

Senna went to bed particularly satisfied at the success

of her festival. She felt admired and appreciated by everyone, even Mister Cole. Senna was glad he wasn't angry. She was sure he had a legitimate cause to complain. Who knew what trouble the festival might give him when it came time to report expenses to the Regent?

Cole was strange in his ways, sometimes unreadable, but occasionally...sweet. What did he mean to kiss her hand in that way?

Probably nothing. Probably women attached hidden intentions to every stray action, where men gave no thought.

Senna let her fantasies run their most primeval course until they became too embarrassing for the privacy of her own head. She considered how often she had wanted to fantasize about Jed, and refused to let herself. Cole seemed more permissible. Which in an objective way made little sense. How realistic was it to form a romance with the Baron of Geid?

CHAPTER TWENTY-ONE

Jed waited alone at the cottage the next morning. He told Rimick he wanted to speak to Senna by himself, which earned him some mild jabs. "Are you going to woo her after all?" Rimick teased. Jed didn't argue, because he couldn't think of another excuse to make Rimick to go away.

By himself, Jed was more anxious than ever. He felt like Dwen on that first day, watching for Senna at the window. She spared him by arriving early. Her hair shook loose in the wind, catching leaves that she stopped to pull out before coming to the door. Jed opened the door so she wouldn't have to pause at the threshold.

Senna gave him a hug as bright and snug as sunshine. "You silly sod, Jed! I'm glad to see you safe and sound."

"Nothing I couldn't handle," Jed bluffed. "Just a little chase. I'm used to it." It was an ordeal that Jed had not enjoyed in the least. He'd spent half the night stuffed underneath a supply cart, and some of his joints had yet to recover.

"You shouldn't have come in the first place," Senna rebuked him.

"What, and miss all the fun? That would hardly be fair. Although I probably didn't earn any friends, breaking up the festival in the middle of it."

Senna shook her head. "It was just as well. The

Guards were getting antsy. If it had gone on much longer, there could have been trouble."

"Nice of you to let me off the hook." Jed laughed. He had expected a more thorough scolding, but Senna seemed in too good of a mood. She busily unpacked a basket of breads.

"Are you feeding me today?"

"Leftovers," she clarified. "For you, or whoever else needs them."

"I brought something for you too." Jed retrieved a bushel of flowers he had hidden under the table.

The praise she gave him was disproportionate to the short time it had taken Jed to pick them. "Jed, how lovely!" She took a deep breath from the petals.

"I wanted to speak with you at the festival. I thought you would look for me."

Senna lowered her eyes, and her brown eyelashes flicked against her skin. Jed unconsciously counted the freckles above her cheeks. Three on one side, four on the other. The familiarity was comforting.

"I feel like I never see you anymore, Senna."

Senna laughed it off. "There's no time."

"No," he agreed. That was the problem, wasn't it? Jed rubbed at the back of his neck, wondering how to phrase his next thought. "Senna, do you think if you told Fenwith you were quitting, he would let you go?"

Senna looked unnerved by this question. "I...I don't know," she said.

"I think it's time you got out."

It was clear from her posture that she didn't agree. "Why?"

"I don't think it's safe anymore."

"It's as safe as it's ever been," she argued. "Our system is perfect. I'm settled in. I know how to run the castle and I've got Fenwith in my front pocket."

"Yes. You think you know how to manage Fenwith, don't you?"

"Well? Don't I?"

222

"I'm afraid he's going to ask you to sleep with him."

Senna gave a short, derisive laugh. "That is *not* a problem," she informed him.

"How can you be sure?"

Senna rolled her eyes. "Fenwith is celibate. Everyone knows that."

Jed wondered if she could tell how much it was straining him to speak of this. "He didn't look that celibate when he was eyeing you at the festival."

Senna looked startled.

"Oh, yes," Jed said. "I was watching him watch you."

"Don't be silly."

"He watched you a lot, Senna."

She turned a little red, but the information did not upset her as much as he thought it would. "I told you it's not a problem, Jed, and I meant it. I can handle Fenwith. Trust me."

"Senna—"

"You need me. You know you need me in there."

"I do need you," Jed answered, feeling an unexpected urgency in his statement.

"Then what are we talking about this for?"

Jed fought with his tongue, which was refusing to take more orders from his brain. He wanted to tell her he needed her. Maybe even that he loved her. Did he love her? How much did you have to care about a person before it turned into love?

Senna was speaking again before he could recover. "It would be stupid to waste all our effort getting to this point. The hard part is over. Nothing can touch us, Jed. I'm telling you, I own this castle. I feel this close to omniscience." She used her fingers to illustrate the distance. "I don't even care if you told me to go, I won't do it. I'm doing a lot of good in that castle."

Jed listened without comprehension. Had he really lost all hold on her? How long ago was it they circled together and swore to fight for each other in the Queen's name? Senna had always been willing to follow his lead. So trusting, so eager to

223

please. Why did he feel like he couldn't trust her anymore?

Comfortable at his desk, Cole ran his eyes over his latest report from the lawyering circle. It informed him of notable events and accomplishments by the townsfolk—marriages, deaths, and so forth. For the most part, Cole eschewed the traditional roles of a Baron, refusing to hold audiences or take petitions. The lawyering circle took care of everything. It was just as well if the tenants of Geid worked through their own disputes without interference from Fenwith.

Today's report showed only one incident of crime—a minor theft of goods that was satisfactorily dealt with. The rest made dry reading.

Senna's footsteps in the hall broke the last of his wandering concentration. Cole was pleasantly disposed to see her. He put the report down and stood to welcome her. Senna was in a less friendly mood. Her posture seemed to anticipate an argument. She approached briskly, folded her arms, and made her demand without preamble. "Let me tell Jed."

It took Cole a moment to ascertain her meaning. When he did, he sat down and picked his report back up. "No, Senna. You promised."

"I promised not without permission. Give me permission."

"No."

"But why? You trust him, don't you?"

"The fewer that know, the better."

"Rubbish! Jed would help."

"He *already* helps, Senna. There's no need for him to know."

Senna's limited temper diminished further. Her nostrils flared. "It's not a question of necessity. It's a question of honor. I can't keep lying to him all the time!"

Cole felt some sympathy for her predicament, but he was careful not to show it in his answer. "So you would filter the lies further downward? You have only one person to lie to, and you would force Jedomar to lie to many? How many people will you include before honor is satisfied? Shall all of Geid be told?"

"You wouldn't have told me if I hadn't caught you interfering with my uncle."

Cole granted her a small smirk. "That's right."

"Aren't you glad you did? I help better this way, don't I?"

Cole gave a grudging nod.

"Well, I think you should give Jedomar a little more credit."

He didn't answer her again, so Senna huffed in disgust and left. Cole read her well enough to know his secret was still safe.

There was no doubt that Mister Jedomar could lie convincingly while he played a part. But in the face of his many friends, where trust and camaraderie ran deep, could he keep himself so aloof? Cole suspected not. On another level, which disliked examination, Cole feared giving Jedomar power over him. Jedomar's enmity was not feigned, and Cole thought it might not be easily overcome.

In her struggle to avoid lying, Senna ended up seeing Jed less and less. Instead she saw Cole a great deal. Senna used to dread the time after her maids left, when the halls were dark and deserted. Now that her isolation was easily remedied, the evening was her favorite part of the day. Senna emptied her dust bucket, laid the wet towels out to dry, and then lit the sconces on her way to the east hall.

Cole was waiting pensively for her by the fireplace. "Senna." He took a sip of wine from a nearby cup. "How was your day?"

Cafia was out sick and the dishwashing girl had broken her wrist, so Senna was more overworked than usual, but she acknowledged none of that. "The horrible little man with the orange hair was here yesterday. I gave him what you asked me, but I wish you wouldn't. Gaultians give me the creeps."

Cole laughed at her discomfort. "Mister Elimilo might not be the finest exemplar of Gaultian greatness."

Gaultian greatness? Senna shivered at the absurdity. She never wanted to see a member of their wicked breed again.

Cole finished his drink and poured another. Then he turned another cup over and poured one for her as well.

"By the way, I'm going to need that birthday letter soon," Senna warned him as Cole handed her the full cup of wine.

"Next Horse-Day," he confirmed.

"How do you know?" Senna balked. She looked into the dark liquid of her cup and wondered if she should drink it. Wine was expensive and generally reserved for nobles. Senna had tasted a few drops here and there, but the flavor had never impressed her.

"I know everything about you. I have it written down in a file."

"You have a file on me?" Senna found she was secretly pleased by this.

"You're my number one spy. Of course I have a file on you."

She wondered if she should demand to see it.

"Your birthday," Cole went on, "as providence would have it, is four months, four years, and fourteen days after mine."

Senna tested her wine as she thought. It was chewy and astringent. "You'll be twenty-four this year."

"Precisely," said he. "Guess how old Fenwith is?"

226

Senna waited for him to tell her.

"Nineteen. Or at least, he would be. I guess the real Fenn didn't make it that far, poor fellow."

"By the Queen, he was a baby!" Senna considered the death of this unknown Baron for the first time.

"Yes. One of the first things I worried about when I went to court—*four years ago*—was how I was going to pass for fifteen."

"And?" Senna tried another sip of the wine and decided it wasn't worth it. She put the cup back on the desk.

"Nobody mentioned it. I must have been scrawny enough to convince them."

Senna nodded. "I should make you eat more."

Cole cringed. "My father used to say that," he said. "He would make me sit for hours in front of a cold bowl of porridge."

That explained why he never ate porridge now. Senna was suddenly curious. "Your father was a steward?"

He nodded.

"Like Corvan?"

Cole chuckled. "Exactly so. Corvan reminds me of my father in some ways."

Senna tried to imagine an older version of Cole bumbling about an estate in Lammark. It suited somehow. "Were your parents good to you?" she asked.

Cole shrugged. "They muddled through. I don't know if they were the most wonderful parents in the world. They were too busy to look after me a lot of the time. Half of my childhood I owe to Lord Gretin."

"Lord Gretin," Senna repeated. The name sounded half familiar. "Was he the Baron of Lammark?"

"Yes, although he was only a half-Baron."

"What's a half-Baron?" Senna had never understood the term.

"He didn't govern the whole county, only a piece of it. Lammark is much larger than Geid."

"What did the Lord do for you?"

227

"He gave me tutors. Let me sit at small court events. I got to eat with him on occasion. It was never public, his treatment of me. Gretin didn't want to embarrass himself. It wasn't as if I was going to inherit anything." Cole paused, and looked thoughtfully to the ceiling. "He was kind to me. He didn't have any children of his own to distract him. I loved him like a second father."

"I guess he died when your parents did."

"No, actually." Cole looked deep into his cup. "Gretin was the one who recommended me to the Queen's Counselours. He was my contact outside the Regent's government until..."

He had to be dead now, though, Senna thought. Her curiosity was burgeoning, but after saying so much in a short time, Cole seemed motivated to change the subject.

"Tell me about your parents, Senna."

Senna bit her lip. Probably no other topic could have distracted her as effectively. "They were good folk," she said. "Good to me and Dwen. And everyone else, really." Senna's heart tightened. "My father used to take in all the strays who couldn't pay for lodging and let them scrub pots in exchange for a bed in the kitchen. We would light two fires in the winter to keep it warm. There were always people downstairs, the whole year long. My father told jokes to keep everyone happy. He said a laughing customer never complains. My mother had a garden, and we raised chickens."

Senna had a picture in her head of her mother standing by the coop in her bare feet, clucking to the birds as she showered them with grain. Laughing as she tossed a handful over Senna's head. The image melted into the drab brick of the office floor. Senna realized her voice had trailed off.

"Was this at your uncle's inn?" Cole asked.

"It was my father's inn before he died. He left it to my uncle."

"Ah," he murmured. "I didn't realize that."

"You weren't here when they died, were you?"

"No," said Cole. "I stopped the hangings the day I arrived, but it was too late to do anything for the first wave. I'm sorry."

She knew that. She had always known it, really. She wanted to tell him that he could have buried them instead of letting their bodies decompose on the castle wall, but she held her tongue. "I always wanted to blame you for it."

"Feel free to use me as a scapegoat. I'm used to it," he said.

Senna shook her head. "No, I'd rather not blame you anymore. I have enough incongruity to deal with already."

Cole shrugged, but Senna could tell he was pleased. He didn't want to be blamed, not really. He gave Senna an unusual stare, penetrating and fraught with emotions she couldn't quite identify.

"What are you thinking?" asked Senna.

"Ah." Cole smiled. "I can't tell you that. You have to play the game yourself."

"What game?"

"The game of reading people. To guess what someone is thinking. And at the same time keep them from guessing correctly about yourself. It's a skill."

"I must not be very good at it. You knew I was a spy, didn't you?"

"I'm not just talking about disguises. Everyone plays this game. And you are too good at it." He gave her a mysterious smile. "Can't you guess what I'm thinking?"

"No." Senna bit her lip. "Or yes...I'm not sure." She feared there was a hidden meaning to this conversation that she wasn't quite grasping.

"That's the unfortunate part," said Cole. "You can never be sure."

CHAPTER TWENTY-TWO

"Three hundred silver pieces! Blessed Queen, if the Baron raises that any higher, I'll turn myself in."

The table at the Ironfoot roared with laughter. "And what will you do with your winnings, Jedomar?"

Jed propped his feet up on the chair beside him. "Buy myself a fancy funeral." Another round of laughter. When the customers couldn't afford to get high on beer, they managed pretty well on good humor.

"Lower your voice, Jed," Senna scolded him. "Do you want everyone up and down the street to know where you are?"

"Let them know. Every man in this building will fight for me."

"That's right!" said Gambad, the innkeeper.

It may have been right, but every man in the building would lose if the Guard decided to rush in and start pounding heads.

Gambad the innkeeper was a large, round-faced man —rounder than most. Gambad seldom went hungry. Senna wasn't sure why he was letting the inn fill with so many nonpaying customers. It might have been to show his support for Jed. She supposed that sort of thing could be good for business.

A servant exited the back room with a platter full of

beverages. There were instant roars of acclaim from the townsfolk. Gambad took the tray from his servant and, with a wink at Jed, took the honor of delivering it himself. Then Senna knew that Jed was paying for the drinks. Gambad would never offer free beer, no matter how watered down it was.

Her disapproval was wasted on Jed, but not on Gambad. He zoned right in to her sour mood. Senna was quite aware that Gambad did not like her. It was still easiest for him to remember her as the daughter of his competitor. Geid was really only big enough for one inn, and the Ironfoot didn't come into its heyday until after the Bonidon Inn was thrown down.

Senna countered his scowl with a wispy smile. "Dear Gambad," she crooned, "so glad to see you're still serving orange beer."

The innkeeper snorted. Gambad had once tried to steal the Bonidon recipe for purple beer. Uncle Wick convinced him that gleeweed was the main ingredient. It made all of Gambad's customers sick for a week.

"Only the best, Madam." Gambad settled his voice just a notch below standard civility. Then he turned away from her and involved himself in conversation with the other guests.

Senna sat at the edge of the table, feeling unhappy and ignored. Jed was too busy sharing a toast to notice her. Hack, who was happily drunk, tipped his cup in her direction. Senna set her eyes in search of more pleasant sights. Hack laughed at her dismissal, and smashed his cup onto the table. Some of the beer sloshed over the rim and moistened the area in front of him. Rimick, sitting nearby with his book, had to lift his hand to keep the pages from being spoiled. He gave Hack a befuddled stare, as if he simply couldn't understand what would drive a human being to such behavior.

Jed reached over and gave Hack a light tap on the head. "Clean up. Or I'll tell your mother." The room laughed. Hack seemed to take the threat seriously. He turned to his cup with a pout and some dubious pretensions about his mother.

"What are you reading, anyway, Rimick?" Jed stuck his head down and read the title aloud before his friend could answer. "The life and times of Olwin the Poet. Mmm. Sounds fascinating."

"I didn't know you liked poetry, Rimick," said Senna.

"I don't. This is about the history of Olwin, not his poems."

Too bad. Senna thought a little poetry would be good for Rimick.

"Rimick just likes to read," Jed said. "I swear he'll read anything he can get his hands on."

"The Baron reads a lot too," Senna observed.

The unguarded comment earned her a handful of curious glances. Rimick raised an eye at her. "Are you implying something?"

She hadn't been, but it struck her now that there were similarities between Rimick and Cole. They shared a certain dry, calculated realism. Cole could be charming when he wanted to be. But Rimick? Ew. Was she that shallow? Was the surface of a person all that moved her?

Another fellow asked Rimick a question about his book. Instead of answering, he put his hand up in an irritated request for silence. Senna rolled her eyes. No, there were other things she disliked about Rimick.

Jed finally gave eyes to Senna's brooding. He switched places with Hack so he could talk to her over the din. "What's wrong, Senna? Is Gambad giving you a hard time?"

Senna shook her head evasively. "Have you heard from the Q.M. lately?" she asked.

"Your uncle is still well," Jed assured her.

"Not that," said Senna. "I meant the Q.M. network. Aren't you supposed to be planning some great revolt?"

Jed downed another swallow of beer and looked dispirited at this line of questioning. "We don't have the best communication," he admitted. "I think someone in Mackabine county is working on it, but there's not much we can do from here."

Senna fell back silently into her own thoughts.

"Don't be so serious, Senna. I get enough of that from Rimick." Jed gave her a cheering smile. "I've got something for you. It's a magic stick."

The tiny twig he presented was so shabby and unimpressive that Senna smothered a snort.

Jed cleared his throat with the aplomb of an entertainer. "Now watch as I make the stick disappear!" He did this by waving his hands a bit.

Senna confessed to being puzzled. While she was looking about for it on the floor, he made the stick reappear. It was a tiny thing, but the trick improved Senna's humor.

"Careful, Jed," she said lightheartedly, "you'll have people thinking you're a witch doctor."

They shared a quiet laugh. "There's the pretty smile I like to see." Jed took Senna's hand and gave it a light squeeze. "You look well tonight. You should relax more often; it suits you."

Senna studied his face, trying to understand the motive behind his words. Senna didn't feel more relaxed than usual. Indeed, her face was hot from receiving this slight compliment. She glanced shyly at the floor. When she lifted her eyes again, Jed had stopped looking at her. He was absorbed in a conversation about someone's goat.

How had she lost his attention so quickly? His fine, thick eyebrows were angled in concentration. Did he really care that Madam Talda's goat was having its third litter in two years?

Senna thought back to what Cole had said about reading people. How foolish that they played the game at all, Senna thought. *How much simpler it would be if we all just said what we meant.*

❖

Senna informed Cole that he was expected in Mackabine the next week while dropping an unsealed pouch on his desk. He frowned briefly. "You're reading my mail now?"

Senna shrugged. "You're the one who told Lodin I could be trusted."

"I'm not sure those were my exact words..." He slid out the contents of the pouch into his hands. Senna pulled her stool close to the Baron's chair as he read the official summons.

"It says there's going to be an announcement," Senna pointed out, gesturing to the letter. "Do you know what it is?"

"I have no idea." Cole dropped the paper with an irritated sigh. "You'd think the Regent would give us a little more advance notice."

"I've been thinking," Senna said, "and I'd like to discuss something before you go." She adjusted her stool as she gathered the determination to complete her thought. "The Q.M. aren't making any progress. Something real needs to be done. And I think you should be the one to do it. You are a Queensman, after all."

Cole looked taken aback. He took a while to process before he gave his answer. "I'm open to suggestions," he said.

"Something has to be done about the Regent."

"Such as?" Cole gave her a cautious stare. "Assassination?"

Senna had considered that. The idea had been tossed around once or twice. Most Queensmen were convinced it wouldn't work. The Gaults had too much power over the Mackabine court. They would just appoint someone else. To win, the Q.M. needed legitimate support from the military. "Not until we have someone to replace him. What we need is a Queen."

"Ah." Cole exhaled, leaning back in his chair. "That would be the thing, wouldn't it?"

According to Jed, it was the only thing that would band Mackabine together and get them to take back their country. "Jed said they wanted to use Queen Benta's uncle."

"Roman?" Cole shook his head. "Roman won't marry anyone without the Regent's permission, which he's unlikely to give."

"But if he did, that woman would be the new Queen."

Cole's face scrunched like he was testing the flavor of a foreign tea. "I suppose the laws of succession could be interpreted that way. Who do you suggest we propose to him?"

That much was far from settled. Gayna of Candige had nominated her own daughter. The Q.M. of Pannerack were supposed to have a handful of candidates in mind. Senna had never heard of any of them. It wouldn't be easy getting the country's numerous and far from unified Queensmen to agree. "I don't know. We'll have to work that out later." Senna didn't really care, as long as the woman was pure-blooded Mackabine.

"Seems arbitrary, doesn't it? Appointing a ruler by fiat."

"What are we supposed to do?" asked Senna. "The Queen's entire family is dead."

"That's what happens when a regime is defeated. The conquering party appoints someone to represent their interests. The Gaults appointed Gote. The Queensmen, if they succeed, will do the same, arranged marriage or not. It's pure arrogance to call that a succession."

Senna felt rather desperate. "Mackabine won't accept a Queen without succession," she insisted.

"No. The best we could do is call a new Regent, and that would lead to civil war. The nobility has been too destructured for anything else. Without a strong leader, the Gaults will simply reassert themselves."

"So you agree we need Roman?"

Cole shrugged. "I'm not optimistic. The man is old. He probably won't live long enough to be useful. And, as I said, he won't cooperate."

"Why? Is he a traitor?"

"Not exactly," said Cole, "but he's not very strong-willed. I think it's merely comfortable for him to do what Gote says."

"I don't understand." Senna stood up and walked around the desk in exasperation. "What do you think we should do?"

Cole took a breath, scratched his neck, and shook his head.

"What does that mean? We give up? We become the next colony of Gault?"

"I know you don't want to hear this, but Gault is hardly a land of deprivation. Putting Mackabine under Gaultian law would improve our lot considerably."

Senna felt her face turn to daggers. Cole had to lift his hand to keep her from leaving. "Senna, I'll talk to Roman."

"You will?" Her anger changed to uncertainty. "How?"

"Directly, I suppose." Cole crossed his arms. "I may have certain means of persuasion."

"Like what?"

Cole gave her a tight smile. "Blackmail, if you must know. I...uh, won't tell you what for. But it's dangerous, you realize. If Roman decides to risk talking to Gote, our chance is shot."

Senna felt a cold shiver down her spine. "What happens then?"

His blank expression made her feel how stupid her question was. Senna suddenly regretted her persuasive powers. She sat back down on the little stool. "Maybe we should rethink this."

"No, you've made a point. If anything is going to be done, it may as well be done now."

"You think it's a good plan?" she asked.

"I wouldn't say it's a good plan. It's just the only one I've heard."

"But—"

Cole interrupted, his mind set. "This is what I signed up for in the first place. Let me try, Senna."

Senna swallowed. Motivations were tricky things. Not all of the things Senna wanted seemed to be compatible with one another. She didn't think she could bear it if Cole never came back.

"Why did you sign up?" she asked him.

Cole shrugged as he thought about it. "At the time, I saw it as good fortune—a chance to make my mark on the world. I would avenge my family and serve my Queen at the same time. I was naive, and blindly patriotic."

"Aren't you still patriotic?"

"Oh...I suppose...it's just—politics give me a headache these days. Sometimes I wonder where I'd be if Queen Benta were still at Mackabine. Tending the stables in Lammark, maybe. By the Queen, I envy a stablehand. It would have been a good life. I could have settled down with someone by now."

"Was there someone?" Senna held her breath as she asked the question.

"No." Cole smirked. "Not unless you count Rebina."

"Who's Rebina?"

"A milkmaid with red hair."

Senna's heart constricted with sudden jealousy. She probably wasn't the sort of woman he wished for in that better life. "Did you love her?"

Cole's smirk turned to a laugh. "Not exactly. I was sixteen. I tried to kiss her in the barn and she threw a milk pan at me."

Senna bit her lip, pleased that the relationship had ended so quickly. "You must have been very brash," she teased.

"That wasn't the problem," he said. "Her family told her that albinos belong to the Otherworld."

Senna noticed his smile disappear. He looked tragically beautiful to her just then. A long moment passed before she thought of something to say. "You use that superstition, you know."

"Of course I do," he said. "Being albino contributes to my image."

"It does," said Senna. "I never met anyone else who could turn me to jelly just by looking at me."

Cole harrumphed. She thought he would have preferred her to disagree.

"Don't worry," Senna said. "You've been demystified. I don't think you can make me go to jelly anymore." That wasn't entirely true, though. She felt herself half jellied at this moment. Cole was so intense, it was impossible not to be affected by his presence. She tried to regain her composure by looking about the room.

Cole drummed his fingers against the desk. "I'm feeding the superstition. It worries me. A hundred years from now people may look to Fenwith as proof that albinos are evil."

Senna couldn't help him with that. She didn't think it was an unreasonable fear. A piece of liquid wax spilled from the candelabra onto the table. Senna pinched it with her thumbnail. "Does it bother you, being albino?"

"It used to. I used to comb through books, looking for answers. Once I met a witch doctor peddler who claimed to have a cure for albinism. I spent my life savings on his potion."

"What happened?"

"I got very sick. My hair fell out." He clicked his tongue. "I never saw that witch doctor again."

Senna wanted to laugh, but she thought it might be rude, so she covered her mouth instead. She had once wanted to buy a beauty concoction from a witch doctor, but her mother forbade it. Perhaps her mother had some greater wisdom.

"You know the sad part?" said Cole. "When my hair fell out, I was *so excited*. I thought it would grow back in color."

"Well, I think Rebina had poor taste," Senna offered.

"I like you the way you are."

A sort of light came into his eyes as Cole looked at her. Senna felt like those eyes might swallow her.

Senna regretted how obvious her comment had been. She hoped her face was not as red as it felt. "I only mean," she stuttered, "I know what it's like to be mocked for how you look. Because I'm so plain."

Cole studied her strangely for a moment. "It's a matter of perspective." He picked up a piece of her hair and ran it over his finger. "I think you're stunning," he said. Then the light in his eyes snapped out.

He dropped her hair as if suddenly remembering where he was. His face showed a flash of plain embarrassment, but he took control so quickly that a moment later Senna wasn't sure what had happened.

Cole closed his book with a bang. "I'm going to bed. I'll have to get up early tomorrow. Make sure you put out the fire when you leave."

The hall door thumped forbiddingly behind him.

Cole was not asleep when Senna came, but he was close. At first, he thought the ghostly light was part of a dream. It hovered disembodied-like in the doorway until Senna raised the lantern and cast a yellow glow across the lower curve of her face. Cole sat up.

"Senna?" The reproach in his voice made her hesitate. "What are you doing here?"

In his room. In the dead of night.

Cole's eyes adjusted enough to make out the contour of Senna's body. She was wearing a white nightgown cut from nearly translucent cloth. It hung off her shoulders and flowed prettily over her breasts onto the floor.

"I thought you might be lonely," she answered.

239

The room was silent as Cole tried to decide if there was a scenario to explain Senna's behavior other than the one which most obviously presented itself. "Actually, no. I was sleeping."

Senna cast her eyes down and tucked her lip between her teeth. She closed the door, set the lantern on the table, and walked slowly towards him. She perched herself at the foot of his bed like she belonged there, and lay a palm on his knee through the blanket. Cole was too transfixed to move. "I meant in general," she said. She lifted her hand and ran her fingers down the side of his cheek.

Cole felt a shiver materialize in his head and zip down his spine to the soles of his feet. He squeezed his eyes tight, thinking that might block out the feeling. "Senna," he cautioned, removing her hand from his face and putting it back in her lap, "you can't do this."

"Why not?" she challenged. "I...I think I love you."

These words had more effect on him than he would have thought possible. The warmth intensified until he was almost on fire. When he opened his eyes again, Senna's eyes met his expectantly. They glowed prettily: soft eyes, big and brown, with just a touch of green.

It occurred to Cole that he was about to do something drastic. Abruptly, he rose from the bed and retreated to the other side of the room. Without thinking, he grabbed his wash basin and dumped it over his head. The water made a resounding splash on the stone floor. It was cold and restored a portion of his sobriety. He took two deep breaths before he trusted himself to turn around.

Senna was motionless on the bed. Her empty hands lay in her lap and she examined them with a mortified expression. "I'm sorry," she said. Her voice cracked as she spoke. "I shouldn't have come. I don't know why I thought..."

"Senna," Cole nearly choked from the effort of speaking calmly, "You are a far worthier woman than I ever expected to think of me. In other circumstances, I wouldn't hesitate."

Senna gave him a look that was so hopeful it was heartbreaking. "Truly?"

"Yes, but not like this."

Senna lowered her gaze while she processed this. When she looked up, it was with very little expectation.

"Senna," Cole picked up her hand and kissed it, "I'm sorry...I wish, I... Why don't I know what to do?"

He wasn't sure in the dim light, but he thought he saw a tear on her cheek. "Because you're a fool and a half," she whispered.

She stood up and kissed him sweetly on the mouth, and then he was sure because he felt the wetness of her face against his own. Cole's eyes were still closed when the bright lantern hovered away.

He sat awake in the dark for a long time after that. He tried to remember why it was he had sent Senna away, because he rather wished she would come back. He even thought about going after her, and got as far as the end of the hall before turning away.

No, someone would see. If not tonight, then eventually. Senna would lose all her influence with the tenants, and with Jedomar. She would become the Baron's mistress, and nothing more. He wouldn't do that to her.

Cole went through the possibilities in his head. Marrying in secret was out of the question. Marrying in public was worse. Senna was right to be pessimistic. The only way they could be together was if the Queensmen overthrew the Regent and if Cole was somehow vindicated in the process. It was by far the least likely scenario.

CHAPTER TWENTY-THREE

Mackabine castle was the fullest Cole had seen since the Revolution. There were nineteen Barons of Mackabine at present, including four half-Barons and one post in vacancy. The Baron of Chatskin was abroad securing a wife. There was some debate among the Barons whether Gote would consider this a defensible excuse.

The nobles traded the latest gossip over dinner while they waited for Regent Gote to make his announcement. Speculation grew wilder as the dishes were cleared. Was the Regent retiring? Would the King of Gault make his ownership of Mackabine official? Very few expected good news.

"Perhaps Lady Orila is with child," one of the younger Counselours suggested. The rumor worked its way around the room until it neared the Regent's table, where it was tidily smothered.

Cole's nerves were wound too well for him to appreciate the dinner. While a servant removed his untouched plate, Cole gave his eyes to Lord Gote's table. Hemmon was seated on the right side, deep in conversation with the Regent. Cole looked away as the Counselour noticed him. Hemmon made him shiver with a loathing that could never be fully disguised.

Hemmon seemed to accept it as a facet of Fenwith's character. He thought Fenwith thin-skinned; he didn't imagine that Cole held Hemmon responsible for the torture and murder of his beloved mentor. Cole put a hand over his heart in silent salute to Lord Gretin.

Roman was seated at the other end of Gote's table, next to one of Lady Orila's waiting maids. Roman was a solemn, inert man with very little hair. He studied his fingernails while the waiting maid exchanged words with a servant. Cole hadn't planned yet how to get close to Roman. He was hoping Gote's announcement would provide a distraction.

The Regent stood up and signaled for silence. "My friends, my friends." He used the term generously. Lord Gote walked to the front of the table, where he could be seen more clearly. "I have excellent news tonight. News that will shake the soul of this court and bring new peace." Cole forced himself to concentrate through Gote's loquaciousness. The Regent's ambassadorial background gave him a taste for long speeches. "A burden has been lifted today, an indignation rooted out."

Cole got out of his seat as unobtrusively as possible. Melding with the standing crowd—family members, colleagues, and assistants not important enough to merit a chair—Cole delicately worked his way through them, his eyes on Lord Roman.

The Regent went on, working up his audience. A traitor was discovered, he declared. Heads lifted and looked about, as if expecting to find the offender among their own number. Cole had a split second to be nervous before Gote pointed to the end of the hall. A young woman was being led out by an escort of Guards. "Here she is," he said. "A relic of the former government—the Lady Anwa."

The room became momentarily silent. Cole's heart skipped a couple beats. Was this a joke? Anwa was the name of Queen Benta's youngest daughter. He didn't have to control his expression; everyone in the room was gawking. Anwa was the only member of the family whose body was never recovered after the Revolution. It was a popular rumor that Anwa had been secretly plotting a return to power. Some claimed to have seen her walking the streets of Mackabine. Cole had never swallowed any of it. It was obvious the girl had been killed during the first weeks of the takeover. Reports of Anwa's revolt had never been anything but the slightest annoyance to the Regent, merely because he was still unable to prove her death.

Fleetingly, Cole considered whether Gote had set out to do just that: arrest a young girl, call her the Queen, and then dispose of her body. But no; there were people in this room who had been at court since Benta's reign. Cole could hear their gasps of surprise. They actually recognized the girl.

Cole had never seen Anwa, of course, but somehow she looked exactly as he liked to picture her. She was tall and strong-looking, with an expression that made her seem older than seventeen years. Tangled honey hair clung to her cheeks in damp knotted locks. Anwa didn't blink in the face of so many accusers. She kept her chin up as if she really were a monarch instead of a condemned soul.

The murmuring was getting out of hand. Gote had to wave his court into silence. With some ceremony, he addressed himself to the Lady. "Anwa, formerly of Mackabine," the Regent said, "you are charged with being a traitor in conspiring with Yfreife to undermine the sovereign rights of this country."

Cole was silent, but the irony was so thick that some people were coughing to cover their laughter. No one could be stupid enough to buy this story. Yfreife was a country on the other side of Gault and too small to do anything without Gaultian permission. Cole was amused that Gote bothered to render any justification at all. He hadn't with Queen Benta.

"Your absence from this court for the last four years is proof of your treachery," Gote continued.

Anwa opened her mouth to refute him and Gote had to halt his speech in order interrupt her. "You are not permitted to speak!" The warning did not stop her and Gote was forced to shout in order to drown out her words. "Stay

244

silent or you'll be removed from this court!"

"I will not stay silent!" cried Anwa, even as the Regent waved for his Guards to take her away. The court grew noisier. A few pieces of her testimony managed to rise above the tumult. "Will not permit...lies about me...you hypocrite...traitor!"

Her hasty exit was indecorous for a Queen, and the court exchanged shocked whispers as the Guards pulled her away. Cole felt like laughing. Queen Anwa had spirit. No doubt Gote had expected her to stand there in disgrace while he presented his speech.

He tried to continue the speech in her absence, but the room was so agitated, no one could bring themselves to listen. "We will overcome these threats to Mackabine," Gote finished weakly, and then he settled into his chair and let the court run away with speculation.

Cole wandered the room, avoiding notice as he absorbed the waves of astonished conversation.

"The princess was alive all this time."

"But where has she been?"

"She's not the Queen, you fool. You heard the Regent."

"She was so young when—"

When her family was killed. And still very young now, but not too young to accept vassals. Cole could scarcely contain his glee. There was no question where the line of succession came now. Gote was a fool to let Anwa's existence be known, even to his own court. He should have killed her in secret.

He pulled Roman's blackmail note from his pocket and ran his fingers absentmindedly along the creases. Then he edged towards the wall and flicked the letter into the nearest fireplace.

❖

Anwa was thirteen when her mother was killed. The revolutionaries broke into the Queen's bedroom on a spring afternoon and slit her throat with a mole blade. Her older sister and several brothers were captured and held for two days before having their heads cut off. Anwa didn't hear about it for three days after that. She was away at Hansetch, staying with friends and pretending to study natural philosophy.

The Queensmen came for her in the middle of the night. They said her life was in danger, and smuggled her away to a safe house. She didn't know where it was except that it was small and dark and had none of the comforts she was accustomed to.

"Stay here, Great Lady, until we come for you again."

Anwa waited for four long years.

The safe house was run by an old man and an old woman. They brought her food and made sure she was healthy. No one had told them who she was, but they guessed soon enough. They kept her secret. They were simple, ignorant people who didn't quite know what to do with her. But they were kind. Anwa did not know what happened to them. She did not imagine that the old couple had betrayed her. Her capture had probably been their death sentence.

Anwa mourned for them now, as she mourned her own life, and her inadequacy as a ruler. She was Queen of Mackabine by right. She should have done more with her time in exile, not kept herself prisoner in an attic. Her studies might have prepared her to lead a country, but not to claim one she had lost. It was easier to keep quiet, to mourn in silence, and to hope that someone would come along who knew what to do. Now it was too late. The country had given its allegiance to their nefarious new Regent.

Anwa shivered as a draft of cold air broke against her skin. She would have been cold if she could have disengaged her mind from her other discomforts. Her wrists were attached by rope to a ring set so low on the post that she was forced to kneel on the hard tile beneath her. She wished she could curl up onto the stone floor and sleep. The Regent insisted they not beat her, but that didn't stop them from hurting her in more subtle ways. Her arms pulsed with bruises where she had been tied, pushed, and dragged over the last few days. She feared a more intimate violation, even though the dishonor of raping a Queen was unthinkable. So far the Guards had given her body no more than hungry looks.

No one in the castle showed respect for Anwa or her mother. She was in the heart of her enemy's fortress. But no, she wouldn't think of it that way. This was her mother's castle. When she crossed the drawbridge that would lead her to the Regent's court, Anwa's eyes moistened at the sight of those familiar spires. It was fitting that she end her journey here, in the same place where it began.

The cell door made a noise, jarring Anwa out of her thoughts. It happened with a suddenness that left no time to put up her mask. The intruders caught her half slouched, mouth gaping and half of her hair in her face. She stiffened proudly and straightened her back against the post, ready to face whoever disturbed the sanctity of her prison.

There were two men. One she recognized from her brief presentation to the Regent's court. The other was a stranger in working garb. He held a nightstick and a large ring of keys.

The second man, clearly the jailer, opened his mouth to speak, but the noble put a palm up to dissuade him. He stared at Anwa with an intentness that frightened her. Anwa had not had the time to study every noble in the throne room, but this one was hard not to notice. His skin looked like ice, as if it would be cold to touch. The noble drew a pouch out of his cloak and held it just out of the jailer's reach.

"I'll double the fee for a half hour," he said.

The jailer narrowed his eyes as he agreed. He took the pouch and locked the door behind him, leaving Anwa alone with the pale-faced man. He regarded her in silence for a minute or more. The young Queen stared back. It was hard not to be curious about a visitor who came through the force of bribes. But Anwa wasn't going to give him the satisfaction of asking what he wanted. Not even if he stared at her for the full half hour.

When he did speak, it was not to her, but to the jailer who had left. "Garin, I've changed my mind. Come back please." He spoke powerfully—not yelling, but in a voice that filled up the space in the small room. The response was immediate. The jailer fiddled with the lock and stuck his puzzled head through the door.

"I asked to be left alone, Garin," the noble stated patiently.

"Yes, but you just—oh," The jailer frowned. "Of course, Baron. My apologies." He left again, and Anwa, listening carefully, heard the sound of the jailer's footsteps carrying down the hall.

Another minute passed. Anwa gritted her teeth and waited. The man took a step closer. His face cycled through a series of unreadable expressions. Then he prostrated himself on the floor in front of her.

"Great Lady," he said, "I am your servant. Whatever you ask of me, I will do it."

Anwa's eyes widened. She was ready to be threatened, insulted, or questioned, but not worshiped. It awakened something long buried within her. There had been a time when men had fallen over themselves for a chance to show their admiration for the Princess Anwa.

She tried to conceal her fluttering spirits. It would not do to jump to conclusions. This Lord could be mocking her. But even as Anwa considered the possibility, she dismissed it. Something about the tone suggested, if not actual sincerity, at least a hope of appearing sincere. But what reason could he have to offer his allegiance? She was a powerless species of monarch, and he was a hand-picked lackey of the Regent. There seemed little prospective for gain.

Anwa drew in a breath and examined the back of the noble's head, his face still pressed to the ground in this display

248

of devotion. She decided to test his resolve. "In that case," she declared, "I command you to jump in the moat."

The Lord was smiling as he rolled back onto his heels to face her. "If you insist, Lady, but allow me to suggest that there are other orders that could prove more to your advantage at the moment."

"Such as?"

"I think I can find a way to save your life."

"How?"

He started to answer her, but Anwa interrupted. "Wait! I have a better question. Why? What do you get out of it?"

"I have no ambition but to serve my Queen," the noble said, and then hesitated, perhaps realizing what an incomplete explanation it was. "I am not entirely what I appear to be. I was entrusted with a commission four years ago, at the start of the Revolution. Counselour Edra wanted someone to watch the Regent's court, so she used me to replace one of his Barons."

"You're a spy!"

"More or less," the noble conceded. "I am not a very good spy. It's about all I can manage to stay alive most of the time. But I never confused my loyalty in my heart."

Anwa knew that common sense should leave her suspicious. She had nothing but this man's word to go on. But Anwa was young and her heart was easily engaged. It latched onto the fragile hope in front of her. "I accept you as my servant. What is your name, friend?"

He told her it was Cole, and then added, as an afterthought, that the Regent knew him as Fenwith.

"Lord Cole, I hereby designate you official rescuer to the Queen."

He smiled again. "Yes, Great Lady. Thank you."

"Now tell me your plan."

Cole told her the names of several Queensmen, and the locations of a few, but he said it would be tricky to contact most of them. They needed someone who could not only protect Anwa, but make use of the power she gave them. In the right hands, she was the key to a new revolution. Lord Cole seemed very excited by this possibility. His faith in her made Anwa feel hope.

Together they settled on Queensman Brock as the logical choice. He was a former member of the Silver Guard and the last formally commissioned Queensman of which the Regent's court was aware. He wasn't high in rank, but he had been in Benta's castle and would recognize Anwa when he saw her. More importantly, he was close by.

Anwa listened carefully as Lord Cole explained his thoughts. She had questions, but there was not time to answer them. The Lord couldn't stay with her.

"There is one more thing." Cole hesitated before making his last request. "Brock will want proof, and I don't know how much he'll settle for. If you could give me something...a sign to verify your trust...it might help. I know it's asking a lot. I will go without it, but—"

Anwa knew precisely what would help. "Yes, yes," she interrupted. "The last pass code for the Silver Guard was 'a good mother hen sleeps on her eggs.' They can't change the pass code without the Queen's approval, so it should still be in effect. He's bound to do whatever you say."

The young man smiled ever so sweetly. She thought him very handsome, in an exotic way. "I don't know what I've done to earn your confidence, but I'm glad of it."

Anwa felt a little breathless at his courtesy. Lord Cole knew how to behave like a courtier, which was more than she could say for any of her company of the past four years.

"Go now, brave rescuer. Do not keep me waiting."

Her champion bowed gently and left at a pace that hearkened to her words.

CHAPTER TWENTY-FOUR

The Regent's best intelligence placed Brock within twenty miles of Mackabine. He was an ongoing nuisance to law enforcement, hiding in the local forest with a small army of discontents. Dozens of trained officers had staked their reputations on finding the Queensmen hideout, but so far all of them had failed. Cole couldn't feel optimistic about his odds.

He stood at the entrance to the Mackabine forest and gazed into the thick, foreboding trees. There were two roads leading from the city into the woods. One was a side-route to Wensor, a southern harbor town, and the other was a layman's trail used for hunting. The hunting trail was smaller and more obscure. It might make more sense for the Q.M. to use the open thoroughfare to hide their numbers. Cole eventually took the smaller track on the basis that *he* didn't want to be seen by anyone who knew *him*.

He spent the morning hours walking steadily. Although the trail split several times, Cole kept to the broadest, most-worn path. Around noon, he stopped to eat a cold lunch of bread and dried fruit. It was then he caught sight of the first souls to share the trail with him: a middle-aged woman with her son. The woman scowled when she saw him and made no effort to hide her revulsion. She put her child behind her to shield him. Cole wondered if her reaction was due to his albinism or merely because he was a stranger in her forest.

"Good meeting, Madam. I'm looking for Mister Brock. Do you know where I can find him?"

The woman dropped her scowl and laughed callously. "Not I," she said. She pulled her son closer and left the trail to pass him at a safe distance.

Cole put the woman out of his mind and wiped the last of the breadcrumbs from his pants.

In the afternoon, the trail became steeper and increasingly difficult to follow. Cole began to fear getting lost. He was contemplating whether to turn around when he was stopped by three travelers on the path. One was a woman, young and slight. The other two were older men, sturdy-looking fellows.

The woman put her staff across the path to get his attention. The man in the middle became spokesperson. He put his arms to his chest and glared at Cole. "I heard you're looking for Mister Brock."

"That's right."

"Are you alone?"

"Yes," said Cole. He was certain they'd been following him long enough to ascertain that.

The man gave an ominous smile. "We'll show you the way to Brock, but it's even odds whether you ever get shown back again."

Cole accepted with a nod.

He had a story ready to spin for them, but they didn't ask to hear it. They split up—two ahead and one behind—as they ushered him off the trail into the trees. They traveled silently, their journey taking them deeper into the forest. Cole became exhausted. He wasn't used to walking all day, certainly not over rough terrain. When he stopped to catch his breath, the man behind bumped purposefully into his shoulder.

"Can we rest for a bit?" asked Cole.

"We're almost there," the man said.

Cole was glad to hear it. He sat abruptly on a fallen

tree and counted on his escorts not to leave him to his own devices.

The man huffed and nodded to the woman, who left them and took off in an easterly direction. They let Cole sit for several minutes while the pace of his heart began to slow. He heard a shout and some voices through the trees and realized that the camp was indeed right at hand.

Rather than waiting for Cole to come to them, a group of people burst through the trees. They murmured in curiosity to one other as they looked him over. Cole didn't have to spend too much time identifying their leader. Brock introduced himself out loud. The Q.M. leader had been built with an emphasis on utility versus aesthetics. He was thick, with hairy hands, and large facial features.

Brock motioned with his pinky, beckoning to a group of reluctant bystanders. "I have three witnesses here who say you're the Baron of Geid. Care to contradict that?"

Cole stole a glance at the informers. He didn't recognize any of them, but that didn't mean anything. "No."

"Excellent!" said Brock. "Any last words?"

"Yes," he said quickly. "A good mother hen sleeps on her eggs."

The Queensman didn't look especially surprised, and Cole feared Brock had long forgotten the ancient pass code. When he spoke again it was in a cautious tone. "Well, that is...very interesting. Where did you hear that?"

"Queen Anwa."

"Anwa is not Queen."

That was a peculiar thing for a Queensman to say, however true it might be. Cole was interrupted before he could answer by a voice exclaiming in disbelief from the edge of the crowd.

"Cole?" it said.

Cole turned with the rest of the crowd towards the speaker. The euphoria of hearing his name was quenched when he saw the speaker. Two brown eyes gaped at him from a familiar face. It was Mister Mole.

In another life, Mole had belonged to a gang of youths in Lammark. If the gang had been organized enough to have a leader, Mole would have been it. The gang used to scour the town looking for victims on which to vent their adolescence. Cole was a few years younger and inherently outcast. He'd spent more than one afternoon hiding from these boys, and almost as many others with bruises because of them. Mole had taken a special dislike to Cole because of the unfortunate rhyming of their names, which brought irritating jests from other youngsters. Cole wasn't likely to forget his old nemesis's name, and neither, it seemed, was Mole.

"Do you know this man?" Brock asked Mole.

"Eh." Mole hesitated. "Just answer me one thing. Do all albinos look exactly the same?"

"Not that I know of."

"Then, yes."

Cole smiled as best he could, but he wasn't sure it didn't look more like a grimace. "Hello there, Mole."

"Ah, you remember me!" said the man, flexing his large arms. A few years had fleshed him out nicely. Mole was burly and well built.

"Who could forget?"

Mole laughed and looked quizzically at Brock. "He's from my hometown. His name is Cole."

Brock glared at Cole with folded arms. "Then you're *not* a Baron?"

Cole tersely explained himself, starting with the events that led to his recruitment by Counselour Edra. There were interruptions from Brock, who wanted to know the particulars of the commission and the adjutant who bestowed it. Eventually he described the Queen's predicament, and his desire to deliver her into the hands of faithful Queensmen such as themselves. Cole stopped himself in time from calling them rebels.

His plan excited the company into a frenzy, with a definite split between those who believed him and those who wanted to gut him on the spot. The Regent hadn't made

Anwa's recovery public. To many of them, the return of the Queen seemed too good to be true.

Without Mister Mole's help, Cole believed opinion would have swung out of his favor. But Mole stood calmly, looking bewildered, and confirmed Cole's story up and down. An adjutant matching the correct description had indeed appeared in Lammark during the Gault Revolution and Cole had disappeared right after.

Mole's character was brought into question. Some suggested that Mole had been planted by the Regent to corroborate the Baron's hokey story. But other witnesses came out and said they had known Mole for ages and that he was a solid fellow, not given to exaggeration.

Brock rubbed his eyes and said that it was just plausible enough to be possible and had just enough holes to smell like a trap.

Cole didn't know how else to convince him. "You have a great deal to gain," he said.

"And just as much to lose," the Queensman snapped back.

Their debate went on past sunfall, by which time there was enough support to prolong the issue to the morrow.

Cole was alloted a place at the dinner table. He sat quietly, observing the Queensmen beneath a guarded exterior. They were former soldiers mostly, judging by their manner and use of arms. But he also saw a smattering of more educated cityfolk and a few farmspeople. Cole counted about forty heads.

The rebels seemed content with their hideout. It was homey as far as a camp in the forest could be made to be so. The wear of the dirt showed they had been there for some time. The cuisine consisted of local game and coarsely milled grain. Not fancy, but filling. Cole was happy to take advantage of it.

Cole recognized the surly woman from the road as one of the cooks. She stood by the roasting stick and offered thick slices of meat to anyone who asked. Cole briefly caught the woman's eye, but she sniffed and looked away. He went back to his meal and was startled by the sudden booming voice of a man settling onto the bench beside him. He looked up to see Mister Mole swinging his legs over the wooden bench. Cole instinctively prepared to defend himself.

"Well, Cole. It's been a long time," said Mole. There was nothing of the old arrogance in his manner. Only curiosity and a rather childlike need for attention.

"Yes," Cole responded noncommittally.

A few others followed Mole into proximity and huddled behind him with examining gazes, shielded by the bulk of Mole's large body. Mole turned to the two closest and identified them as his best friends. "That's Dograth. He's a merchant from Banth. And Shaw, a loudmouth, also from Banth."

No one from Lammark, Cole noticed out loud.

"Yeah," admitted Mole. "I kind of had to leave Lammark too. Got into trouble there." His expression turned repentant. "Listen, I'm sorry about—you know—those pranks and things when we were young. We were just playing around. Not much of an excuse, I guess, but uh... No hard feelings?"

Cole was pleased to find that Mole's outlook had matured along with his muscles. "None at all." He offered Mole his hand. "I'm the last man to hold a grudge. I've no right to it, believe me."

Mole shook Cole's hand with a vigor that matched the delight on his face. "People sure wondered where you'd got to. By the Queen! A real spy. Wait 'til I tell folks." Cole's expression must have matched his enthusiasm for that idea. Mole's smile faded quickly. "What I mean is, I'll never tell anyone. The Otherworld couldn't drag it out of me."

Cole barked a short laugh. He was looking forward to discussing more about Lammark, but their conversation was cut short by the arrival of a gray-haired woman.

"Mole," she called, "let me have a word with this one."

Mole hastily shut his mouth and gave way to the

newcomer. The woman rubbed her slender jaw as she waited for the privacy that Mole and his group were quick to give her. Cole had already heard her name and knew who she was. Marwen was a former Counselour and Brock's right hand. In Benta's time, most Counselours were women, but Gote had dismissed all of the female officials when he took power. The Gaults disapproved of female leadership.

"I knew Edra, your recruiter," Marwen began without preamble. "She had that really big wart on her chin."

Cole was glad of his ability to pass this small test. "Actually, it was on her forehead."

Marwen nodded casually. "Yes, that's right. She must have given you a code name?"

Unlikely to help. "Do you know mine?"

Marwen smiled. "No."

"But you believe me."

"I think so. I know Edra put people undercover. Some came back to us eventually. Others disappeared. I never thought she had anyone as high-profile as a Baron."

"Gote may know what you know. It could still be a trap." Cole said aloud what he supposed the woman was thinking.

Marwen only shook her head. "We have our own spies in Gote's circle. We know that Lady Anwa was presented in chains to the Mackabine court yesterday. I believe the Regent is too preoccupied in dealing with her to fashion schemes right now. Also, from what I can gather, the Baron of Geid isn't known for his artifice."

Cole savored his satisfaction as Marwen got up and inclined her head in an invitation to follow.

Marwen led Cole to an outmoded gray tent. It was probably former equipment for the Silver Guard, but it had been used under hard conditions long enough that its emblems were torn or faded. Brock raised his eyes as they entered, looking none too pleased to see them. He was seated next to a woman in a clean, modest tunic.

"Since everyone's against me on this, there doesn't

seem to be much point in resisting," Brock said.

Madam Marwen ignored his comment. "Mister Cole, this is Madam Eold. She is our spy in service at Mackabine Castle."

Eold was elderly but mild-looking. She had no physical defects—a requirement for service in the castle—although her hands were well weathered.

"You work with the morning household," said Cole as he sat.

The woman sucked in her breath as if he had wounded her pride.

"You didn't do anything to draw attention," Cole assured her. "I inferred from your dress." It would be impossible to memorize the face of every servant in Mackabine Castle. A useful camouflage, that. But it was obvious the Madam knew Cole by sight. She was one of the earlier witnesses against him.

Mister Brock interrupted the introductions. "Anything you can get to Eold will get to us."

"That should work," said Cole.

There was a shadow and a rustle outside the tent. Brock tapped the fabric wall and barked an intelligible reprimand. The curious eavesdroppers fled.

Brock turned back to Cole. "All right, fake Baron. Let's suppose you bring us the girl. What then?"

"What do you mean, what then?" Eold interjected.

Brock crossed his arms and scowled darkly. "I mean what good does it do us to add one adolescent woman to our rank?"

Eold's eyes flashed angrily. "She's our Queen!"

Marwen put a pacifying hand on her leader's arm. "We'll have the country's attention, Brock. People will flock to our company when they hear Queen Anwa leads us."

Brock grunted, considering. "That's not enough though, is it? Not with the Gaults defending their claim. What say you, Mister Cole? Will little Anwa convince the Gaults to leave Mackabine?"

"Hardly," Cole answered.

"Then what will?"

Cole was pleased to be asked so directly. He answered without hesitation. "Jade Hammar."

The suggestion made no impact, even to Marwen, who was presumably well-educated enough to know that Jade Hammar was a city-state on Gault's northern border. Cole persevered over their confused silence. "Gault has a lot of small wars going on right now. Mackabine isn't their highest priority."

Brock looked marginally insulted.

"It's a good thing, trust me," Cole said. "Jade City has been semi-independent for decades, but Hammar is offering to defend it, which puts it in the way of a civil war. Gault intends to take the city with an overwhelming force."

Brock squinted more intensely. Cole decided to spare them the political details. "It doesn't matter," he said. "What matters is that the bulk of the Gaultian army will be elsewhere. Regent Gote has been informed to expect it."

"The Gaults are planning to withdraw from Mackabine?" asked Marwen.

"Not withdraw, entirely. But if something were to happen during that window, there wouldn't be reinforcements. Not for weeks."

Marwen hummed a strain of appreciation as she absorbed the ramifications. She exchanged a look with Brock that sprang from well-acquainted understanding. Cole wasn't able to read into it.

"If we defeat the Gaults stationed here, there'll be no more coming?" asked Eold.

"Right," said Cole. Not for a while, anyway.

"It sounds good to me," said Madam Eold. "If they want to conquer us, they'll have to do it from scratch. Honestly this time."

In the quiet moment that followed, a joyful hum of voices breached the walls of the tent. "Anwa is alive. The Queen will save us!" News was out. Gote wouldn't be able to

259

hide it when she escaped.

Brock glared at Cole, as if blaming him for upsetting the quietude of his camp. "And how are you going to be any help from *Geid*?" Brock said Geid as if it were the name of an unpalatable beverage that he had just sampled for the first time.

"If I need to send a message through Q.M. channels, I can do that from Geid as well," said Cole.

"How?" asked Brock.

"I have Queensmen near me. Jedomar. You've heard of him?" Cole presumed. Tales of Queensmen were popular, especially to one another.

"Jedomar." Brock tested the name, shrugging and nodding at the same time. "What makes him Q.M.?"

Cole shrugged back. "Self-declaration, I suppose."

Brock snorted. "Being a Queensman used to mean something. Now it applies to any riffraff who skirts the law and cheers for someone other than the Gaults."

Cole felt a spark of contempt for Mister Brock. "Unlike some, Jedomar chose the role of Queensman. He didn't merely inherit it."

Marwen smiled at his words, and even Eold seemed amused. Privately, Cole wished Rimick and Jed were there to lead the revolt instead of Brock. He thought Jedomar would have done a far better job.

Brock grunted softly. Far from insulting him, the outburst seemed to cool Brock's animosity. He hunkered down with the promise of discussing plans well into the night.

Cole was relieved to find Anwa in one piece when he went down to the jail. The young Queen brightened at the sight of him. She was so brave and lovely a thing, it was hard not to feel affection for her beyond her mere importance.

"My Lord rescuer! Did you succeed?" she asked as he cut away her bonds.

Cole put a hand to his lips. "Quickly, quietly, like the mouse visiting the wolf."

The reference to a children's poem made Anwa smile. She obeyed with an alacrity that demonstrated her good sense.

Outside the cell, Anwa started just briefly at the jailer's dead body on the floor. It was the first person Cole had ever killed with his own hand. He'd been afraid he couldn't do it, but it was altogether easier than expected, much like stabbing a peach off a plate.

They climbed the stairs and passed the upstairs cells without arousing alarm from any other occupants. They followed the last hallway to its end, where a drain at the stone wall's base afforded its only outlet. Cole had already removed the grate, revealing a hole half a span in diameter.

"What's that?"

"The exits are too well guarded. You'll escape by the sewer."

"Oh." Anwa stared stupefied into the dark orifice.

Her reaction was no less than he expected. The sewer was the worst place he could think to put any person, much less a Queen. Cole quickly dispensed instructions.

"The tunnel extends about ten spans until it hits a fork. The right tunnel leads downhill, but you cannot take that one because it opens into the moat. You must take the left tunnel slightly uphill. It will lead you to another fork. Turn right, then it takes you down. With any luck, you'll see torchlight at the end. It will be a tight squeeze at the exit, but we've broken the stone away to make room for a small person. Queensman Brock will be waiting for you."

Anwa had stopped breathing, but the determined look on her face convinced him she was listening. "Rats?" Anwa whispered.

"Rats are small foes compared to the Regent's Guards," Cole observed wisely. The rats were nothing compared to the smell, but he didn't mention that either.

"You're not coming with me?"

"No. I will shut the grate behind you."

"Lord Cole—" She hesitated. "That is your title, isn't it?"

"No, Lady. I have no noble blood in me." He held out a hand to invite her to kneel down.

Anwa looked slightly disappointed. "Oh," she said. "Mister Cole, you may call me Anwa," she said.

Cole smiled. "Yes, Great Lady."

Queen Anwa stuck her chin up. "I insist, please. There are no great words for people who crawl through sewer drains."

Cole hoped his whisper conveyed a sense of urgency. "Yes, Anwa. Go quickly now, please."

The girl took a breath, and accepted his arm. He lowered her onto her stomach.

"You remember the way?"

"Left, then right."

"Good. Good luck, Anwa."

The Queen slithered into the sewer with the courage and determination of a young person. Her bare feet vanished and he replaced the grate, sealing her in.

CHAPTER TWENTY-FIVE

To infiltrate Mackabine Castle, the Queensmen had to breach two gates. No one gave Brock's team, disguised in Guard's uniforms, a second glance at the first gate. The second gate required them to show papers declaring their orders and station.

Brock felt an insect at his elbow, and started to swat it, then pulled back for fear the gesture would make him look nervous. The Gate Guard examined him, aloofly at first, then with slow suspicion. "I don't recognize you," he said, his eyes combing the disguised Queensmen behind him.

Brock repeated the lines the albino spy had coached him to say. "We just transferred from Aog. Captain Hadrett said we could keep together until Guardsman Derrow decided what to do with us."

"Ah, yeah." The Gate Guard nodded. "I saw you guys get off the ship this morning. Thought there were more of you?"

Brock clenched his teeth a little. Mister Cole had pointedly specified five men. The albino might have been wrong, or this Guard might be less observant. Either way, Brock didn't care to commit himself. "How many Guards can it take to watch an inner gate?"

Somehow it ended up being the right thing to say. The

Guard laughed. "The Captain's been paranoid since the Regent's announcement," he said.

The alarm came then, from the main Guard station. Indecipherable at first, the call was repeated by every ear it reached until it grew clear.

Prison breach. All Guards wake and report!

The Guard in front of them said a little prayer to the Otherworld. Brock fidgeted, wishing he could do the same. Couldn't the damned albino have waited two more minutes?

"Should we go?" Brock offered reluctantly.

The Guard snapped at them like they'd suggested a dereliction of duty. "Get to your post. The wall needs to be secure."

Brock didn't need to be told twice. Brock had served in the Silver Guard for ten years and he knew the castle as well as any Guard here. He led his Queensmen past the tower junctions to the grate just below the jail.

"Now what?" said Marwen. Marwen's uniform had been adjusted to obscure her female physique. It might fool other men's eyes, but it only succeeded in stirring Brock's loins. Marwen was the most fetching figure of a Guardsman in full harness and chain that he had ever seen.

"Brock!" Marwen prompted when he didn't answer. "This is the right sewer outflow grate, isn't it? How will we know when she gets here?"

Brock hesitated. "Perhaps we should bend down and check."

"Don't you think that would look suspicious?"

Brock glanced around the empty courtyard. In the general sense of chaos following the alarm, no one seemed to be watching them.

The girl made their hesitation unnecessary. She stuck her little fingers through the holes in the grate. "I'm here. Help me out," she ordered.

Marwen sensibly extinguished the torch nearest their location. The rest of them yanked away the heavy grate and pulled the princess out by her armpits. She was skinny and filthy and shivering from the cold.

"Are you Brock?" she asked.

Brock merely grunted. There would be time for introductions later.

He wrapped the girl in a dusty blanket, covering her from head to toe. With a few apologetic words, Brock picked the princess up and bore her over his shoulder. The girl took up no more room than a sack of day-riding cargo, and that was what she looked like when they strapped her, blanket and all, to the back of a horse.

The gate custodian was gone, and no one paid their group any mind when they passed the checkpoint. The authorities couldn't decide whether or not Anwa had left the castle. They were sending waves of Guards out the main gate to search roads.

"Excuse me?" a small voice came muffled from the roll at Brock's back.

Brock concealed his impatience. "I'm sorry, Lady. It's best if you stay where you are for now."

"Obviously," Anwa answered. "But my feet are cold, and I think they may be showing."

An inspection of his gear revealed the protrusion of a human toe. Marwen quickly readjusted the blanket, pulling an extra fold over the back of the horse.

Another patrol of Guards passed beside them on the right. Brock wondered why he had ever been nervous to come here. No one remained from the old days to recognize a former Queen's Guard. He passed Marwen a wink of confidence.

She nodded towards the road, where they blended in seamlessly, riding in the direction of freedom.

"Fenn, come in. Don't linger in the doorway.

265

Someone will think you're a statue and try to dust you."

Cole settled his nerves as he moved to obey. Speaking to the Regent was one of his least favorite things to do and he had already done it twice today.

"I owe you a commendation. My Guardsman tells me you alerted him to the disappearance of that," Regent Gote searched for an appropriate term, "woman."

"It was nothing, Uncle. I saw some suspicious figures leaving the dungeon. I thought it was worth reporting, that's all." Cole was hesitant to take too much credit. His account had sent the Guards in the wrong direction. Hours later, Cole was comfortable in his opinion they would find no trace of Anwa. The Guards' continued assurance that they would find the Queen was based on self-preservation more than optimism. Anwa was either safely in the arms of Brock's Q.M. or she was drowned in the bowels of the castle sewer. Cole tried very hard not to dwell on the latter possibility.

"Even so. That's the sort of vigilant thinking I look for in my Barons. Well done, Fenn." Gote appeared distracted. He picked a portion of his breakfast from between his middle incisors. "While we're at it, I wanted to ask you: how are things in Geid?"

"Adequate, Lord."

"Safe for travel, I assume?"

Cole hesitated only briefly. "Of course, Lord," he said, providing what could be the only acceptable response. Cole hoped this wasn't going to turn into another conversation about Jedomar. Surely Gote had other things on his mind?

"I have a sudden ambition to take a journey into the southern counties. I anticipate staying with you in Geid for a number of days."

"Indeed, Lord?" Cole was alarmed, and very much surprised. He had never known Gote to venture out of the capital since the Revolution.

"No need to trouble yourself, Fenn. It will be a short visit. Ambassador Jefrause requires my presence in Banth. While I'm on the way, I may as well take the trouble to benefit from the bounty of your county. I hear Geid has some of the richest farmland of Mackabine."

From this speech, Cole immediately perceived two things. One, that the Gaults were forcing him to make this sojourn. Two, that Lord Gote expected to be kept in the high comfort to which he was accustomed.

Cole gave his most graceful, aristocratic bow. "I understand completely, Uncle."

"Thank you, Fenn. I'm sure I can count on you." His mouth twitched up slightly, turning his smile from merely pleasant to amused. "I'll bring Lord Hemmon along for you as well. You always seem to find something charming to say to him."

Cole's mood lightened as Geid Castle came into view over the crest of the hill. His journey home had been more enjoyable than usual. Every travel inn had a new version of Anwa's escape, each outperforming the last in scope and inaccuracy. Cole's own Guards fell under the spell as they communed with the locals, joining in a hushed adulation of their Mackabine Queen. Cole observed it all with silent satisfaction.

Cole left his escort at the last waystation. The Guards would follow in an hour or so, but he wanted to savor the last stretch of road on his own horse. He urged Whip into a run, relishing the wind in his hair as the ground swept away beneath him. Cole was smiling as he cleared the gate into the castle, and had to wipe it off his face as Corvan came out of the stables to meet him. Cole gave Whip one affectionate pat on the neck as he dismounted.

"Where is Senna?" Cole asked Corvan.

The steward was unmoved by his unorthodox question. "She's within." He put out his hand, calmly awaiting the receipt of the horse's reins. Cole silently surrendered Whip to the steward.

He entered through the back entrance, something he seldom did, hoping to surprise her in the kitchen. The smell of warm bread greeted him, but Senna did not. He called her name softly, half-fearing the kitchen maids had overstayed their shifts, but his voice only echoed against hollow walls. He followed a trail of freshly lit lamps through the dining room, down the hallway towards his office. Senna was standing on a stool, poised under a lamp that was too high to reach by tiptoe.

"Senna," he called.

She turned around, and had two or three seconds to register his presence before he reached her. He seized her low under her waist, pulled her off the stool, and spun her full circle. Senna made a cry of surprise and delight. Her face showed that she was glad to see him. Cole put her down before it became apparent how much it was straining him to carry her.

"Senna, when this is over" —Cole reveled in the conviction that it *would* be over— "will you marry me?"

"Yes," she said without hesitation.

Cole was surprised by how easily she took his question for granted. He hadn't even broken the good news yet. He stopped himself from asking, "Really?" Instead he said thank you, which wasn't much better. But she smiled as if that had been the right thing to say.

It was a few moments before Cole was able to break himself out of the spell. "I have something to tell you."

"I can see that." Senna awaited the good tidings. His tone of voice promised nothing less. Cole had never had such good news, nor been so eager to tell it.

"I found Anwa of Mackabine."

Senna became still in his arms. This was clearly beyond her best expectations. Her eyes went wide as she considered the implications. "You're not serious. Queen Anwa? She is alive? You *found* her?"

"Well," he amended, "it is truer to say that Regent Gote found her. I only rescued her."

"You rescued the Queen?"

"I did. She is well and whole and staying with the very sturdy Queensmen of her county, with whom I am now in direct contact."

Senna put her eager hands to the sides of Cole's head. "Have I told you that I love you?" she asked.

Cole smiled again. "Yes, you did. I haven't forgotten."

"Can I kiss you?"

"Please do," Cole barely managed to say before Senna was upon him, warm and pressing and passionate.

CHAPTER TWENTY-SIX

Senna walked into the courtyard from the road very early on a Horse-Day morning, startling Guardsman Perr on the verge of ending his shift. He barked a couple of insults which she scarcely heard, and she gifted him a breakfast roll as she passed. Despite having slept little, Senna was refreshed and fortified for the day. She had spent the night at Carly cottage, most of it in deep conversation with Jed and Rimick. Jed had stayed with her by the fire long after Rimick and Hack had gone to bed, sharing their memories of Dwen, and reminiscing the good times as children.

Cole was waiting for her in the kitchen. He sat irreverently on her bread board, feet swinging childishly over the side.

"There is a stool, you know," said Senna, as she closed the door and twisted the lock for privacy.

Cole didn't look particularly chastised. "What did Jedomar think of your news?"

Senna scoffed. "He didn't hear it from me. I think everyone in the country must know by now."

"So what's their reaction?" Cole leaned forward rather eagerly.

Senna smiled to herself. He looked like Madam Emwid, waiting to hear the gossip of who said what to whom. She set down her overnight basket and flicked her hands at

Cole, chasing him off her clean counter. "Excitement, naturally," she said. "Disbelief, from some. Jed sent Grath to Candige to see what Gayna knows. There's a connection somewhere to Brock's group, but it's tenuous." Senna began unpacking the contents of her basket. She untied a loose bundle of wildflowers and spread them over the counter.

"These are nice." Cole picked up a flower with a curious expression.

"Jed picked them for me."

Cole showed his teeth and drew in air between them.

"What?" asked Senna.

"I just experienced an unusual feeling. I think it was...jealousy."

She laughed. It wasn't a novel emotion for her, although she couldn't remember ever being the source of it before. "Well, why don't *you* give me flowers?"

Cole seemed to think it over. "I will. Someday."

Senna resolved not to hold her breath. "Anyway, the general feeling is that the Queen is going to sweep Regent Gote out of Mackabine any day. It's pretty intense. I think the town is ready to storm the castle and overthrow you, if Jed asks them to."

Cole shrugged rather ambivalently. "I hope the Queen can act soon, then."

"Before they do?" Senna teased. She reclaimed the truant flower from Cole's hand and put her bouquet into a cup of water.

"Before their fervor fades. They're going to need it. Jed didn't know about the Regent coming, did he?"

Senna shook her head. "No, that was news to him. Although we barely talked about it. It seemed strangely insignificant after the return of the Queen."

"I wonder," Cole mused to himself, "if the Regent's visit will calm people down or inflame them further."

"Why *is* the Regent coming?" Senna interrupted. "I've never heard of him leaving Mackabine before."

"He doesn't much, since the Revolution. Apparently

the Gaults want him to hold a conference in Banth. I suspect it's some sort of punishment for Gote. The Gaults are unhappy about this incident with Anwa, but I'm not sure they realize her real importance."

"Anwa." Senna rolled the name over her tongue for the hundredth time. Queen Anwa. It was exciting to think about. "What was she like?"

"I can't say I know her very well. I only spent an hour with her."

"Will she be a good Queen?"

"Any Queen is better than none," answered Cole. "A lump of dirt would suffice if we could get people to follow it. But yes, to answer your question, I think Anwa will do well. She seems resolved. Inexperienced, of course, but as long as it doesn't get her killed, that will cure itself quickly. Brock has sent me two letters already, and he complained about her in both of them. Headstrong, I think he called her."

"Is she pretty?"

Cole huffed. "Why do women always ask that question? Yes, she's very pretty."

Senna humphed. It didn't bother her that Anwa was pretty, but that wasn't why she asked. She had braided her hair in a particularly clever fashion this morning, and Cole was stubbornly refusing to notice. Even Jed had given her a little compliment about it.

"Do you think you're up to cooking for the Regent?" Cole asked.

Senna was proud of her cooking, and couldn't help feeling a little insulted by the question. "I'll feed him moss and goat's tail," Senna said archly. She was joking, but the shadow in her eyes gave him a moment's concern.

"You're not serious, right?"

Senna rolled her eyes. "Of course not." She whopped him lightly.

"Well," said Cole, "we need to appear in good form. If you want to hire more people..." Senna put her hands to her hips defensively and stared at him. Cole trailed off. "Never mind," he said, laughing. "For a moment I forgot I actually had a skilled housekeeper."

Senna flashed him a forgiving smile. She would look for more help tomorrow. "Your old housekeeper wasn't so skilled, I take it?"

"Melga? By the Queen, she was a witch of a woman. Nowhere near as attractive as you. In fact, unattractive is about the nicest way I can think to describe her."

"Did you really have her killed?" Senna recalled rumors that had rolled around the time she left.

Cole made a disgusted face. "No. I told her I was going to, and then I 'accidentally' let her run away." He paused, picked up a peach that Senna had left on the counter, and rolled it back and forth between his hands. "She was the sort of vindictive, greedy woman the world would probably be better without. But that's hardly my place to judge, is it?"

"You killed Guardsman Toby," Senna pointed out, perhaps more accusingly than she intended.

Cole stopped. He put the peach down. "Yes...but he was a very bad man."

"Oh." Senna was surprised. She hadn't known Toby except in the most passing sense.

Cole looked intently at her. "You don't know what he was capable of, Senna. He would have hurt people. Even without a position of power." Senna was more than satisfied by this explanation, but Cole continued to try and justify himself, in a manner so urgent it revealed some internal strife. "I don't want to tell you what he did, but any court would have determined as much."

"Cole!" Senna interrupted firmly. "It's all right. I believe you."

He became sufficiently calm, and Senna chased him out of her kitchen with a kiss.

❖

273

Cole raised a hand to massage a knot from his neck but lowered it when he found his office door blocked by a large, sturdy subordinate.

Guardsman Rofus's chest was broad enough to be an obstruction. The rest of the space he defended with a strategic spread of his legs. The Guard refused to move at first glance, and Cole was forced to address him.

"What—" he started to say, then decided this was too much invitation and amended his salutation to "*Who are you?*" In fact, Cole knew every member of his Guard on sight, though he pretended not to.

Rofus gave his name, bowing in introduction, and politely requested a private audience.

"No," said Cole bluntly. He did not have individual conversations with his Guard.

"What I have to say is important."

Cole took a moment to admire his steady decorum. "Important enough to risk my considerable wrath?"

"Yes," the Guard stated.

Cole sighed in a show of irritated defeat. He pushed Rofus aside—a maneuver the Guard politely allowed. Cole casually brushed some papers off his desk and collapsed nonchalantly into his chair. "Then by all means, proceed."

Rofus came to his point quite forwardly. "You should remove Lodin as Captain of your Guard," he said.

Cole coughed a laugh, not attempting to conceal some genuine amusement. "Is that so?"

"I am sorry, Lord Baron. He is incompetent. He commits frequent breaches of order. He accepts bribes from the tenants to overlook their infractions."

Cole waved a hand. He had no doubt it was true.

"I would make an excellent replacement, Lord Baron," Rofus put forward without blinking.

"Your impertinence is impressive, Guardsman. But it isn't what I look for in a Captain of the Guard." Cole scarcely knew how to react to this kind of audacity. What *would* Fenwith do? He was torn between rewarding the Guard and throwing him in the dungeon.

"On the contrary, Lord," Rofus continued, "boldness is what you require. Your county lacks order. The Queensman Jedomar operates unchecked in the town. The tenants talk evil behind your back. You have enemies, self-proclaimed, who walk openly in the streets. It is not well to have these threats uncontrolled while expecting a visit from the Regent."

Cole said to Rofus with minacious gravity, "I think I might kill you for saying this." He tried hard to think of an alternative solution to the problem. All he knew was, he would rather have a thorn in his foot than Guardsman Rofus for a Captain.

If Rofus feared for his life, it didn't show. The Guard thought he was full of hot air. It had been too long since Fenwith asserted his reputation. It was past time to make an example. Cole grimaced, shying from the convenient choice in front of him. He couldn't help thinking that the Q.M.'s rebellion would soon make these power struggles moot.

Cole made a cautious gesture of invitation. "Do you have reason to fear some violence against Lord Gote?"

Rofus hesitated for the first time, but he could admit to no special knowledge, only a general sense of danger.

Cole watched Rofus evaluate him with his eyes. The Guardsman was trying to understand what drove his Baron to make irrational, or at least ineffectual, choices. Cole did not appreciate the scrutiny.

"There is some value to what you say," Cole began carefully. "I'm not ready to turn over the captaincy just now. But perhaps there's something you can do to prove yourself."

A slight turn of the mouth was the only sign of Rofus's disappointment. He waited, aware, at least, of an opportunity.

"I need a liaison between my men and the Regent's Guard during his visit. Lodin may not be up to the task. You, on the other hand, appear to have a way with people. You could prevent difficulties." Rofus was sure to see the potential for gain in that arrangement. At any rate, he had no recourse other than to bow in acceptance.

"As you wish, Lord."

Cole watched the troubled Guardsman march away. There was a shrewdness in Rofus. None of the careless cruelty found in Guardsmen Skole or Garbe, but something far more dangerous.

CHAPTER TWENTY-SEVEN

Jed crouched beside the wall on the west perimeter of the castle, watching the kitchen door Senna used to go in and out. A cluster of bushes would obscure him from view if anyone happened to be looking. Not that he was overly concerned about being found. The castle yard was essentially empty.

Jed recalled their last visit at Carly cottage a few nights prior. Senna was so self-assured lately, so vibrant. When he held her hand, she had seemed scarcely to notice. The change attracted him powerfully. Jed had thought of little besides Senna since then. He stared at the kitchen door, willing it to open. He wanted Senna claimed, so that everyone would know she belonged to Jedomar and no one else.

The door unfastened eventually, rewarding his shaky patience. Senna had her arms full of a slop bucket, and didn't notice him as she passed Jed on her way to the garbage pit. Jed straightened his tunic as he waited for her to finish her chore. Even his natural confidence couldn't squelch a jittering of nerves when she turned.

"Jed?" She smiled. "Is that you?"

Jed returned her smile and presented a warm, sweet peach he'd brought as a negotiatory offering. If Senna had a weakness, it was peaches.

Senna was surprised, but not as condemning as he'd

feared. There was no scolding for appearing on the castle grounds in broad daylight. She merely flipped her hair and accepted the peach.

"That's two presents in one week! How generous." Senna scrubbed her hands and the fruit thoroughly with her apron before taking a bite from the fruit. A trickle of juice ran down her chin, which she shyly wiped away.

"I'm always generous," Jed teased. He gave her his most winning smile, the one that was supposed to make young ladies melt.

It worked like a charm; Senna blushed and smiled at the ground. "Yes, you are," she agreed.

Jed cleared his throat. He hadn't realized how difficult it would be to start this conversation. "Senna," he began, "Senna, we've always been friends, haven't we?"

Senna looked at him, too absorbed in the business of her peach to answer, but waiting for him to expand his thoughts.

He cleared his throat again. "Have you ever thought, maybe, we could be more?"

Senna's chewing slowed. The answer to this question was obvious to both of them, but neither of them seemed to have the courage to answer it. Senna's eyes grew rather large and watery. Finally she remembered to swallow her bite of peach. "No," she said, lifting the tone of her voice like a question.

Jed smiled at the preposterous lie. "Well, maybe you could think about it now," he suggested.

The wateriness escaped and formed tiny rivers down her face. "No," she said again.

Jed began to feel confused at the firmness with which she spoke. "Senna, I...I haven't always been...I mean, I haven't always known that I loved you. It came on so slow, I didn't know what it was at first. But when I think about not being with you, it shreds my heart right up. I've seen your strength and your courage and your ragdog determination one too many times. You're the one for me. I know it, Senna."

278

"Stop!" The cry was so urgent it made Jed's heart jump. Senna looked like she was in pain. Her hand was curled as if still holding the peach, even though the fruit had fallen from her grasp. "Don't," she said, in a whisper rather than a shout.

Jed didn't know what to do. He held his arms open and Senna fell into them, clung to him, and wept soundly.

"I'm sorry, Senna. I didn't mean to be such a fool. I know I made you wait too long. Do you want to get married straight away? I was thinking we could go to Candige, sort of as a holiday. Your uncle will be there. He might like to see you get married."

He felt her shake her head against his chest. Then she pulled away.

"No, Jed," she said, "I won't marry you. I'm very sorry."

She tried to leave, but Jed grabbed her arm and held it fast. "Senna, wait. You're serious?"

"Yes," she replied. Her face was red and tear-streaked, but her voice was steady. "I know this isn't what you were expecting. But I can't marry you. Let me go, please."

Jed released her arm with a sort of unthinking obedience. Senna looked at him another moment, then turned away and walked back into the castle. Jed stood, exposed on the open grass, struggling to understand.

Rimick was trying to take his mind off Jed's personal life. He poked at a small foot trap for rabbits. The contraption hadn't caught anything for days, and should probably be realigned. He knelt down over the trap and tried to pull the loop free of the trap spindle. It was a challenge to size a loop large enough for the rabbit to fit into and small enough that it would tighten before the animal leapt away.

Rimick pulled his ear, thinking. It wasn't supposed to be his business who Jed married or when. Rimick had no special objection to Jed's choice, but Senna's position complicated things. She had become a visible figure in Geid.

The recent emergence of the Queen made Jed's timing especially bad. Was Jed planning to marry Senna openly, or would he hold off for a hopeful resolution to Anwa's succession? There was a half formed fear in his mind—that the pair might run away together, abandoning Geid to Rimick's inadequate ministrations. He didn't really expect that of Jed, but even in the best scenario, a married Jedomar would have less time for their work.

"Hah!" Rimick cried as the trap released accidentally. The string pulled tight around his finger, pinching his skin. He pulled it back and started over.

Rimick never intended to take a wife. He was past the expected age and he didn't want anyone attempting to check his habits. Jed yearned for the intimacy of a woman. Rimick could understand that. A woman was hard to come by any other way in Mackabine country. Anything besides marriage would result in social ostracization. Rimick knew this wasn't the case everywhere. There were foreign societies with less stringent attitudes. Under other circumstances, he might have suggested Jed migrate to one.

The distraction could prove as disastrous to Senna as it did to Jed. Senna needed her wits about her. She was a cool-headed woman, and possibly more valuable than Jed in that respect. Jed liked to call himself Queensman, but his real pleasure was in the role of hero. He had little appetite for the down and dirty business of battle with an enemy who wanted your head as much as you wanted theirs. While Jed might hold back at critical moments, Rimick had no doubt that Senna would do what was necessary when decisiveness counted.

The crunch of someone treading on vegetation in the distance warned Rimick he had a visitor. Rimick put his trap and twine aside. He quickly scaled a tree to make certain it was Jedomar and not an unwelcome intruder. He dropped down as his friend came into view.

"Well, then," Rimick said in welcome. Jed was back sooner than Rimick expected. "Did you ask her already?"

Jed turned his face away. He threw his cloak haphazardly at the log beside him.

"Congratulations," said Rimick, feeling a little confused. He would never understand. If Jed wanted to marry the girl, why did he look so angry?

"She said no."

Rimick waited patiently for an explanation but Jed offered none. "What does that mean?" he said finally.

"It means she said no!"

Rimick thought he had better confirm for the sake of clarity. "She said no?"

Jed was more agitated than Rimick had ever seen him. "That's what I said, isn't it?" he snapped.

"She won't marry you? Are you sure she understood the question?"

Jed drew his breath in so ferociously that Rimick decided to stop asking. "Well...well." Rimick did not know what else to say. He was very surprised, and irked at himself for failing yet again to predict human behavior. Inwardly Rimick was relieved, though he realized it would be a social blunder to say so. "That's a sad way, my friend."

"Forget it. I don't want to talk about it. Ever." He plopped down next to Rimick.

Rimick carefully followed Jed's advice. He would have liked to talk about something more useful. Like the Regent's upcoming visit, or their proposed trip to Candige. Jed deflected his minor attempts, however. No other topic seemed safe for discussion, so they stayed silent for several minutes. Eventually, Rimick went back to adjusting his foot trap.

"How did I not see this coming?" Jed mused.

Rimick paused to confirm that Jed expected an answer. "People are fickle things. They change their minds from hour to hour. I certainly don't understand it. I don't see why you should."

"Change her mind?" Jed snapped up hopefully. "That makes sense. I should have thought of that." Without the smallest glance at Rimick, Jed hopped up and left, barely remembering to take his cloak with him.

Senna's reservations against revealing Cole's secret were gone, evaporated like so much water in a puddle. Jed deserved to know. She had already decided to tell him. But she was so angry, so venomously angry, that she hesitated. If Jed couldn't figure out why she was unhappy, then he deserved to be confused.

She threw the last tablecloth into her basket with a grunt. Senna found no satisfaction in taking her vengeance out on the laundry. All those years of waiting. Didn't Jed realize she would give him up eventually? Her heart fluttered momentarily at the temptation to change her mind.

Senna glanced along the secluded wall by the porch, her eyes slipping to the spot that Jed used to sneak in. She half expected to find him standing there still. Of course, he was not. There was nothing but a branch bent by frequent passing. She picked up her basket and carried it across the courtyard towards the basin. The day was suddenly cold and the sun didn't feel as nice on her back as it had an hour ago. Her gaze was tightly focused on her goal and she gave a start when a man suddenly blocked her view.

"Oh," she breathed. Senna checked her momentum in time to keep from running into him.

Captain Lodin gave her with an appraising look. Senna wasn't sure what she had done to draw his attention. She often did her work outside when it was warm enough. "Someone hurt you, Madam?" Lodin asked.

Senna reflexively put a hand to her face and drew it back doused in tears. "Oh," she answered, nervously making an effort to wipe them off. "It's nothing."

Lodin continued to look quietly concerned. Senna had been nice to him once or twice. Apparently that was enough to put him on her side. It was strange, how many things in this castle had morphed from one thing into another, when she came close enough to see them properly.

Senna felt a wavering smile cross her lips. "I'll be fine," she assured him. "Really."

Lodin nodded in grim acceptance. "I can't do much about the behavior of our Lord, but...if something happened, you'd let me know?" His eye wandered suspiciously towards the stables. Cole was there with a bridle in hand, dispensing instructions to Corvan.

"It's not that," she promised. She started to excuse herself back to work, but Lodin was no longer looking at her. She followed his gaze towards the stable. The old steward had collapsed. He clutched feverishly at his chest while the Baron bent over him.

Senna started running the same time Lodin did. Her laundry basket rolled in front of her, scattering garments into the dirt. She leaped to avoid tripping over it.

Lodin arrived before her, but she was in time to hear the Captain's first plea to the Baron. "Lord Fenwith, what happened?" he asked.

"I don't know," Cole answered. "He just fell." Cole was out of character, his voice apprehensive. Senna spared a glance at Lodin to see if he noticed, but his focus was likewise on the trembling steward.

Corvan was rigid and gasping for breath. He was so old, Senna thought his body wouldn't take much. She put a hand to the steward's forehead and found it layered in sweat.

Cole swung his head briefly towards the Captain. "Send for the witch doctor," he ordered.

His voice seemed to revive the steward slightly. "Master," he said, hacking out words in slow pieces, "I never finished putting the rosemary in."

"You finished it yesterday," Cole lied. "The garden is

283

perfect. You did everything right." Cole took the old man's hand.

The approbation brought a smile to the steward's eyes, and contentment lingered there as they closed for a final time.

When Cole checked the steward's pulse, his stony facade returned. There was a moment of contemplation, then Cole backhanded Lodin with surprising force. Senna winced as Lodin covered his smarting cheek. "Forget the doctor," Cole snapped. "Get rid of the body."

Senna watched Lodin waver between confusion and offense as Cole marched away.

CHAPTER TWENTY-EIGHT

Jed went hunting in the deep forest across the river. For a day and a half he reflected on the problem while he ambled, unaccompanied, over the faint hunting trails. When he was a boy, Jed's father used to take him shooting when meat was too expensive to buy. Hunting was less common in Geid than in other counties. The timbi deer didn't range this far south. But there were always rabbits and the occasional wolf. He made enough kills to keep a family or two in meat this week.

The exercise focused Jed's mind. It was true he hadn't responded well to Senna's overtures in the past. At first, Jed thought she meant to punish him, but he later pushed that notion away. He understood Senna's character well enough to see that her refusal was sincere. It could only mean she had given up. Senna didn't trust herself to hold his affection.

The realization made him feel very bad. The solution was simple, however. Jed needed to give Senna the good turn she deserved. He meant to see her again as soon as he could. Do some proper wooing this time. His head fashioned more and more elaborate ploys guaranteed to enchant a woman.

When his romantic aspirations didn't consume his attention, Jed reflected on the state of the Q.M. movement. Madam Gayna wrote message after message. She'd confirmed every rumor of Anwa and added a few of her own to the mix. It was a very exciting time. The Queensmen were posing to dismantle the regime. Jed wasn't sure what he would do if it actually happened.

The last message from Gayna included an assignment. She wanted Jed and Rimick to assassinate the Regent when he passed through their county on his way to Banth. Gayna admitted that the idea wasn't sanctioned by any other Q.M. circles, but she seemed to think it would precipitate the Queen's plans.

Jed and Rimick discussed it at length, but in the end, they decided against her request. Jed wasn't anxious to engage in premeditated murder. He had killed in self defense, in the urgency of a moment. But he'd never deliberately planned to take another person's life. Not even a useless tyrant like Gote.

Jed was nonetheless determined to get a look at the Regent as he passed. He found a patch of road with the best view and settled comfortably into a tree to wait. The morning was muggy, but not terribly chilly. Jed snoozed for an hour until a flock of birds woke him, screeching curses of surprise at the envoy's approach. Jed straightened his spine at the upcoming spectacle and congratulated himself on having come. The Regent's carriage was a sight worth seeing. It was led by a full Honor Guard, and followed by court escorts and supply wagons for a hundred spans down the road. The Guards were smartly dressed in the dark blue of Mackabine county, their armor clean and well maintained. To his disappointment, the Regent's carriage windows were obscured, depriving Jed of seeing its star occupant. Jed wondered if an arrow would make it through the window shade. Likely not, Jed thought. There would be glass underneath. An assassination attempt would never have succeeded. It would take an army to match this group.

It took several minutes for all the wagons to pass. Jed leaned out a bit after the last horses went by. In the road ahead, he spied a small group of women walking towards the envoy. Like Jed, they'd come to enjoy the spectacle, only they were being less subtle about it. It was hard to make out details from a distance. Jed thought he recognized Yamat and Etta at the head of the group. Yamat had been married for several months now, but she still kept company with some of the younger and sillier girls. The women lined up along the road and cheered as if for a parade. This reckless behavior triggered an unpleasant result. The Regent's carriage slowed. Jed watched with paused breath as the shades were lowered. A hand extended languidly from the window and waved for the women to approach. Yamat was too pretty for her own good. The witless girl came forward without hesitation.

At that point, some of the Guards shifted position and Jed lost what visibility he had. He slid down his tree onto the forest floor. The underbrush was thick enough to hide him from the road, but he held his breath as he slipped past the dozens of armed men to his left. Jed found another tree closer to the scene and climbed it soundlessly. His reward was a first rate view of Regent Gote.

Gote wouldn't have been worth looking at if he were anyone else. He was moderately sized, well fed, and his nose was slightly off center. The Regent's air of nobility did nothing to disguise the lust in his eyes. The carriage door was open and Yamat was hanging through one side of it with her elbows on the ledge, chatting to the Regent without a care. Jed didn't see how Yamat could be so foolish. The other women had enough sense to hover at the edge of the road.

The Regent said something that made Yamat's posture change. She tried to disengage herself from the carriage window, but Gote grabbed her chin with his large hand. He stuck out a long tongue and wiggled it against her cheek. Yamat screamed.

What happened next was what Jed would be known for the rest of his life. He would later consider that, of all the significant actions of his life, this one was undertaken with the least forethought. He put an arrow in his bow, drew it, and shot Lord Gote in the face.

Jed's bow was medium range and low power, fashioned for shooting rabbits. If his shot had been a fraction higher, it would have grazed the Regent's skull and done no permanent damage. Instead it caught the man in the soft tissue of his eye. The arrow embedded itself six inches into his head. Gote didn't have time to make a sound. He convulsed once and then landed in a heap beside his carriage.

The abhorrence of what he had done washed over Jed. Yamat was screaming and so were most of the Guard. Jed lowered his bow. He felt some mild surprise to find his muscles still working.

The initial outburst subsided, and the cry went out for the Guard to search the trees. Jed knocked himself back into reality. He jostled himself out of the tree into freefall. The ground jolted him and knocked him flat on his knees. Jed rolled to his feet in time to see the first men crash through the brush towards him.

Jed could not have been less prepared. He scrambled to his feet just in time to be knocked back to the earth. The superior numbers of enemies defeated his chances before he got started. Two Guards locked his arms in a vise grip. They dragged him, kicking and grunting, out onto the road. He stopped his futile thrashing as he realized how irretrievable his situation was.

The Guards gathered to gawk at him. They looked more curious than angry about the fact that Jed had just accomplished the death of the man they were paid to protect.

"That was unforeseen," someone said. Jed tried to place the speaker in context. He was a stately man with dark hair and a set of costly-looking cloaks. The man appeared entirely unaffected by the Regent's demise. After a moment of uncertain recognition, Jed realized he was Counselour Hemmon, the inspector he's spied on last year. Hemmon took command, through sheer self-assuredness, or perhaps due to a lack of clarity exhibited by everyone else. He ordered the Guards to wrap Lord Gote's deceased body.

"Yes, Lord," one of the Guards answered.

Yamat, still wailing, managed to make the most noise of anyone. She knelt near the Regent and alternated between scooting towards and away from the body on her knees, trying to make up her mind whether he was really dead.

The Couselour briefly directed his attention to Jed. "What a loathsome woman. Did you actually care what happened to her?" he asked rhetorically.

Without missing a beat, Hemmon walked over to Yamat, took her by the hair, and dispassionately slit her throat.

Jed closed his eyes with a shudder. He had done worse to Yamat than Regent Gote would have done. Of all the emotions coursing through him, guilt was suddenly the heaviest. Jed lifted his eyes in search of the other women, and was glad to see they had fled in the aftermath.

"Was he alone?" Jed heard Hemmon ask.

"We believe so." The Guards were still regrouping, but the man who answered sounded confident. Jed realized that, since no one from Geid was in the party, they did not yet know who he was. That wouldn't last.

The next Guard announced that Baron Fenwith was riding out to welcome them. "A shame he's missed the show," the Counselour mused in a mild tone.

Jed didn't see Fenwith, but he overheard Lord Hemmon addressing him from a distance. The Counselour filled him in on recent events. Jed flicked his eyes up. It didn't take them long to settle on his familiar nemesis. The Baron held himself taut, inspecting the scene with wide, rather disbelieving eyes.

"Do you recognize the assassin?"

Fenwith looked too furious to answer right away. He kicked his horse, which he still hadn't bothered to dismount, and had to regain control before he could speak. "Yes," he said grudgingly. "That's *my* damned Queensman."

Hemmon chuckled, as if he'd suspected it. "Bit of an idiot, isn't he?" he said. "I wonder why it is you couldn't catch him sooner."

Jed could think of one or two retorts. He willed himself to use them, to show bravado with a smirk. Instead it was all he could do to keep his legs steady underneath him.

The Guards tied Jed up, using an inordinate amount of

rope. Jed decided struggling would encourage them to do a better job, so he held as still as could. Someone drew a gag through his teeth that smelled of old urine and made it difficult to breathe.

Hemmon and Fenwith began to argue over who held custody of him. The Guards appeared unaffected by their argument. They picked Jed up and secured him in the back of the wagon. He had a small wedge of space to crouch aside crates of luggage and horse feed. Thankfully, the Regent was being stored elsewhere.

The convoy moved without warning. Jed was rocked backwards with a suddenness that jarred his neck and shoulders. Jed wished he could turn back time by half an hour, walk away, and never lay eyes on the useless Regent.

CHAPTER TWENTY-NINE

The Regent's arrival caused more upheaval than Senna expected. She found out why when she got a look at the funeral board that was conveying him into the cellar, bloody sheet and all. Senna was too astonished to be pleased. She nearly tripped over the floor tiles with the bowl of clean water she had brought to refresh her guests. The surviving nobles bandied details amongst themselves. Senna hung close by to catch what she could.

"Shot in the face like a treeskunk."

"Good aim," someone else mused.

Their emotions ranged from shock to woe to various degrees of half-concealed glee.

It took a little longer for Senna to sort out the story enough to realize that Jed was the one responsible. She wondered about his motives. Did the Q.M. have a plan to redirect the Regent's successor? How long had Jed been planning this? Senna pushed her ruminations aside. Despite the Regent's removal, there were still arrangements to be made. A handful of clerks and Counselours required rooms. Dinner would still be served.

She helped the servants direct some of the luggage upstairs. On her way down the hall, a hand grabbed her arm and tugged her into one of the empty rooms. Senna almost shrieked until Cole put a hand to her mouth. Then he pulled back to let her speak. She wanted to ask what had happened, but that would take too long. "The Regent's death. Is that good or bad for us?"

Cole looked surprised at her choice of question, but he answered it willingly enough. "I don't know. It escalates things. It could be either one. Probably bad."

Senna put a hand to her forehead. "What was Jed doing?" she whispered, mostly to herself, although Cole certainly heard her.

He responded dramatically, throwing his hands over his head in a show of aggravation. "I would like to know that myself. Damn that man! He could have had better timing."

Senna shot Cole a withering glance. "Well maybe if he knew who you were, he would have asked your opinion."

"I notice he didn't ask yours."

Senna bit her lip. She hadn't spoken to Jed since the afternoon he told her he loved her. He might have been avoiding her, but the truth was, she'd made at least as much effort to avoid *him*. Somewhere in the confines of her stomach, a little knot of bitterness turned to guilt. "At least he got away," she said aloud to reassure herself.

Cole gave her a funny look. "Who told you he got away?"

Senna felt her pulse began to race. No one told her. She had assumed. Senna put both hands to her face and nervously massaged her cheeks. There were contingency plans in case any of Jed's people were ever captured. Senna knew them. She took a pair of deep breaths through her nose and emerged slowly from a cloud of panic. She realized Cole was still talking to her.

"I need you to find Rimick. Find out what went wrong and see if they have a plan in mind."

Senna nodded without really thinking. "You need to talk to Jed," she said, in as commanding a tone as she had ever managed.

Cole nodded grimly. He looked out of his depth. Senna could see the worry collected beneath his steady expression. "It's going to be okay, isn't it?" she asked, desperate for reassurance.

Cole avoided her eyes. "I need to talk to Hemmon too," he said. He left before Senna could question him further.

Hemmon took command of the Regent's party with an equanimity that felt premeditated. As the senior Counselour present, it was his right to do so. Cole was only disconcerted when he tried to extend that command to Geid Castle. Hemmon gave imperious orders to Captain Lodin and ensconced himself in Gote's room without permission.

It was obvious Hemmon intended to make a bid for Gote's place. He wouldn't do so without an expectation of success. Cole let Hemmon get away with it while he played host to the other guests. A few minor adjutants vied for attention over minor matters. Cole excused himself as soon as it was polite to do so.

A hunch led Cole to the east office, where he found Hemmon composing the messages that would convey this tragedy to the Mackabine court. The Counselour looked comfortable occupying Cole's desk, and he didn't bother to stand when Cole entered.

"Fenn, do come in. I need to speak with you." Hemmon casually put down the letter he had been working on.

"I suppose many individuals will be vying for the Regency now. Ambitious of you to get a head start."

"I admire your penchant for transparent insults," Hemmon said dryly. "One of your few redeemable qualities, Fenn. Did you know I had a conversation with Gote regarding you on our way here? Quite amusing. He was perturbed by the signs that your tenants put along the road to welcome us. *Gote the Goat* and *Go Jedomar!* Had you known about those?"

Cole swallowed. He had not.

"He made a handful of rash vows—said he was going to get rid of you if you didn't catch that Queensman by the time he was through here. If Gote had predicted the circumstances, he might not have been so eager."

Cole was off guard. The plan of attack he had prepared no longer seemed appropriate. He clenched his fists, trying to regain his mental footing. "Your authority is not as broad as you want it to be, Hemmon. The Gaultian Ambassador will select the next Regent."

Hemmon smiled like a man confident in his course. "Gote had outlived his usefulness, Lord Fenwith. To the country, to me, and especially to Gault. After that tomfoolery with the child queen, I was able to make an agreement with a few key officers.

"Did you know it was I who urged Gote to stage his public condemnation of Anwa? I knew it would make Gote even more hated than he was, which would leave the people happy to accept my leadership. The child's escape was not part of that plan. Nonetheless, it did move things along. I had a promise from Ambassador Jefrause that Gote would not be making the return journey from Banth." Hemmon could be lying, but something in his posture told Cole he was not. "As a matter of fact, your Q.M. saved me a bit of trouble. I should thank him, really."

"You've just told me you committed treason." Cole said. This shift in power was worse than he feared.

"Who are you going to tell, Fenwith? Nobody listens to you."

Cole could think of nothing else to say. Hemmon let him stew for a minute before continuing.

"Let us come to the point. I don't like you." Hemmon smiled again; he was obviously aware the feeling was mutual. "But as satisfying as it might be to hang you next to your Queensman, I've decided that executing the first Baron in my vicinity isn't the smoothest way to start my tenure. I've decided to give you another chance...unless you give me an excuse. Order in your county does seem to be hanging by a thread."

Cole realized it was time to retreat. His opponent was too strong. "You must have a lot of planning to do, Lord Hemmon," he said, poised to turn.

"About your Queensman, Fenn." Hemmon's tone ordered Cole to remain.

"I'll take care of him my way," Cole promised.

"I think not," Hemmon continued. "Your little cliff-tossing ceremony is no good. I need to take the man's head back to Mackabine."

Cole felt his stomach drop. He had foreseen this request. "I like my cliff-tossing ceremony."

"Yes, it's very nice," Hemmon mumbled, "but it doesn't leave me with a head, now does it?"

Cole tried to come up with a more reasonable objection. "It helps me control my tenants. They fear it."

"Your puny county is not a factor here. This Queensman murdered the appointed Regent of Mackabine. A crime of that caliber requires a public display. The skull will give me something to point blame at." Hemmon flicked a bit of congealed ink off his pen. "Unless you want me to put the blame on you instead."

Cole stood mutely, processing his defeat.

"Don't look so glum, Fenn. You do want to put on a show, don't you? The cliff isn't a good place for a public gathering. You should start your preparations in the square. I want it ready by tomorrow morning. I'll be leaving after the execution. For your sake, I expect a calm and orderly affair."

A cry drew Lodin's attention from the checklist he was confirming with Guardsman Rofus. His Guards were pooled in a huddle at one end of the courtyard, separating themselves from the new arrivals. He noticed some of them giving eyes to the cloudless sky. He asked the closet Guard what had happened.

"A crow turned around. Nothing to worry about."

Lodin scanned the sky and shivered. A crow changing course was an omen for dark times. Lodin nodded to smooth the worries of his men, but he knew better. That crow was sending a cold wind and a piece of death, and it was coming this way.

"You! Geid Captain."

Lodin turned around, angered at the disrespectful tone used by the Regent's Guard. He didn't like taking orders from these capital riffraff. Everything about the Regent's Guard annoyed him, from their formal speech to their arrogant manners to the gleam of their unused swords. "Yes?" he answered neutrally. He hadn't tried to tell the new Guards his name. He didn't think they would make the effort to remember it.

"We're going to need all of this space. You local Guards should try to bunk in town. You'll know where the best spots are."

Lodin thought it was a poor excuse to kick his men out of their lodgings. But he didn't have a better alternative. Castle quarters would barely house the forty men the Regent had brought with him. He gritted his teeth and agreed. "As you say, sir." Lodin already knew which room he would be demanding at the Ironfoot.

The rest of the Guard would be unhappy mingling in the town. The capture of Jedomar had sent the mood of Geid on a morose turn. Several townsfolk had come to the castle to ask about Jedomar. After the first few were arrested, they stopped coming, but the town's spirit was damaged. It would only get worse.

The Regent's Guard had barred the dungeon, and refused to let anyone from Geid inside, including Lodin. It would be interesting to see what sort of punishment got dished out to a man who slaughtered a Regent, even if it was a

Regent that no one particularly liked.

Lodin got a quick look at the Queensman when they brought him through. Jedomar was stoic, but defeated. No swagger or hope of rescue in his eyes. He would die well if they didn't torture him first. As long and hard as Lodin had worked to apprehend Jedomar, now that he was caught, Lodin felt rather sorry. He wasn't the one who captured the Queensman. There was no credit for himself or any of his men. To have the deed done by the Regent's Guard was merely annoying.

Lodin handed the checklist back to Rofus, trusting him to get it into the proper hands.

A pair of Guards tried to hide something hastily as Lodin passed them. He noticed a glint of metal catch the sunlight as Daggin closed his hand. "What's that?" demanded Lodin.

Guardsman Daggin tried to hide the trinket, but the Captain's notice could not be undone. Lodin put his hand out and motioned firmly. Daggin grudgingly parted with a small brass ring.

"It belonged to Jedomar," Patch interrupted. Daggin looked like he wanted to punch him.

"Small loss," Lodin said to his Guard. "It's cheap metal."

Daggin grunted.

Even if the ring had no real value, Lodin decided it might be worth something, considering it had belonged to the infamous Queensman. He tucked it within the confines of his cloak.

CHAPTER THIRTY

Jed felt the Baron's approach before he heard it. Floating, as he had been for hours, on the boundary between waking and sleeping, he sensed a presence and turned an ear towards the stairwell until it caught the deep reverb of boots against stone. A single pair. *Calump calump*. He didn't open his eyes until they stopped.

It was the face he least wanted to see in all the world. Jed remained unmoving so as not to rattle the chains that held him to the wall, and worked to keep his face free from expression. Jed had never been one for humility, but he wondered how much his face would betray by the time this was over.

The Baron was giving Jed an unusual stare. It was devoid of triumph and seemed to be looming on the verge of...sadness. Jed had made a habit of studying the Baron, but he decided this particular expression formed a new category.

"I don't even know what to say," said the Baron. He put a hand to his forehead in a show of frustration. "I had safeguards in place. And you—" Fenwith laughed painfully "—you manage to get caught with half the Mackabine Guard sleeping in my castle."

So far the Regent's Guards had not been kind, and Jed was alarmed to think that Fenwith's plans for torturing him were so intense that he felt inhibited by their presence.

"Sorry to spoil things for you," said Jed. He meant to be brave, but his sore jaw slowed his speech, and he was afraid he sounded pathetic.

Fenwith frowned. "You look terrible," he said.

Jed pulled his swollen lips into a taunting smile. "Really? I feel great."

"I'm sorry. The worst should be over, I think."

Jed couldn't tell if the Baron was mocking him or if he was trying to trick him into giving something away. The latter was pointless. The former was strangely effective.

"I don't suppose you have some magical plan of escape hidden in your sleeve?" The Baron glanced around as if seeking assistance from the walls of the dungeon.

"If you don't want me here, you could always let me go." Jed managed to keep most of the sarcasm out of his voice —just in case the Baron had *actually* lost his mind and was prone to suggestion.

"I will, if you ask me to."

The way he managed to say this with perfect sincerity chafed at Jed's innards. If he had a hand free, he would have punched the Baron sideways.

"I'm going to tell you everything," Fenwith said. "And when I'm done, you're going to tell me what to do."

Jed could tell him what to do with himself right now. Even so, he prepared to hear whatever tale the Baron was ready to spin for him. Fenwith began slowly, working his way into a story with such coolness and detail that Jed supposed he must have spent a long time preparing for it. Fenwith claimed to be secretly working with the Queen. It made about as much sense as a fly in a cup of beer. Jed wished Rimick and Hack were around to hear. It certainly showed more imagination than Jed ever gave the Baron credit for. Jed smothered his disbelief as long as he could, not wanting to interrupt the diversion.

Fenwith gave him a carefully restrained smile. "I can see you're skeptical."

"What do you think you're going to get out of this?

Torture would be more effective."

"And much more messy. I suppose I could threaten to throw you over the cliff into the Otherworld. But then you would just swim away to your underground pool." A twitch of fear seized Jed, and left him defenseless for the next words, which seeped out of the Baron's mouth like poison. "The one hollowed out beneath Mister Grath's house."

The Baron waved a hand as if to wipe the horror off of Jed's face. "Don't worry, Jedomar. I've known for years. That's why I chose that method of execution in the first place." Jed thought he was a liar, but he struggled to process as Fenwith went on. Each sentence the Baron spoke was more astonishing than the last. "You connect with the other Q.M. through Madam Gayna in Candige. You have meetings at the Carly house every Curse-Day, at a minimum. The major participants are Haw, Grath, Madam Jortha, Dohack, plus a few more. The innkeeper on occasion, and, oh—Senna, naturally. Shall I go on?"

It was the worst torment imaginable, to hear your worst enemy spill out all your secrets to your face. Reality realigned itself as Jed began to accept the significance of such knowledge.

Burning blessed Queen. It was true! The Baron was on their side! This was somehow so wonderful and so horrible at the same time that Jed felt he might suffer some kind of spasm. Another notion fell into place and Jed's lips cracked open before he could stop them. "Senna," he whispered.

"She knows," the Baron assured him. "She's known for over a year now. I use her to leak information to you. In return, she tells me where you're hiding so I can confidently send my Guard in the opposite direction."

"Damn her. Damn you, you bogsnatching skunk." Jed felt sick.

"Do you hate me more now than you did before?"

"It's not possible for me to hate you more than I did before. But I hate you *almost* as much." Jed twisted and pulled his chains out a few pitiful inches from the wall. "You used me. You played me for a fool."

Fenwith's jaw stiffened until he looked more like the old Baron, the familiar one, who was cold and stoic and revealed nothing. "That's not true," he said.

"I was your puppet and you sat in your castle, pulling my strings." Jed laughed bitterly. It wasn't funny, but he did want to laugh. He laughed and coughed at the same time. "I thought I was some kind of a hero."

"You are a hero, you fool," Fenwith told him. "Do you think I could have done this without you? It was your choice to do what you did. Nobody dropped into that bay was going to rescue themselves. I couldn't do it, and if you hadn't, they would have died. Your life is your own making, Jedomar."

Jed listened, but his thoughts were far away. They were full of a brown-haired woman, turning away while he reached for her hand. "Senna once called you Cole by accident," Jed murmured. "She brushed it over, pretended it was nothing. I didn't think much of it because the name didn't mean anything."

The Baron tilted his head at him. "Don't be too hard on Senna. She wanted to tell you. I made her swear an oath of secrecy. She asked many times for permission to tell you. I refused."

Jed didn't appreciate this explanation. All it meant was that Senna cared more for her oath to this man than she did for him. By the Queen, that stung.

"Do you love her?" Jed asked.

The Baron gave a start. It didn't appear to be a question he was expecting. But after a moment's hesitation, he responded that he did.

Jed wanted to be angry. It was another reason to hate this man—best one yet, in fact—but instead he felt the fight drain out of him. "Are going to marry her?" he asked, without the sarcastic venom he had intended.

Fenwith looked deeply uncomfortable. "I hope to, after Lady Anwa reclaims Mackabine."

The mention of the Queen rekindled Jed's concentration. "You're really in contact with Queen Anwa?"

The Baron nodded.

"Since when?" Jed asked.

"Since she was taken prisoner by the Regent."

Jed's eyes widened in sudden understanding. "You helped her escape."

Fenwith nodded again.

"You must be invaluable to her." There was a long silence. Jed closed his eyes. Trying not to regret his own tongue, he spoke quickly. "I should tell you: the new Regent will probably kill you if you let me go. He was talking about it earlier. He thinks you're an imbecile."

Fenwith winced. "I know. He told me too."

Jed was disgusted. An hour ago it wouldn't have bothered him in the least for his escape to trigger Fenwith's comeuppance. He would have called it the cat's luck. Now it prevented him from leaving.

The Baron shook his head. "Forget Hemmon. I'll go into hiding."

Jed thought an albino with his history was going to have a hard time finding a hiding place, but he decided not to mention it. "Who will rule Geid then?"

"Someone new."

Perhaps that would be a blow to Geid, perhaps not. Jed thought he and Rimick could handle it. "And the Queen?" he asked. "Is she depending on you?"

The Baron didn't answer immediately, but Jed could see that the answer was yes. "It's likely the revolt will take place anyway. My involvement doesn't guarantee victory or failure."

"You should stay."

Fenwith let out a long breath. "You're clever, Jed," he whispered. "Think of something!"

"What about the cliff?" Jed asked hopefully.

"It won't pass. Lord Hemmon wants to take your head back to Mackabine."

"You could just assassinate the new Regent," Jed suggested, conceiving of the obvious.

The Baron sighed. "That is an almost delightful option," he said. "However, losing two Regents in succession would destroy any possibility of my keeping the Baronship. The subsequent investigation would reveal more than I could afford, if not in fact my actual guilt."

"You think they would suspect you?"

"Oh, yes." Fenwith nodded. "The motive would even be apparent. Hemmon and I are known enemies."

"If he dislikes you, won't he just replace you?"

Fenwith shrugged. "He could, but the court might disapprove if he does so without cause."

Jed was too overwhelmed to come up with another suggestion. "I guess I shouldn't have killed the old Regent," he said.

Fenwith pinched his lips together. "I wasn't going to bring that up, but for all the Otherworld, Jedomar...why *did* you?"

Jed decided it was better to look mysterious than bone-headed. "I have my reasons," he answered shortly.

The Baron said nothing. He stared as if he expected something more. Jed wanted to shake the thick-headed Baron. What did he think he could do, change the Regent's mind? The Baron's eyes were focused on Jed. They were as empty and colorless as ever, but they conveyed an emotion that startled him. It was beyond pity or esteem; it was trust. With a start, Jed realized that what this man had told him in the beginning was true. He would do whatever Jed asked of him.

Jed nearly bit his tongue. He was afraid. Every time he evaded the Baron's Guards, he somehow believed that he was invincible. Danger was exhilarating, but the reality of death had never faced him the way it had today. Jed understood now how a person could give anything, betray anything, just to save his own skin.

Jed swallowed before he spoke. "I've spent my life trying to serve my Queen, and this is the best way to do that now. You have the power to do something no one else can. So that's your obligation. Serve the Queen. Forget about me."

The Baron looked at the floor. "With you gone—" he started.

"With me gone, Rimick will take over. Have no fear of that."

Fenwith held very still. He seemed to be studying the irregular patten of stones on the prison floor. "I think I would rather die than kill you," he whispered.

Jed laughed again. He couldn't help it. "You're a marvelous actor."

"I'm not acting!" The Baron jerked his head up.

"I know," Jed said. "At least, I think I do. I meant before. Either way—you acted then or you're acting now—you are a marvelous actor."

Fenwith smiled thinly, without amusement.

"It doesn't matter," Jed continued. "There are more important things at stake here than your conscience."

"There's your life," the Baron added weakly.

"I want to do this," Jed lied. He recalled the words of the witch doctor, foretelling the fate laid out for him: *Break the kindling, not light the fire.* Senna, Rimick...the Baron—they would finish what Jed started.

Fenwith finally nodded. "Your execution is scheduled for noon tomorrow. It will be a short hanging."

Jed repressed a shudder, though the sentence was more merciful than he expected.

"I probably won't see you again, so if there's anything you want...now's the time."

"You'd do something for me?"

"Anything."

"Make Senna happy."

The Baron gave a meaningful nod. He left without looking back.

CHAPTER THIRTY-ONE

Senna caught his eye as soon as Cole entered the main hall and tossed her shoulder at the kitchen to show that she wanted to speak with him. Cole ignored her. The Regent's attendants were fanned out like wolves, waiting to receive him. It was not a good time to cater to the whims of his serving girl.

Counselour Lallimus was the first to offer him a cup of wine. "Despite it all, Fenwith, I suppose congratulations are in order for catching your Queensman."

"They are," he murmured coolly, before downing the liquid in one gulp.

Lallimus raised an eyebrow to show his approval. "I've never seen you drink so freely, Fenn."

Cole pressed his lips into a thin, even smile. In his mind he referred to it as the wicked smile. It made him feel dirty. He hoped the wine made him drunk, and quickly. "I'm celebrating."

"Rebel tell you anything?"

Cole nodded. "He doesn't think so, but he did." He offered Lallimus his empty cup. The Counselour took it, choosing to ignore this overt sign of arrogance. "You have to know how the man's mind works. He thinks he's a martyr; he'd suffer anything just to spite you. But there are other ways of getting to the information."

"You must tell me, Fenn. You have me on the prick of a pin."

Cole shook his head mysteriously. "You can't have all my secrets, Lallimus. But don't worry, his Queensmen friends won't be far behind."

Lallimus nodded with a sniveling smile. The Counselour was dubious of such boasts. He had heard them all before. *Keep smiling, you insufferable prick,* Cole thought at him.

Senna walked out of the hall and back in several times, shooting angry looks in Cole's direction. It was starting to draw attention. Cole gritted his teeth and decided he should give in before her impertinence grew so obvious that he had to punish her publicly. He excused himself from the Counselour and felt the room watching him as he left. He could only pray Senna would have the good sense to look busy for a few moments before she followed him.

She didn't. He found her waiting in the larder.

Cole backed her up against the pantry doors and whispered furiously, "Senna, this is not a game."

The woman was unperturbed by his attitude. "You saw him," she said, almost as an accusation.

"Yes," he admitted grudgingly.

"What's the plan?" Her eyes shone with confidence. Brave little Senna.

"There is no plan."

The shine faded slightly. "What do you mean, there's no plan? What are you going to do?"

"Nothing. That's what I'm going to do."

The next few moments echoed heavy with silence. Senna looked as if her mind had wandered off and gotten lost. "I don't believe you," she said finally.

The words stung him, not because she was upset, but because she spoke them in earnest. Senna really didn't believe he would leave her friend to be sacrificed. Cole regarded her helplessly. She searched his expression for a long time, looking for some clue to validate her faith in him. But in the end, she read him too well.

Her voice trembled, betraying itself. "You can't, you wouldn't, you can't."

Senna's horror affected him more than his own. He took her arm to console her, but she broke away angrily. "No!" Rage made her face fluorescent. "I'll save him myself if you won't," she vowed.

He took her arm with a grip too strong for her to slip out of. "You will not," he whispered dangerously, "or I'll lock you in your room until tomorrow. This is his choice, Senna. You should give him the honor of respecting his decisions."

"You—you—you—" Failing to find an insult severe enough, she slapped him. The shock of it made him release her. "I don't love you," she swore. "I could never love you." Then she was gone.

In the dungeon corridor, a damp, cloying odor made Senna clear her throat. *Ahem.* A pause. *Ahem.*

"Excuse me," Senna called finally, when the Guard refused to acknowledge her. She held up the tray of cold meat and biscuits in her hands.

The Guard was bright enough to know it wasn't for him. He looked at Senna as if she were an imbecile. "The prisoner is in no condition to eat."

Senna sighed. "I think that's the point. The Baron doesn't want him to eat. He just wants him to see it."

The Guard still looked suspicious.

"Don't ask me to explain the Baron's sense of humor. Do you want me to go back and tell him you disapproved?"

The Guard rolled his eyes and moved to let her pass.

Jed flinched when he felt another set of footsteps descending to the dungeon. It had been several hours since any of the Guard had come to gawk at him. Jed didn't want to see who it was, and he pretended to be unconscious until the visitor put her hands around his neck. He recognized the smell of her. "Senna!" he said, full of sudden gladness. "Does Fenwith know you're here?"

Senna broke away, her eyes confused. "He said he told you."

"Told me what? About his damned commission to the Queen? Yes."

She put her hands against the sides of his head. "Did you believe him?"

"Had to. It's true, isn't it?"

"But you called him Fenwith."

Jed scoffed. "I don't really care what his name is."

"Oh." Senna buried herself in him and pressed her nose into his neck. Her softness melted some measure of his pain. Jed breathed her in, content to let this be the last pleasant moment of his life.

"No, he doesn't know," Senna said, answering a question that seemed to have come years before. "He...he's such a...I hate him!"

Jed felt slightly cheered by this sentiment. He laughed. "Good girl, Senna. I knew you were on my side."

Senna tightened her grip. "I'll get Rimick. We'll find a way to get you out of here."

Jed cracked an insincere smile for her benefit. "If I know Rimick, he is furious with me. You'd better leave him out of it. No, I mean it," he urged, interrupting the protest on her lips. "Stay out of this, Senna. Don't try to rescue me."

Senna gave him a wild-eyed stare that was far from acquiescence. Jed wasn't sure what more he could do to convince her.

The door above them moved ajar and released a clang

as it hit something solid in the doorway. A Guard's voice called churlishly into the dungeon, "What's going on down there?"

Senna loosened her grip on him. Jed didn't want her to go. There was so much he needed to say to her. He called her name, but she didn't answer. She moved urgently to obey the Guard's summons, taking the stairs two at a time.

When Jed spoke again, it was to an empty room. "Senna...goodbye."

Senna vanished rather suddenly from Geid Castle. Where she went, Cole was unable to determine. He made a few discreet inquiries, but did not trace her steps too closely, nor do anything to draw attention to her absence. The last thing he wanted was to provoke a search for his housekeeper on the eve before she was likely to do something stupid. The rest of the temporary staff fell into a turmoil that was obviously painful, and strangely silent. Somehow they managed to keep the affairs of the castle from crashing like a felled tree.

The day passed in stagnant agony. Cole placed himself on automatic, aware of the necessity to appear unmoved. He awkwardly facilitated the order of the servants, and spoke foolish platitudes to the Counselours. Inside he felt like he was being crushed by the weight of several oceans. He had to remind himself occasionally to breathe.

When evening came, Cole was eager to retreat to the solace of his room. But there was no repose in silence. It left nothing to distract him from his thoughts. Cole wound himself into a ball on the farthest corner of the floor, determined, by some kind of perverseness, to make himself as uncomfortable as possible.

There was no one in the world who Cole respected

more than Jedomar. He had always regarded the Queensman as a sort of secret partner. To him, the fact that Jed was unaware of their partnership was part of the fun. But that had only been an artful illusion. Cole was not surprised to learn that Jed did not see it this way.

What tortured Cole most was the knowledge that he could *still* act, if he chose to. The scenario played out wonderfully in his head. He would go downstairs and order the Guard off. Jedomar would vanish into the forest and have a good laugh. The Fenwith character would balk and then mysteriously disappear. In his generous fantasies, Cole even allowed himself the privilege of escape.

It was the right thing to do, he was certain. A good man would make this choice, and damn the consequences. A few weeks later, when the King of Gault gave his summons, and there was no one to deliver intelligence to the Queen, Cole did not think he would even feel bad. He would have done his part. The Gaults might rule another ten years, but eventually politics would swing again. Wars came and went and people died by the thousands no matter who was in charge. Who said he had to be the one to alter history?

But the judicious part of Cole believed that Anwa of Mackabine would soften death tolls. If he traded one life for a thousand, that made sense, didn't it? By sheer mathematics?

I am not a good man, decided Cole. *I'm a calculating man.* It was not complimentary, but it was so. He stayed in his room until morning.

CHAPTER THIRTY-TWO

Morning came no earlier than usual, but the lethargy of the castle made its arrival seem ill-timed. Mackabine attendants were used to late hours.

"Gote would have let us sleep in," one of the adjutants murmured as he straggled into the dining room. There were polite chuckles around the table. Hemmon continued to take his meals in private, which felt like a demonstration of authority.

The kitchen staff put forth a heroic effort for breakfast, filling the dining room with a variety of foodstuffs. Cole thought for a minute that Senna must have slipped back into duty, and he asked one of the maids as she brought out a basket of rolls, "Where's Senna?" The fearful look on her face told him she didn't know, so he cut her off before she could answer. "Never mind, just bring me some water."

"Yes, Lord."

He turned his attention back to his breakfast companions.

"Senna? Is that your housekeeper?" Counselour Lallimus felt compelled to comment. "Pretty little thing. You're fond of her, aren't you, Fenn?"

Cole shrugged. "She's a good cook. Why? Do you want her? Two weeks taxes and she's yours."

Lallimus laughed at the ridiculous price and turned to

hear Mister Ingaro describe the cuisine of some cook he'd encountered in the south of Gault.

It was within character for Cole to ignore most of their conversation. He grabbed one of the rolls off the table and excused himself to check on the Guards' arrangements.

The courtyard had ceased to thrive without the tender care of its steward. Naked dirt made the yard look bare despite the number of Guards. The sense of desolation felt appropriate. Cole found Lodin standing near the dungeon entrance, rolling a piece of metal around his fingertips.

"Lodin," Cole called, startling the Captain into dropping whatever he was holding. Cole didn't have the energy to reprimand him. He waited until Lodin recovered his trinket from the ground and made his perfunctory bow. "What's going on?"

"Nothing, Lord. Everything is under control."

"Tell me the situation, in your own words."

Lodin compensated for his discomfort by looking down. "The prisoner is secure. The square has been cleared of vendors, and the platform is being set up now. We had to scare some people away from the site. The town is a little on edge."

"Don't let the town get riled up. I want every Guard in the square today. No one takes the day off, understand? The Regent's Guards will do as they like. Let them stay in charge of the prisoner, but—what is that?"

Cole pointed to Lodin's fist, still fidgeting with something.

Lodin hesitated before revealing his palm. "Nothing, Lord. It's just a ring."

"It's Jedomar's ring," Cole clarified.

Lodin swallowed dolefully as Cole motioned for the ring, like a child who'd been asked to surrender his favorite toy.

Cole felt his patience with Lodin wearing thin. It wasn't always useful to have a sulking simpleton for a Captain. "Nothing can go wrong today, Lodin." The words would have been less painful if he hadn't meant them.

"Yes, Lord."

"*Yes, Lord,*" Cole mimicked Lodin's rote response. "I'd expect the same answer from you if I asked you to walk barefoot across the sea. Don't say it if you can't do it."

"Yes, Lord. Nothing will go wrong. You can count on it."

The Captain took off with some eagerness as Cole dismissed him. Cole took a bite of the roll in his hand, but the bread felt like wool in his mouth. He spit it out onto the ground.

A few spans away, a Guard was staring at him. Cole didn't know him. One of Gote's. Hemmon's. Whatever. Cole acted on a vindictive urge, and threw the remainder of his roll at the Guard's head. He wasn't a very good shot. The roll bounced painlessly against the Guard's chest. It was enough to shame the man into bowing away.

Cole felt astonished at his own temper. *Well,* he thought, *at least that was in character.*

A troupe of discontented citizens lined the edge of the road and watched the execution procession advance. Rimick stood fast in the midst of them, arms linked with two others who seemed to draw on him for comfort. Rimick had hoped there would be fewer Guards escorting Jed to the square. But apparently they decided to err on the side of preparedness. Every one of the Regent's Guards was standing to march with their prisoner, and most of the county Guards were poised to follow. The rest were already in the square, making final preparations.

The people nearest Rimick shuffled in trepidation as the procession came into close range. Some of the crowd was there at his request; others merely because they couldn't

313

restrain their curiosity. Rimick stood out no more than any other man along the road, but Jed's searching gaze discovered him soon enough. They communicated briefly with their eyes. Rimick sensed Jed's apology, but Rimick had no message to convey other than determination.

The booing began promptly.

"Shame!"

"Go home, Mackabine Guards!"

The Mackabine Guards didn't tolerate this sort of confrontation the way the Geid Guards would have. The formation drew their spears and advanced towards the crowd.

Without looking, Rimick signaled to Grath, and felt the weight of a drenched cloth pass into his hand. A trickle of alcohol dripped down the length of his finger. He quickly wrapped the cloth around a branch and lit it on fire. The rush of heat was instantaneous. Rimick turned his face away and launched the torch at the approaching Guards.

The distraction worked as intended. People screamed and trampled off in unexpected directions. The line of Guards faltered. Some went after the fire, a few more after the fleeing crowd. For a few seconds there was only one Guard holding onto Jed's arm.

Now, thought Rimick, willing Jed to take the shot. *Go on, hit him!*

The odds weren't good. They were unarmed and outnumbered, even if you counted the men in the mob who might have helped them. This momentary burst of chaos was still the best chance Jed would get. Except Jed wouldn't take it; he held his ground. The only clue he gave Rimick was a slight shake of his head.

The moment passed. The fiery wad was stamped out. Guards regrouped. Rimick stepped back and let himself be swallowed by the crowd.

❖

It was a warm day for an execution. One of those rare, midsummer spurts when the sun shone straight and hot into Geid. Cole donned a cloak to shield himself from the glare, despite the heat an extra layer would add.

"The dais is this way, Lord Fenwith."

Cole turned to see who had addressed him. The sunlight accosted his eyes painfully. He put a hand between his face and the speaker.

"What's wrong, Fenn? Are you blind?" It sounded like Counselour Lallimus.

"Merely incommoded," he drawled.

He managed to get onto the dais, where a cloth had been draped to shade them from the sun. From there Cole was able to survey the scene below.

The square was hardly recognizable, gutted except for the platform temporarily erected across from them. The stage was already fitted ominously with a noose. An unnatural silence filled the air, despite the sizable number of people. Every soul in Geid had come to witness the execution of their hero. They crammed into the square, spilling over each other like too many chickens shoved into a henhouse. There should have been shouting and jeering and arguing, but instead there were solemn whispers. The people of Geid didn't care that Lord Gote was dead. All that concerned them was the fate of Jedomar. Cole noticed several tenants attempting not to cry, and some were not succeeding very well, even though the Guard had threatened to remove anyone who showed sympathy for the criminal.

Cole settled into the central chair that had been reserved for him. He considered yielding it to Lord Hemmon, but that was showing more submission than was probably good for him. This was still his county.

"There's nothing like a good short hanging, is there?" the adjutant next to him opted to say.

Cole made a gesture of agreement. Many times since

taking the role of Fenwith, Cole had been forced to put his behavior at odds with his feelings. Now more than ever, he felt the benefit of several years' practice.

Short referred to the length of rope that was used, not to the time involved. A long hanging was over very quickly because the victim's neck snapped on the way down. But short hangings were arduous, and could take hours, depending on the strength of the victim. Death by suffocation. Cole had seen it before. It was not pleasant, and he definitely didn't want to see it now.

From his seat in the corner, Counselour Lallimus made a noise of disgust. "What is it about an execution that gets everyone riled up? It's so gruesome."

Lallimus glanced sideways at Cole, forcing him to add an opinion. "You misspeak, Counselour. Death is the only natural part of our existence."

The adjutant on the other side of him laughed. "What would you do, Lallimus? Let the criminal go free?"

"Of course not," Lallimus said. "That Queensman is stirring up trouble that will no doubt continue until he is dead. I just don't want to watch it happen."

Lord Hemmon arrived. He climbed the steps of the dais rather daintily, holding the length of a decorative cloak in a formal pose at his side. He was fragile-looking for so venomous a man. Hemmon settled contentedly into a seat at Cole's right hand and waved for a manservant, who brought them each a basin of water and a towel.

Cole relinquished to Hemmon the honor of presiding over the execution. However, Hemmon found it beneath him to address the crowd personally and directed the Head Guard to do it for him. The Guard made a formal presentation of Lord Hemmon as the new Regent. Hemmon didn't have the humility to wait until the court resubmitted the title. Cole wished that Jed's shot had hit Lord Hemmon in the face instead of Gote. That might have been more useful.

Hemmon's Guard gave a small speech about justice and punishment. Any person who resisted Mackabine law would meet the same fate as Mister Jedomar, and so forth. Cole doubted his tenants would find it convincing.

The last of the noise halted when Jedomar was led out. The Queensman held his head up. Jedomar looked over the crowd carefully, perhaps searching for faces he knew. Eventually, he met Cole's eyes and nodded. It was a deliberate enough gesture that the audience took note of it, although no doubt they interpreted it differently. The Guard led Jedomar up the platform and turned him towards the crowd. There was a ghost of a smile on his face, as if he were taunting death, or life, or those fools on the dais who condemned him.

Hemmon voiced his observations to Cole. "I don't think you did a very good job of breaking that man. At least your tenants seem appropriately subdued. Perhaps you can keep them that way now."

There were several placatory responses to this, but Cole was unable to summon the strength to voice any of them. He prayed for a miracle to halt the proceedings. A storm, an army, an invasion from the Otherworld—none of these seemed likely.

Another of the Regent's Guard, designated a hangman for the next few minutes, slipped the rope over Jedomar's neck and tightened it. Cole was unable to stall his duty any longer. He sauntered slowly to the head of the dais. Eyes shifted from the platform to him until Cole felt the gaze of everyone present. He had the feeling he would go down in history as the man who had murdered Jedomar. It was the worst legacy he could possibly imagine. Jedomar would be remembered as a great hero and a martyr. Cole would have given anything to change places with him.

Cole raised his arm at a right angle. Prisoners were not supposed to speak, but Jedomar did not let that stop him. He watched Cole's gesture and timed it well. As Cole dropped his hand, the hangman withdrew the block, but not before Jedomar had screamed his last words with pride. "Long live Queen Anwa!"

Pandemonium ensued. Spectators rose to their feet,

echoing the mantra. "Queen Anwa!" they shouted. "Long live the Queen!"

Cole would reflect later that Jed's outburst came from good intentions. He thought it would invigorate the townsfolk. He may not have thought through the other consequences.

A man near the front tried to climb on top of the platform, kicking through the line of Guards at the bottom. They pulled him down to push him back into the crowd, but as more people threatened to swarm them, the Guards drew their swords. One swipe of metal and the man fell down, his hands spread over the gash in his chest. Children screamed. People scattered. Hemmon stood up and joined him at the head of the dais.

"Stop this!" Cole yelled futilely. He gripped the rail to steady himself. But there was no way to prevent the frenetic riot that unfolded. The townsfolk surged against the platform in one quick, violent wave. They stood no chance. The Regent's Guards outnumbered his own threefold, and their combined strength was quite effective against a smattering of untrained tenants. Cole watched in dismay as they took off the head of a young man who tried to flee the scene.

It was over in a few seconds. Fear reasserted its hold over the townsfolk. They surrendered as quickly as the Guards would let them.

Hemmon chuckled next to him. "Not a bad show."

"Yes," Cole managed, his voice thick with irony. A measure of shock spared him from immediate emotion.

The square was one great communal moan. Tenants held their hands over their heads, wailing in grief. Mothers, sons, and wives mourned the loss of the insurgent dead.

Above them, Jedomar's body kicked convulsively, until it very slowly weakened and stopped.

CHAPTER THIRTY-THREE

Senna did not come back.

Hemmon and his troupe of attendants brushed out of Geid as quickly as they came in, leaving in their wake worn floors and a few rooms of used linens. Their brief presence left a lasting mark on the town of Geid. Lodin reported the extent of the damage done in the square. A few Guards were bruised up. Nothing serious. At least four tenants had been killed, and several more were grievously wounded. More blood on Cole's hands. If not on his hands, at least seeping out from under his shadow. There was no sign of Rimick or anyone else eager for vengeance at the loss of Jedomar. The town was quiet and more law-abiding than usual.

Cole expected Senna as soon as the last wagons rolled away, but she didn't present herself at dinner. Nor was she there the next morning. A day passed, and another, with no sign of the castle's housekeeper. Cole fell into a deep depression. He stood for hours at the upstairs hall window, staring at the road below, waiting for her figure to stride over the hill.

It had to be obvious to the staff and the Guard that Senna was missing, but as Cole ignored the subject, no one was anxious to bring it up in his presence. He wandered aimlessly through the castle, neglecting his business, speaking to no one, and second-guessing himself constantly. Nothing made sense. Nothing was right anymore. He had five years of morally ambiguous decisions weighing him down. Jedomar was only the last and most brutal of them. Perhaps he should not have asked Jedomar for his opinion. If Cole left him ignorant, the Queensman would not have hesitated to escape. Then again, perhaps Senna was right all along: he should have told Jedomar the truth ages ago.

The last thing Cole tried to think about was Senna. His mind was eager to invent a dozen reasons for her disappearance—the least of which was merely that she hated him and didn't want to see him again. He didn't like to imagine that she had been kidnapped, or eaten by wolves, or been so distraught by Jedomar's death that she threw herself off the cliff into the ocean.

On the third morning of silence, Cole caught a glimpse of himself in his dressing mirror. The reflection drew his attention and he stepped up to it. To his consternation, he no longer saw himself. He saw what everyone else saw when they looked at him. Fenwith looked sick, angry, and ill-natured. He had dark circles under his eyes that showed how little he had been sleeping.

I am not you.

The image stuck his lip out and trembled with disgust. Fenwith hated him as much as Cole hated him back.

You created me, remember?

Cole remembered. It had seemed like such an achievement at the time. He'd spent hours in front of this mirror, practicing lines, crafting a persona that would fit the image of a spoiled, antisocial young man. He thought he could slip in and out of character at will. It worked at first. Somewhere along the line, things had gotten blurred. Sometimes Cole couldn't remember when he was being Fenwith and when he was being himself. It was bound to happen. It wasn't healthy being someone else most of the time.

I don't want you anymore, Cole told the reflection. *Go away!*

You still need me.

Cole was past caring about that. *I said go!*

Fenwith shook his head and smiled the wicked smile. *You can't get rid of me, silly. I'm more you now than you are.*

Cole picked up a chair, the only solid object in the room, and rammed it seat first into the glass. The mirror shattered into a thousand flashing slivers. They showered onto his skin and clothing before raining down to the floor. Cole dropped the chair and stared bewildered at the pieces, trying to decide how much of his mind he had lost.

Senna had been alone a long time. She sat on the great old stump, a monument in the middle of the forest, easily located by those who knew it. She and Jed used to play here as children: hide-and-seek and round-the-run. She was taller now —the stump was much easier to climb. She dug her fingers into the familiar knots. Any tears Senna had come to shed were long since spent. She huddled quietly, oblivious to the sounds of the forest or the dampness of the wood beneath her.

Jed's death she had witnessed from an obscure corner of the square, wrapped in a cloak to avoid recognition. Since then, she had spurned human contact, wandering from place to place, and even sleeping outside a couple of times—an impossible feat in winter, but in the heart of summer, only deeply uncomfortable. Her backside bore the marks of scratchy moss. It would be nice, she mused, to return to the rickety bed that awaited her at Geid Castle.

Rimick's voice unexpectedly broke through the barrier of her mind. She hadn't seen him arrive.

"Are you all right?" he asked.

Senna didn't respond, but her expression must have answered in the negative. Rimick wasn't very adept in the role of comforter. He probably had little enough sense how to comfort himself. Still, she gave him some credit for trying.

Rimick tried again, "Senna, you should think about what Jed would want."

The implication was that Jed would not want her to mope unproductively upon a tree stump. The truth of it hardly moved her.

"Are you going to retake your post at the castle?" Rimick prompted.

Her face flushed, conveying emotion her tongue did not. Senna should have realized sooner. Rimick didn't care about her. His only motive was to secure her talents for his later use. Senna gave him the only answer he was going to get. "Rimick, get away from me before I bite your nose off."

She was too far away for that, but Rimick decided to take her malice at face value. "All right, Senna, you know where I am if you need me."

Rimick left.

The damage he had done remained, however. Her spell of isolation was broken. Senna craved the company of someone who loved her. She sighed in a mixture of relief and defeat. With Jed gone, there was only one person who still fit that criterion.

Senna knew the Baron was in the east hall from the glow of the fire within. He had his back to the door and didn't see her come in. She called his name once. He jerked as if he had heard a ghost. She tiptoed farther inside.

"I'm sorry," Senna began. "I didn't mean to be gone so long. I had some things to figure out. I'm better now."

"Senna," Cole said again, quite hoarsely.

By the Queen, it was good to see him. He looked as if he had missed her quite a bit. She shouldn't have left without any word. At first it had seemed a just punishment, but now she just felt sorry. She tried to take one of his hands, and noticed they were covered in thin red marks. Senna gasped. "What happened to your hands?" She picked one up, examining the tiny wounds. Cole pulled it back in embarrassment. She hastily seized the other, held it under her face, and stroked it pityingly.

"I got in a fight with my mirror," he said.

"Who won?"

He huffed a little. "I'm not sure, but I don't think it was me." Cole looked like he badly wanted to say something else. He spoke very slowly, tripping over the words. "Senna, I...do not...know what to...I'm sorry—"

"Don't. Let's not apologize anymore." She gently opened his palm and pressed it to her cheek.

He closed his eyes and fell silent. His fingers were warm on her face and she liked the feel of them. Cole was not nearly so cold as he looked.

"Senna," he said, "if it's possible, I want to win you back."

She slid effortlessly into Cole's embrace. "You never lost me," she said. She felt him shudder in relief. They held each other in silence until Senna summoned something to say.

"Lodin tried to pick a fight with me on my way in here. I told him I was back from 'personal leave.'"

"Good. I'll tell him I gave it to you."

She smiled, and assembled the nerve to ask her next question. "Cole? If Jed had asked you to help him, would you have?"

Cole pulled back from her. He looked offended. "Of course, yes. By the Queen, I wish he had."

Senna had thought as much, but hearing him say it was a healing stroke for her. She forgave him, and released her hold on Jed in the same moment. "Poor Jed," she murmured. "I think the idea of martyrdom must have appealed to him. He wanted to meet the Otherworld on the grandest terms— with everybody watching." A sense of urgency overtook her

323

and she pulled on Cole's shirt, pulling his body against hers. "Don't die on me, Cole. I couldn't take it. Will you promise?"

Cole didn't seem to want to answer her. He was too literal-minded.

"Just say it," she insisted. "It doesn't matter what happens, say it anyway."

He did promise. Although his tone of voice was not very reassuring.

CHAPTER THIRTY-FOUR

Guardsman Falk splashed water over his face and patted it dry with a towel. Then he picked up his breakfast dish and wiped it down with the same cloth. The towel was so dirty it smeared filth around the rim. He studied it a moment, wondering if it had been that way before he used it on his face. Grunting, he threw the towel into a corner in the hope that someone would wash it later. The bowl he refilled with grain and carried into the back room.

Falk was a Regent's Guardsman of the first order. The title had lost some of its stigma in the past week. Lord Gote had always been something of a boor, but the new Regent was accomplished and sophisticated. Lord Hemmon intended to mollify the people through good deeds. His first speech to the people of Mackabine had been a call for decency. He ordered the Guards to treat citizens of Mackabine with respect. He had even recalled some of the mining teams from Pannerack, diverting them from silver excavations back to farming. Guardsman Falk was impressed by the stratagem. The people might cease to rebel against a government that wished them well. The idea depressed Falk. What a waste of a good revolution that would be!

The door to the back room was old and poorly hung. Falk had to use all the force of his weight to open it. The door screeched in complaint, grating against the floor on one side.

In the everyday commotion of a busy warehouse, it was unlikely anyone concerned themselves with the noise. Even so, Falk was careful to latch the hook behind him.

The Queensman in the back room was awake and alert. He had been unconscious, or near to it, the last time Falk checked on him. It was a miracle the man had survived these long days of deprivation and confinement. Still, the fellow's demeanor left much to be desired. He studied Falk with an expression of unmitigated gloom.

"Snap up," Falk suggested. "By the Queen, good fellow. You look as if you were going to be hanged." He slammed the bowl down and laughed at his own joke.

The man called Jedomar raised his head uncertainly toward Falk. He blinked a few times, trying to bring his eyes into focus. "What do you want with me? Who are you?"

Falk wondered how much memory he had of their first meeting, when Falk had stuffed his half-expired body into one of the late Regent's luggage chests. "My name is Falk. I'm a Guard to the Regent. Although perhaps not for much longer. I heard Lord Hemmon intends to replace us with his own Guards." He admitted this last part regretfully.

The Queensman stared at him. "Did you save my life?"

"That depends. Are you alive?"

Jedomar considered the question with far more solemnity than it deserved. "I think so," he said.

"I must have done, then," said Falk.

It had not been a sure thing. Hanging a man was a delicate process, and the margin for error was broad. Falk knew of cases where a hanged man was presumed dead and then reanimated hours later. Falk thought it might be possible to engineer the results deliberately, and so he experimented, cutting the Queensman down a little early. It was a risky scheme. If anyone had checked the body after Falk declared him dead, they could have hung together the next day. But that had not happened. Instead he smuggled Jedomar to Mackabine in the back of Lord Hemmon's wagon.

Falk started to describe this process to Jedomar, but he stopped when the Q.M. broke eye contact and resorted to examining the floor. The Queensman looked very well thrashed.

Falk had expected more panache from the slayer of Regent Gote. He felt some respect for this Queensman. Not because he had killed Gote, but because he was held in such high regard by the town of Geid. The man must have done good there to merit such devotion.

"Where am I now?" Jedomar asked.

"This is Mackabine. The city herself. You're in a warehouse that services the Regent's castle."

The Queensman smiled with weak irony. "Always wanted to visit Mackabine."

"You'll get that chance soon enough. For now, let's talk strategy."

"Strategy?"

"For your rebellion, right?" Ever since Guardsman Falk learned of Lady Anwa's survival, he had been aching to join the cause of the Queensmen that followed her. Until now, he lacked only opportunity. Jedomar was Falk's ticket into the Q.M.

Jedomar gazed blankly in contradiction.

"You don't trust me yet?" Falk asked, only slightly disappointed. Queensmen were known to be suspicious fellows.

Jedomar frowned. "There's no rebellion. At least, none that involves me."

There's got to be, Falk thought. He couldn't bear to be wrong. "Why not? Everyone knows the Q.M. are planning something. And you're a Queensman. Most famous one of them all, after last week."

Jedomar blinked and rubbed his temples. He spoke as if no one were listening. "I'm not supposed to be here."

Falk tried to be mellow as he laughed his agreement, but the Queensman's obstinacy was starting to get to him. He began to fear he'd made an error in judgment. "Where are you supposed to be?"

"I didn't ask for your help," the Queensman murmured.

That was a fine piece of ingratitude, if Falk ever heard one. "Look here," Falk started.

"No, you look!" Jedomar interrupted. "I'm not a Queensman. I mean I was, but—I don't know anything, all right? I can't help you, and I wouldn't bother."

Falk was aghast. His temper threatened to manifest itself as a slug to Jedomar's nose. He kept it in, but only just. Did Mister Jedomar think it was easy, dragging his inert body across three counties? Falk wondered if it was feasible to change the man's mind, or how much effort it would be. "Will you at least introduce me to Lady Anwa?" Falk begged.

Jedomar laughed as if he'd made a bad joke. "Did you not hear what I said? I couldn't find Lady Anwa if I were the last Queensman in Mackabine. I'm useless to you! Leave me alone."

Exasperated, Falk took a breath. He had no taste for keeping a hostile and despondent Queensman. "In that case, you'll have to leave," he said.

This seemed to be the attitude Jedomar was looking for. He calmed down as Falk helped him to his feet. Falk gave him a common Guard's uniform. It was the only spare garment available. It would serve as practical camouflage until the man found something better. The uniform had a high collar, which would hide the hideous bruise around his neck. The black eye and roughened face would pass as tokens of a brawl, but the rope mark could only be recognized for what it was. Jedomar quickly ate the bowl of grain after he donned the new clothes.

The man was silent as Falk led him through the warehouse to the closest exit. Before going, he gave Falk a belatedly apologetic look. "I don't think we Queensmen are as organized as you seem to assume."

Falk sighed. He was about to let the most famous Q.M. in Mackabine walk out of his sight, and there wasn't a thing he could do about it. "How disappointing. Good luck to you, Mister Jedomar, Queensman or no."

Jed was not pleased to have cheated death. You could cheat at cards, you could cheat your taxes, but you ought not cheat fate. The Otherworld would be offended. Would it deign to take Jed a second time? Was his spirit doomed to wander as an outcast?

Jed glanced behind, startled by a gust of wind. No ghostly spirits followed his trail. A line of schoolchildren giggled as they passed on the left. A man ran too quickly from behind a stand and nudged his shoulder against Jed's. "Pardon me, sir," the man bowed as he scurried out of Jed's way.

Jed felt distracted and light-headed. Even fascination for his new environment was barely enough to keep him from lying down in exhaustion. He couldn't stop seeing the faces of the people in Geid square. How many died because of him? Some, at least. Maybe more than some. He hadn't really seen most of it.

Jed explored the streets of Mackabine city in a sort of baffled stupor. He was in the heart of the capital, a few hundred spans from Mackabine Castle. He could see its spires towering in the distance over the outer walls. It was the largest building Jed had ever seen, more like a mountain than a thing built by men.

The folk around him were intent on their business. They passed one another with indifference and occasional nods of meeting. It could have been like walking through the marketplace after harvest—but only if Geid market was twelve times as large, smelled of strange perfumes, and was full of people he didn't know.

Searching the faces, Jed saw one that roused his sensibility. It was the old witch doctor, the same one he had communed with in Geid on a calm autumn day. Jed recognized his bone necklace. Fate had not abandoned him!

The wizened man was sitting on the edge of a platform, as solitary and mystical as the first time Jed saw him. Jed almost tripped over his own feet with his urgency to reach the old man. The witch doctor yelped as Jed stirred the dust that he was using to sort a cup of beans.

"Forgive me, wise one." Jed knelt down to gather the scattered beans. "I didn't mean to startle you. I seek your counsel."

The witch doctor still seemed upset by his greeting. He looked Jed up and down with distrust. "You want wisdom?" he grunted. "Make a contribution."

"What? I don't—" Jed's hand moved automatically to his pockets, and he was surprised to find a smattering of coins collected there. The Regent's Guard must have left them as a gift. Feeling foolish, Jed selected the largest denomination of coin and offered it to the old man.

After verifying its authenticity, the witch doctor relaxed. His face settled into a serene smile. "What mysteries do you face, young man?"

Jed was caught off guard again as he realized that the witch doctor did not remember him. It was possible the witch doctor was not fully aware of the spiritual powers that guided him.

"I don't understand what's happened," said Jed. "Or what I should do now."

The old man gave him a subtle smile. "There is a time for doing something new, and a time for doing what you have always done."

What did that mean? Jed stared with a wrinkled brow until the witch doctor decided to try again.

"You seek revenge against those who have hurt you," he said.

That didn't feel right. Who would he take revenge against? The Guard who had helped him? Jed touched his bruised face, worried that his appearance might have confused

330

the witch doctor. "Tell me what fate wants me to do," said Jed. "No conundrums, just instructions. You have my promise I'll obey, no matter how drastic it seems."

The old man hesitated a while before speaking again. "If you must take action, then drastic action may be taken. Request a transfer from your Captain. Take up your post in a new city. Only then will you find the answers you require."

Jed felt like he had tried to run through a wall. His head physically hurt from the impact. Jed wasn't really a Guard; he was just dressed like one. But the witch doctor didn't know that. The witch doctor didn't know anything, except how to spout riddles in exchange for money.

I can't cheat fate, Jed realized, *I make my own fate.*

Jed let loose a sigh, and was surprised to find it more full of more relief than disappointment. The universe flipped itself upside down, and then came out all right again on the other side. "Thank you," he told the witch doctor, half sincerely.

The old man gave a sagely nod as he waved away another satisfied customer.

Guardsman Falk rested a wet clump of clay on his forehead and tried to recite the calming chant his witch doctor had recommended. The clay was doing nothing for his headache, and the chant only reminded him how frustrated he was. *Good things come to those who plan.* Not necessarily, he thought. Falk leveled his head back, one leg propped up against a table.

Just when a sense of relaxation was starting to descend, the back room door shuddered open with a thunk. Falk's leg dropped abruptly, offsetting his balance until he lowered both feet to the floor. His forehead clay dislodged with a slurk, trailing down his nose before it squished to the floor.

"You again!" Falk barked at the sudden intruder. "Back so soon?"

Queensman Jedomar was hardly the same man who had left him an hour ago. Propelled by some bottled-up energy, he burst over the table before Falk could finish standing up to greet him. "Falk! You want to be a Queensman, don't you?"

Falk gripped Jedomar by the arm. "Not so loud," he whispered.

"Sorry." The foolish Queensman grinned wildly, not looking reproached at all.

"What happened to you?" Falk asked, mistrustful of the Q.M.'s incredible change of mood. Falk's headache returned suddenly.

Jedomar made a couple attempts to explain. Something about dying too many times and finding his destiny. At the end of it, Falk still had no sense of the man's logic. But he did understand that Jedomar was ready to join him in the Queen's cause. That was good news. Falk hoped.

Jed sat down at the table and helped himself to another bowl of grain while Falk sealed the door behind them. The Queensman opened a dialogue in between eager bites of grain, and outlined what he described as their options. Falk listened for a few minutes until he realized that his goal of joining the Queensmen was no closer to being realized. Jedomar had not understated his usefulness.

"The Mackabine Q.M. won't recognize me," said Jed. "I've never been here before."

Falk felt his hope drain. He should have realized this. Anyone could claim to be Jedomar raised from the dead, but the Q.M. would have to be pretty stupid to believe it, wouldn't they? What a joke.

"They have to be recruiting. They must need people," Falk contended.

Jed raised his hands in apology. "If I was recruiting for the Queen, the last place I would look would be in the

Regent's Guard," he admitted.

Falk swore angrily. Being a Guard used to be an honorable position. Taking an oath in the Regent's Guard seemed a logical thing after the Gault Revolution. Queen Benta was dead. Who else could be said to be the rightful ruler of Mackabine?

However, once he learned of Lady Anwa, Falk felt his service must revert instantly back to her. It puzzled Falk why people didn't rise up and instate Anwa that very day. Wasn't it obvious she was their Queen? Were they not Mackabines?

"I do have some pass codes used by the Q.M.," Jedomar offered. "We could distribute letters, and hope one gets into the right hands."

They wrote a few letters, on the spot, until Falk's pen ran low on ink. He folded them into the deepest pocket of his cloak. Despite the disappointing circumstances, it felt good to finally have an accomplice.

CHAPTER THIRTY-FIVE

Cole sat at his desk for the last time, sorting a stack of reports he was glad he would never see again. It was his last chance to set his credit book in order. He was taking the responsibility seriously, even if it meant the normally neat area looked like a flock of birds pecked through it.

Senna tutted in mock disapproval from the doorway. "I'm not picking this up," she said. She tiptoed through the mess of paper on the floor and handed Cole another letter for the stack.

It was a report from Lodin on the disappearance of Guardsman Rofus, recommending he send out a notice of desertion. Cole saw no point. Rofus was out of his hands one way or the other. None of Geid's problems would be his for very much longer.

"I want to go with you," said Senna.

Cole gave her a glance that he hoped would dampen expectations. "You would be in the way," he said. It was true; he didn't need another distraction.

Senna hefted the saddle bag from upstairs onto the desk. "I can't sit here and do nothing!" she exclaimed.

Cole critically examined the bag's bulging form. "When you offered to pack, I didn't think you'd attempt to include everything I own." He resolved to repack the bag later tonight.

"You should take what you can," Senna pointed out. "If all goes well, you won't be coming back."

Cole felt a moment's satisfaction at Senna's remark. If it didn't go well, he wouldn't come back, either. There was something cheerful in the thought that no matter what happened, he would never again have to occupy this voluminous office.

Senna pressed her case, reminding him that she could make her way to Mackabine with or without him. He certainly wouldn't be there to stop her.

"Geid needs you here, Senna. Aren't you going to lead the revolt against Captain Lodin?"

Senna had to smile at that notion. But she took his point. "Fine. Then I'll meet you in Mackabine after the Regent is gone."

Cole frowned. He had already advised Senna to meet him in Rodenark. It was an out of the way village in the lower forests of Anseth, about thirty miles from Geid. A neutral rendezvous point. The capital was too large, and too hard to navigate. How would he find her?

"It's not safe," said Cole. "There's no telling what the roads will be like. Transitional governments are dangerous." Cole tucked a pinkie into the side pocket of the saddle bag and tugged out a ridiculous silk cloak that he remembered vowing to never wear. "What is this for?" he asked.

"I can take care of myself," said Senna. She took the silk cloak from him and helpfully restuffed it into the bag.

"It's not you I'm worried about," Cole replied, half truthfully.

Senna's hands halted. "Why? The Queen will pardon you, surely."

"That's assuming she survives. We're assuming a lot of things."

Senna wrung her hands again. She didn't want him to die. He liked that. In a strange, uncharitable way, it was nice to have someone else made miserable at your misfortunes.

335

"But if you're going to travel all that distance, you should just come back to Geid," she said finally.

Cole shook his head. He didn't plan to return to Geid if his life depended on it. He chose Rodenark because it was remote, and because it had access to a small port on the coast of Anseth. If all went well, the Q.M. could give him safe escort to the village. If not, it was a convenient place from which to leave the country.

Senna seemed to accept this explanation when he gave it, but she still looked unsettled. She bit her lip in thoughtful anguish.

He kissed her quickly on the cheek for comfort. "I love the way you bite your lip," he observed.

Senna looked genuinely confused. "I don't bite my lip," she protested.

Cole could only chuckle. After a slight hesitation, she slipped close and tried to bite his lip too. He pushed her gently to a safe distance.

Senna sighed. "You're just so disciplined, aren't you?"

"Senna..." Cole was determined to keep Senna an honest woman until marriage was an option.

She pouted and bit her lip again. "Fine," she said, "I'll wait."

"In Rodenark," he said. He didn't want to show up and find her not there.

Senna capitulated. "In Rodenark."

Falk's warehouse was one of seven storage units serving the city center. It was dubbed the Guards' warehouse because the goods within primarily went to the upkeep of the Guard—not, as Jed first thought, because it was attached to the Guards' post, a short distance from Mackabine Castle. Intermittently stocked with goods, its numerous crawl spaces and minimal entrances made it an ideal hideout. Jed wandered freely, giving courteous nods to whoever he saw. No one thought he looked out of place in his borrowed uniform.

Guardsman Falk checked in daily, bringing food and prospects from the outside. Today Falk brought a bottle of orange beer to make up for his lack of news. They shared it at an empty table, under the soft glow of paper lanterns. Mackabine Guards had the means to drink a good deal more than Jed was accustomed to seeing in Geid. "I have to give it to you, sir. Mackabine beer is nearly as good as the beer in Geid."

"Hah! You wish," said Falk. "I tasted your backwater swill while I was there." Falk poured himself a second cup and topped Jed's off while he was at it.

Jed was finding a fast friend in Guardsman Falk. He was a little dogmatic, but far more easygoing than Rimick.

The second shift of Guards came in after duty. The arriving Guards brought their own bottles, and they nodded a brief acknowledgment before helping themselves to places at their table.

One of the Guards gave Jed a mild pat on the back. "I saw you around here earlier. You're that Guard from Geid, right? New transfer."

Jed glanced at Falk and saw him nod significantly.

"What's your name?"

Jed responded awkwardly, "Er...Lodin."

The Guard gave himself and the others a lackluster introduction. There was some light taunting, and avowals of the superiority of second shift, then someone in the group produced a pack of cards.

"Want to join in?" a Guardsman called Shuck invited them. "Straight Dinigo. No limits."

Falk took a spot, and Jed decided he might as well. He never really played Dinigo. In fact, he barely knew the rules. But what better way to learn than to be trounced by a few half-drunken Mackabines?

The first round was dealt overhanded to discourage

cheating. Jed had a good hand, but he sighed and brooded with the rest of them. This was tradition as much as it was a strategy to throw off the other players.

"So...since we're all off duty here," Falk got a conspiratorial glint in his eye, "anyone heard whether the Q.M. are planning to start a rebellion?"

Jed wanted to slap Falk. His eyes shot nervously around the table of armed men, but the comment drew forth little more than snickers. "They're always trying that, aren't they?" said one. "Doesn't mean they're going to succeed any time soon."

"Except they have *her* now," said Falk.

Some shrugs and murmurs conceded the observation.

It was surprising to Jed how many of these Guards were lukewarm in their loyalty to the Regent. So far, Jed had avoided open conversation with other Guards, but he managed to overhear snips of whispered speculation. The Guards were as interested in the fate of the young Queen as anyone else.

One of the older Guards lowered his voice. "There's a lot of tension among the poorer folk. Like they're waiting for something."

The Guard next to him banged his fist. "Well, chase my tail and call me crazy. Let's go tell the Regent!" The table laughed heartily. A short interval of silence went by. Two players made matches and passed the turn.

"Almost makes you want to be a Queensman, doesn't it?" The words were out of Jed's mouth before he could stop them. By the Queen, his tongue was looser than Falk's! He held his breath, waiting to be condemned for treason.

The Guard beside him gave a lazy answer. "That depends. If the Queen wins, sure. Who wouldn't want to be a Queensman then? If she loses, I'd rather stay where I am."

There were nods all around.

Guardsman Shuck threw his cards face down. "Shut it. Someone change the subject or I'll report the lot of you."

Falk immediately complied, bringing up horses or

gambling, or both. Jed stopped paying attention. He couldn't stop thinking how easy it would be for Anwa to persuade the entire lot of them to her side.

In Mackabine Castle, a host of candles cast a yellow glow over the great hall. One hundred and forty-four candles, most likely. Multiples of sixteen were considered ideal. Lord Hemmon's taste was less ostentatious than Gote's, but not lacking in dignity. The effect made the dance hall unnaturally warm and afforded an illumination never meant to be attained in the dead of night.

While the call to Jade Hammar was mostly military, local Ambassadors were taking advantage of the Gaultian withdrawal to visit their families. The castle filled to capacity with the departing and those wishing them well. Guests, diplomats, and officers from the Gaultian ships all milled about, smiling, drinking, and engaging in useless conversation.

Hemmon stood at the far end of the hall, chatting casually with the Admiral of the Gaultian fleet. It was hard to argue how flawlessly Hemmon had appropriated his new position. A few favors to the right people, lip service to the rest, and the court was ready to pledge their devotion. Cole hadn't heard one mention of the late Regent since he arrived.

Cole accidentally brushed the sleeve of a servant setting out early refreshments. He glanced at the servant's mark on her apron as the unfamiliar woman bowed out of his way. He wondered if Madam Eold was present in the congregation. He didn't want her to accost him the way she had yesterday, dragging him into a closet so she could pass on Queensman Brock's incessant demands for information.

Cole spent every spare moment since he arrived chasing specifics on the state of the Regent's forces. He took a lesson from Senna and loitered near the scheduling office, but all he'd gotten there were curious looks. At least here his presence was expected, immersed in the smell of meat and sweet cakes.

The Regent's party held its own breed of tensions. The Gaults were in an uproar over their action overseas. Rumors said that the Hammars were arresting Gaultian citizens in Jade City as a pretense to steal their wealth. Cole held himself very much removed from it all. *It's probably the way the rest of the world feels about us,* Cole thought. *Mackabine: a regrettably oppressed country, but distant and unworthy of much thought.*

"*Marquebine* is beautiful land here." This opinion came from a full-bearded man who appeared mysteriously at Cole's side. He pronounced Mackabine in the Gaultian style, with emphasis on the wrong syllable.

"It's tolerable," Cole told him, hoping his tone would chase the friendly Gault somewhere else. The man was probably in Mackabine for the first time, based on his limited use of the language.

A passing servant offered Cole a cup of Sequie wine, and he took it willingly. The Gaults were from a land of grapes. But wine was expensive in Mackabine, reserved for nobles and special occasions. Cole had developed a taste for it. It had a more subtle flavor than beer, and it was sweeter.

The Baron of Pannerack intruded unannounced, giving eyes to the Gaultian at Cole's side. "Lord Renton." Cole turned slightly to acknowledge him.

Renton gave an austere bow. "Fenwith," he murmured with equally low enthusiasm. He appeared to have something to say to the Gaultian. "How are you finding your visit to our country, sir?" Renton asked him.

The Gaultian gave a gracious, if broken reply. He smiled at a servant who tiptoed nearby, delivering delicacies borne on elaborately inscribed dishes. The servant made an obvious effort to offer them a treat.

"What is it?" Cole asked.

"Fermented loul-bean," said the servant. "A Gaultian delicacy. It's buried underground for one hundred days, then soaked in oil prior to serving."

Cole wrinkled his face at the foul-smelling paste. He shook his head.

Renton gave Cole a superior smile as he accepted one of the samples. His jaw paused in mid-chew, and his lip quivered as he rendered judgment. "Delightful," he said. Without further comment, Lord Renton covered his mouth and walked hastily in the direction of the washroom.

The Gaultian laughed good-heartedly. "As well, I eat no loul. Bad for stomach."

Cole glanced back at the man. He looked eager to continue practicing his Mackabine. "Tomorrow you sail with the fleet?" Cole asked him.

The Gaultian nodded, proud of his role. "I am, how we say, part-part Admiral. *Eu dezvauthu.*"

Weapons requisitioner. That explained Renton's attention. It got Cole's as well.

"Are you well-armed for your venture?" he asked impertinently.

The Gaultian looked confused by Cole's choice of words. Cole rephrased his question into Gaultian.

"Yes!" said the Gaultian. "I took from your *Marquebine* armories. It be you need no much, I think?"

"From the main armory or the second? The second armory must be more convenient for loading your ships, being close to the harbor." Cole held his breath. The location of the armories was one of the things Brock most wanted.

"No? Think you some other armory. Take from other side the city, not harbor side. Next to church. Underground."

Cole sifted his thoughts for the man's meaning. He had to mean the helping shrine. The statues and fountain would make it seem the equivalent of a Gaultian church. Cole gave the Gaultian a grateful smile.

A small boy of four or five careened into the room from the hallway. He ran recklessly into the Gaultian's knees and latched himself onto his leg cuff. "Ah, this my son," the man explained, introducing Cole to the small assailant. His

341

speech reverted to Gaultian while he admonished the boy to wait in the side room with the other children.

The youngster spat off a list of wrongs the other children had made against him. Cole caught about half of his rapid explanation. It occurred to Cole that he had been trying to learn Gaultian longer than this boy had been alive. It hardly seemed fair.

"Excuse, please," the man said, taking his son in tow.

Cole turned his attention back to the center of the hall. He spied Lady Orila resting in one of the chairs against the wall. The woman was overlooked for the first time in many years. You could tell it was not agreeing with her. Earlier, he heard Lady Dolas invite her into a parlor game, but even that may not have been a kindness. Orila had only a minimal command of Dinigo. Cole tried to avoid catching her eye as he worked his way through the preening crowd. But the Lady saw him and called until he was forced to attend her.

"Hello, Aunt," Cole said coolly. He came to a halt near the hem of her wide golden skirt.

"Fenn." The aggrieved woman looked close to tears as she spoke. "They said you were there when...when Gote was killed. Were you?"

Cole strove to arrange the best answer to her question. Was it possible that Lady Orila actually cared for her husband? "It was over quickly," he said honestly.

"Yes," the Lady said. She looked moderately comforted. "I thought so. I...I could use something to drink."

"I'll fetch you something, Aunt," he promised.

The beverage table was within easy hearing distance of Regent Hemmon and the Gaultian Admiral. They were speaking Gaultian, which made it difficult to follow. To Cole's untrained ear, Hemmon's Gaultian sounded flawless, indistinguishable from a native. Cole took his time perusing the drink options, and picked up enough words to surmise an understanding.

"The delay would only be a few hours," the Regent urged upon his companion.

The Gaultian officer held his wine close to his chest. "I have friends in Jade City right now," he said. Cole watched the Admiral grimace. He seemed torn between apology and disdain for the conversation. "Abandoning them to the Hammars is not an option."

"Naturally," Hemmon answered. "But an hour is gained or lost at sea without regard. How can a few more signify?"

"A few hours makes a decisive difference in battle. I am sorry, Lord Regent. Your harbor will survive until your reinforcements arrive. I cannot wait."

Hemmon noticed Cole in proximity and gave him a rather indifferent glance. Cole backed off. He hadn't overheard anything he didn't already know. He still had to learn what reinforcements were expected, and from what direction.

Pannerack was the closest county capital. Cole spied Lord Renton emerging from the washroom, only slightly worse for wear. Cole caught him before he had a chance to merge back into the crowd. "You look like you could use this." He offered Renton the drink he'd poured for Orila.

"Oh," said Renton. He took the glass hesitantly, suspicious of Cole's goodwill, but downed it nonetheless.

"Too bad about the transfer," Cole hazarded, "but I guess with the mining drop, you don't really *need* that many men, do you?"

"That's none of your business, Fenwith," Renton snapped quickly, then raised his chin as he gained control. Cole observed Renton's temper with glee. He had guessed right. "For your information, the transfer is temporary, and I'm being reimbursed for it."

Cole pressed forward. "How much for fifty Guards? Enough to buy a new coat?"

"Don't be ridiculous. The compensation's not in money. And it's only thirty Guards. Which still leaves me with twice your number, I suppose." Renton departed with a smug expression, somehow under the impression that he had gained the advantage of the conversation.

CHAPTER THIRTY-SIX

Hedian walked along the hallway of Mackabine Castle in the poised posture her aunt had taught her—chin uncomfortably high, hands uncomfortably stiff. Her fingers itched like she was holding a wad of pepperweed. She technically wasn't allowed upstairs. She had only joined the castle staff four days ago. However, servants' places were blurred in the chaos of the evening. Given the lateness of the hour, Hedian hoped no one would notice her.

Hedian rubbed the message in her hand as her eyes explored the splendor of the recently emptied dance hall. She wished her aunt would magically appear. Aunt Eold hadn't shown up in their shared room last night. No one in the servants' quarters seemed to know what had happened to her.

Hedian wanted to believe that her aunt was free from harm. Eold often had errands that took her away on either castle business or Queensman business. But why would she leave without telling Hedian first? The message in her hand was supposed to go through Eold. Hedian had been warned not to open it, but what else was she to do? She tried not to read what the message contained as she scribbled her own line hastily at the bottom: *Eold missing. Please help.*

Hedian knew nothing about her target except that he was albino and he was attending the party. Of the ten or twelve persons still left in the dance hall, there was one fitting the description. As it seemed unlikely that there were two such persons in the building, Hedian approached him with confidence.

"Excuse me, Lord; are you the Baron of Geid?" Hedian raised her chin some more and hoped her appearance looked official. She was almost proud of the speckless servant's tunic she had donned for the occasion.

The albino glanced sidelong at Hedian and turned his back without answering.

Hedian started, but recovered before the Baron left hearing distance. "I have something for you." She held her message out.

The Baron took the necessary steps in Hedian's direction, snatched the paper, and opened it rather angrily. There was no change in his deportment as he read the note. "I'm not interested in any celebration committee." He immediately surrendered the note back into a confused Hedian's hands.

"Uh..." Hedian protested warily.

"Go on!"

Aware of the many eyes directed at her, Hedian unhappily obeyed.

She spent the next several hours performing the grueling services of her job. Hedian wasn't considered good enough to serve guests at the party, but she was good enough to help clean afterward. It was quite late—past morning—when she retired, limp and sore, to the servants' rooms. The rooms were windowless so that servants could sleep at all hours. Hedian carried a candle to find her way. Once there, she wrapped a strip of gauze around the new blisters on her palms, souvenirs of vigorous scrubbing.

When she finally lay down, a crinkle underneath Hedian's head jolted her back into wakefulness. She reached in surprise for the paper concealed in her pillowcase. Excitement overcame fatigue as Hedian relit her small candle. She crouched at the foot of her bed, where the light would not disturb her sleeping bunkmates.

Dear Madam, please take this letter immediately. I will look for Eold.

Hedian gulped. The rest was not intended for her eyes, but Hedian skimmed it anyway. Its import struck her immediately. The Gault ships would leave on the early tide! Did Eold already know? Hedian tucked the letter into a secret pocket and put her shoes back on her feet. There was no chance for a restful sleep until she reached Mister Brock.

Jed held the feather tail of an arrow to his eye and admired the uniformity of its length. The arrow's shaft was made of ash, a better-quality wood than he used in Geid. It would be nice to test the arrows in a real weapon. He considered the practicality of setting up a practice target in a room with such a low ceiling.

Jed told himself not to complain. He was warm and well fed, feasting on bread and meat for every meal. Many a man might have enjoyed loafing about, masquerading as a Guard without having to do any of the work involved. The idleness was making Jed crazy. He added the arrow to the abundant pile at his feet.

The door shifted suddenly, startling Jed from his thoughts.

"What?" Jed said to Falk. "I thought you were on duty all day."

Falk didn't answer right away. He grabbed a helmet and sword off the wall in a single motion. "Time to go," he announced. "We just got a summons. The Queensmen are attacking the castle."

Jed tipped his bench in his haste to get up. A score of arrows, partially fletched, spilled over the floor. Jed tripped as they rolled underfoot. He regained his balance barely in time to follow Falk before he disappeared. The warehouse was strangely empty as they passed through the rooms towards the exit. They stumbled out into a host of confused Guards arguing in the street.

Falk filled Jed in on what he knew, which wasn't much. His patrol had been in the lower market when some men stormed down the street, screaming heyday about an attack at the castle. The disturbance cleared out the market in a panic, overturning some vegetable stands. Falk looked rumpled by the experience. "I was nearly crushed by the combination of running feet and rolling melons," he said.

Jed questioned the others nearby and got half a dozen conflicting reports—an attack on the harbor, the Mackabine River being barricaded, the Regent's warehouse gone up in flames. No one could agree to what extent the Q.M. were involved. To top it off, the Captain had gone missing and left them without a line of command. One of the more senior Guardsmen finally stepped up. His bellowing voice took effect on the Guards closest to him. "We need to know what's going on before we decide anything else!"

Jed stepped up to volunteer. "I can scout the castle and be back in time to sneeze," he said. After passing as a Guard for almost a week now, it was peculiarly simple to fit into that role.

The ranking Guardsman didn't have any idea who Jed was, but that didn't seem to matter in the present cacophony. He ordered Jed to take a second. Guardsman Falk put himself forward, and they left together. Jed hadn't walked the street since that first day in Mackabine. The street was considerably less crowded now. The few folks they saw got out of the way at the sight of their uniforms.

"Do you have a plan, Mister Jedomar?" asked Falk.

Jed had as much plan as a dog on a mouse hunt. He answered his friend with a cocky smile. "Don't you trust my sense of strategy?"

Falk gave a short bark of a laugh. "Are you joking? After you lost all my money playing Dinigo, you mushcake?"

The deserted market gave Jed an eerie feeling in his

bones. The street was dark, as shadows fell densely among the tall, closely-packed buildings of the city. Just north of them were the castle gates, which they found solid and unbreached. The great walls appeared undisturbed by the chaos about them, standing as they had for hundreds of years. A great slab of wood towered at a central point before the gates, erected for wielding decrees. Jed glanced casually at the notice, which read in bold letters: *Jedomar, slayer of the Regent Gote.* The sign was affixed to a pole, which his eyes followed balefully upwards. A severed head, barely recognizable as such after days of decay, stuck skewered a few spans in the air.

"What!" Jed cried involuntarily. For a brief moment, he actually believed his head had gotten up there somehow without him.

"Oh-ho," said Falk. "That's nothing to worry about. Lord Hemmon insisted on having it, so I cut off another fellow's head for him. He never noticed the difference."

Jed took a pair of deep, soothing breaths before giving Falk a sidelong look. "I hope the other fellow wasn't using it at the time."

"Nah..."

Jed decided not to question further. He studied the head suspiciously. "Doesn't look a thing like me."

"He did, before he started decomposing."

"Not funny," said Jed, unsure whether Falk was joking.

They were interrupted by the sight of a lone Guardsman hustling towards them from the opposite direction. The man had lost his helmet and his harness was loose. He paused for breath when he was close enough to speak. "Where are you two headed?"

"We heard Queensmen were storming the gates."

The other man shook his head. "The castle's fine. The Q.M. planted spies to spread false rumors."

"How do you know?" said Falk.

"I just came from the harbor. Captain Stine's post. The whole place is lost. We managed to capture a couple of the rebels and squeeze out what they knew. We need to get to the underground armory before they do." He tossed his head meaningfully back towards the market. "I could use the help; I was the only one of my unit who got away."

"The second armory?" Falk looked unaccountably astonished. "Do they know where it is?"

"Looks like they found out somehow."

"By the Queen," Falk swore. "Even I don't know where it is."

The other Guard took off at a run, trusting them to follow.

"I don't understand," Jed said to Falk as they moved to catch up. He leapt to avoid a pile of litter in the road. "Doesn't the Guard have enough weapons already?"

"The main armory is inside the castle." Falk's chest heaved with the effort of keeping up with the Guard ahead of them. "There's a backup outside in case of a siege. But Jed...what do you think will happen if the Q.M. arm the general populace with heavy weapons?"

Jed's initial gut feeling was that this was a terrible idea. "Aside from cutting themselves apart?"

"This rebellion isn't going to be bloodless," said Falk.

Lord Hemmon inhaled the scent of flower water that lapped gently against his ears. The boy cleaned and trimmed his nails while another servant covered his skin in a sequence of precious oils. His morning routine kept Hemmon centered. A healthy body was a focused mind. He spent the hour meditating, and revising the intricate plans that spun constantly in his mind.

The latest easements were having an appeasing effect on the country's populace, and money from the mines was still flowing almost as profusely. Hemmon smiled smugly.

Oppression had a damping effect on people's memories. He didn't have to restore Pannerack to what it had been under Benta's reign; he only had to improve conditions above what they were now, and the county would kiss his feet for the favor.

A knock rang against the chamber door, startling the boy, who nipped painfully at Hemmon's skin. Hemmon opened his eyes to see the boy's face pale in terror. Hemmon reserved the greater part of his anger for whichever person dared interrupt his ritual in private chambers.

"What is it?" An echo of his voice rang back at Hemmon across the empty space. *This room needs more tapestries for sound absorption.* Hemmon added it to the mental list of demands on his schedule.

No answer was forthcoming. The servants hastily fulfilled his order for a dressing robe. Hemmon left damp footprints on the tile on his way to the door.

The Head Postman was waiting by the door, his arms folded stiffly across his chest, his face wrenched in distress. Hemmon had given the Head Postman his position only the week prior, after dismissing Gote's untested man. The new Postman, unfortunately, was not yet broken in to the grandeur of his role.

"Explain your presence, Mister Orgelio."

"Lord Regent." The Postman bowed low.

Hemmon raised his hand in mild rebuke. "My name will do fine, please." Hemmon preferred to distance himself from the title of Regent. He didn't want history to confuse him with Lord Gote.

"Yes, Lord Hemmon." The Postman looked as if he did not know where to start. "My messengers have located a spy in the castle."

Hemmon's annoyance evaporated. He was glad to have given the Postman the benefit of the doubt. "What sort of spy?"

"A woman. An overservant in the upstairs quarter."

Hemmon nodded. There were probably dozens of

such spies among the staff. Hemmon was prepared to congratulate Postman Orgelio on his discovery.

The Postman wasn't finished, however. He winced as he confessed the gravity of the affair. "It seems someone has been altering incoming and outgoing reports."

"One servant?" said Hemmon. "That seems unlikely."

"We think she had help. We're questioning her now, but it may take some time to uncover her crimes."

"How long has this been going on?" Hemmon tightened his robe, and motioned for the Postman to walk with him to his dressing room. His routine appeared to be over for the day.

"Several days, I believe."

Hemmon stopped abruptly, his annoyance returning. "And you only bothered to bring it up now?"

"No, Lord, of course not." The Postman, who had hardly been comfortable at the start of this conversation, sank into confirmed melancholy. "The misinformation has only now been realized. It became most apparent this morning, however... Lord Hemmon, there have been some disturbing messages."

A messenger chased them into the hallway at that moment, rather confirming the legitimacy of this notion. He was a young man, scarcely old enough to escape being called a boy, but the colors of his uniform vouched for the importance of his station. The messenger gave the Head Postman a cursory bow, and then flung himself at Hemmon's feet. "Lord Regent," the messenger blurted, "the Queensmen are rebelling."

The Postman's response to this news was summarily dismissive. He flapped one of his hands in exasperation. "That's the fifth same report I've heard in an hour."

Hemmon's blood grew oddly cold. His eyes descended dangerously over the incompetent Postman. "Is there a reason you didn't start with that?"

The Postman was quick to defend himself. Nothing had been confirmed, he insisted. The first report was retracted as an error. The second as a reckless joke. The rest were in disagreement about which Queensmen were at fault and where they had chosen to strike. "I sent members of the first Guard to get proper information," Orgelio said, "but as yet, they are unreturned."

Hemmon chose to cease recognition of the doomed Postman. He turned his gaze instead on the young messenger at his feet. "Finish your report. You say there are Queensmen rebelling. Where? Which ones?"

The messenger was obviously nervous about responding, but his voice did not waver when he answered, "All of them."

CHAPTER THIRTY-SEVEN

Long before they reached their destination, it became clear that the underground armory was cleaned out. The Queensmen had distributed crossbows, swords, and many thousands of arrows to anyone who looked willing to make use of them. The resulting ruckus made it hard to tell an actual Queensman from the random sailor, merchant, or rabble-rouser—assuming there had been very much difference to begin with.

The result was anarchy. Jed and Falk lost the guide they had been following. Folk crawled out the walls looking for attention, information, excitement or whatnot. The city Guards clumped and scattered alternatively. Some wasted time confiscating weapons from the city folk, which they then had to either carry or leave carelessly unattended. Jed squeezed his way into the largest collective of Guards he could find, which amounted to about fifteen. Then he lost track of Falk for several minutes. Eventually he spied him weaving about at the edge of a crowd, where he had to fight his way back past a horde of quarreling fish-sellers.

"I think it might be time to get rid of these uniforms," Falk observed.

Jed more than agreed. The fish-sellers were giving them eyes in an uncomplimentary manner. Any moment one of them might choose to make use of their newly acquired swords.

A horn blew loudly, forestalling the threat of violence. The crowd cleared to make room for a large group of Mackabine Guards who marched in proper formation along the road. Suddenly outnumbered, the city folk averted their eyes. A Captain on horseback, a man with stern, weathered features, led them. He snapped his fingers, inviting the remaining stragglers to join the formation. The scattered Guards obeyed instantly, merging seamlessly into the tail end of the marching line.

Jed and Falk had no choice but to follow suit. Falk gave Jed a gentle push. "We're in for it now. That's Captain Abelle, a top Gaultian officer. Last one still in Mackabine, maybe."

"Gaultian, is he?"

Jed was hushed by a tap from a disapproving Guard. However, a lot of the Guards were as confused as they were, and not all submitted to being silenced.

"Where are we going?" one insisted.

An eager-looking man in the middle of the line answered. "Abelle knows where to find the Q.M. leaders. We're going to stop this thing at its heart."

Jed was at least heartened to hear he was going the right way.

The march moved them ponderously through the web of city streets. The roads were dirtier than any Jed had seen— not with dirt, but piles of trash and human waste people had left there. A swarm of gnats hovered over the corpse of an animal. None of the other passersby gave it a glance, so Jed did his best to ignore it. Jed assumed he had seen most of Mackabine in his first glimpse, but he couldn't have been more wrong. The city had no end. Row after row of stone and wood buildings went by. The houses were clumped so tightly in places that they melded together, sharing walls. Some rose two or three stories in the air, climbing over the others in a struggle for dominance. *How can people live like this?* Jed wondered. Did they never see trees?

After a long time, the houses thinned. The road widened, revealing the outskirts of the city. There were signs of destruction on many of the outer buildings. Fires had been started and hastily extinguished. City folk fled at the sight of the Guards' formation, shouting and sobbing, some with heads wrapped in bloody rags. Jed's throat felt tight. How much of this had happened while he was hiding in the bowels of the warehouse, useless and oblivious?

Their goal became clear as they entered the open flatland of Mackabine County. The Queensmen were congregated at the bottom of a clear green hill, hunkered down amid makeshift stockades built from trading wagons. Dead bodies peppered the ground in between. Whatever struggles had already taken place left hollow cries from the wounded and grief-stricken.

Jed felt a hand of dread grasp his shoulder. The Guards were outnumbered, but that could easily be made up for in training and discipline. Jed estimated there were perhaps fifty of their number to one hundred Queensmen. He clutched a standard-issue sword that someone had given him —he hardly remembered when. Why had he ever thought his help would be somehow precipitous? The situation was far out of his control.

"Have you ever been in a battle, Mister Jedomar?" Falk asked quietly behind Jed's shoulder.

Jed didn't answer. He wasn't sure his experience would count for much in this setting.

The frontmost Guards opened with a volley of arrows that downed a dozen Queensmen in seconds.

Jed fought his way to the front of the formation just as the Captain issued a call to charge. Jed sprinted, trying to put distance between himself and the horde of attacking Guards. But he felt the footsteps of the others a few paces behind. To anyone watching, he would look like the leader of the invading force.

"Bogsnatching...bog—" Jed grumbled as he searched for a better expletive. This was not going according to plan. It might've helped if he'd had a plan.

The first Queensman Jed came to was crouched with arms clasped around a wounded comrade, who he was attempting to drag to safety. Jed lurched to a halt, his shoes sliding in the mud. The soot-streaked Queensman paused, looking up at Jed in terror. Another Guard advanced, brushing past Jed's shoulder as he raised a sword to strike.

Jed's own sword felt heavy but he managed to lift the weapon in time. The sword slid through the Guard's torso, bypassing his scale armor and lodging in soft flesh. The wounded Queensman squawked as the dead Guard fell limply onto his feet.

Jed bent over to retrieve his sword. The nearest remaining Guard screamed curses at him, expressing equal parts wonder and vengeance. He rushed Jed, forcing him to dodge and lose his balance. One of his arms caught the attacking Guardsman's harness as he stumbled. The Guard was too inexperienced to use this to his advantage. Jed fortified his grip, yanking the Guard's torso to his level. Jed's sword went through his neck with a sickening squish.

Jed's apparently treasonous behavior was drawing serious attention. The Captain actually turned away from what he was doing and issued a secondary order to have him killed. The Guards' flank shifted slightly. Jed had a brief second to feel gratified at the advantage this would give the Q.M. before he turned and fled the battleground in the most promising direction.

Most of the Guards had already exhausted their arrows, which was the only thing keeping Jed alive at the moment. A few came around to close on his position from the front. Jed stopped to face one. He was spared the fight when an arrow pierced his foe from behind. Another Guard took a shot in the arm, convincing him to fall back. Both arrows had come from the field of Mackabine Guards rather than the Q.M. Jed was confused until he spied Falk, waving at him with a crossbow. No one else seemed to have noticed his aim.

By now, the Q.M. were meeting the Guard head on,

distracting their attention. Jed's identity was lost in the scuffle. He scanned the battlefield, trying to decide what to do. People were dying everywhere, but some of the Guards were already arguing for surrender. He heard a call go out for Queen Anwa.

Jed's eyes caught a slender young woman being dragged by her wrists away from one of the stockades. She was dressed in good skirmishing gear, but it was obvious she didn't know how to fight. Her kicks were aimed ineffectually at the thighs of the Guard who held her.

Jed used the hilt of his sword to strike the Guard in the head. He let go of the woman, and fell to his knees groaning. The man glared at Jed with one eye. The other was covered by the hand cradling his bleeding skull. "What's wrong with you? Stupid son of a dogfish!" he said.

"You can insult me if you like," Jed replied, "but please leave my mother out of it."

No one else came to the stricken Guard's rescue. Guards were turning on one other all over the field. Jed wondered if Falk's example had been helpful. Much later, when the corpse of the Gaultian Captain was examined, they found he had been shot in the back by his own ranks.

Jed leaned over and offered a hand to the woman. She was petite, somewhat less than twenty, and had amber-honey hair. "Are you all right?" he asked. The woman tried to pick herself up without his help, but her shoe slipped on the mud and Jed was forced to grab her to keep her from falling back down. "Don't worry, little Madam," he said, gripping her shoulder. "Stay close to me."

"You!" The howl of an angry Queensman made Jed turn. "Let go of her!" the man demanded—fruitlessly, since Jed had already done so. Jed was prepared to explain, but the Queensman tried to sock him in the face. Jed dodged in time, and readied himself to do so again, while the Q.M. puffed himself up importantly. "You dare!"

The woman interrupted sharply, "Don't bother, Brock." She brushed a glob of dirt from her blouse. "He doesn't know who I am."

"Who is she?" Jed was moved to inquire.

"Queen Anwa," said the man.

Jed drew in his breath. As a host of ramifications ran through his mind, Jed unconsciously said aloud the one that struck him most severely. "She's beautiful!"

The Queen laughed. It was a light, effervescent sound that saved Jed from over-embarrassment.

"Forgive me," said Jed. He bowed as low as he could without falling over. He dared not apologize for the compliment.

"Stand away from her," the Queensman threatened again, "you false-hearted brute. Easy to make obeisance now, is it?"

Jed glanced over the rest of the field. The battle was over. It had been very brief. A handful of Guards retreated. The rest were laying down their swords in surrender. Jed realized he still had his weapon, and he carefully knelt down to remedy this.

"Be civil, Brock," said Anwa. "That's the Guard who stirred them up in the beginning. He turned sides before the battle even started."

The man's name finally seeped through Jed's befuddled skull. He was talking to the leader of the Mackabine Queensmen, the man that Jed and Falk had been trying to find. "Mister Brock, is it? Good meeting! I'm actually a Queensman. I was only pretending to be a Guard."

Brock squinted in obvious disbelief.

Jed was saved from having to elaborate by a pair of thick, hairy arms. They seized him before he had a chance to see who they belonged to. "Jed! Jed, Jed! You poor skunk, I thought you were dead."

Jed pulled back to see who was talking to him. The large face was pleasantly familiar. "Inwick?" Jed cried in delight. In a trick of the tongue, Jed almost called him Uncle the way Senna did. "What are you doing here?"

"I came to Mackabine for the revolution, what else? I was in the field and I saw you running down here with all those Guards. I thought I was dreaming. You must have some tale to tell, Jedomar."

More Queensmen arrived to watch the exchange. They gathered in a protective circle around Brock and Anwa.

"It's a...long story," Jed answered.

"Jedomar?" the Queen mused over the syllables of his name. "Are you the Q.M. who slew Lord Gote?"

Jed admitted this was so. He still believed he deserved more criticism than praise for that deed. But the group around him was appreciative. They accepted Jed immediately. "Well done" and "Good riddance" were the general opinions proffered.

Anwa's sentiments were more inquisitive. "They say your head is on display in front of the castle."

"A small misunderstanding, Great Lady," said Jed. The listening crowd grew larger by the moment. Jed couldn't see more than a few spans behind him. "Where is Guardsman Falk?" he cried.

Heads turned, a few calls went out, and Falk was brought forward.

Jed pointed dramatically. "This is the man who saved my life. A former member of the Regent's Guard whose first desire was to serve his Queen since the moment he learned of her existence. I think you will find a surprising number of friends among these Guards, Great Lady."

Falk turned positively blue. He confirmed his loyalty with fervor and not much elegance. The Queen took it in stride. She climbed upon an overturned wagon and loudly announced a public pardon for any Guard willing to follow her. The proclamation was exceedingly popular. Almost all the surrendered Guards took up her offer.

"You are a damn lucky fellow, Mister Jedomar," Falk whispered in Jed's ear when he was able to get close. "Damn lucky fellow."

❖

Hemmon impassively observed the Queensmen's barricade through the pieced glass of his third-story window. Everyone else was avoiding the sight of the angry, lawless rabble at their doorstep, but Hemmon had ordered his servants to turn his writing desk around so he could have the best view of the rebels. The barricade had been erected overnight, putting the castle into effective quarantine. The Queensmen weren't equipped to take the castle by force, but they could starve it into eventual surrender. A few nobles tried to leave this morning, and the Queensmen slaughtered those who refused to turn back.

Mister Orgelio, the Head Postman, stood at the end of his desk. Hemmon hadn't yet had a chance to replace him, although it was on his list of priorities. The short-sighted Postman could have taken steps to prevent this, back when action was still possible, but instead he chose to believe the less sensational story. Hemmon was still crafting an appropriate punishment. From his timid quaking, it was likely Orgelio knew this.

Hemmon ignored the Postman as he peered through the office window. The Q.M. jeered impudently, raising their stolen swords like prizes at an entertainer's show. Hemmon's window was too high for the mob to see him, but he imagined the rebels targeting him with their taunts. Earlier Hemmon had ordered a few hundred arrows launched into the crowd. Lines of Q.M. rioters dropped satisfyingly onto the gritty pavement below the gate. Most of the bodies still graced the pavement, creating a no-man's-land between the castle and the Q.M. horde. It hadn't discouraged the rest of them. There were more rebels than there were arrows, and Hemmon was saving what he had left.

Postman Orgelio wiped his chin, preventing a bead of sweat from falling on the Regent's Revordian carpet. Hemmon slid one set of fingers over the other and finally issued the invitation to speak. "Did one of our messages get through to the Gaultian fleet?"

"Yes," said the Postman. He relayed the Gaultian Admiral's formal response. The answer was unsurprising. The fleet was too committed to their present course to be persuaded into returning. The Admiral expressed annoyance with Hemmon's inability to keep order. He offered neither aid nor advice.

"Shall I prepare a return message?" Orgelio's voice was less than hopeful.

Hemmon didn't bother to respond. He waved a finger for a servant, who passed him a cup of spiced tea. He breathed the aroma before he sipped.

For a man in his situation, Hemmon comported himself well. That was a tangible, if small, consolation. Hemmon knew he was ruined. The full extent of the damage lay before him. The entire country was swept up in the spirit of rebellion. Even if he somehow managed to assassinate their pathetic child Queen, the people had turned against Hemmon. They would never again accept his rule as Regent. Not willingly, at least. The hard-earned progress made by Regent Gote had been wiped out. The only way forward would be to break them again, crush their spirits...but Hemmon wouldn't get that chance. It was only a matter of time until the siege broke, and what little power he retained was wrenched away.

"There's another small matter of interest, Lord Hemmon," Orgelio whispered to him. The Postman mistook Hemmon's blank look for permission to proceed. "A Guard has arrived from Geid. He claims to have extraordinary information he wishes to put to your ears."

"Who is this man?"

"His name is Rofus, Lord. He managed to sneak into the castle while the barricade was still going up. He's been detained by the Guards since last night, but I checked his documents, and he appears to be who he says he is."

"Send him in, then."

The Counselour had the Guard waiting outside. Hemmon's eyes narrowed as he studied the disheveled-looking Guard. "I remember you," said Hemmon. "You tried to gain a position in my service, while we were staying in Geid. My Head Guardsman complained of your impertinence. Now you come to Mackabine begging a personal audience."

The offending Guardsman maintained an aura of self-control. "The news I bring will be worth your inconvenience, Lord Regent."

"Then tell me."

"It's about Lord Fenwith," said the Guard.

Hemmon's interest remained quite low. "What about him?"

"He's dead."

Hemmon raised an amused eyebrow. He had seen Fenwith in the main hall not an hour before. "That's good news, if true. But I would hardly have to rely on *you* for such paltry information."

"You misunderstand me, Lord." The Guardsman bowed. "Fenwith died five years ago, gutted by some Queensmen in Aog harbor, shortly after stepping off the boat. I don't know who that man is downstairs, but he is not who you think he is."

Hemmon had to summon some willpower not to drop his cup of tea onto the fine grace-wood desk. He set the cup down with a firmly controlled hand. "How do you know this?"

The Guard told his story. A week or so past, he caught a wretched-looking Gaultian named Elimilo on the grounds of Geid Castle, skulking by the kitchen entrance. Rofus turned some ungentle persuasion on him, and got the Gaultian to confess his errand. He learned that the Gaultian was once acquainted with the real Fenwith and he had been extorting money out of the Baron's housekeeper in exchange for keeping this vile secret.

"I went to Aog to confirm the story before coming to you. Of course, I regret that now, seeing how..."

Seeing how the delay had rendered his information nearly useless. Nonetheless, from the Guard's perspective, it had been the proper thing to do. Hemmon wrestled to understand. How bizarre. How could such a thing go unsuspected? Also, why had Fenn—or supposedly, the impostor—not simply killed this meddling Gaultian and had done with it?

The Guard informant offered his opinion on the matter when asked. "I'm not sure," he said. "I can only assume he was too soft-hearted for the task."

Soft-hearted. Fenn. That made Hemmon want to laugh.

"Lord Hemmon," Postman Orgelio found the courage to volunteer, "Lord Fenwith attended a war meeting the other day, before the farewell dinner."

"Why?"

"It *was* strange, Lord, but we saw no reason to kick him out."

"Are you suggesting that the *alleged* spy—the one you're all so fond of casting blame upon, the one who subverted our messages during the initial revolt, and prevented us from knowing we were under attack until the harbor and the main gate were already taken—was *Lord Fenwith?*"

The room was silent. Of course, no one had suggested anything. But even his most foolish advisers must be coming to this conclusion. Hemmon felt a coldness in his chest that locked his splayed fingers against the wooden table. No possible display of rage was sufficient. It was better to give none.

"Orgelio," Hemmon said finally, "instate Mister Rofus into my personal Guard, please." It was hardly much of a reward at this point. The new Guard was unlikely to relish his position for very long. But Rofus seemed to take some satisfaction from the offer.

"Yes, Lord Hemmon," Orgelio ventured slowly. "Do you...want me to detain Fenwith?"

Hemmon's face tightened. "No," he said. "Watch him. Get someone to tail him. Be discreet. But make sure they understand, whatever else happens, that albino does not leave this castle alive."

Anwa released an involuntary coo of pain as her head jerked sideways from a tangle. "I'm sorry!" The skittish serving girl dropped the brush a second time. She jumped away and scrambled under a chair after the brush.

"It's okay," Anwa said, wishing she could remember the girl's name. She remembered being fussed over long ago, by servants whose lineage made them suitable. They knotted her hair into intricate forms that vaguely mimicked animals or geologic formations. Those servants never dropped the brush, nor treated her as if she were a tempestuous beast that might bite them. Anwa never tried to remember her servants' names back then. She had been proud and stupid. She understood better now.

Anwa claimed the brush from the girl's frantic hands, and stroked a shoulder to calm her. "Don't worry," Anwa said.

Every person here was more real to her than those silly school friends whose faces she scarcely recalled. Anwa's throat tightened whenever she compared this life to that other. In any gathering from her childhood, she had been a pretty afterthought, an heir third in line—something to keep on hand, but not involve in anything important. Now, no matter where she went, she was the most vital person in attendance. This whole camp of refugees existed for her sake.

Not for her, Anwa reminded herself. For Mackabine.

The girl looked more uncomfortable than soothed by Anwa's forgiveness. Was she hoping to improve as a hairdresser or would she really just rather be somewhere else? Anwa couldn't tell. "You can go. I'll finish up by myself."

The girl looked relieved at Anwa's suggestion. With a quick bob, she was gone.

Anwa turned to the tiny mirror on the wall. It was barely big enough to see her whole face at the same time, let alone her hair. When she lived in the safe house, the old woman cut Anwa's hair short every few months—a measure to keep dirt and lice to a minimum. Now her hair was starting to grow again. The longest strands curled outward against her shoulders. She ran the brush through twice, roughly, and decided that was good enough. She wondered what the old man and woman would say if they could see her now. What of her mother? Would Queen Benta be pleased that Anwa was taking her birthright by force?

The Q.M. tried to keep Anwa out of the fray, but she insisted on being close to the city. Her presence encouraged and rallied everyone they came across. She couldn't ask others to defy the Regent's Guard if she wasn't willing herself. Counselour Marwen had agreed.

Anwa left her tent and walked across a stretch of field to Marwen's personal tent. The Counselour was an invaluable source of advice and comfort. Marwen had been a contemporary of her mother's. Perhaps, it could be said, a distant friend. Marwen told Anwa that she reminded her very much of Lady Benta. Whether that was truth or a ploy to ingratiate herself with Anwa, it worked just the same.

The early morning dew seeped through her shoes. Anwa trod slowly so she wouldn't slip on the wet grass. The atmosphere of the camp was greatly relaxed after their recent victory. Anwa found neither Guard nor herald to announce her arrival at Marwen's tent. She took an uncertain step inside.

There had been some late night festivities after the last Q.M. victory. A lantern lit the walls with a gentle glow, revealing the unkempt state of the tent. The Counselour sat at a small table littered with bones and used cups. Clothes and blankets were strewn about carelessly, as if people had been sleeping any which where.

Marwen was faced away from her. The salt-and-pepper hair that fell braided down her back made her identity unmistakable. The gray hair made her look older than she was.

366

Marwen was not yet forty. Brock sat on her right, hands resting comfortably on the top of his head. Brock was older by a few years only, but his hair also showed signs of losing its color.

"Since we destroyed the postal system, we have as much trouble as the Regent getting messages to the other counties. We may face unknown battles against nonlocal forces," Marwen said to her companion.

Brock also had his back to the door, an imprudent tactic, Anwa thought. The pair had no idea of her presence.

"Shouldn't we wait for the girl before we discuss?"

Anwa relied heavily on her advisers for these sorts of decisions. She tried to recall her education in economy and warfare, but it was so long ago, and she hadn't been paying the attention she should have.

"I merely wish to consolidate our thoughts before we present her options to the Lady," Marwen said. "Still, I'm glad to see your attempts to control her every move have declined."

Brock grudgingly waved a hand. "We could do worse."

"It's good to see you come around to my way of thinking," said Marwen.

"Ha!" Brock scoffed noisily. "What's that nonsense about you shaping me into an independent mind, if you only want me to think like you anyway?"

Anwa was beginning to feel it was ignoble to eavesdrop. The conversation had taken such an interesting turn.

Marwen ignored his comment as she continued. "Part of the problem is directing our manpower in an organized direction. I was thinking we use that man Jedomar as our spokesperson."

Anwa recalled the handsome man from the battlefield. He was the best example of the new breed of Queensman: wild and rustic.

Brock grunted. "Could we have a more uncourtly spokesperson?" he asked.

It was a fair observation, yet Anwa felt offended on the man's behalf. There was a charm to his address, and a straightforwardness she found refreshing.

"Jedomar is immensely popular," said Marwen. "The future court of Mackabine is likely to be much less refined than Lady Benta's, or else it will develop new fashions and manners to be called refinement. Anwa is young enough, I think, that this doesn't bother her."

"It may," Anwa interrupted. "I haven't decided."

Brock was startled out of his chair. Marwen maintained her composure with more success. Both wore conflicted expressions as they considered how to greet her. Was she a teenager spying on her caretakers? Or a monarch observing a meeting of state?

She was both, Anwa decided. She lifted her chin as she crossed the threshold to join them.

CHAPTER THIRTY-EIGHT

Unable to sleep in the heart of night, Senna roved the familiar spaces of the castle. She ran a finger over the top of her kitchen counter, struck with longing at the thought she might never see it again. The counter held two bundles of dried peaches, presents for Emwid and Cafia, along with notes of gratitude. It made her remember the letter she'd written to Rimick, telling him where to find Geid's treasury. She wondered what the safest way to give it to him would be, without having to speak to him, if possible.

A noise interrupted her thoughts. Senna turned in time to see the backs of two Guards pass by her door. They were breaking protocol by entering the castle while their Lord was absent. Senna hesitated briefly. It was too late at night for their intentions to be innocuous. Her eyes caught sight of a heavy serving tray with iron handles, resting in its cubby, and she seized it on her way out the door. It could be used as a weapon if needed, and would look unthreatening if not.

Senna followed the sound of footsteps to the main hall and paused at the entrance threshold. She peered slowly around the corner and watched Guardsman Skole drop into the Baron's audience chair.

"Wow, Skole. I'm gonna tell Lodin."

Senna recognized the second Guard by his voice. Guardsman Hoke had a deep timbre that reminded Senna of

369

her uncle. Hoke disliked being by himself, and could often be seen following around other Guards who would tolerate him.

"Pff." Skole spun sideways and draped his legs irreverently over the side of the chair. "I dare Lodin to speak to me. I'll give him a close look at my fist."

Senna saw Hoke start to shake his head, and she pulled back so that he wouldn't see her in his periphery. "You can push Lodin over in a lot of ways," Hoke said, "but not with a fist."

Senna leaned her head against the stone with her ear as close to the entrance as possible. The Guards' voices echoed freely through the archway.

"How that crust-faced nincompoop ever got to be Captain is beyond me. He's even taking orders from the housekeeper."

"Fenwith told him to," Hoke explained.

"And he listened!"

Senna had likewise not expected Lodin to take this charge seriously, but the Captain had approached Senna several times to ask if she had any tasks for him. So far she hadn't made any demands.

"When Fenwith gets back..." Hoke began.

Skole interrupted. "Fenwith's not coming back."

"What makes you so sure?"

"Rofus told me."

"Rofus?" Hoke murmured, half audibly.

Skole was too deep in his soliloquy to answer. "Things are coming to a head. You saw that letter from the Captain in Anseth? The rebellion with the Queensmen might be here or might be there. I don't care. I'm getting out while the distraction holds." He made a rustle that made Senna think he must have changed position. "And I'm not leaving empty-handed. It's time I squeezed something out of this odious little town."

"Sure," Hoke observed indifferently, "but what can you squeeze?"

Senna heard a thud and imagined Skole jumping to his

toes. "I'll start with that sniveling innkeeper."

"Gambad?"

"What an annoying little echo you are. Yes, Gambad. Come with me, Hoke. We'll slit his stomach and take back the month's salary I paid him last week."

Galvanized by the subject, Senna involuntarily turned her eyes back towards the room. Skole had his face and his arms both raised to the ceiling, like a madman calling a spirit from the Otherworld.

"You can't just rob the town citizens," Hoke said.

Skole turned to his companion as if only just noticing who he was. "Forget you. I'll get Perr to join me." Senna withdrew again, just in time, as Skole spun his heel towards the door. "I'm more than enough for some simple townsfolk, anyway."

A few footsteps later, Skole's forehead was upon her, and Senna bashed it with the tray. She put everything she had into the blow, and felt her bones vibrate with the impact. Skole vibrated too, enough to make the fat of his cheeks jiggle. His eyes landed on her without focusing, and he crumpled to the floor.

Hoke made a cry of surprise that morphed into delight. "Hah!" he laughed. "Would you look at the little housekeeper bring down mighty Skole?" He tugged his harness and stretched to his full height, eyeing Senna as if daring her to try her tray on him.

Senna lowered her tray carefully to avoid it clanging on the stone. "Help me drag him to the dungeon," she directed. "You can tell Lodin he's there in the morning."

Hoke didn't argue a jot.

There was no sign of Eold to be had in Mackabine Castle. Cole questioned everyone but the Postman himself, then concluded that the Madam was very likely dead.

His original intent was to leave Mackabine at the same time as the Gaultian navy, preferably before the Queensmen made their first move. When Eold's disappearance prompted him to remain, Cole lost his window. There was no longer any question of leaving. No one was allowed to come or go from Mackabine Castle, on pain of death at one end or the other. Half of the court was fortifying themselves in their quarters, and the other half was going on as if nothing had happened.

Cole limited his forays to the emptiness of the early morning, especially when his route took him along well-traveled paths, such as the one next to the Regent's office.

With his eyes half cast down, Cole sensed rather than saw someone come to rest in front of him. When he looked up, he was surprised to find that his obstruction was the Lord Regent himself. Hemmon looked inexplicably pleased to see him.

"Fenwith, Fenwith," Hemmon sang, "where are you going?"

Cole turned himself sideways to squeeze past. He excused himself vaguely, barely managing to show the Regent his due deference.

"Ah, forgive me," said Hemmon. "I know that's not your real name."

A superb actor would have not betrayed alarm. Cole was superb, but he was also distracted, and he flinched. It was impossible to feign disinterest. His left foot pivoted back in Hemmon's direction. "What are you talking about?"

"Step into my office and I'll tell you." The Regent pointed elegantly to the room behind him. A Guard opened the door at his gesture.

Cole gave the Guard a hard look. He would rather have turned and run, but he suspected that was no longer an option. It was possible that Hemmon was guessing. Unlikely, but possible. Cole traced Hemmon's footsteps into the office.

The Regent opened his dialogue unemotionally, sighing as he wandered towards his desk. "Something came to light recently. Evidence of a distressing nature. I'm sure it will be of interest to you. It seems Lady Orila's nephew was murdered out of port five years ago." Satisfaction gleamed in Hemmon's eyes as he relayed this information. He stroked the back of his chair but did not sit in it.

"Really, Hemmon?" Cole forced a shadow of a laugh into his words. "Do you hire someone to spin these stories for you?"

Hemmon ignored his outburst. "The shock of it, when I heard! A stripling boy of not sixteen years, chased down and slain by a mob of nasty, heartless rebels. All of this was very regrettable, but then it did beg the question: who are *you*?"

The facade of five years disappeared. It fell off in layers, peeling like scales off a dried fish. Cole shuddered as he felt it go. There was nothing to hide behind now—no Fenwith to take control, no way to retreat into the shadows of his soul. Cole crossed his arms, wishing the gesture would shield more of himself from Hemmon's view.

Hemmon stepped up, prompting Cole to take an involuntary step back. The Guard held an arm out, blocking the exit. "No need to protest," Hemmon crooned. "We're beyond that. I admit your performance was impressive. I never suspected Fenwith to be the spy. He was always so boorish."

"It's too late," Cole contended finally. "Your reinforcements are already turning. Queen Anwa will take your place within the week."

"You're quite right. By all accounts, I have lost. My only consolation lies in taking everything I can down with me. That now includes you. I wish I had killed you in Geid when I had the chance. If you knew how much I regret that..."

Cole shrugged disinterestedly. "I hope you find my death satisfying." He observed this wish without sarcasm. Cole had no emotion left for the defeated Regent.

"Indeed," said Hemmon matter-of-factly. "I still don't know your real name. Would you care to enlighten me?"

Cole couldn't think of a reason to. A welcome sense of

detachment settled over him. He admired the colors of Hemmon's window.

"Well," Hemmon continued, unruffled, "Mister—whoever you are, I am particularly attentive when it comes to revenge. Your death is not the only vengeance I intend to exact. In fact, I spent all of yesterday devising the appropriate punishment for you. Would you like to know what I came up with?"

Cole remembered well what Hemmon had done to Lord Gretin. Kindly, wise, elderly Gretin was the best Baron ever to serve Lammark, or possibly any other county. Cole knew he should have been terrified. Instead he felt like he wasn't really there anymore.

"I have just sent a letter in your name—well, not your name exactly, but the origin was clear—to the Admiral of the Gaultian fleet. It extends an offer to continue your services as spy in the new court of the Mackabine Queen. To play both sides against the other, as it were; it's a skill for which you've shown considerable aptitude. It will be intercepted, of course, by the Queen-plying bandits guarding the road."

Cole stared at Hemmon, not comprehending his motive. "How in the Queen's name does that help you?" he asked.

"It doesn't. The point, Mister, is to sully your name for history. In the eyes of pretty much everyone, you will die a traitor."

Hemmon clearly expected this to bother him. The Regent's eyes bored into Cole, waiting for him to flinch. Cole felt only mild irritation, and even that he was able to hide behind an indifferent gesture.

Hemmon was obviously disappointed, but he continued his speech, which he had taken pains to prepare. "That is not all. I've also taken out a contract with the Rose."

Cole almost laughed despite himself. The Rose was an assassin's guild. A good one, by reputation; Gaultian in origin, although not actually associated with any government. "On me? That's a little redundant, don't you think?"

"Not on you." Hemmon displayed a very small, rather nasty smirk. "On Geid."

Cole did not completely understand this, but he felt free to scoff. "That's absurd. You can't take out a contract on a county."

"For the right price, my friend, you can take out a contract on anything."

Surely even Hemmon wasn't that rich. Cole tried to assuage his fears while the Regent explained his arrangement. The assassin had been sent an appropriate portion of Darleath —an expensive and potent form of dragonweed. This poison, if administered to the well, would infect the town's drinking water, and decimate the population over a period of two or three weeks. "I paid a small bonus for the irregularity of the job," Hemmon drawled, "but nothing obscene."

"What," Cole asked him slowly, "makes you think...that I care one *half-piece* about *Geid*?"

Hemmon's stare bored into him. "Do you know, I'd rather assumed the opposite. But Guardsman Rofus seems to think that you might. I'm pulling at stray vines here. Hoping to seize one that rattles you."

Cole felt his head swim. It was possible that Hemmon was lying, but he couldn't think of anything that made the scheme implausible. Cole clutched the fireplace for support, and ground his hand into the scattered ash on the manteltop. The children would die first, and the elderly. After word spread of the outbreak, people would avoid the town. Perhaps some lives would be spared. But the town itself would probably never recover.

"I framed you for that too, if it matters," the Regent added.

Cole no longer felt any apathy towards Hemmon. He wanted to detach Hemmon's head and use it as a wagon wheel.

Hemmon laughed in delight. "Your composure fails you, nameless one. Not that it needs to, but I find it satisfying nonethe—"

Hemmon did not finish because Cole flung his fistful of ashes into the Regent's face. Hemmon shrieked, clutched his eyes, and tipped backwards. Luck was with Cole just then, because Hemmon was close enough to the doorway that his Guard tried to catch him, and the movement left a space just wide enough for Cole to dart through. The Guard made a half-hearted lunge for his sleeve, but he tripped against Hemmon's flailing form. Cole gained a few precious seconds' head start.

He ducked into the first room he found, which was a Lady's sitting room. The ladies exchanged frowns at the sight of him, and then squealed as he leapt up on top of their card table. Cups of wine tipped, the contents splashing onto the women's clothing. Cole ignored the cries of indignation as he launched himself from table to window ledge. It was a broad window, which let in a good deal of light, and gave the ladies a pretty view of the garden. Cole steadied himself on a hook that some industrious person had fastened to the wood for hanging flowers.

His resolve wavered when he saw the distance to the ground below. However, the immediate appearance of the Guards behind him left no choice but to release his hold on the ledge. He fell feet first onto the sill of the window underneath. The blow against heavy stone jolted him, and his legs slipped, but he managed to keep both arms over the ledge of the window.

Overhead, the Guards pushed the excited ladies out of the way. Hemmon ordered them not to fire any arrows. Apparently, he didn't think much of Cole's odds of escape. Flailing like a fish out of water, Cole dragged the rest of his body into the room below. It was blissfully empty. Cole got up and worked his way into a slightly less obvious room. The third floor was a maze of hallways, which might take a search party some time to navigate.

Cole seized a decorative sword off the wall, felt its weight, then discarded it under a table. He barely knew one end of a sword from the other. Hiding would be difficult under the circumstances, and he wasn't especially swift-footed. If he could get to a horse, he might stand a chance, but it was a long way from the courtyard to the stables.

Cole pressed himself against the wall and peered out into the dim light of the passageway. The ruckus upstairs grew louder. Cole suspected some of the Guard had already found their way down the stairwell at the end of the wing. He was steeling himself to flee down the corridor when Lady Rona walked into the room.

Her eyes brightened, and she seemed momentarily speechless at the good fortune of finding him first. Cole thought she had come on purpose to rat him out. But she took his hand and pulled him out of the room. "Come!" she whispered sharply.

Cole was too surprised to protest. He followed Rona's lead to a private bedroom. The room was unmarked by anything to indicate its owner. A wardrobe against the wall hung open a crack, revealing a bare space. Rona opened the wardrobe door and gestured him into it.

Cole raised his eyebrows at her. He was half inclined to refuse, but Lady Rona's plan was better than anything he had ready. He crawled inside without comment. Rona closed the door and turned the key to the wardrobe. Cole wondered if this was actually her room or if her designs on her hosts extended to thievery. She had a key to the outer door as well, and he heard her turn the door latch to the room as she left. Then she let out a wild shriek.

"Guards!" the Lady cried out over and over again until the thud of boots indicated they had responded. Cole fully believed she would turn him over then. Such nicely wrapped prey was bound to earn her a reward. He held his breath while the Guards entered into a discussion with Lady Rona. He couldn't make most of it out, but he overheard the words "Lord Fenwith" repeated once or twice, and something about the way he had gone. After a moment, the noise receded down to the end of the hall.

Cole waited. His breathing seemed loud to his own

ears; he only hoped it wouldn't be heard outside the wardrobe. Time passed. How much, Cole wasn't sure. His eyes grew accustomed enough to the meager light to let him discern imperfections in the grain of the wardrobe's interior. He wondered what he would do if Lady Rona failed to come back. Eventually, he heard the sound of a turning key announce her return.

She swung open the wardrobe, crossed her arms, and gave him a triumphant look. He asked her the question she was obviously expecting. "Why are you helping me?"

"You're with the Queen, right?" Rona queried, her arms still crossed.

Cole nodded.

"I want amnesty. I'll help you escape, and in return I get to stay in the castle after the Queen takes her place."

Cole was fleetingly amused. This woman liked to cover her bets. "I'll do what I can," he promised.

It was enough to satisfy the Lady. She helped Cole disentangle himself from the wooden prison. He steadied himself at the foot of the bed and tried to work feeling back into his legs. The hall was clear, Lady Rona assured him. There was still the problem of getting free of the castle, but Rona had an idea about that, too. She beckoned imperiously.

Cole followed the Lady around a corner and down a flight of stairs he had never seen. The hall was barren of traffic. Cole wondered if Rona had arranged a distraction to keep the passersby elsewhere. On the ground floor, they reached one of the servants' entrances. It had an oversized door for passing large loads—furniture, or the like. A pair of storage rooms stood off to the side. Rona herded him into the closest one.

A single occupant awaited him there. He recognized her first by the unmistakable scent of her perfume. "Oh, Fenn!" Lady Orila spread her arms across her velvet-lined skirt. She pulled Cole into a tight hug. "You poor boy. I'm not going to let anyone hurt my only nephew, am I?"

Cole gave Rona an exasperated look. It was hard to say

378

whether Orila had been properly informed. He decided it wasn't the best time to enlighten her.

"Lady Orila is going to smuggle you out in her carriage," Rona explained.

"Thank you, Aunt," said Cole. He took her hand and kissed it with some sincere gratitude.

The storage area had its own small entrance that led to the garage where Lady Orila's carriage was parked. Cole nodded a brief farewell to the ladies, mounted the carriage, and stuffed himself into the box underneath the seat. It was a space even less commodious than the wardrobe, but he was not in a position to complain. Lady Orila arrived several minutes later. He felt her weight settle on the plank, and heard her order the carriage towards the outer gate.

The horseman argued with her a little bit. There was no place to go, he said reasonably. No one was allowed to leave the castle, by Lord Hemmon's orders. He avoided mention of the horde of Queensmen laying siege outside the walls. After several insistent refrains, the Lady was eventually obeyed.

Their ride lasted only a couple of minutes. Orila poked softly at the seat as she vacated the carriage. "I think it's safe to come out, Fenn."

Cole hesitated, suspecting that Lady Orila might not have the best sense of what conditions were safe. He rolled out of the seat and peeked cautiously through the carriage window.

"Rona said you would need a horse."

The carriage was parked against the outer gate, where a pair of Guards' horses were tethered. Lady Rona was as smart as he gave her credit for. "Thank you," said Cole.

Orila's carriageman eyed him suspiciously as he crawled out of the carriage. Cole didn't much care for his opinion. Once he got on a horse, he doubted anyone would be able to catch him.

"I don't understand why everything is so confused these days," Orila said. She trailed fecklessly behind him as he approached the horses. Her voice cracked emotionally. "If only Gote were still alive, none of this would be happening."

Cole would have liked half an hour to sit down and disillusion the woman. The most he could be bothered to say for the moment was a quick and distracted, "Goodbye, Aunt."

He took command of the swiftest-looking horse and turned it towards the barricade. The Queensmen's barrier lay fifty spans ahead, a collection of roughly cut logs and unevenly armed soldiers. They gathered in curiosity at the sight of the Lady's carriage. Cole aimed for the most open spot and urged the horse into a gallop. The animal responded well to his body posture. It was a trained warhorse, accustomed to riding without flinching. Cole's charge took the Queensmen by surprise. He cleared their barricade with a kick and the trace of a war cry. A few arrows were fired lazily in his direction, but none of them met their mark. He heard a few shouts from the frustrated Queensmen in his wake.

Cole smiled in elation as the wind whipped over his ears. *I'd like to see Hemmon try that!*

Jed saw it from a distance.

He was too far away to affect anything, but he recognized the man tumbling out of a carriage in the middle of the field. Jed dropped what he was doing and ran over. He watched the Baron mount a horse and rush the barricade like a madman. He was fifty spans off, and by the time he reached the barricade, the Baron's horse had already cleared it. "Hey! Hey, wait!" he called, but he was too late. The man next to him lifted his bow. Jed seized his arm and pulled it down. "Stop shooting!" he howled at them. His manner carried enough confidence that most of them obeyed. The rest were not quick enough or lucky enough to hit their target.

"Come back, you! Damn Baron," Jed spoke this

appeal to the empty air. The horse was too far away for the man to hear. Jed stared after the vanishing rider, feeling more than a little perplexed. Where in the world did that albino think he was going?

CHAPTER THIRTY-NINE

Sable licked the last crumbs of bread from his napkin as he watched the road wind off into the horizon. The road had been remarkably busy, filled with refugees, loyalists, opportunists, and Queensmen alike. Hack said the Queen's Revolution would offer prospects to ambitious young men.

Sable spared a glance at his two companions, both napping on the grass after their generous lunch. They were lucky to have the tranquility of mind to sleep. Sable couldn't stop worrying about his parents, whom he had not informed before embarking on this expedition. His note didn't tell them where he was going, but there were only two roads out of Geid, and it wouldn't be hard to guess which one he had taken.

Sable watched a figure on horseback in the distance. Although the road stretched ahead for miles, only parts of it were visible at a time. The rider disappeared and reappeared at the crest of every hill. Sable began to feel a suspicious sense of familiarity.

Reaching over, Sable cautiously prodded the body of his sleeping friend. "Hack," he said. Hack was lost in his nap, and responded only with a weak grunt. "Dohack, wake up for a minute. Is that the Baron of Geid?"

Hack wasn't awake enough to give the question proper

consideration. He raised his head, shrugged disinterestedly, and lay back down without opening his eyes.

Sable turned his attention back to the road. The rider had been moving at urgent speed, but he slowed as he reached their group, and brought his panting, sweat-drenched horse to a halt. Sable was astounded. It really was the Baron. He watched, mouth open in surprise, as the Baron dismounted next to their tethered horses, and took his pick of their youngest animal.

"Hack?" Sable felt justified in giving his friend a good kick. "He's stealing your horse."

That news woke Hack up in a hurry. "What?" he blurted, sitting up. His face went very red when he saw the Baron. The Baron had already mounted, and the horse reared up in their faces as it turned towards the road. Hack tried to make a run at the horse, but all he got for his trouble was a face full of dust.

Hack's language devolved into an incoherent mess of curses. "What are you standing there for, you sod?" Hack cried at Sable. He quickly untied Chet's horse and mounted it without permission.

Chet was awake now too, and quicker to react than Sable. He hesitated a moment at his missing horse, and then took Sable's horse instead.

Sable stood nonplussed in the road, watching his friends gallop away. The Baron faded out of sight long before Hack and Chet did. Sable turned to the exhausted horse left behind. The animal gave a shuddering breath, too tired to look at him. Sable gave it a sympathetic pat.

The Q.M. takeover of Geid was so smooth, most people didn't realize it had happened until it was over. With their Baron gone, the Geid Guards stopped patrolling the

383

town and kept to the castle as reports of Q.M. victory rolled in from every quarter.

The town appointed Rimick the new Judge by popular opinion. He would be in charge of Geid until the new Queen could appoint someone. Rimick accepted the position, even though he feared he was miserably suited to it. Never had there been so many people in contest for his attention. The townsfolk seemed to think he was entitled to a show of deference. They brought him gifts and endless questions.

"Mister Rimick, can I get you some tea?" a man offered.

Rimick forced himself to answer politely. "No, thank you, Mister Pom," he opened a hand to dismiss the man as he listened to the more important counsel of Madam Jortha. On Grath's advice, Rimick tried to adapt his bearing to appear more receptive, and less taciturn. He couldn't tell if it was working.

"The next business is to send someone to the other villages. Let them know what's going on, if they don't know already. Tell the local Judges to hold tight."

Rimick nodded at the elderly woman across from him. Madam Jortha was the most senior member of the lawyering circle, and the person on whose opinion Rimick placed the most weight. She would have been Judge, by all rights, if the town had not insisted on Rimick.

"Brade came back from Indor this morning," Madam Haw added, "with good things to report. It should be done in an official capacity."

The door jostled noisily, bumping the empty barrel they had rolled there to block it. The room wasn't large enough to accommodate everyone who thought they had a right to attend—namely, half the town. Rimick realized he would have to post guards at the entrance. The door shuddered again and the barrel gave way. There was a press at the entrance as the crowd struggled to determine who should enter. One of Grath's boys was small enough to squeeze through the spaces between adults. He made the first announcement. "The Q.M. from Candige have come!"

Rimick stood up as a tall, battle-wearied woman followed at the boy's heels. With a toss of her chin, she discouraged those behind her from following. Rimick recognized her as Gayna's eldest daughter, although the name momentarily escaped him.

"Captain Werd," the woman introduced herself. "Newly commissioned by the Queen's adjutant in Candige," she added. Her mother was the first to give her the title of Captain. She looked proud that it had ceased to be honorary.

"You have word from Candige?" One of the farmers addressed the Captain out of turn. The man had more riding on the matter than anyone else, since his daughter's family had emigrated there some years ago.

Werd gave a stiff nod. She slid into a chair that Madam Haw politely vacated for her. She took cautious care of the weapons at her side, one for each hand. "Once the Baron of Candige figured out what was happening, he sent his Guards to massacre us. Those who weren't slaughtered were those who fought back. The streets were red as tinted paper." Werd lifted her eyes and eyed Rimick a little enviously. "Your county seems to have weathered the change more easily."

"We're hoping to keep it that way," said Rimick.

Candige had over a hundred Guards and access to mercenaries in port. It made sense to see resistance on both sides. "The last I heard, the fighting was mostly over," said Rimick. His fingers searched reflexively for the latest letter from Gayna, still open on the table in front of them.

"The Q.M. took control of Candige Castle on Talent-Day. The last flares of violence were dying down when I left."

"How is your mother?"

"She lives," said the Captain, "which is enough to be said for a woman of her age."

On the other side of the table, Madam Tamonda whispered under her breath, "How many children does Madam Gayna have?"

Werd's ears were good enough to catch the remark. It

made her smile. "Just enough to accomplish what she bids them, Madam." Werd's smile made her look much like her mother. They were similar types of women.

The Regent had done away with female Captains after the Revolution. Gaults thought it unseemly for women to hold positions of leadership. In the past few years, some Mackabines had fallen to the same persuasion. Rimick was curious to see whether former customs would reassert themselves under Lady Anwa.

"What did you do with the Guards at Candige Castle? Did any of them surrender?" asked Madam Jortha. The Guards were a topic of contention for their circle. The townsfolk of Geid were neither angry nor organized enough to come after them, but it didn't seem fair to leave them in possession of the castle.

"No soul was spared," Werd said blandly.

Someone at the end of the room looked perturbed. "You executed all the Guards?"

"Not just the Guards. All the Baron's staff. Down to the last humdrum clerk, I'm afraid. Your young friend Dwen has been well avenged. You may rejoice in that, Mister Rimick," said Werd.

The mention of Dwen recalled Madam Senna to his mind. She had disappeared several days ago, and no one had seen a sign of her since. "Have you heard anything from the sister, a woman called Senna?"

Werd shook her head, not indicating whether or not she recognized the name.

"We still haven't confronted our Guards," another member of the lawyering circle pointed out.

"That is why I came here," offered Captain Werd, "to help you establish order for the Q.M. I have some people with me, if there's any fighting that needs done."

Madam Jortha was the first to answer. "Our Guards haven't been seen for days. They're just sitting up at the castle. I don't know what they're living on in there."

"What about your Baron? Is he in Mackabine?"

They answered in a series of grumbles and nods. "And lucky for him, too," someone grunted.

"He won't fare much better there," Werd promised them. "The castle in Mackabine has already been taken."

Rimick steered the conversation back to their first problem. "I managed to speak with Captain Lodin earlier today," he said. "He's agreed to step down."

This wasn't news to the rest of the table, but Werd looked quite impressed. "What about the rest of the Guards?" she asked.

Rimick shook his head. "Lodin refused to talk to them. Since he relinquished his role as Captain, he claimed it was no longer his duty."

Snickers escaped around the table. Captain Lodin had all the spine of a cucumber.

"Lodin isn't important," said Rimick. "We can send a separate missive to the rest of the Guard. Promise them amnesty in return for cooperating."

"All of them?" Madam Tamonda grew sullen.

"A few should be punished, but most of them are witless tools." The voice of reason came from Madam Jortha, who had already given this argument several times.

"That's fine," said another, "but let the punishment be exile, not death."

"What about Guardsman Skole?" Tamonda protested. "I want his blood."

Captain Werd looked bemused by their leniency. "If you're going to make an example of someone, it ought to be the Captain," she suggested.

Jortha disagreed firmly. "Captain Lodin is harmless. He's the most witless one of them all."

Everyone was talking at once. Rimick didn't know how to make them stop. He wished Jed was here instead of him. Jed would know how to handle these people and their conflicting opinions. He got up from the table, stunning the room into momentary silence. He ignored their stares and strode out of the building to seek a moment alone.

The crowd had cleared since Werd's arrival. Rimick was met outside only by a brisk wind. It felt natural, more comfortable than the stuffy smoked hall. Folk had gathered in the square around the rest of the Candige Queensmen, who were sharing their beer, telling stories of rebellion, and enjoying the attention. Market stalls hung heavy with the smell of meat and ripe fruit. A flock of children played "chase your uncle" near the well. Not much had changed, Rimick thought. Werd had reason to be jealous.

A boy approached shyly from the recess of the adjoining porch. "Rimick? Er...Mister Rimick?"

"Yes, what?" Rimick snapped, regretting his harsh tone.

It was the same boy who broke through to announce Captain Werd. Rimick knew him from association with his parents. His name was Thuder. He was Sable's younger brother. Thuder was deemed too young to participate in schemes with the Q.M. Perhaps the boy would get more attention now that Sable had run off seeking his fortune in Mackabine.

"Are you all right, sir?"

Rimick meant to nod, but he shook his head instead. Then he laughed, which was uncommon for him. He wished errantly that Jed were there to hear it. Others in the square pointed as they noticed his presence on the porch. There was no escape from it, Rimick realized. He put a hand on the boy's shoulder and led Thuder back into the hall with him.

CHAPTER FORTY

In a good carriage, with ideal weather, it was a comfortable four day journey to Geid from Mackabine. Cole made it in a day and a half. He passed the turnoff to Rodenark with some reluctance. Was Senna waiting there now? As much as he could have used the help, Cole didn't think he could afford the extra days it would take to fetch her.

At the same time, he was glad Senna was out of danger, and not just from Hemmon's assassin. From what he'd seen of the country, Mackabines were celebrating their freedom a little too freely. Near Redcone, he watched a mob of villagers burn someone on a bed of kindling fueled by tax receipts. Cole prayed the chaos would dissipate soon. No doubt Anwa would also expect her subjects to pay taxes.

Cole crossed the border into Geid county a little after dawn on Forward-Day. His mare was reaching the limits of her endurance. She wheezed and tossed her head crossly. The mare was his third horse, and Cole was driving her longer than the others. He tightened his grip on the reins, determined to coax her into the last few miles, but the mare had had enough. She stopped abruptly and reared into the air. It caught Cole unawares. He tumbled off her backside into the soggy road.

Cole was too stunned to move right away. His back ached, but he didn't think anything was broken. When he opened his eyes, he found a face hovering curiously above him. It belonged to a squat, dull-looking woman of too many years. Her eyes rolled a little and her mouth was stuck in a sort of witless grin. Cole ran her face through a mental catalog of townsfolk. Madam Gareb, perhaps? Or Cadweth?

The old woman tilted her face sideways at him. "Man fall down. Down, down, down," she garbled.

Cole decided she wasn't a heavy threat. He picked himself up and slapped the mud from his knees.

The mare was too tired to run away. She stood panting with her snout near the ground. Cole wasn't going to try to mount her again. He unbridled the horse and led her to a patch of frosty grass to chew. The woman gnawed her fingertips as she watched him discard the bridle over her front gate.

"Madam Cadweth, is it?" said Cole. A glimmer of recognition told him he had guessed correctly. "Good meeting to you."

Madam Cadweth showed no indication of knowing who he was. Her mind wasn't all there. "Meeting...meeting," she mumbled. She lost interest in him and set her eyes on the panting mare. Cole left them to each other in the hope they would get along. He wandered around the side of the tiny house and helped himself to a shawl and some gloves that he found on the drying line. He thought briefly to offer the Madam some reimbursement, then realized he had no money. He settled for not being seen, and wrapped himself thoroughly before taking to Geid on foot.

At first glance, the town appeared untouched by the havoc that the Q.M. revolt had wrought over the rest of Mackabine. No one seemed to be hiding, or preparing for anything life-threatening. Someone had tied strips of decorative colored ribbon to the posts of their fence. Madam Magg was handing out her morning surplus of eggs to stray passersby. "Praise the Queen," she told each recipient. She offered one to Cole. He almost refused until he realized how stupid that would be. He cracked the egg open in front of her and sucked down the cool raw substance. It was his first meal since Mackabine.

Cole tried not to make eye contact with anyone. The day was warming, making Cole's disguise of heavy clothing less convincing. If anyone thought him odd, they made no comment. He followed the growing crowd headed to market and listened to the distracted chatter of the townsfolk closest to him.

"I don't think the Queen has so many appointments as people hope for," said a man to his wife. "She's not going to give one to everyone who asks, is she?"

"If she gives one to a Geidman at all, I'll be astounded," the woman answered.

No one challenged Cole before he reached the town square. His eyes shot to the well, situated in the middle of human activity. He had to restrain himself from issuing a warning, as he saw the first folks line up to draw water. It was tempting merely to hang a sign that read *Poisoned Well: Do Not Touch.*

Beside him, a pair of handsome women linked arms as they passed. The first woman wore a giant hat. She flipped it casually off her head to fan away a swarm of flies. "Where is Mister Rimick going to put the new Queensmen who came?"

"I wish they would stay at our house," her companion answered. "There's some nice-looking young men among them."

"You're so silly, Efina." The hatted woman grinned. "We don't have the spare room for a treeskunk!"

Their laughter brightened the space around them. Cole felt an unexpected pang of fondness for these townsfolk. After five years of pretending to be their Baron, he had developed a sense of ownership towards them. He would not forgive himself if anything happened to them.

Cole settled into the doorway of an abandoned shop to think. He'd set out to Geid with very little plan in mind. His first though had been to stand guard by this well until the assassin appeared. Cole was confident he had arrived first— assuming Hemmon hadn't made the whole thing up.

However, there were a lot of points against this plan, which Cole had slowly come to terms with. First, there was no guarantee Cole would recognize the assassin when he appeared. The movement needed to slip poison into a well might be fairly subtle. Second, Cole was no match for an assassin, even if he caught him. And third, if he sat down, Cole was fairly certain he would fall asleep.

No. He needed to alert the new authorities of Geid, whoever they were, to the danger—without tipping off the assassin. It wasn't enough to quarantine the well. The assassin would target whatever water supply they diverted to.

Cole wasn't looking forward to enacting this new plan. He gave eyes to the building that housed the lawyering circle and tried to picture what Madam Jortha would be doing inside. Mister Rimick might also be nearby, given what Cole had heard of the women's conversation. Rimick was a logical fellow. He might be made to see the big picture if Cole explained it to him, step for step.

Feeling sick with indecision, Cole watched the morning business of the square move forward. A stranger approached from one end of the square. Strangers were not unusual at present. This wasn't the first person Cole hadn't recognized today. It made sense that refugees would come to Geid seeking shelter from fighting in other areas of the country. This stranger, however, looked perceptively foreign. He lingered a long time near the well without having any apparent business.

Cole inched closer. A merchant called out loudly, waving to a group of folk that appeared from the road. Cole recognized the entire group as friends to the Q.M. Walking freely in the open, at the head of the party, was Mister Rimick. Cole let himself smirk. That was proof of the favorable state of things. After some quick words with Grath, Rimick gave his eyes to the stranger at the well. Cole decided against attracting Rimick's attention at present. He relocated to a place where he was able to overhear their conversation.

"Good meeting, stranger." Rimick's greeting was

friendly enough. "How did you come to be in our town?"

"Is there a problem?" the stranger said.

"I'm the Judge here. We're just checking to see how many newcomers we have. Where they're coming from, and so forth. We have volunteers offering food and lodging to those who need it."

Cole wondered if Rimick was sifting for foes among the refugees. He shifted uneasily. If Rimick was questioning strangers, he would probably look this way next. The stranger dissembled expertly, lowering his bag to the ground as he spoke. Came into Mackabine for some business that went sour when the rebellion hit, the stranger claimed. It sounded plausible enough. Cole had no solid reason to suspect him as the assassin.

The stranger turned his hands out to draw attention away from his feet, which he used to gently push his bag into the underspace of the stall behind him. Cole watched it settle dustily a few inches from the rickety panel on the other side. He edged his way along the outer circuit of stalls, approaching the stranger's booth from the south side. Hidden by the panel between them, Cole crouched and thrust his hands into the man's bag. His search was rewarded after a few seconds with the discovery of a small vial. Cole pulled the top off and took a whiff of the contents. The pungent odor confirmed it was poison. It was a smell every castle steward was trained to detect. Cole had never smelled Darleath, but he presumed it was similar to the scent of dragonweed.

He slipped the vial into his sleeve and took a few steps back without raising the alarm of anyone present. Cole sent a fast prayer of gratitude to the Otherworld for his luck. He managed to leave the market with only mild urgency.

Cole took the shortest path out of the town, uphill towards the cliffside. It would be a fitting place to dispose of the vile liquid. Cole's feet made deep prints in the loamy soil. His mind roiled as he walked, and his relief slowly faded. Snatching the poison might not be the end of it, he realized.

As far as Cole understood it, contracts were bound to

the agent on which they were assigned. If by some luck the target managed to kill the assassin coming after him, the contract was considered filled, and the instigator would have to pay anew for a second attempt. But Cole hadn't actually stopped the assassin. All he'd done was pilfer an instrument.

Cole shook his head. He was bone tired, not thinking clearly, and still looking for an excuse not to reveal himself as Baron Fenwith. The assassin wouldn't go home until he fulfilled his task, not even if he had to wait to secure more poison.

Cole paused, eyeing the cliff coming into view ahead of him. Perhaps he should turn around and take the poison to Rimick. Would it serve as evidence? Would Rimick believe a single word he said?

A shuffle of boots broke Cole's concentration. He glanced back to see a figure tracing his footsteps on the hill below. Cole cursed under his breath. It was almost certainly the assassin. He gripped the vial through the fabric of his sleeve. He kept his course steady, trying to look unaware of any threat to his plans. After a few spans, he heard the assassin's footsteps quicken. Cole gave up and broke into a run. He was close to his goal now, but the assassin was fast. Cole heard him gaining ground with each second. Cole desperately pulled the poison out of his sleeve and launched the vial with all his might. It narrowly cleared the edge of the cliff before it disappeared. The assassin hollered in rage. His body fell into Cole, pitching him to the ground and pinning him there.

The assassin pulled Cole's cloak away and got a good look at him. "You!" he shouted, incredulous. "You must be the spy Lord Hemmon found. How did you get here?"

Cole squirmed under the weight against his chest. It was pointless, and the assassin cuffed him for his trouble. He looked over Cole's diminutive figure. "You're rather short for a spy, aren't you?"

"You're rather poisonless for an assassin, aren't you?" Cole retorted.

The assassin took his wit with a smile. "What's your name?"

Cole told him, surprised the assassin cared.

The assassin released his grip and backed off. Cole stood, cautiously gauging the assassin's movements. "What about you?" he asked, trying to keep the assassin distracted while he searched for a weak point.

"The Rose doesn't give out names."

"Of course not," Cole said acerbically. Assassins didn't have weak points.

"That was smart of you, to get away from Hemmon like that. To get the poison, too. Very shifty. It doesn't change anything, though." The assassin's hand shot out with the precision of a viper and wrapped itself around Cole's throat. Cole choked as the assassin lifted him up by the neck.

"I'll let Hemmon know I finished his job. Maybe I get a bonus." Smiling grimly, he eased his arm out over the edge of the cliff.

Cole was suffocating. He pried at the fingers against his throat to no avail. He tried clawing at the assassin's arm, leaving feeble scratches, desperately trying to get him to release his hold. Then the worst thing happened. He did.

Cole fell through vacant air for several seconds. He saw the black void below and knew what was coming. He prepared himself mentally for the embrace of the ocean. The cold struck like a mallet over the head. Cole had never been immersed in water before. He had imagined it would be peaceful, not like this...consuming nothingness. There was supposed to be a way to navigate. He was supposed to swim. He had some vague notion of how this might be accomplished, but his arms and legs didn't respond the way he wanted them to. It felt like a thousand tiny arrows drilling into his skull. This was a terrible way to die. Which way was the surface? How long did it take for a man to drown?

After thrashing about to no particular effect, Cole grew still. The reality of defeat settled in. He wouldn't have minded so much, if not for Senna. He conjured a vision of her face to comfort himself. All beautiful hair tumbling over soft cheeks…the image called out to him, telling him to fight. Cole decided Senna was worth fighting for, and he stretched out one more time. To his surprise, his hand broke free into the air. Another jolt of effort propelled him to the surface. Cole sucked down a mouthful of air. The relief was short-lived. The water claimed him again when he stopped moving. He had to kick and struggle to maintain a minimal relationship with the surface.

Cole didn't notice the movement of the ocean was pushing him towards the cliff until he looked up and saw he was about to be smashed into its jagged face. Where was that accursed passage?

The current knew, even though Cole did not. As he neared the wall, his feet were sucked into a tunnel, and he surrendered to the tug of the ocean. The passage became obvious once he found it. Serrated rocks abraded his skin, but he used every part of his body to shove and haul his way forward, until finally he arose in a shallow pool. Cole drew great, gasping breaths of air as he dragged himself out of the biting water. He had no idea this experience would be so horrible. He was wholly ashamed to have ever inflicted it on anyone else.

Madam Haw's basement cavern was mostly dark. Only a faint glow came from the firepit, where a few coals had been allowed to smolder. Cole dragged himself over to that meager warmth. He was shaking so badly it was impossible to walk. He threw in as much kindling as he could find, and watched a flame build up over the coals. He was half stunned into uselessness, and it took a force of concentration to look around. In the growing light, he gradually made out the irregularity of a natural formation that had been connected to a room. There were a pair of cots, shelves for storage, and a stock of blankets and dry clothes. Cole forced himself to undress and dry off. Then, too exhausted to do otherwise, he fell asleep for an indeterminate length of time.

He was still alone when he woke. There was no sign

that anyone knew he was down here. Sleep had cleared the worst fatigue from his mind and body. He rummaged through the shelves for some bread and dried fruit, which he devoured like a starving child. Then he sat in front of the dying fire and let his thoughts tumble about loosely for another half hour. Eventually there was only so much inaction the situation could tolerate. Cole took his pick of the best clothes that would fit. Then he staggered up the tunnel that connected the cavern with the house.

The family was sitting down to a meal when Cole walked into their front room. He had to move a broom away from the door to get through, and the sound made them look up as he opened the door. They stared at him like a treeskunk would stare at a viper who'd blundered into its burrow.

Madam Haw dropped her spoon, handle-first, into her soup. It splashed a bit of vegetable onto her face, which clung there unnoticed while she ogled him down. One of Grath's sons stood up. Grath looked like he wanted to pull the lad back into his chair, but all he did was flap one hand flaccidly against the boy's shirt.

"Ahh...I'm sorry," said Cole, wishing he had the presence of mind to say something better. "Please excuse me." He edged his way to the door, feeling very awkward. None of the family managed to find their voice before Cole found the handle to the door. He fled the house without looking back.

CHAPTER FORTY-ONE

Captain Lodin's mind wandered in conjunction with his feet, up and down the halls of Geid Castle. Its walls felt strange to him—familiar, yet surreal. His last orders from Fenwith were to hole up inside the castle if there was trouble, and wait until things improved. They'd seemed like odd instructions at the time. Lodin wondered what sort of trouble Fenwith had been suspecting, and if it bore any resemblance to the current state of things.

The first hint of a problem came days ago, in the form of a letter from a Captain in Anseth. He mentioned Queensmen in the capital, and warned the county Guards to quench rebellion at the first sign. Lodin shrugged the concern away. He never saw any signs. Soon after, the posts stopped coming. News came in the form of travelers, weary, war-stricken people who spoke of dethroned Barons and the rise of Queen Anwa. The other Guardsmen asked for action. Send a scout, they urged. There was no shortage of volunteers. In the end almost half the Guard abandoned Geid Castle on reconnaissance. Lodin let them all go, although he doubted he would see any again. The town was out of his hands. He was a relic, waiting to be replaced and shipped elsewhere. Lodin wouldn't fight, but he would stay in the castle until someone kicked him out.

He heard a noise echo down an empty hall, and held

his breath a moment in trepidation. Should he investigate? Was it his place? Did it even matter anymore? Lodin's feet carried him unconsciously to the east hall. What he found made him question whether he was dreaming. Lord Fenwith sat cross-legged on the floor, hunched over in deep concentration. He had poured out the contents of his desk and was going through the papers. He looked unkempt and his hair was damp. Lodin half believed the little albino was a returned spirit or, failing that, he was at least crazy.

The Baron was so involved in what he was doing that he didn't notice Lodin come in. Lodin stopped beside the desk and looked down at the scattered mess of notes. Fenwith started a little when he looked up. "Oh! Lodin," the Baron said, unconcerned. "I'm looking for a letter with the seal of the Rose. It's a little red mark with thorns that sort of weave around the bottom. It might have come while I was gone. Have you seen it?"

Lodin couldn't remember for the life of him. He'd stopped paying attention to those kinds of things. He shook his head.

The Baron sighed in frustration. He opened a chest against the wall and pawed through the things on top. "No, no," Fenwith mumbled to himself. He momentarily took notice of Lodin again. "Lodin, I want this chest delivered to the lawyering circle. Will you take care of it?"

Lodin obediently picked up the chest and started to take it outside. He got all the way to the main hall before he remembered that he no longer worked for Lord Fenwith. After some hesitation, he set the chest down and went to inform Mister Rimick that Fenwith had returned to the castle.

Cole was almost outside the gates when a young voice begged him to wait. He turned around to see Guardsman

Cafin running across the courtyard. He wanted to flee, or maybe tell Cafin to go away. But Cafin's cry had roused several other Guards. They seethed out of the Guards' quarters like ants swarming an invader. Cole slowed his footsteps as the men inevitably converged on him.

"Lord Fenwith, where have you been?" asked Cafin. "What happens in Mackabine?"

Cole opened his mouth and realized he did not know what to say. Fenwith's ego failed to materialize on command. It was gone, melted somehow into the floor of Hemmon's office. All of a sudden he felt very insecure addressing his Guards as anyone but himself. "Uh," he stammered, "well..."

The Guards were as confused as he. They were expecting orders against the revolt. Rimick had probably sent them instructions to disarm and await the judgment of the lawyering circle.

"What should we do?" asked one.

A more brazen Guard gave his opinion. "We'll fight for you, Lord."

"No," Cole said quickly. "Don't fight. You'll only get yourselves killed. Just surrender. Or leave. Some of you have families in other counties. You should go back to them."

There was a heavy pause while the Guards considered his words. "What about the Regent?"

"There is no Regent. Mackabine will shortly be filled with nothing but Queensmen. My advice is to try to fit in."

These words silenced further objections. Cole picked up the crossbow he had set down and laid it gingerly against his shoulder.

Cafin wouldn't let him leave without saying one more thing. "Lord Fenwith, forgive me, but...you seem different."

Cole nodded in acknowledgment. "That's nice," he said. He turned and walked away, and gave thanks to the Otherworld that none of them tried to follow.

❖

Rimick winced mentally as someone called his name on the road. He forced himself to slow down as Mister Rell hurried to catch up.

"What is it?" Rimick asked the fellow who fell into step beside him.

Rell was panting from the effort of catching him. "You know that big stranger from the market? The one who got robbed?"

"Yes, what about him?" The stranger called himself Urgan. He caused a bit of a ruckus in the market a few hours ago when someone reported a thief rifling through his bag.

"He's a murderer," Rell exclaimed. "I saw him throw someone off the cliff!"

Rimick stopped walking altogether. "Are you sure?"

"Sure as the Queen is Lady Anwa, sir. I saw it happen."

Rimick sighed. The victim was probably the thief from the market. Urgan said he wanted to deal with the problem himself. He'd convinced them not to try to intercept the thief. Rimick had been too busy to argue. Now he had a murder on his hands and it was only his second day as the town Judge.

Then Rimick recalled the devastation described by Captain Werd in her home county of Candige. He was glad wandering criminals were the worst of his problems.

"Did anyone else see this?"

No one had, but Rimick believed the older man. Rell described the scene with impassive detail. Rimick wasn't sure what to do. With the local Guard disbanded, there was no one to carry out orders for an arrest.

"I watched him a little ways," Rell confessed. "He slipped into the forest behind Carly cottage. I was scared to go farther than that."

"That's just as well," Rimick told him. He thanked Mister Rell and excused him back to his home.

Since Rimick was near the cottage anyway, he decided

to look around. Without a clear point of origin, it could be impossible to pick up a trail. But there was nothing lost in trying.

A light rain had made the ground soft and susceptible to imprints. There were footprints all over the road near Carly cottage. Some were far too old. Some were recognizable as persons he knew. But he did find one set that was interesting. The prints were especially large and made by an expensive cut of shoe. Instead of leading towards the town, they veered away into the forest some spans west of the cottage.

Rimick hesitated only slightly before following them. It was strange to think that law enforcement had suddenly become his business. He couldn't remember a time when he had been on the proper of government before.

The forest floor was familiar and comforting. Rimick moved slowly, placing his feet to minimize any noise. He ventured deep before his search bore results. A tumble of crushed leaves in the distance told him someone was nearby. Rimick took his time pulling closer, inch by inch, until he began to catch fragments of a conversation.

"...have to leave...back with more poison...maybe some bodyguards." Rimick recognized the deep, accented voice of Mister Urgan.

A lighter, younger voice answered him. "So the Mackabine revolt has been successful, after all."

Rimick wanted a closer look. He stepped into the shadows of a bush whose dense foliage shielded him from the eyes of the men he stalked. He peered through a jumble of leaves into a makeshift camp. A flimsy-looking tent was propped against a tree beside a firepit still under construction. "I knew it would be," Urgan grumbled. "It doesn't matter. Our reputation compels us to complete the assignment regardless of Hemmon's fate."

"How were you seen, master?"

Rimick detected a trace of condescension in the younger man.

"Never mind—" Urgan started to snap, then he

402

stopped. "We're being watched."

Rimick didn't know how he had been discovered. He hadn't done more than breathe in his hiding place. He started to back up, but Urgan was surprisingly fast for a man of his grand size. He closed the distance to the bush and reached his arm through the wall of leaves that separated them. A hundred tiny branches snapped against his body as the man pulled Rimick into the clearing. Urgan threw him furiously to the ground.

Rimick's instincts made his body react swiftly. He rolled as he hit dirt and bounced reflexively to his feet. The stranger was expecting it. His drawn fist rammed explosively into Rimick's jaw. The second man caught Rimick as he stumbled and sent him flying back. Rimick tripped on his way and Urgan moved aside to let him collapse on the ground.

Rimick didn't stay down long. He swung one foot underneath and launched himself violently at Urgan. Rimick was angry and alert, but for the first time in his life, he was truly outclassed. Urgan interrupted Rimick with a blow that sucked the air out of his chest. He bent over gasping. Rimick tried one last time to get up, but Urgan pushed him into the earth with his heavy boot.

He kept Rimick pinned with one foot while he kicked him repeatedly with the other. When he finally lost enthusiasm for that method, he bent down and went to work on Rimick with his fists. Urgan kept going until Rimick literally begged him to stop.

"Done?" Urgan asked.

Rimick didn't move again.

"You're the new Judge, aren't you? You're the second man that's tried to tail me today. A pretty foolish business, you see."

"*Who are you?*" Rimick whispered, but his voice was so weak he didn't think the stranger heard him.

"You stupid, insignificant little Mackabine. You don't deserve to be killed by me." Rimick watched his blood seep into the dark earth as he listened. "Thought you could take me by yourself? Well, that's the last mistake your town will have to suffer for, at your hands, anyway."

Rimick found the strength to struggle again as Urgan drew a long knife and dragged his damaged body up the trunk of a tree.

An unexpected voice intruded at this moment, sounding clearly across the clearing. "Drop him," it said. Rimick's first assumption was that Urgan's assistant made the demand, but his eyes passed over the stupefied assistant to see him gawking in the other direction. He followed that gaze to the new arrival.

Rimick couldn't think of a person he less expected to see. It was Baron Fenwith. The Baron stood boldly, legs apart, holding a crossbow it looked like he barely knew how to use. "Did you hear me?" said Fenwith. "I said let him go."

Urgan did not let Rimick go, but he did lower the knife. "You? I don't believe it," Urgan said. His disbelief appeared genuine. "Do you actually know how to swim?"

"I figured it out."

Then Fenwith shot him.

Rimick gave Fenwith credit for not dallying around. On the other hand, his aim was rather poor. The arrow hit Urgan in the breastbone, wounding him superficially before it bounced to the ground. It did get Urgan to release his hold on Rimick. Rimick slunk ungracefully to the ground.

The assistant came to his senses and made a move to rush Fenwith. His ankle passed near Rimick's hand, and Rimick seized it, yanking the younger man to the ground. The assistant grunted, more annoyed than anything, but he underestimated Rimick. Rimick nimbly took the knife from the assistant's belt and plunged it through the young man's ribs. The assistant gurgled in surprise as he died. Rimick looked up to see Fenwith desperately attempting to reload his crossbow.

Urgan still had his knife, and he looked quite dangerous for someone who'd just been shot in the chest. He glared murderously at Rimick for killing his companion. Then he decided the albino was the larger threat, and he turned to deal with Fenwith first. Wrong choice, thought Rimick. He removed the knife from the corpse in front of him and tossed it into Urgan's exposed back. Urgan went down howling.

It took him longer to die than his assistant. He fell and lay on his side, bleeding from both front and back. "You piece of garbage, foreign dogfish," he spat, furious in the throes of death. "I'll scrape the eyes out of your head and feed them to your children!" Fenwith stared at Urgan in fascination as his curses faded into groans. His body twitched and gradually grew still.

Rimick struggled to stay conscious. After several moments, the Baron came to stand over him. Rimick's offhand plan was to choke the life out of Fenwith with his bare hands, but the albino kept a cautious distance. He lowered the crossbow in his hands.

"Well done," said Fenwith. "I don't know if you knew this, but those men were trying to kill every soul in Geid."

Rimick stared at him, his mouth waiting to form one of the many questions in his head. None of them came. He closed his eyes instead. But he remained at least fractionally aware as Fenwith arduously dragged his body up and heaved him over his shoulder.

CHAPTER FORTY-TWO

Cole struggled to keep upright as dense branches threatened to trip him at every step. It didn't help matters that Mister Rimick weighed almost twice as much as him. He trudged awkwardly through the brush in what he hoped was the proper direction.

Rimick made a grinding moan into Cole's shoulder. "Hey." Cole prodded the sagging head, hoping to elicit some response, but Rimick remained soundly unconscious. Cole might have dropped the body anywhere, but Rimick had been beaten so badly that Cole feared he might die without help.

After some minutes, Cole stumbled across a trail etched tenuously into the forest floor by hunters and wandering livestock. Cole couldn't tell if it was the same trail that brought him here, but he assumed it would lead them to civilization. The track became familiar when it merged with a wider one. Cole confidently took the right fork towards town. He intended to leave Rimick within sight of the first person he saw.

With the assassin brought to a satisfactory end, Cole could be clear of Geid in under an hour. The thought kept his feet moving.

A noxious aroma told Cole he has nearing the tanner's shop. The shop sat on the outskirts of town, where the stench could waft harmlessly into the trees. When it came into view, he spied a pair of women huddled on the stepway of the shop. Cole made a curt appeal for help from the side of the road. The women cried in alarm at the sight of him, and took off in the opposite direction.

He watched them for a moment before he realized that his hood had been knocked askew in the strain to keep Rimick balanced. After a frantic moment of indecision, he settled on this spot as the best place to leave Mister Rimick. The man was so heavy that Cole feared he bruised Rimick further by dropping him too fast.

Cole grabbed at his cloak. The hood was long gone, lost somewhere in the bowels of the forest. He could arrange a new covering, but that would take precious minutes, which it turned out he did not have. The distress of the women had drawn an immediate response. The tanner's stepway suddenly filled with people. Cole took an apprehensive step backwards. How many customers did the tanner have?

Then he caught a sight that made his heart drop. It was Whip, his beautiful stallion, led by a Geidman around a curve in the road. Cole had left Whip tethered and saddled in a glade not far from here. If the townsfolk found Whip and brought him here, did that mean they were looking for his owner?

Cole could see no other recourse, so he began walking calmly and self-assuredly towards his horse. Rimick's inert body created a temporary distraction. Several people rushed past him to attend to their friend on the ground.

"It's Mister Rimick!" he heard them call. No doubt they would blame Cole for his damaged condition.

The townsfolk were in disarray. A few shot Cole dirty looks, but whether from a lack of certainty or general authority, no one actually stopped him.

The man holding Whip was a farmer named Timbad. By reputation, a supposedly timid fellow. Cole had never verified this, but the farmer looked deeply intimidated by his approach. He released his hold on the stallion's reins. Whip threw back his head, pleased by the freedom, and trotted blithely towards Cole. By the Queen, he loved that horse.

"Are you crazy?" someone said. "That's Baron Fenwith."

"Somebody get him!"

Cole had a hold on Whip's reins before the crowd finished forming its resolution. He pulled himself into the saddle and was out of their reach in a matter of moments. He paused a ways off, and looked back from the perch of his horse. The townsfolk stared back at him, wide-eyed and accusatory.

A few waved towards some bushes beside the road, where a pair of riders appeared on horseback. Cole could not immediately place them in context. They were strangers to Geid, but they had adorned their shoulders with sashes to mark themselves as Queensmen. Cole studied the Q.M. as they addressed themselves briefly to the townsfolk. When they turned in his direction, he decided it was time to leave.

Cole urged Whip into a gallop. The quickest way out of Geid was straight through the center of town. The townsfolk in his way got out of the road when they saw him coming. Cole could hear the Q.M. giving chase behind him. They were decent riders, but Cole's head start was more than sufficient. He was light, and Whip was bred for speed. By the time he reached the other edge of town, Cole settled confidently into a more comfortable pace.

The main road angled southward, away from the ocean, where it would eventually fork into two paths. The obvious one led towards Candige, and eventually Mackabine. The smaller path led inland to Anseth, towards Rodenark and Senna. Cole wasn't sure which path the Q.M. would expect him to take.

Cole almost missed the glimmer of the trip wire in front of him. It flashed in the ebbing sunlight, less than a dozen spans ahead. Cole jerked back on the reins slightly. Whip slowed into a turn, limiting the force of the trap. Cole closed his eyes reflexively. He flew a good ten spans, then rolled another five.

When his vision cleared, Cole checked himself for injury. He had lost his wind and a little skin, but nothing serious. Cole remembered his horse and gave eyes to the road behind him. Whip looked more riled than put down. The stallion had pawed his way back to his feet. Cole could see the red line where the wire cut across the cannon of his leg.

A man and woman emerged from the brush alongside the trip wire. They blocked his access to Whip. Their sashes were cut from the same fabric as the earlier Queensmen's. The pair showed no remorse for risking serious injury to his stallion. They didn't approach, but they clearly weren't going to let him leave. The Q.M. that chased him earlier arrived in force at that moment, along with two more he hadn't yet seen. The air of triumph that had buoyed his spirits a moment before began to fade. Cole saw no way to fight his way past six armed Queensmen.

"Haris! Well done." A woman with dark hair came to a stop at the forefront. If her manner were not enough, she marked herself as Captain by a leather badge affixed to her sash. "It seems that ousted Guard Captain was correct, after all." She dismounted officiously and circumnavigated the wire still affixed to the undergrowth.

Cole used the interlude to beat the dust out of his cloak. Betrayed by Lodin; that was a fittingly ironic finale. He glanced at the Captain and wondered what to say to her. The woman didn't look open to persuasion. His breath was fast and ragged enough to grant some excuse for silence and the Queensmen were disciplined enough not to engage in smug repartee. They stood silent and immobile until their Captain spoke again.

"Well, Lord Baron of Geid, I think your tenure has run out."

"Who are you people?" Cole asked out of curiosity more than stratagem. Their authority was likely self-appointed, but that didn't mean it wouldn't hold its weight in this climate.

"We are appointees of the Q.M. of Candige. I am Captain Werd."

Cole knew the name. She was more official than Cole had hoped. Gayna's daughter would be acknowledged by association.

The Captain waited longer, but if she was expecting a response, she didn't get one. Werd studied him another long moment. "We set our Baron on fire while he was still alive," she said.

What a lovely thing to share. Cole scanned the road in both directions, looking for what sort of aid, he couldn't imagine.

"Look here, Baron. I'll give you a choice. We can dispense justice here and now," the Captain put her hand on her sword for effect, "or if you prefer, we can take you back to Geid and let them deal with you."

The offer surprised Cole. He half expected the Q.M. to beat him up before they dragged him away. He searched the Captain's face for malicious intent, but found none. The woman regarded him with something between pity and disgust. Maybe she hadn't enjoyed watching the Candige folk burn Baron Selweck.

"I don't have a preference either way, Baron," said Werd, "but I won't lift a finger once I hand you off to your tenants."

Cole found himself considering the Captain's offer very seriously. He truly did not want to go back into Geid. The notion of standing trial by the lawyering circle did not raise a lot of pleasant expectations. Cole examined a pattern of crossing wheel tracks in the road while he thought. He might buy time by telling the truth, while waiting for a reprieve from the Queen which may or may not come. Cole doubted whether he would even attempt it. If Senna were here, she would have spoken for him, and they might have listened to her. Right now there was no one, and very little evidence on his side. He would be lucky to get a short hanging. Cole continued his train of thought until he could see the Captain's patience growing thin. "All right," said Cole quietly, "I'll take your justice. Thank you."

410

The Captain obviously didn't expect him to answer any differently, but the *thank you* made her squint.

Cole walked over to his horse, ignoring the man who defiantly held Whip's reins out of his reach. He ripped strips from the edge of his borrowed cloak and used them to clumsily bandage Whip's front legs, still bleeding from contact with the trip wire. He felt the eyes of the Q.M. on him, but they didn't object. A trained noblehorse was not cheap.

"May I have a last request?" Cole asked as he stood. He made the appeal before they could get into the details of his execution.

The Captain's squint deepened suspiciously. "What?" Her tone foreshadowed refusal.

"I want to write a letter."

"To whom?"

"A woman. Senna. She's waiting for me at the bridge into Rodenark. She'll be alone, and she's not dangerous. Will you take it to her?" Cole asked boldly, as a man seeking a favor from a friend. He would save begging for later if it came to that.

The Queensmen gave each other bemused looks. The Captain looked annoyed at being asked to do something out of her way, but to Cole's surprise, she agreed. "You have fifteen minutes." She ordered some paper and let Cole sit unmolested under a tree.

The fifteen minutes were generous, and Cole treasured them, but they passed very quickly. He relinquished the letter still unsatisfied with its contents. The Captain again guaranteed its delivery. A messenger would have been sufficient, but Captain Werd put the paper in her own cloak and vowed to do it herself. Cole could only hope she was telling the truth.

The Queensmen were finished with delays. They kicked the loose leaves off a flat piece of earth. "On your knees," the Captain ordered.

Cole obeyed. In the distance he heard someone call for a man to hold the Baron still and the man complained about

411

getting blood on his clothes.

"I won't move," Cole promised. He didn't waste time observing their reaction, but they seemed to take him at his word because they gave him a wide berth.

One of the men wiped a sword unceremoniously on his saddlebag. The man looked strong enough to make a clean cut. Cole certainly hoped so. Partial beheadings were not pretty. He wondered if he would end up on a pike somewhere, like Jedomar in the Mackabine market.

Cole had his eyes closed, but he sensed the man take position behind him. Sensed him raise the heavy weapon. His ears were sharply attuned to these sounds. He felt wind whistle behind him, a fast rush of air, and he suddenly had his nose in the dirt.

It took Cole half a second to realize that he had ducked. It was instinctual. The Queensman's sword passed through empty air. Some of the Queensmen thought it was funny, but the Captain sounded irritated. She cursed at the man laughing next to her.

"Haris, for heaven's sake, hold him down!"

"I'm sorry," Cole said. He was quite embarrassed. The Queensmen paid him no mind. A pair of them grabbed him roughly and tucked his arms behind his back. They pushed his neck low to the ground, but the sound of an arrow shooting over their heads stopped them from proceeding further.

Cole froze, supposing they were under attack, and took a moment to consider whether or not that might be a good thing. Unable to look up, he listened as the hooves of several horses galloped into range.

"Hold there!" someone called in a strong voice. "Is that the Baron of Geid?"

By this time, the Queensmen were more interested in what was going on than they were in holding him down, so they allowed him to sit up. The new arrivals brought their horses to rest in a semicircle. A brief glance told Cole they were Queensmen, and far more official-looking than this group. They had actual uniforms with the Queen's crest stitched on the breast. Cole felt dizzy from sudden hope.

The two Captains faced each other. Gayna's daughter took her time evaluating the second group. "It is," she said finally.

The new Captain was a short, stocky fellow, with a big beard that made him look robust. He raised his head importantly. "You're to deliver him into our custody. Special order from the Queen herself." He waved a paper in the air.

Cole watched Captain Werd walk over and snatch the paper, which she read with an indignant air. The other Captain addressed her disapprovingly. "Why didn't you take him into Geid?"

"This way seemed less messy. The Baron requested it," she said, nodding at Cole.

The bearded Queensman frowned critically at him. *Are you crazy?* his face seemed to say. Cole could only agree.

Werd furrowed her brow at the paper in front of her, as if she couldn't understand the purpose of the order. "You have to execute him yourself, is that it?"

Cole waited for the new Queensman to contradict it, but instead he nodded. "Queen wanted to make sure it got done, so she sent us special. You're welcome to stay and watch."

Cole's hope sank to the pit of his stomach. If this was true, he was sorry he had lived to know it. He focused his last energies on cursing Hemmon and his deceitful letters. *Two-headed, scum-faced, lying fiend of a dogfish.*

"I'd appreciate that, actually," said Captain Werd.

New hands took possession of him. They shoved the other Q.M. away, like bullies taking a toy from smaller children. Cole was pulled uphill with an impatient vigor. He dragged his feet the whole way, making them work for every span.

A short time later they were on a ridge clear of trees. A man perched Cole on the ridgeline with a clear view of the Candige Queensmen below, and the spot where he had nearly been beheaded moments earlier. Someone put a long block of wood into the crook of his arm with the bottom resting in his left hand. Cole tilted his head to examine this inexplicable log. It was a few inches wide and arranged vertically against his body so that the top just reached his shoulder. A hand tapped him and motioned for him to face forward.

Cole looked uncomprehendingly into the eyes of a well-humored Queensman. The man winked at him.

"Don't worry, Step is an excellent shot." He jerked his head back slightly. Cole watched an archer taking position at close range. "When the arrow hits, I suggest you fall over."

Understanding began to dawn. With the sunset behind them, they would be largely silhouetted to the group of Queensmen below. The others got out of the way. One Queensman held a cloth up to shield the archer from the sun.

The arrow flew true and struck the log dead in the center. He had seen people shot before, and Cole thought he mimicked the event convincingly. He lay still, breathing shallowly, until someone came and lifted his body off the grass.

"Stay dead," the man warned. "They're still here."

Cole was thrown onto the back of a horse, where he dangled uncomfortably with his face in the animal's stomach. The horse walked forward in a direction Cole could not guess. Several minutes passed before someone lifted his head by the hair and asked in a voice that was slightly concerned, "You're still alive, right?"

"Yes," Cole answered.

"Good, because I think the Queen would decommission me if I killed you accidentally."

"Can I get up now?"

"I think so," the Queensman said. He offered his short, brawny arm for Cole to steady himself against as he rose into a sitting position. Cole took the reins gladly. He felt instantly better, in control of his own horse.

"I'm Captain Ritt." Cole shook the man's extended hand. The Captain used his left hand to shake. The other hand was misshapen, ending in two blackened stubs and a gnarled version of a palm. Frostbite damage, Cole noted. Not an uncommon sight in these parts.

Ritt turned around and introduced the rest of his group. There were four of them including the Captain. The two besides Tale were called Step and Darkin. Darkin was on foot since Cole had overtaken the use of his horse. Cole nodded at each of them. "I'm Mister Cole," he reciprocated.

"We know your name," said Step.

"We've only been chasing you for three days," Darkin added. He looked tired from the task.

"Not a damn moment too soon," Ritt scoffed, "Do you realize how close that was?"

Cole suppressed the urge to rub his neck. He didn't want to think how close.

"It's a good thing we didn't stop to let you piss, Tale!" Ritt yelled in a heavy voice. Tale wrinkled his nose like a man who still had to go. "Anyway," the Captain went on, "I think that charade went rather well. If those Queensmen go back into Geid and report what they saw, maybe the town will stop howling for your blood."

Cole was unnerved by Ritt's choice of words. They weren't actually howling, were they?

"Anwa wanted me to fake my death?" he asked.

Captain Ritt looked momentarily offended by his use of the Queen's given name. He shook it off with a shrug and a scoff. "No, that was my idea. But you've been sighted in the vicinity, and there are a lot of indignant folks sending out search parties. Let's face it, you're not exactly easy to camouflage. But——" Ritt pulled another document from his coat pocket "——in case our strategy fails, you should hang onto this. It's your pardon."

Cole unrolled the paper and examined it with a sense of awe.

"Full exoneration for any and all deeds committed while acting as the Baron of Geid," Ritt clarified. The Queensman sounded as though he disapproved of the idea, but he gave a conciliatory smile as Cole looked back up. He jerked his head toward the river below them. "We're going to camp down here," Ritt announced. "We've been riding with no sleep since Banth."

CHAPTER FORTY-THREE

Cole did his part setting up the tent and gathering wood for the fire. The simple labor put him in a good mood. The other Queensmen nodded and smiled like they were glad to see him. It did him a great deal of good.

He waited until dinner was cooked and eaten before he informed Ritt that it was necessary to take a detour through Rodenark before they could deliver him to the Queen.

"Rodenark? That's out of the way."

"I know, but there's someone waiting for me there."

"Out of the question." Ritt spoke with an authority that didn't care to admit argument. He leaned back against the tent post and unlaced the restraints of his vest.

Cole cleared his throat. "It's very important. I gave her my word."

"Who?"

"My—" Cole broke off as he searched for the correct term.

"Lover?" Ritt guessed. He nonchalantly put a blade of stiff grass into his mouth.

Cole scowled at him. "My...friend," he finished weakly.

Ritt laughed. "Whoever heard of a woman friend?"

Cole decided to ignore this rather strange question. "All right," he conceded, "I want to marry her. But I have to fetch her first. It'll only take a couple of days."

"It would take four days," Ritt said. "Two there and two back!"

Cole didn't argue the point. Instead he said, "Four days isn't that long."

The Queensman shook his head. "The Queen was very specific. I'm supposed to deliver you straight away. After that, she can let you go to Rodenark if she chooses."

Cole refused to accept this. Senna would wait a long time, but not if she thought he was dead, and word of that was sure to get around the county. "That will take weeks."

Ritt raised his eyebrows a couple of times, as if he was winking for a prostitute. "If the lady loves you, then she'll wait for you," he snipped.

Cole could see that Ritt had nothing but contempt for his love life, but he seemed to be taunting Senna more than him. It made him angry. Cole gritted his teeth and leaned forward. "I will go by myself if you won't take me."

"You will not leave my sight. Not if I have to tie you up and carry you." Ritt was struggling to keep their conversation light, but his threat was no jest and Cole knew it. The Queensman lowered his voice. "Look, I can see you're serious. But my orders are serious too. I gave my word to the Queen that I would take you to her as fast as humanly possible."

"It won't be as fast as humanly possible if I'm fighting you every inch of the way, will it?"

Captain Ritt's thin veil of civility reached its breaking point. He turned cherry red. "What sort of Queensman are you, anyway? Willing to fight to disobey her orders?"

The words cooled Cole's temper rather quickly. He lowered his eyes. "I don't think she would begrudge me this."

"You don't *think*," Ritt spat at him. "Your high and mighty Baronship! What gives you this glorious insight into the Great Lady's mind?"

Cole turned his head away, but Ritt wasn't finished with him. "Do you want to know what I think? I think you are a spoiled puppet who wormed his way into the Queen's good graces because he wanted more power. I think you've stepped on the backs of hard-working people for so long, you don't have a notion what it feels like to be one of them. You're a little too used to getting your own way, Baron."

None of what he said was true. Not enough to trouble Cole. The only trouble was that Ritt thought it was true, and that Cole would have to deal with it. Cole stared into the fire. He felt the eyes of the other Queensmen boring into him.

It stayed quiet until they started to turn down beds. Cole offered to take first watch, given how no one else had slept recently, but Ritt shot him down again. "You're not one of us, Mister Cole. You're just the cargo."

Cole lay down in the blanket Darkin gave him and pretended to sleep, until sleep eventually came.

Ritt made his way to the stream in the dark. His feet squished noisily, collapsing marshflowers as he walked. He was fuming so bad he doubted he would be able to sleep, despite how tired he was. Exhaustion made him angry, and anger made it hard to rest. He was angry at himself for losing control. But there was plenty of anger left over for the stupid Baron, and some to spare for his Queensmen, who kept frowning to show that they disapproved of his foul mood.

He started to undo his pants with his good hand when a shadow passed over the light from the fire. One of his men followed a few steps behind. Ritt whirled around and snapped at the intruder, "Go shove yourself down the river, Tale. I'm trying to take a dump!"

Tale was unmoved. He folded his arms to give weight to the lecture he was about to impart. "You were a little hard on him, don't you think?"

"What do you know, Tale?"

"I know if Ethine was waiting for me somewhere, I would want to go to her."

Ritt rolled his eyes. Tale couldn't see the gesture in the darkness, but he couldn't mistake the tone of his voice. "Oh, please."

"Just 'cause you never had a woman, Ritt!"

"I've had plenty of women!" A fact Tale knew very well.

"Right. Plenty. But never *a* woman."

Ritt sighed heavily.

"A few days won't make much difference," Tale argued. "And if Cole has the Queen's ear, which seems to me is the case, then she might be angry at you for not helping him."

This was a valid observation. It galled Ritt that it was so. "I don't trust the man."

"The Queen said he was good. Don't you trust her judgment?"

Ritt ground his teeth together. He adored Anwa because he adored his country, but the Queen was only eighteen years old. How much judgment could she have? "Look, Tale. I'm extremely tired," he said, falling back on the truth. "I regret what I said, okay? I'll take the fool to Rodenark if it will shut you up. For pity's sake, go away."

"Sure thing, Ritt. Sorry to interrupt."

Werd couldn't fathom why the Queen would send a special envoy just to get rid of one Baron. Part of her was miffed at the implication that she had not done the job properly. But mostly, she wondered what Fenwith had done to Anwa to warrant this particular piece of attention.

The Judge was annoyed as well; he had wanted to speak to Fenwith. Mister Rimick awakened shortly after her

Queensmen returned, grumbling and trying to get out of bed against everyone's advice. Werd approved of Rimick as the temporary Judge. The man was fair, if a bit rough around the edges. Werd thought he would probably be glad to give up the post when he was asked to.

Gayna had sent them to Geid for nothing. The local Q.M. had organized a government on their own, and no one was starving, so they didn't have to organize a food drive. Werd was glad enough for that. She had seen more than her share of war in recent days.

Restless and not yet ready to return to Candige, Werd took her errand to Rodenark. She had read Fenwith's letter as soon as the man was dead, so that she could decide whether or not to deliver it. It left her curious. The letter was signed with an alias, which concerned Werd that he was trying to impersonate another man. She decided to deliver it, and to make sure the recipient understood where it came from.

With good weather and a fresh horse, the trip was barely more than a day. Rodenark was actually closer to Geid's capital than its own. It was roughly the same distance from Mackabine as Candige, though it lay along a path far less traveled. Anseth was the largest county in Mackabine, and its many villages were hard to keep track of.

Werd removed the traveling cloak from her shoulders as she stopped for water. The Baron's note, tucked into a top pocket, crinkled inside the fabric as she tried to fold it. Werd withdrew the paper and read it for the tenth time.

Good, gentle Senna,

For the last time, I must beg your forgiveness. I did everything I could to live up to my promise. Everything else is done. I had only to come to you, but circumstances have a tendency to hedge up a man one way or another. I have always believed this day was coming. Somehow it feels like justice to me. Perhaps you will feel pity enough not to hate me for it.

I wish I had more time to say everything to you. Now I know what it means when they say there are not enough words. I am embarrassed to put this to paper, knowing that my courier will almost certainly read this letter, but I ache to tell you what you must already know. I love you. I love you. I love you.

Do not grieve long, Senna. The world is open to you and you will yet find happiness in it. For myself, I regret nothing. We won, and the victory is sweet. My time is gone. I pray this reaches you. My last thoughts will be of you.

Cole

It was phrased well enough to please a sweetheart, if that was its goal. Not that Werd was any judge of fancy writings. The last part unnerved her a bit. What could the Baron have won? Had he sabotaged something? Werd was anxious to speak to the woman when she found her.

The bridge outside Rodenark was scarcely more than a few logs, splayed over a stream the width of a carriage. It was prettily situated at the base of a hill, about a mile before the town opened up. On the far side of the bridge grew a small walnut tree. It could only have been there for maybe a decade, because it was no more than ten spans high, but it offered the only shade between the bridge and an acre of open land. A dingy woman camped underneath it.

Werd thought at first the woman was sleeping, but she bolted upright when she heard the horse's hooves on the bridge. After she had a proper look at Werd, she lost interest, and lay back down, her body spooned away from the road.

Werd led her horse to the woman's side. The tree was too small to offer shade at midday, and her shadow fell directly over the woman. If she wasn't asleep, then she must be aware of her presence. But despite their proximity, it wasn't until Werd used her name that the woman showed any interest.

"Are you Senna?"

The woman sat up and fixed her gaze on Werd with absolute attention. She rose to her feet without moving her eyes. "Yes. Who are you?"

"Werd. I'm a commissioned Queensman."

Madam Senna did not look especially impressed. Werd

let her expectations simmer while she got off her horse and brushed the dust of twenty miles from her cloak. Finally she produced the letter in her right hand. "I have something for you."

The Madam took the proffered parchment without looking at it. "Where is Cole?"

The woman relaxed slightly as she saw that Werd recognized the name, but Werd's hesitation reagitated her. Werd asked who she thought this person was.

The question brought the Madam close to hysteria. "He has also been known as Fenwith, Baron of Geid. Do you know where he is?"

"Yes," Werd answered succinctly. "He's dead." Werd watched closely for the Madam's reaction. At first there was none. Then her limbs gave way and she crumpled to the ground.

Werd couldn't remember why she'd thought it was important to question this woman. If she wanted to sleep with tyrants, then she knew what she was about. "His last act was to write you that note," Werd informed the woman. She turned and began to remount her horse. Her left foot was into the stirrup when a hand took hold of her shirt and pulled her back down.

"You don't have any idea!" the Madam cried. When Werd faced her, the woman seized her collar. Werd used her elbow to disengage, then spun the woman and pinned her arms to her sides.

"Stop it!" the Madam screamed, struggling against Werd's efforts to pacify her. The harder Werd worked to keep her still, the harder the woman fought. "Don't touch me! Don't touch me!"

Werd finally let her go, and the woman fell down again. She beat the ground with her fists, then rocked forlornly back and forth on the grass.

"For all the Queen's land, calm yourself, woman." Werd watched her writhe on the grass, somewhat fascinated by such behavior. "You'll ruin your letter."

The Madam stopped as if the wind had been knocked out of her. She brought her hand to her face and studied the paper crushed between her fingers. The parchment was so worn Werd feared it would disintegrate under so much abuse. With trembling fingers, the woman reverently opened the letter face down, smoothed the edges, and folded it into halves and then quarters.

"Go on and read it then," Werd urged.

The Madam shook her head. "I can't. It's the last thing he'll ever say to me. If I read it, then he's gone."

Werd sighed distastefully. She was ready to ride into the village. She wanted to get a drink, and to see how Rodenark had fared in the transition. Anseth was one of the largest and most sparsely populated counties. It would take time to reestablish the Queen's law everywhere. But Werd could see, from the gaily decorated banners peeking over the hilltop, that freedom had already been declared. County villages tended to follow their capital towns rather quickly.

"It cost everything," the Madam said, more to herself than to Werd. "It wasn't worth it. I should have let the Gaults win!"

"Sorry," said Werd.

Madam Senna guessed at her imperfect sincerity. Her mouth twitched in enmity. "Go away," she ordered.

Madam Senna took no notice as Werd mounted her horse a second time. She was no more aware of Werd than she was of the sky, or the road, or the town behind her that was celebrating the demise of its own despot.

CHAPTER FORTY-FOUR

The first thing Cole saw when he opened his eyes the next morning was the stern face of Captain Ritt staring down at him. Ritt announced in a loud voice that they were going to detour their expedition through Rodenark.

Cole had spent much of the night devising arguments. He was determined to reach Rodenark, even if he had to get there by kicking and screaming. Ritt's unexpected declaration saved him a lot of trouble. Cole got to his feet, folded his hands, and pretended he had never intended to be anything but perfectly obedient.

They ate a fast breakfast while Step went to requisition another horse from the Geid stables. Cole recommended he ask for the dappled brown. Ritt grumbled about the delay, then moved them along at the pace of a lame goat. Cole tried to ignore the sulking Captain. It was true the road to Rodenark didn't suit well for speed. It was a meandering, infrequently kept road. Horses couldn't run on most of it.

Ritt pulled up briefly alongside Cole's horse as they left their campsite. "Let me know when you're ready to set down for lunch, Baron."

"Stop calling me that," said Cole.

"What?" Ritt pretended ignorance.

"Baron."

"It's a term of respect." The Captain straightened defensively on his horse.

"I'm not that dense, Ritt. If you want to show me respect, you'll have to mean it."

The Captain shut up.

The other Queensmen proved more affable as the journey progressed. Tale and Step were especially curious to hear of Cole's role in the rebellion. He told them the history of how he came to impersonate the man called Fenwith, which they both seemed to find particularly interesting. The pair shared their stories in return. Step had been a farmer in one of Mackabine's outer villages. Tale, a dockworker.

"Until I pursued the more prestigious career of Queensman. All of—what, two months ago? I jumped on the bandwagon late. So did Step. But Ritt has been a Queensman since before Anwa's return." Tale made an effort to engage eye contact with Ritt. He got a small huff from the Captain.

The Q.M. shared the latest news from Mackabine. The castle fell the same day of Cole's departure. Tale seemed to think the occupants were being sorted in an orderly manner. Lord Hemmon was dead. He had tried to smuggle himself out at the last moment, but ended up betrayed and turned in by one of his own Counselours. Afterwards he sued for peace with Anwa, but the Queen had none of it. She ordered him slain in front of her. Cole was pleased to hear it.

There weren't a lot of surviving Counselours in the nobility, so Queen Anwa formed a temporary council out of common Queensmen. It was said the Great Lady was endowing titles left and right. Cole sobered as he listened, even though it was what he expected. It would mean an infant aristocracy, built out of the most vehement leaders of the revolution. He feared it might not be very stable.

The Queensmen had other stories, some of them quite wild, and Tale admitted that many of them might not be accurate. The favorite rumor was the Queensman who rose from the dead. Jedomar, the slayer of Regent Gote, had appeared miraculously to aid the Queen during a battle.

Cole had to laugh when he heard that one. Superstition and hero worship never died. He hoped Jedomar would catch wind of it from the Otherworld.

"Any chance you heard of a servant named Eold?" Cole asked.

The grim look on Step's face made it clear he didn't have to describe her further. Step exchanged a look with Tale. "They say she's the reason Anwa wouldn't show mercy to Hemmon, because of what he did to that Madam."

Cole brought his horse to a stop. He hadn't known Eold well. He hadn't even particularly liked her. He'd assumed she lost her nerve and ran away. If she had been captured, two days before the Queensman action... Cole had difficulty keeping a neutral face. Two days. An unwelcome memory flashed in his mind—Lord Gretin's broken body, shipped out to sea after Hemmon was done with him. The image was worse somehow, when it was a woman.

What was two days in theory took scarcely more than one day in practice. They rode late and started early the next day. It was just after midday the second day when their group approached Rodenark. A mile outside the village, Cole stopped them and asked to go on alone. "I'll only be gone an hour," he promised.

Cole's request was wishful thinking; he fully expected to be refused. Ritt turned so red, Cole thought he would explode with more browbeating, but instead he shrugged and agreed. Tale and Step both looked a little shocked.

"Thank you," said Cole. He pushed his horse forward before Ritt could change his mind. Tale called after him, but Cole didn't look back.

It took mere minutes to reach the border at a gallop. The bridge crossed a brook that curved twice around a grassy hill before it descended into the town. In the distance, Rodenark's rooftops glittered with reflected sunlight. The tree beyond the bridge was young enough that it bent under the light wind. Cole slowed his horse to an easy walk.

Senna was curled up very tightly beside the tree's

427

slender trunk. She didn't move when he called her name, and her posture was so unnatural that Cole began to fear she might be ill. "Senna?" he called again.

His eyes landed on a piece of crumpled paper hanging from her fingertips. Surprise jolted his stomach.

"Senna," he breathed again, almost falling off his horse. Cole landed ungracefully on his knees and rolled towards her. Senna moaned as he lifted her limp body off the grass. She dragged her head up and groggily parted her eyelids. He parted her hair and smoothed it away from her face. "Senna, wake up."

Senna did not recover easily. She trembled at his touch. "Cole?" Her warm breath receded as she pushed his face away to examine it. "Cole, am I dead?"

"No," he told her.

"Are you dead?"

"No," he told her, smiling with amusement.

Senna sat transfixed for a few seconds. Her stillness was perfect and rather beautiful. Then she hit him. "How could you *do* that to me?" she yelled.

"Ow!" Cole laughed. "I'm sorry, Senna. I didn't mean to," he said, although he was too happy to appear very contrite. Truly, it astonished him that the letter had arrived before he did. Captain Werd was a woman of her word.

"How long have you had that?" he nodded at the paper fallen in the dirt.

She looked confused. "I don't know. Maybe an hour." She glanced at the position of the sun. "Maybe less."

Cole glanced furtively behind him. He wasn't anxious to run into those Candige Queensmen again.

Senna wrapped her hands around Cole's wrists as if fearing he might disappear. "Tell me everything," she said.

"It's too long to tell just this moment."

"Is it safe?"

Cole figured he was as close to that state as he would get. "I've got a Queen's pardon in my vest pocket."

Senna released a long sigh. He felt the tension fall

428

from her body. "I should never have listened to you. I should have gone on to Mackabine."

"Actually, I wish you would have stayed in Geid."

"Geid? Why?" Senna made a scornful expression. "There was *nothing* happening there." Cole had no time to answer before she moved on to her next accusation. "And why did you write me that horrible letter?"

Cole retrieved the discarded letter and smoothed it over his palm. A glance confirmed that the writing had not been altered. "What's the matter with it?"

Senna narrowed her eyes, struggling to come up with an answer. "You told me not to mourn you."

He raised an eye. "You wanted to mourn?"

"Yes!" she cried. "I'm not a potato."

"I see."

"What if something happened to me?" Senna asked. "Would you move on? Forget all about me?"

"Yes," he said, matter-of-factly. "I would feel sorrow for a while, and then I would recover."

"You dogfish."

Cole smiled tightly. Somehow it did not surprise him that Senna preferred him to wallow in grief forever if she died.

Senna sighed. "That wasn't the problem. You shouldn't have sent it at all."

"You would have preferred nothing?" Cole asked.

"No," she turned her head. "If you really had died, I would have treasured that letter. But to send it when you weren't going to die, that was really unkind."

"If it makes any difference, I fully intended to die."

"I know. And I'll never forgive you for that either." Senna stopped his snort with a nasty glare. "You should have fought harder. Did you tell the Q.M. you were working for the Queen?"

His hesitation revealed everything. Senna looked mightily furious.

"They would not have believed me," he offered.

"You should have tried! For *my* sake, Cole."

"I'm sorry," he said, and meant it. He *should* have tried. It was only pride that stopped him.

There was nothing else said for a while. Senna buried her face in his chest while Cole stroked her back. They stayed this way a few minutes without stirring. Senna looked as if she never meant to stir again, but eventually Cole began to shoot looks towards the road. He expected Ritt's men to follow him at any moment.

"Senna, will you marry me now?" he whispered.

Senna's forehead bumped against his chest in a nod.

He pulled away against her body's protests, and started gathering her things together.

"Do you mean *right* now?" she asked.

"Rodenark must have a Judge, yes?"

It took him a few seconds of rummaging to untie the parcel at his waist and remove the item he kept safe there. The parcel was in good shape, considering that it had survived the entire journey from Mackabine, including a dump into the bay. Senna froze when she saw it. "Where did you get that?"

Cole tried hard to read her still expression. He wanted very much to impress her. "I made it," he admitted. Senna reached for the circlet of wire and colored ribbon. "It's mostly brass," he said, "but the leaves are silver. I scrounged a bit of coin and had it melted."

"It must have taken you weeks," she said. Her fingers caressed the tiny carvings.

Cole was silent. Months was more like it, since he'd been careful to do it in secret. He waited for her to render judgment.

"It's beautiful," she said, with a quaver in her voice that made him believe her.

He smiled. "It's not quite finished yet." Cole took a pouch from his pocket and unwrapped a handful of miniature white flowers. They'd been picked on the road this morning and were only slightly crushed. He fastened the bud stems into prearranged slots on the side.

Senna had tears in her eyes as she watched him work.

"Oh Cole, it's perfect. No one ever had anything so wonderful."

That was probably going a bit far. Cole put the crown on her head. "No one would look more wonderful in it." He must really be in love, to say such foolish things.

Senna laughed. "I've been crying and I haven't bathed, and I've been sitting in the dirt for days."

"Would you rather wait?" Cole didn't want to wait. He wanted Senna to be his; he wanted it official and he wanted it now. If the opportunity wasn't seized, who knew what might arise to impede them next?

Senna shook her head. "Now."

Senna had second thoughts almost as soon as she agreed to the plan. "What if someone recognizes you?" she whispered.

Cole waved a hand in dismissal. "I've never been here," he said.

That didn't mean no one from Rodenark had ever visited Geid. Cole was already drawing attention. Senna blushed at every stare that followed them down the road.

When they reached the inn, Senna hung back while Cole requested permission to marry from the local Judge. One of the patrons whispered conspiratorially to the host. Senna distinctly caught the word "Baron." Cole heard it too and he laughed easily.

"I get that a lot. Not many of my kind get to be Barons, I suppose. Cross my heart, I'm a stablehand from Lammark." He made a comical pout to show how he whimsically viewed the idea. "Anyway, you don't think the Baron of Geid wants to get married, do you?"

It was so well done that the patrons laughed, and the mood in the inn lightened instantly. "No," the Judge said, laughing back, "I think not."

Senna watched Cole sign the marriage papers, confident and cheery-eyed. He really was a good liar.

It wasn't difficult to recruit citizens of Rodenark to be witnesses. Word went around quickly in such a small place. The villagers seemed happy to celebrate a romance in their midst, even that of passing refugees. The inn filled up with curious bystanders. They cheered when Senna climbed up onto the table.

"Senna," Cole called up to her, "you are the finest woman I know. I want to make you happy for the rest of my life. Will you have me?"

Some women argued a bit at their weddings, pretending to need greater persuasion before they stepped off the table. Senna only paused before she answered in the affirmative.

"Jump down, then," he said.

The patrons echoed the order. "Jump, jump, jump!" they encouraged her.

Senna bit her lip. Cole almost looked too fragile to hold her weight. She stepped gently off the edge of the table and Cole caught her before her feet touched the ground.

The inn erupted in cheers. It was done. She was married. Senna pinched herself to be certain.

Cole wanted to take Senna upstairs right then. All he needed was an hour of uninterrupted bliss. The innkeeper would expect it. It was probably already arranged. Cole wondered how long it would take the Queensmen to come into town after him. Sadly, the answer came through the door that minute, bringing Ritt, Tale, and Darkin along with it. They took it all in at a glance: the paper lace, the witnesses, Senna's crown.

"Mister Cole," Ritt hissed through clenched teeth, "what do you think you're doing?"

Cole took Senna's hand in a presentory manner. "Friends, may I introduce my wife, Madam Senna."

Senna was all smiles and courtesy. She approached the Queensmen and took their hands one at a time. "I'm so pleased to meet you," she said. "It's an honor. Really, I'm so happy, I could kiss all of you."

Cole hadn't coached Senna to do anything, but she couldn't have courted them better. Her sincerity was obvious and her warmth was totally disarming. He could see the sternness melt slowly out of the Queensmen.

"Madam Senna," Captain Ritt grunted, "the honor is ours." He bowed a little.

Senna made good on her threat. She took the Captain's big head in her hands and kissed his nose. "Thank you for bringing my husband."

Ritt turned bright red.

CHAPTER FORTY-FIVE

Senna spent her wedding night on a riding cloak with her husband on one side and Captain Ritt on the other. If Cole was bothered by any sexual frustrations, it didn't show. He slept like a stone, wearing a smile that must have come from good dreams. It consoled Senna to see her new husband happy. It seemed strangely uncharacteristic of him.

Senna had never traveled until recently. Her bottom ached from riding after the first day. The next day was even worse. The Queensmen showed little inclination for rest. Senna tried not to mind.

For her, the road had always been like the ocean: mysterious and infinite. A conduit to places she had heard talk of but never been. It was exciting to have those mysteries suddenly unveiled.

As their road widened and merged with a larger one, they began to pass other folk seeking shelter or adventure. The travelers stood to the side of the road while they passed, giving instant obeisance to the Queensmen in uniform. A few children pointed and cheered at Senna. She blushed, cognizant of her wedding crown. These early days after her wedding, she should have been visiting the homes of her friends and family, receiving food and gifts from the older generation. Senna was sad that she couldn't perform the traditional bridal practices, but she wore her crown just as proudly.

The Queensmen tried to give Senna the attention due to a bride. Even Darkin, the youngest and shyest of the Queensmen, gathered the courage to compliment Senna on her wedding crown.

"Thank you," she replied. "Cole made it himself."

Mister Step was visibly impressed. "Did he? How many grooms make their bride's wedding crown themselves?"

Tale answered, "Not many, I imagine."

"I didn't have much choice," said Cole. "I couldn't buy one."

Wedding observance ended on the third day, the night before they reached Mackabine. Senna reluctantly removed her crown and packed it lovingly into a box. Someday she hoped she would display it in her home and receive compliments from visitors.

The reality of Mackabine left Senna underwhelmed. Someone once told Senna that Mackabine was to Geid as the ocean was to a spring puddle. But to her it seemed a dirty, crowded, depressing place. The buildings along the road looked no bigger than those she grew up with. Many were ruined or abandoned, or overrun with occupants who didn't appear to belong to them.

"This isn't really Mackabine City," Cole explained to Senna, reading her expression. "It's just the outskirts. The Queen is camping here until the castle is deemed safe again."

They stopped at a round enclosure with a guarded entrance. It was certainly not a castle, but it was larger than any other building nearabouts. Ritt sent Tale inside to report their arrival and receive orders.

"I want to look around," said Senna.

"You are looking around," Cole said.

Senna took a breath. The sights and sounds were nearly overwhelming to her. While Ritt gave Cole some last instruction, Senna stepped aside to watch the traffic in and out of the Queen's camp. She noticed hungry looks from ragged men on foot. Senna scanned faces, wondering if it were possible for her to recognize anyone walking by. Someone else recognized her first.

"Senna!"

Hack was in front of her before she could turn around to see who had called her name. He gave a cocky hoot of triumph, and shook her shoulder impulsively. "What are *you* doing here? Is anyone with you? Have you seen this place? Did you hear about Jed? Did you hear about Fenwith? Did you know the Queen is in those tents over there? I mean, right there! She's maybe two hundred spans away."

Senna pushed Hack's sticky hand off her shoulder. "Dohack. I should have known you'd be chasing trouble. What do you mean about Fenwith?"

"The Queen pardoned him. Can you believe that? He did some stuff here against the Regent and now he gets off. What a sham, eh?"

Senna laughed mentally at Hack's reaction. She wondered what the rest of Geid would say once rumors reached that far. She rather wished she could be there to see it. "I'm glad for it," she said.

"Really? You know how nasty he is. Albinos should be burned as soon as they're born."

"Let's not speak poorly of albinos, please. My husband is one."

Hack started visibly. "Since when?"

"Since he was born, silly."

"But—" Hack sputtered in annoyance. "When did you get married?"

"Let's see." Senna pretended to think. She ardently wished they had arrived a day sooner so she could have shown him her wedding crown. "Let me ask him. Cole? Oh, Cole!" she called over the tents separating them from view of her party.

Cole was in hearing range, and came willingly to her summons, although he looked for an explanation once she landed him in front of Hack.

The look on Hack's face was priceless. Senna was

tempted to poke him to see if he'd fall over.

"Who is this?" Cole asked, unable to understand why he'd been called over.

Senna playfully slapped her husband's arm. "Don't you recognize your former tenants? This is Mister Dohack."

"Oh," said Cole. His interest appeared to rise slightly. "Aren't you the fellow who tried to have me poisoned?"

Hack did not answer, although his mouth fell open a little.

"If you're done having fun, Senna, we should go. The Queen is ready to see us."

Senna gave Hack a wide mocking smile as Cole pulled her away.

When they were out of range, he admonished her not to do that again. "I can see you think it's funny, but it could also be dangerous."

"Oh, bogsnatch," she answered. "I won't be able to do it for very long anyway. News spreads too fast. Hack will tell everyone, just you see."

Jed's post was finally empty for the moment. The last batch of recruits he submitted was being processed for the Queen's growing regiment. He leaned against the table, stretching his legs as he looked over at the Queen's camp. It would be a few minutes, at least, until Marwen brought the next wave of opportunists.

Dohack noticed Jed watching him and ran across the road. Jed grinned to see the expression on his friend's face. He was twitching like an upside-down treeskunk.

Jed waved away Hack's urgent exclamations. "I saw," he said.

His eyes were still fixed on the former Baron, hunched in conference with a circle of Queensmen. The ashen hair was easy to pick out of a crowd. Senna was less obvious from a distance. His eyes took their time studying the profile of his longtime friend. Jed braced himself for a resurgence of those emotions that had plagued him a few months ago. They did not come. The yearning he felt for Senna was gone, leaving only a comfortable, companionable urge to surprise her.

"Gave you a shock, did she?" Jed smiled to himself. He'd also had fun scaring the daylights out of Hack when he'd found him the other day.

Jed waited for Senna to look his way, but she was too busy interacting with her group. It looked like the Queensmen were about to lead her into the Queen's inner sanctum. Jed didn't want to wait that long. He abandoned his post and crossed the road. Hack gave a meager protest, which Jed ignored.

Jed's approach caught the attention of the group at roughly the same time. Jed had hoped for a stronger reaction from the Baron. The most that could be said for Mister Cole was that his mouth opened a little, and that he stared.

Senna's reaction was more dramatic. She had just taken a cup of water from one of her companions and was draining it blithely. Her eyes dilated when she saw him. Then her drinking slowed, and the bulge in her throat became larger as she forgot to swallow. Water spilled freely over her chin until she finally dropped the cup. Then she screamed.

She might have been witnessing a murder, for the sound she was making. Its intensity made the Queensmen beside her back up. Cole tried to calm her, and she flailed her arms at him.

"Senna!" they both called in unison.

Senna was silent for the time it took her to gasp for breath. Then she screamed again, with less shock and more anger. "Jed!" The accusation burned out of her. "You're not dead? You—dogfish! Dogfish from the Otherworld!"

Jed felt rather vexed as Cole put his arms around Senna. But when he got close, Cole handed her over quite readily. Senna fell weeping against his chest. He might have enjoyed this display of feminine compassion, if her unhappiness didn't make him feel guilty. He really hadn't had an opportunity to inform her of his survival any sooner. He took care to point that out to her now.

Senna pulled away to look at him. She poked his cheek, testing its solidity.

Mister Cole's curiosity overcame his reluctance to speak. "How in the name of the Otherworld did you do it?" he asked. "Was it Rimick? That man is more clever than anyone realizes."

Jed would have been gratified to explain, but the Captain interrupted. He was under orders to get them to Lady Anwa, and apparently very low on patience. "Mister Cole, does your wife have no end of friends? Can we move the next ten spans without interruption?"

Married already, was she? Covering his embarrassment, he asked Senna quickly, "Are you excited to see the Queen?"

Senna wiped the last tears from her eyes. "Jealous, Jedomar?" she asked.

Jed relaxed at her gibe. If she felt well enough to tease him, then he was forgiven. "Not really. I saw her this morning," he said. This was true, but he was jealous anyway. Jed could look forever and still not see enough of Lady Anwa.

One of the other Q.M. in the group, to whom Jed had not given any notice, blinked with an impressed air. "You're the Queensman Jedomar? Truly?"

Jed offered a dignified nod. He was getting used to this sort of shocked admiration from strangers. He would have said more, but the Captain forbade another word. Jed let them push past. The albino hesitated as if remembering something. He ignored the fierce glare of the Captain as he rummaged through his pockets. The item he retrieved was too small to identify until it reached the palm of Jed's hand. "You probably want that back," he said.

"What do you know?" Jed said softly. He caressed the familiar imperfections of the metal before slipping it onto his finger. "My ring."

Senna was still reeling from meeting Jed when the Queen's Guards led her into the tent. *I shall expect to see my brother next,* she thought in jest. Her heart felt light. She was proud to be allotted a glimpse of their new sovereign.

Someone ushered them up to the front of a line. "Glad you're here. The Queen was ready to send another party after *you*, Ritt."

A uniformed Guard raised a curtain to admit them into the Queen's chamber. The area was spacious and splendidly arranged. It felt less like a tent and more like the receiving room of a castle. Senna's eyes singled out the Queen without difficulty: a radiant, slender woman poised on the edge of a small dais. She looked every one of her eighteen years, and precisely no more.

Ritt steered Cole to the forefront.

"Great Lady." He bowed low. "I brought you your stray Queensman."

Queen Anwa smiled, a gesture that intensified her beauty. Senna caught her breath in admiration.

The Queen glided regally down the four steps of the dais, and paused in front of Cole. The Lady's smile assured Senna that all of her intentions were favorable.

Cole bowed as low as he could without kneeling. Anwa waited until Cole had righted himself. Then she took his chin in both her hands and kissed him full on the mouth.

Senna's buoyancy fell into a ball at the bottom of her gut. The room became unbearably silent.

With his back to her, Cole seemed calm as ever. Senna would have given anything to know what he was thinking. She could not fail to notice how poorly she measured up to the competition. The Queen outranked Senna in every

440

conceivable quality.

Captain Ritt sensed her agitation. It was only as Ritt clenched her hand in his own that she realized she was shaking. Senna returned the gesture, clutching the Captain's fingers like a child in a nightmare.

An eternity of seconds passed before Cole took the arms of the Queen and lowered them from his neck. There was some stiffness to his voice as he spoke. "Great Lady, allow me to present my wife."

Every eye in the room turned to examine Senna. She couldn't imagine what she must look like to them. She felt like a poached hen on display.

No gaze was more bewildered than Lady Anwa's. "Your wife?" she repeated.

"Yes," Cole said.

The Queen's eyes moved from Senna to Cole and back again.

Senna had never thought of Anwa as a woman. But as the Queen transformed before her eyes into a quivering wisp, Senna was suddenly aware how very mortal a person she was. A person on whom Senna's freedom and happiness depended absolutely.

Anwa covered her mouth with her hand, and wordlessly left the room.

CHAPTER FORTY-SIX

If Cole had not known how to measure his status before coming here, he knew less now. The silence did not lift with Anwa's departure. The candid welcome of the Queen's staff turned to hardness and embarrassment. Both ahead and behind, the assembly of Lords and Q.M. looked on Cole and his wife with fascination. What had Anwa said to her court? He didn't think she told them that she planned to claim him as her consort. They looked as aghast as Cole felt. Once his head cleared, he remembered to glance at Senna.

Cole reached back to touch her hand. "It's going to be fine."

"Is it?"

Cole consulted his estimation of Anwa's character, limited as it was. "Yes," he affirmed.

Cole was very glad he had already married Senna. The situation was awkward enough without that uncertainty. He gave his wife's arm a comforting squeeze, then went to the tent flap Anwa had used to disappear.

"I'll go talk to her," he told the woman guarding it. The Queen's attendants gave each other guarded looks. Cole could read their silent uncertainty. *What kind of authority does this man have?* No one knew. Consequently, no one stopped him.

Cole swept aside the curtain and found Anwa in a

sitting area adorned with her personal effects. He took a fraction of a moment to verify that she was alone, then he lowered the curtain behind him.

The Queen didn't react to his approach. Cole moved close enough to see her face, but didn't dare do more without invitation. She had a hand over her mouth and was crying silently.

"I'm sorry," Anwa volunteered quickly. "I feel so stupid. Your wife will hate me now, I think."

"You couldn't have known."

She shook her head. "I don't know...I assumed..."

A span of silence passed that Cole did not choose to break quickly. But Anwa seemed too shy to speak again, so he eventually selected one of the questions weighing on his mind. "Counselour Hemmon told me he sent a false message, implicating me as a Gaultian agent. To destroy my credibility. Was he lying?"

Anwa murmured distractedly, "No, we got that."

"How did you know it was forged?"

"Oh," she said dismissively, "I knew you would never do something like that."

Cole smiled at her naivety. "I am touched, Great Lady." He bowed a little. "You've done well. Your country is proud of you."

Anwa slowly recovered some of her verve. She spoke to him about Brock, about the trauma of the rebellion, and the choices she was facing for Mackabine. It was a plea for normalcy, which Cole was happy to grant. They seemed to come to a silent agreement never to speak again of her mislaid kiss.

"I have a gift for you," Anwa said. She clapped her hands, and the side of the tent opened. It took a moment for Cole's eyes to recover from the brief burst of sunlight. When they did, he found a young attendant in stable gear presenting a familiar stallion. Whip snorted joyously at the sight of him.

Cole was astonished. "Thank you, Lady," he paused to give Whip an affectionate welcome, "but this horse was born in the stables of Geid. I think he must belong to the rightful Baron of that land."

Anwa hesitated longer before speaking again. "The previous Baron left no heirs. I can't think of anyone with more right to the title than you."

Cole could scarcely fathom his own horror. He felt ready to fall over. "Lady," he said with great effort, "I beg you not to ask that of me."

Anwa looked confused. "I would make you a magistrate, and give you title over five times as much land." When his expression of dismay did not lessen, she offered him the northern lands, if Geid did not suit him.

"Great Lady, I thank you for the honor. But I've had my taste of nobility for one lifetime."

Anwa looked distressed. It may have been the first time she'd offered land to someone who didn't want it. "How can I repay you, then?"

"Your gratitude is sufficient."

"Gratitude?" Anwa looked from Cole to the stallion. "At least take the horse!"

When Cole related to Senna all that occurred during his exchange with Lady Anwa, it had two effects. First, it softened Senna towards the Queen, and second, it aroused ire against her husband.

"Don't I get a say?" Senna griped. "It's my future as well. I don't think I would mind being a Lady. And you would make a decent Lord if you gave up your tyrannical ways."

Senna saw she was defeated before she began. Cole's shudder was visible from across the room. "Well, what *do* you want to do?" she asked.

Cole considered his answer a moment before speaking. "I'd like to go back to Lammark. See if there's anyone left there I remember."

Senna had little notion of where Lammark even was. She imagined it in some bleak, remote corner on the far side of Mackabine Island. "Oh bother." Senna slumped onto the bed in the tent the Q.M. had assigned to them. "And I could have been a rich woman!" she lamented.

Cole flashed a frown at her. "You don't really care about being rich, do you?"

"Who says?" Senna was pretty sure she had never said so. Perhaps it was not vital to her happiness, but it certainly couldn't have hurt.

He grunted at her discontent. "You should have married better, then. All I have in the world is a secondhand noblehorse."

Two hours later, Senna was back in the Queen's waiting area, preparing for her own audience with Lady Anwa. Senna would have avoided the encounter, if possible, but when the Queen of your country asks to see you, you don't have the option to refuse.

She distracted herself by admiring the opulence of the tent. Senna's cushion was textured with silk pleats that felt like water under her hands. The best furnishings of the castle must have been brought here to serve Anwa. It struck Senna how nothing matched, in color or in taste.

The call for her attendance broke Senna from her wonderings. She stood up, startled out of the anxiousness that kept her twisting her hands against her cloak.

The attendant led her through the empty audience room into the private chamber beyond. Senna smoothed her hair and belatedly thought to untie her cloak. She had barely decided which shoulder to lay it over when the Great Lady was suddenly before her.

"Madam Senna, good meeting to you. Please come in." The Queen's greeting was more warm than formal. She gave a bob of welcome as she invited Senna forward. Anwa had laid a small breakfast spread, as any woman in Mackabine might do for her neighbor.

"I owe you an apology. As your Queen, I know you will be forced to accept it. But if it pleases you, we may choose to be friends."

Senna stood dumbly for a moment, wondering what answer would give the monarch the least offense.

Anwa looked humbly at her hands. "It was a silly thing. A young girl's fantasy. I loved Cole since the moment he walked into that cold dungeon and told me he had come to save me. He was so gentle and courageous."

Senna bit her lip to keep from laughing. She marveled at Cole's ability to leave very different impressions. Perhaps the cure to the Queen's ailment would be to see Cole bark at his Guards in the morning or throw goods from a merchant's stall into the street. Then she could decide how gentle he was.

Lady Anwa raised her head again. "I will smother these emotions. I only wonder...I wonder at the strength of them from so brief an acquaintance."

Senna felt her jealous heart warm itself. A country could not suffer from so honest a ruler. "You are very young, Lady." As if that accounted for it! As if Senna were qualified to make assessments on love!

"So I am told," Anwa agreed. The Queen sat down to the breakfast, an inviting cue for her guest to do the same. "They told me you've only been married a few days. It seems unfair to take your wedding crown off so soon, when you've only been traveling."

"Oh." Senna bit her lip.

"I know it's cheating, but...perhaps you'll let me see you wear it sometime?" said Anwa. Her eyes held a mischievous glint.

They shared a giggle. Senna felt a rush of affection for the young Queen.

"I was unable to bestow a reward on your husband for his service," said Anwa. "I thought it would help to consult your feelings. What are your plans? What does Cole want?"

Senna was forced to confess that—as far as Cole had ever confided in her—his greatest visions for happiness involved refuge in a town that was so small and so far away that no one had ever heard of it. Or more importantly, of him. "He wants to be a farmer, I think. Not that he knows how, but he would try to learn." Senna's brow furrowed as she envisioned it. "Or a stablehand. He would enjoy that. And be good at it, even though it would mean living somewhere noticeable enough to have horses."

"Oh my," said Anwa.

Senna could only agree.

"I don't suppose I know him very well," the Queen observed. "It's strange, how you can love someone without knowing anything about them."

Senna had to pretend to understand this sentiment. Embarrassed, she leaned over the breakfast spread and took a nibble from one of the tiny honey cakes. Anwa continued her thoughts out loud.

"Your divulgence makes me uneasy of my next question. I pray you will forgive me. Honor and hope both compel me to extend it."

Senna looked up, honey still on her lip. She wondered what sort of question could require such a preface.

"You have also been a champion to my cause. Your name is on the first document of intent released by the Q.M. As my loyal supporter, would you accept Baronship over the county of Geid?"

"Ah..." Senna's mouth fell open. A torrent of doubts dropped on top of her. She tried to figure out which one to present, until she realized how irrelevant any of them were to the question. Senna put her chin high, the way she envisioned a Baroness might do. "Yes, I would."

Senna followed her escort through the camp without paying very much attention to where she was. The Guard

447

brought her to a conference tent. Outside it looked much like the others, made from the same corded fabric. Inside she heard soft murmurs of conversation. Senna spotted Cole through the door, seated at the head of the table near a single lamp. He smiled at her.

"Your husband is here, Lady."

Senna looked round and identified the others that had gathered to converse with him. Jed was at the forefront, along with Hack, Step, and two others Senna didn't know. They turned to look as the Guard steadied her over the threshold. Hack got the first word. "Did he just call you Lady?"

Jed looked excited. Cole looked concerned. Someone got up to offer Senna a seat next to her husband.

Senna nodded as she sank into the chair. She felt strange and stiff. Was that the way a Lady nodded? She wondered how she was going to inform them further, as she couldn't imagine saying her title out loud.

The Guard behind her offered assistance. "She is the new Baroness of Geid."

"No," Cole whispered. He lay his forehead onto the table and covered the back of his head with both hands.

The rest of the table erupted in congratulation. "Wow," said a teenager to her left. Senna glanced at the youth and realized that it was Sable, grown half a foot since the last time Senna had seen him.

"It should be you, Senna," said Jed. "That feels right."

"We need more Ladies in the Baronship." This commendation came from the unfamiliar woman who had just surrendered her chair.

"Cole," Senna put her chin on the table so that he would hear her. "You can still be a stablehand. I'll have the title. You don't have to talk to anyone if you don't want to."

"That's not how it works, Senna. Being married to you means I get the title too."

"It won't be that bad," she promised. "People will get used to the idea."

Dohack cleared his throat. "I don't know, Senna."

Senna reared on him, temper blazing. "Stall your ugly mouth, Hack!"

Jed covered a chuckle as he tossed a nod to Hack. "That's your Baroness talking."

Cole lifted his head and whispered with her. "If you ask, it might be possible to get some other county. I think Pannerack needs a Baroness?"

"No!" Senna hadn't realized how eager she was to return to Geid until she considered doing otherwise. That castle had her name on it. Her heart swelled at the thought of the plans she had in mind.

Cole sat back, silenced. There was a long conversation in store there. Senna hoped it would hold until they were alone.

She searched for an alternate thread of discussion. "What have you been talking about while I was gone?" Senna addressed herself to Jedomar.

"History," Jed answered, "The goings on in Geid, over the past several years."

Sable piped in, "Like how he knew about our underground cave."

Senna remembered asking those questions herself. "Corvan, right?" she said.

Jed nodded. "Apparently, the steward was friends with Sable's great grandfather."

"Rumor was you poisoned the old steward," Hack interjected. "Didn't he fall down dead out the blue?"

"By the Queen!" Jed frowned at Hack. "We just told you the steward was older than a tree!"

Sable nodded sagely. "That's enough to kill anyone."

Cole was putting all his energy into sitting quietly and it didn't look like anyone would be breaking his focus soon. The conversation wouldn't hold, Senna realized. "Would you excuse us?" she asked, starting to rise. "I need a word with my husband."

"We'll go," the woman behind her answered with authority. "You stay."

Jed hopped up obediently at her signal, ushering Hack and Sable before him. "Lady Marwen," Jed bowed as he passed the elegantly dressed woman.

The woman bestowed a sympathetic smile on Senna before she drew the tent door shut and tied it behind her.

Senna let the tent sit in silence for a few seconds to see if Cole would speak first. He didn't. With a sigh, Senna hiked up her skirt, crawled hand and knee up to the tabletop, and swung her legs over the side in front of him.

The maneuver got his attention. Cole made eye contact, though his face was still mostly vacant. "You'll be an excellent Baroness, Senna."

Senna halted the speech that had been building inside. "I will?"

His eyes fell to her butt resting on the tabletop. "Your decorum needs some improvement first."

Senna scowled, tried to decide how serious that comment was, then moved on. "Emwid will be our housekeeper. You'll apologize for yelling at her, and then stay out of her way until she realizes how polite you can be and forgives you. We'll have festival twice a year, and we won't lose money because we'll charge admission. You'll keep me in check, and run the books. You'll keep a low profile at first. Everyone will strive to catch a glimpse of you, because your tale is so interesting that every man, woman, and child in the whole of Mackabine will hear it.

"Eventually you'll grow tired of the constant questions, and you'll end up talking to someone, probably making friends. They'll introduce you to their other friends. News of your charm and modesty will spread. Sooner or later, dear husband, I'm afraid you will end up well known and fairly well liked."

Cole's stupefied expression dissipated the longer she talked. By the end, he looked defeated and a little annoyed. "It can't be helped," he said, "The only thing I know for certain is that I'll be wherever you are."

Senna released a breath she had been metaphorically

holding since she left the Queen. It was nearly unthinkable for a Lord to refuse to take residence with his Lady. Nonetheless, Senna admitted that she had been a little worried.

She put the tip of her nose against Cole's cheek, willing her happiness to transfer via touch. Cole accepted her, pulled her in, hands climbing over her skin and body. The tension that had been building over days erupted into sudden, giddy desire.

"Do you think...anyone is going to disturb a Baroness without warning?"

Cole answered in between caressing her neck with his mouth. "This is our tent, Senna."

Senna looked past the table for the first time, into the shaded depths of the shetler. Her eyes, adjusted to the dim light of the lamp, began to perceive the outline of a bed.

Cole pulled back enough for their eyes to meet. "We're alone," he whispered, "truly."

Finally, thought Senna.

CHAPTER FORTY-SEVEN

Jed had lived twenty-six summers in Geid. But none were ever as beautiful as this one. Jed smiled at the sight of increasingly familiar trees. His feet were sore from walking, but he didn't mind. Last night's rain sparkled over the pebbled highway. Every leaf washed in sunshine was a bright green jewel, bedecking the forest. Home was within grasp of the next half hour.

"Jed," the young man beside him said, "wait until you see your memorial block. It's the biggest one Geid ever had."

Jed only answered that they'd better take it down, quick as they could, now that they knew he was alive. The spirits of the Otherworld were sure to dislike such a thing.

"I suppose so," said Sable.

Until recently, Jed had a clump of fans following him from Mackabine. He managed to ditch the bulk of them at the last waystop, sneaking away in the hour before dawn. Only Hack and Sable remained with him now.

The first landmark of Geid came into view then. Hack gave a whoop of triumph, calling their attention to the castle with a great wave of his arm. "Jed, let's build a new one!" he said.

The castle had never looked inviting to Jed, and even today's buoyant mood couldn't change that. But its neglected walls did seem less foreboding than they had previously.

"That'll be Lady Senna's business," said Jed.

"I still can't wrap my head around that," said Hack. "Senna was a lousy inn maid. How can she be a Baroness?"

"Should've gone to Jed," said Sable.

Hack rolled his eyes. "She offered him another one, didn't she?"

Jed didn't have to remind them that he'd turned her down. The thought of his last meeting with the Great Lady quickened Jed's heart. Every detail of that conversation was burned into his memory. The gleam of recognition in Queen Anwa's eye when he entered. The disapproval of her attendants, when she asked them to vacate the chamber. It was an immense honor to be left alone with the Queen.

In truth, he should have seen her offer coming. But no, he'd been too focused on her physical person to consider why he was there.

"I've heard good things about you, Mister Jedomar," Anwa began. Her skirt was blue and her tunic a strong earthy green. A good combination. It brought out the color of her face. "You have done much for the name of Queensman, both here and in Geid. You are a man of some capability."

Senna told Jed she'd put in a good word for him. Jed was pleased to learn it had not gone to waste. "I don't listen to rumors, Lady. Unless they're all about me and they make me sound wonderful."

Anwa's mouth flicked upwards involuntarily. Jed was delighted to see she was not immune to his charm.

"Mister Jedomar, I owe you a personal debt. You helped rid me of a powerful enemy."

Of course she meant Gote. He bowed. "Glad to be of service, Great Lady. Although he was hardly any trouble. And not worth it, if you ask me."

"He was a fiend who murdered my mother. Did he shake in fear at the end?"

Jed sensed a real vehemence behind her words. He hesitated, then gestured thoughtfully towards one eye. "To be honest, I don't think he saw it coming."

If that disappointed the Queen, she recovered quickly. "I wish to reward your service. I apologize that your home county has been spoken for. Would you permit me, instead, to grant you tenure of the county of Anseth?"

Jed stared for a moment, hardly understanding what she asked. Then he laughed aloud. "You wish me to be a Baron? The Baron of Anseth? That would make quite the image! I feel almost tempted, but I think I'll say no. I am hardly qualified."

Anwa seemed strangely pleased by his refusal. "That is an honest answer," she said. "Many of my appointments these days are...underqualified."

"I hadn't thought of it that way."

"We are all learning together." The Queen looked thoughtful, and hesitated before speaking again. "If you remained in Mackabine, I could see that you receive training. Perhaps after a time, you would feel ready to take up an office in the capital?"

Jed felt a lightness all over his body. "Yes! I need to go home first and see my friends. But then, Lady, I would swim to the moon and back if it meant I could be near you."

Anwa shifted her gaze uncomfortably.

"Lady, forgive me. I know you must receive flattery of all kinds, from all quarters. Mine must seem very trivial to you. I speak only for my own sake. You are a more worthy Queen than I dreamed possible. I would face the Otherworld to do whatever you asked of me."

Jed had fine-tuned this speech many hours in advance of their meeting. It was only as he finished saying it out loud that he realized what a fool he'd made of himself. "Uh..." Jed fumbled and clasped his hands "...except for what you asked me just now, and I said no."

Anwa looked in turn embarrassed, pleased, and puzzled. Finally she laughed. It was a wonderful sound, womanly and beguiling. The memory of it tried to hold him, even as a voice returned him to the present.

"Mister Jed, is that really you?" Their first Geidman met them with an armful of produce he was carrying in the direction of the castle.

"Mister Timbad, good meeting!" Jed responded gladly. "How is your family?"

Timbad grinned. "We heard you were alive, but we weren't sure if we should believe it."

On the hill, a young girl shouted and ran down the slope, cloak flapping in one hand. Jed waved, but picked up his stride, eager to meet the town before news outpaced him.

The walk through town brought out all the breadth of exclamation Jed was looking for. There was too much noise to parse all of it. Some cries were exuberant, others too soft to be overheard. Jed's eyes made sense of what his ears couldn't.

"Can it be?"

"It's Jedomar! He's come back!"

Jed gave his neighbors a magnanimous wave. He expected the hushed awe to get old at some point, but for now, he enjoyed every bit. He shook hands, kissed cheeks, laughed, and greeted every face by name. Alongside exclamations of "Jed!" there was at least one exclamation of "Sable!"

"That'll be your mother, lad," said Jed.

Sable ducked his head. Madam Haw fell on the boy with a fervor and kissed him as hard as she scolded him.

"Where's Rimick?" Jed asked Haw.

A chorus of voices tried to answer at the same time. Rimick was acting town Judge, they informed him. Must be inside the lawyering circle again.

Jed hadn't been inside the circle since before the Gault Revolution. He had to get directions from the crowd. Too excited to give him privacy, they followed him to the door. Some of the townsfolk got inside before Jed could.

Rimick was talking to Madam Jortha and he didn't sound happy. The sight of his friend in profile hit Jed with a shock. Rimick looked worse than Jed did the last time they saw each other. Jortha saw him first, but she was too stumped to alert Rimick.

Whatever Rimick's recent argument was about, it didn't leave him in a mood to entertain visitors. He turned harshly on the invading townsfolk. "The next person who tries to tell me Jedomar is back from the dead—"

"Rimick," Jed called.

The sound drew Rimick's eyes to his spot at the back of the room. They were badly swollen, one to the point of being bandaged shut. The remaining eye opened and closed, as if trying to reset itself.

"By the Queen, old friend! You look like someone washed you up with the laundry. Or mistook you for a rug. Or just...told you to stand there while they hit you with a stick."

Rimick, true to form, had little to say. He stared at Jed, wheels rolling in his overactive head. Jed tried to get closer. The crowd allowed themselves to be pushed aside.

Jed very much wanted to hug Rimick, an action Rimick generally forbade. But in this instance, Rimick didn't protest. He even sort of hugged back.

"Rimick? You're not crying?" Jed pulled back to look at him. "I didn't think you *could* cry."

"I can't. I don't," Rimick protested. And in fact he didn't, but it looked to be a close thing.

"It's all true, then?" Jortha asked. Her whisper carried a streak of delight. "About the Baron? He engineered your escape?"

A grimace crossed Jed's face. He opened his mouth to answer, then shut it again. What was the point? "True enough."

"Rimick has been quite the doubter," Jortha said.

Jed nodded understanding. "It's hard to believe Fenwith was less scum than he appeared."

"I believed that," said Rimick. "There wasn't much doubt after Lodin showed us that chest with all the monetary evidence. I feel dull for not seeing it sooner, in fact."

Jed raised his eyes in surprise.

"But I never believed a man I saw hanged would walk

into town on two legs and shake my hand."

Jed was still holding Rimick's right hand, so he shook it again with a cheerful fervor. There was so much to tell one another, and plenty of time to tell it.

Made in the USA
San Bernardino, CA
19 April 2020